MAD AMOS MALONE: THE COMPLETE STORIES

ALAN DEAN FOSTER

WFP
WordFire Press

QUOTES

"Best-selling author Foster brings his creative storytelling to the Old West, with a fantasy twist."

—from *True West Magazine*

"Alan Dean Foster is the modern-day Renaissance writer, as his abilities seem to have no genre boundaries."

—from *Bookbrowser* (for *The Mocking Program*)

"One of the most consistently inventive and fertile writers of science-fiction and fantasy."

—from *The Times* (London)

"Alan Dean Foster is a master of creating alien worlds for his protagonists to deal with."

—from *SFRevue* (for *Sagramanda*).

Cover design by Janet McDonald
Kevin J. Anderson, Art Director

Published by
WordFire Press, LLC
PO Box 1840
Monument CO 80132
Kevin J. Anderson & Rebecca Moesta, Publishers

WordFire Press Trade Paperback Edition 2019
WordFire Press Hardcover Edition 2019
Printed in the USA

Join our WordFire Press Readers Group for sneak previews, updates, new projects, and giveaways
Sign up at wordfirepress.com

CONTENTS

DEDICATION

To my beautiful wife JoAnn, who sparked the idea of Mad Amos and whose spark is still burning brightly. With much love.

INTRODUCTION

In 1981 my wife and I and our dogs and cats moved from Big Bear Lake, California, into a historic single-story ranch-style house in Prescott, Arizona. We remain today in the same house, surrounded by native vegetation, visited frequently by coyotes and owls and occasionally by bobcats and deer, and bedeviled by chipmunks and pack rats. We chose the place for its location at the terminus of a dead-end road and for the redoubtable materials used in its construction.

At the time, I was vaguely aware that while it did not possess the same name recognition as Tombstone or Deadwood or Dodge City, Prescott could boast of its own substantial Old West lineage, most notably for being the home of the world's oldest rodeo. This meant nothing to me, as I was not and am not a rodeo fan. When I look at a bull rider, I see hamburger, not a sport.

But the longer we lived here, the more aware I became of Prescott's unique heritage. Virgil Earp, Wyatt's brother, was the town sheriff for a while. Big Nose Kate, Doc Holliday's longtime mistress, is buried in one of the local cemeteries. Silent film star Tom Mix had a ranch here and shot some of his films in the area. On a completely different note, the fine western painter Irish McCalla lived here during her last years. Those who recognize the name will more likely remember her as Sheena, Queen of the Jungle. Even as a senior, she still looked the part. Ran into her on Cortez Street one day but was too shy to say anything.

That has nothing whatsoever to do specifically with Prescott or the Old West, but viewers of fifties TV will understand why I mention it.

Despite living in a town parts of which could (and have) doubled for a film set (see *Junior Bonner,* with Steve McQueen and Robert Preston ... or maybe *Billy Jack,* or the remake of *The Getaway*), I never drew any story inspiration from our initial visits nor immediately after we moved into our new home. My ramblings tend to take place on other worlds, or in lands of pure fantasy.

One day my wife and I were standing together contemplating adding incidental items like furniture to our new den. This exercise was complicated by the fact that we had no money, having sunk every bit of it into the house itself. We were also struggling to decide what to put on a second-floor landing that led to a single small upstairs room before continuing onward to, curiously, dead-end against the far wall. I commented that the large empty space over our heads needed something: perhaps a fake stuffed bear.

"Why not a dragon?" JoAnn responded.

"Don't be silly," I said. "There were no dragons in the Old West."

She eyed me archly and without missing a beat shot back, "How do *you* know?"

Which, as such observations are wont to do, got me to thinking. The result was the first Mad Amos story. I had no thought of doing more than the one.

That was, as those of mathematical bent will note, eighteen stories ago.

It is a pleasure to have them all gathered together here in one volume, like so many chocolates. Or, as Amos Malone would say, shots of whiskey. Feel free to drink deep.

Amos Malone didn't exist when I began to write Folly. As hinted at already, the story's genesis involved a dragon. A Chinese dragon, to be precise. I made him a visitor from the Far East because I get tired of your standard European dragon and because such an origin allowed me to place him in the context of the Chinese laborers building the western portion of the first transcontinental railroad. Add in the dragonish affection for gold and ... well, the story began to take form from there.

But how to deal with such an intimidating intruder? Who, in the Old West, could handle a dragon? It would have to be someone with knowledge of such creatures, someone unafraid, yet someone who belonged to the environment. I couldn't just import a white-bearded wizard in a pointy hat to magic a dragon away with a wave of his wand. So ... no pointy hats. No wands. No long white beards.

The exploits of the mountain men in the early American West often read like magic. Why not a mountain man who could work a little magic himself? An outsized talent in every sense of the word, but one who retained his essential mountain manness. I'd have to equip him with the right weapons, the right attire, an appropriate mount, and a pair of saddlebags capable of holding, should a particularly sorceral situation arise, more than hardtack and salt pork. Locals would be sure to find such a character passing strange. Maybe even a little bit ... mad.

So Amos Malone came into being as a foil for an expat Chinese dragon. And after that, wouldn't you know it: the dadgum half-crazy sonuvabitch and the worthless steed he rode in on just wouldn't go away.

WU-LING'S FOLLY

Hunt and MacLeish had worked for the Butterfield Line for six and seven years, respectively. They'd fought Indians, and been through growler storms that swept down like a cold dream out of the eastern Rockies, and seen rattlers as big around the middle as a horse's leg. All that, they could cope with; they'd seen it all before. The dragon, though, was something new. You couldn't blame 'em much for panicking a little when the dragon hit the stagecoach.

"I'm tellin' ya," Hunt was declaring to the Butterfield agent in Cheyenne, "it were the biggest, ugliest, scariest-lookin' dang bird you ever saw, Mr. Fraser, sir!" He glanced back at his driver for confirmation.

"Yep. S'truth." Archie MacLeish was a man of few words and much tobacco juice. He was tough as pemmican and as hard to handle, but the incident had turned a few more of the brown-stained whiskers in his copious beard gray as an old Confederate uniform.

"It come down on us, Mr. Fraser, sir," Hunt continued emphatically, "like some great winged devil raised up by an angry Boston temperance marcher, a-screamin' and a-hollerin' and a-blowin' fire out of a mouth filled with ugly, snaggled teeth. 'Twere a sight fit t' raise the departed. I gave it both barrels of Evangeline." He indicated the trusty ten-gauge resting in a corner of the office. "And it ne'er even blinked. Ain't that right, Archie?"

"Yep," confirmed the driver, firing accurately into the bronze-inlaid pewter spittoon set on the floor beside one corner of the big walnut desk.

"I see." The Butterfield agent was a pleasant, sympathetic fellow in his early fifties. Delicate muttonchop whiskers compensated somewhat for the glow the sun brought forth from his naked forehead. His trousers were supported by overloaded suspenders that made dark tracks across an otherwise immaculate white shirt. "And then what happened?"

"Well, both Archie and me was ready t' meet our maker." Hunt was deadly earnest. "You got to understand, Mr. Fraser, sir, this varmint were bigger than coach and team together. Why, them poor horses like t' die afore we coaxed and sweet-talked 'em into town. They're bedded down in the company stable right now, still shakin' at the knees.

"Anyways, this ugly bird just reached down with one claw the size o' my Aunt Molly's Sunday dress and plucked the strongbox right off the top o' the coach, snappin' the guy ropes like they was made o' straw. Then it flew off, still a-screechin' and a-brayin' like the grandfather of jackasses toward the Medicine Bow Mountains."

"God's truth," said the driver.

"This is all most interesting," Fraser mumbled. Now, while known as a sympathetic man, the Butterfield agent would have been somewhat disinclined to believe the tale to which his two employees were swearing, save for the fact that MacLeish and Hunt were still standing in front of his desk rather than cavorting drunk and debauched in the fleshpots of Denver, spending free and easy the ten thousand in gold that the missing strongbox had contained.

And, of course, there was also the confirmation afforded by the stage's three passengers, a reputable Mormon rancher from Salt Lake and two of his wives. At the moment, the ladies were under the care of a local physician who was treating them for shock.

"Couldn't it have been a williwaw?" he asked hopefully.

"Nope," said MacLeish, striking with unerring accuracy into

the spittoon a second time. "'Tweren't the likes o' no wind or beastie I ever seed nor heard tell of, Mr. Fraser. I kinna say more than the truth." He squinted hard at the agent. "D' ye doubt our word?"

"No, no, certainly not. It's only that I have no idea how I am to report the nature of this loss to the company. If you'd been held up, that they would understand. But this ... There will be questions. You must understand my position, gentlemen."

"And *you* should've been in ours, Mr. Fraser, sir," Hunt told him fervently.

The agent was not by his nature an imaginative man, but he thought for a moment, and his slim store of inventiveness came to his rescue. "I'll put it down as a storm-caused loss," he said brightly.

MacLeish said nothing, though he made a face around his wad of fossil tobacco. Hunt was less restrained. He gaped at the agent and said, "But there weren't no storm where we was comin' through, Mr. ..."

Fraser favored him with a grave look. Hunt began to nod slowly. Meanwhile, MacLeish had walked to the corner and picked up the ten-gauge. He handed it to his partner. The two of them started for the door. And that was the end of that.

For about a week.

"Another month, boys, and I think we can call it quits." A bulbous nose made a show of sniffing the air. "Snow's in the wind already."

"Damned if you ain't right, there, Emery," said one of the other men.

There were four of them gathered around the rough-hewn table that dominated the center of the cabin. They were spooning up pork, beans, jerky, dark bread, and some fresh fowl. It was a veritable feast compared to their normal cold meals, but they had reason to celebrate.

Johnny Sutter was an eighteen-year-old from Chicago who'd matured ten years in the twelve-month past. "I," he announced, "am goin' to get me a room in the finest whorehouse in Denver and stay stinkin' drunk for a whole month!"

Loud guffaws came from the rest of the men. "Hell, Johnny," said one of them, "if'n yer goin' t' do that, don't waste your time doin' it in a fancy place. Do it in the streets and let me have your room."

"Dang right," said another. "You'll get yourself too stiff t' do what you'll want t' be doin'."

"Not stiff enough, mos' likely," corrected the mulatto, One-Thumb Washington. He laughed louder than any of them, showing a dark gap where his front teeth ought to have been. He'd lost those two teeth and four fingers of his left hand at Shiloh and never regretted it. Two teeth and four fingers were a fair enough trade for a lifetime of freedom.

Wonder Charlie, the oldest of the four, made quieting motions with his hands. His head was cocked to one side, and he was listening intently with his best ear.

"What's wrong with you, old man?" asked Johnny, grinning at all the good-natured ribbing he was taking. "Ain't you got no suggestions for how a man's to spend his money?"

"It ain't thet, Johnny. I think somethin's after the mules."

"Well, hellfire!" Emery Shanks was up from his chair and reaching for his rifle. "If them thievin' Utes think they can sneak in here the day afore we're set t'—"

Wonder Charlie cut him off sharply. "'Tain't Utes. Ol' Com-it-tan promised me personal two springs ago when I sighted out this creek bed thet we wouldn't have no trouble with his people, and Com-it-tan's a man o' his word. Must be grizzly. Listen."

The men did. In truth, the mules did sound unnaturally hoarse instead of skittish as they would if it were only strange men prowling about the camp. It if was a grizzly, it sure would explain the fear in their throats. A big male griz could carry off a mule alive.

The miners poured out the cabin door, hastily donning boots and pulling up suspenders over their dirty long johns. One-Thumb and Emery fanned out to search the forest behind the hitch-and-rail corral. The moon was swollen near to full, and they could see a fair piece into the trees. There was no sign or sound of a marauding grizzly. One-Thumb kept an eye on the dark palisade of pines as he moved to the corral and tried to calm the lead mule. The poor creature was rolling its eyes and stamping nervously at the ground.

"Whoa, dere, General Grant! Take it easy, mule.... Wonder what the blazes got into dese mu—"

He broke off as the mule gave a convulsive jerk and pulled away from him. There was something between the camp and the moon. It wasn't a storm cloud, and it certainly wasn't a grizzly. It had huge, curving wings like those of a bat, and wild, glowing red eyes, and a tail like a lizard's. Thin tendrils protruded from its lips and head, and curved teeth flashed like Arapaho ponies running through a moonlit meadow.

"Sweet Lord," Johnny Sutter murmured softly, "wouldja look at that?"

The massive yet elegant shape dropped closer. The mules went into a frenzy. Wonder Charlie, who'd been at Bull Run as well as Shiloh and had emerged from those man-made infernos with his skin intact, didn't hesitate. He fired at that toothy, alien face, the rifle *kaboom*ing through the still mountain air.

The aerial damnation didn't so much as blink. It settled down on wings the size of clipper ship toproyals and began digging with pitchfork-sized claws at the watering trough just inside the corral. The mules pawed at the earth, at each other, at the railing in a frantic desire to crowd as far away from the intruder as possible.

One-Thumb ducked under the sweep of a great translucent wing and shouted in sudden realization, "Curse me for a massa, I think the monster's after our gold!"

Sure enough, several moments of excavation turned up a small wooden box. Inside lay the labor of four men sweating out the riches of a mountain for a year and a half, a glittering horde of dust and nuggets large enough to ensure each of them comfort for the rest of his life.

Monster bird or no, they'd worked too damn hard for any of them to give up so easily that pile they'd wrested from the icy river.

They fired and fired, and when it was clear to see that guns weren't doing any good, they went after the intruder with picks and shovels.

When it was all over, a somber moon beamed down on a scene of theft and carnage. The gold was gone, and so were the bodies of young Johnny Sutter and One-Thumb Washington and a mule named General Grant....

There were not many physicians residing in Cheyenne at the time and fewer still who knew anything about medicine, so it was not entirely coincidental that the one who treated the Mormon rancher's wives would also become conversant with the story related by the unfortunate survivors of the Willow Creek claim. He brought the information to the attention of Mr. Fraser, the local Butterfield Line agent who had seen to the care of the distraught passengers. Now these two comparatively learned men discussed the events of the week past over sherry in the dining room of the Hotel Paris.

"I am at a loss as to what to do now, Dr. Waxman," the agent confessed. "My superiors in Denver accepted the report I sent to them which described the loss of the strongbox on a mountain road during a violent, freak storm, but I suspect they are not without lingering suspicions. My worry is what to do if this should occur a second time. Not only would the cargo be lost, I should be lost as well. I have a wife and children, Doctor. I have no desire to be sent to a prison ... or to an asylum. You are the only other educated citizen who has been apprised of this peculiar situation. I believe it is incumbent upon the two of us to do something to rectify the problem. I feel a certain responsibility, as an important member of the community, to do something to ensure the safety of my fellow citizens, and I am sure you feel similarly."

A thoughtful Waxman ran a finger around the edge of his glass. "I agree. Something must be done."

"Well, then. You are positive these two men you treated yesterday were confronted by the same phenomenon as the one that afflicted my drivers?"

"There seems to be no doubt of that." The doctor sipped at his sherry as he peered over thick spectacles at the agent. "With two of their companions carried off by this creature, I should ordinarily have suspected some sort of foul play, were it not for the unique nature of their wounds. Also, they are Christians and swore to the truth of their story quite vociferously to the farmer who found them wandering dazed and bleeding in the mountains, invoking the name of the savior repeatedly."

The agent folded his hands on the clean tablecloth. "More than citizen safety is at stake in this. There is a growing economy to consider. It is clear that this creature has an affinity—nay, a fondness —for gold. Why, I cannot imagine. What matters is that next time it may strike at a bank in Cheyenne or some smaller community when there are women and children on the streets. But how are we to combat it? We do not even know what we face, save that it surely is not some creature native to this land. I suspect a manifestation of the Devil. Perhaps it would be efficacious for me to have a talk with Pastor Hunnicutt of the—"

The doctor waved the suggestion down. "I think we must seek remedies of a more earthly nature before we proceed to the final and uncertain decision of throwing ourselves on the mercy of the Creator. God helps those who help themselves, whether the Devil is involved or not.

"I have had occasion in my work, sir, to deal with certain individuals whose business it is to travel extensively in this still-wild country: Certain acquaintances sometimes impress themselves most forcefully on these bucolic travelers, who are usually commonsensible if not always hygienic.

"In connection with unusual occurrences and happenings, with unexplained incidents and strange manifestations, one name recurs several times and is uttered with respect by everyone from simple farmers to soldiers to educated citizens such as ourselves. I have been reliably informed that this person, a certain Amos Malone, is presently in the Cheyenne region. I believe we should seek his counsel in this matter."

The Butterfield agent stared across at the doctor, who, having finished his sherry, was tamping tobacco into a battered old pipe. "Amos Malone? Mad Amos Malone? I have heard tell of him. He is a relic, a throwback to the heyday of the mountain man and the beaver hat. Besides which, he is rumored to be quite insane."

"So is half of Congress," the doctor replied imperturbably. "Yet I believe we need him if there is to be any chance of resolving this business."

The agent let out a long sigh. "I shall defer to your judgment in this matter, sir, but I confess that I am less than sanguine as to its eventual outcome."

"I am not too hopeful myself," the physician admitted, "but we have to try."

"Very well. How are we to get in touch with this individual? These mountain men do not subscribe to civilized means of communication, nor do they usually remain in one place long enough for contact to be made."

"As to that, I am not concerned." The doctor lit his pipe. "We will put out the word that we require his presence and that it involves a matter of great urgency and most unusual circumstance. I believe he will come. As to precisely how he will learn of our need, I leave that to the unknown and ungovernable means by which the breed of man to which he belongs has always learned of such things."

They waited in the doctor's office. Just before dawn a light snow had salted the town. Now the morning sun, hesitantly glimpsed through muddy dark clouds, threatened to melt the serenely pale flakes and turn the streets into a boot-sucking quagmire.

Sitting in the office next to a nickel-and-iron stove were the Butterfield Line agent and a distraught, angry, and bandaged-up Wonder Charlie. Wonder Charlie wasn't feeling too well—his splinted right arm in particular was giving him hell—but he insisted on being present, and the doctor thought the presence of an eyewitness would be vital to give verisimilitude to their story.

The clock on the high shelf chimed six-thirty.

"And that's for your mountain man," snapped Fraser. He was not in a good mood. His wife, an unforgiving woman, had badgered him relentlessly about risking an attack of colic by tramping outside so early in the morning.

Dr. Waxman gazed unconcernedly at the clock. "Give him a little time. The weather is bad."

There was a knock at the door. Waxman glanced over at the agent and smiled.

"Punctual enough," Fraser admitted reluctantly. "Unusual for these backwoodsmen."

The doctor rose from his seat and moved to open the door, admitting a man who stood in height somewhere between six feet and heaven. He was clad in dirty buckskin and wet Colorado. Two bandoliers of enormous cartridges crisscrossed his expansive chest. In his belt were secured a bowie knife and a LeMat pistol, the latter an eccentric weapon favored for a time by Confederate cavalry officers. It fit the arrival, Fraser thought.

The man's beard was not nearly as gray-speckled as Wonder Charlie's, but there were a few white wires scattered among the black. His eyes were dark as Quantrill's heart, and what one could see of his actual flesh looked cured as tough as the goatskin boots he wore.

"Cold out there this morning," he said, striding over to the potbellied stove. He rubbed his hands in front of it gratefully, then turned to warm his backside.

The doctor closed the door against the cold and proceeded to make formal introductions. Fraser surrendered his uncallused palm to that massive grip gingerly. Wonder Charlie took it firmly, his age and infirmities notwithstanding.

"Now then, gentlemens, word's out that you folk have got yourselves a little gold problem."

"Bird problem, ye mean," Charlie said promptly, before Fraser or the doctor could slip a word in. "Biggest goddamn bird ye ever saw, mister. Killed two o' my partners and stole our poke. Took off with m' best mule, too. Out o' spite, I thinks, for surely One-Thumb and Johnny would've made the beast a good enough supper."

"Easy there, old-timer," Mad Amos said gently. "It don't do to make your head hurt when the rest of you already does. Now, y'all tell me more about this gold-lovin' bird of yours. I admit to being more than a mite curious about it, or I wouldn't be here."

"And just why are you here, Mr. Malone?" Fraser asked curiously. "You have no assurance we are able to pay you for your services or even what extremes of exertion those services might entail."

"Why, I don't care much about that right now, friend." He smiled, showing more teeth than men of his profession usually possessed. "I'm here because I'm curious. Like the cat."

"Curiosity," commented Fraser, still sizing up the new arrival, "killed the cat, if you will remember."

The mountain man turned and stared at him out of eyes so black that the agent shrank a little inside. "Way I figure it, Mr. Fraser, in the long run we're all dead."

With the doctor and the agent nearby to assist his memory, Wonder Charlie related his story of the devil-thing that had attacked his camp and killed two of his partners. Then Fraser repeated what his set-upon driving team had told him. He and Charlie argued a little over details of the creature's appearance, picayune disagreements involving color and size, but basically they and their respective stories were in agreement.

When they'd finished, Mad Amos leaned back in the rocking chair into which he'd settled himself. It creaked with his weight as he clasped both hands around a knee. "Shoot, that ain't no bird you're describing, gentlemens. I thought it weren't when I first heard about it, but I weren't sure. Now I am. What came down on you, old-timer," he told Charlie, "and what lit into your stage, Mr. Fraser, weren't nothin' but a full-blood, gen-u-wine, honest-to-goshen member of the dragon tribe."

"Your pardon, Mr. Malone," said the doctor skeptically, "but a dragon is a mythical creature, an invention of our less enlightened ancestors. This is the nineteenth century, sir. We no longer cotton to such superstitions. I myself once had an encounter with a snake-oil salesman who guaranteed to supply me with some powdered unicorn horn. I am not unskilled in basic chemistry and was able to prove it was nothing more than powder from the common steer."

"Well, y'all better readjust your heads a mite, 'cause that's what got your gold, and those stealings ain't no myth."

"He's right, there," Wonder Charlie said sharply.

"I had thought perhaps a large eagle that normally resides only among the highest and most inaccessible peaks ..." the doctor began.

"Haw!" Mad Amos slapped his knee a blow that would've felled most men. His laugh echoed around the room. "Ain't no eagle in this world big enough to carry off a full-grown mule, let alone twenty pounds of gold in a Butterfield steel strongbox! Ain't no eagle got bat wings instead of feathers. Ain't no eagle colored red and yellow and blue and pink and black and everything else. No, it's a true dragon we're dealing with here, gentlemens. By Solomon's seal it is!"

The Butterfield agent spoke up. "I cannot pretend to argue with either of you gentlemen. I have not your scientific knowledge, sir," he told the doctor, "nor your reputed experience in matters arcane, Mr. Malone. The question before us, however, is not what we are dealing with but how we are to be rid of it. I care not what its proper name be, only that I should not have to set eyes upon it." He eyed the mountain man expectantly.

Some said Malone had once been a doctor himself. Others said he had been captain of a great clipper ship. Still others thought he'd been a learned professor at the Sorbonne in France. General opinion, however, held to it that he was merely full of what the squirrels put away for the Colorado winter. Fraser didn't much care. All he wanted was not to have to explain away the loss of another strongbox filled with gold, and there was a shipment of coin coming up from Denver the very next week.

"That's surely the crux, ain't it? Now, you tell me, old-timer," Malone said to Wonder Charlie, "how many appendages did your visitor have streamin' from his mouth? Did he spit any fire at you? Was his howling high-pitched like a band of attacking Sioux or low like running buffalo in the distance? How did he look at you ... straight on or by twisting his head from one side to the other?"

And so on into the late morning, Malone asking question after question until the old miner's head ached from the labor of recollection. But Charlie persisted. He'd liked Johnny Sutter and One-Thumb Washington, not to mention poor ole General Grant.

———————

Canvas tents pockmarked the side of the little canyon, their sides billowing in the wind. Piles of rails and ties were stacked neatly nearby, along with kegs of spikes, extra hammers, and other equipment. Thick, pungent smells wafted from a single larger tent, while others rose from the far side of the railroad camp. One set of odors indicated the kitchen, the other the end product.

The line from Denver to Cheyenne was comparatively new and in need of regular repair. The crew that had laid the original track was now working its way back down the line, repairing and cleaning up, making certain the roadbed was firm and the rails secure.

The muscular, generally diminutive men swinging the hammers and hauling the iron glanced up with interest as the towering mountain man rode into camp. So did the beefy supervisor charged with overseeing his imported workers. Though he came from a line of prejudiced folk, he would brook no insults toward his men. They might have funny eyes and talk even funnier, but by God they'd work all day long and not complain a whit, which was more than you could say for most men.

"All right. Show's over," he growled, aware that work was slowing all along the line as more men paused to track the progress of the hulking stranger. "Get your backs into it, you happy sons of heaven!"

The pounding of hammers resumed, echoing down the canyon, but alert dark eyes still glanced in the direction of the silent visitor.

They widened beneath the brows of one broad-shouldered worker when the stranger leaned close and whispered something to him in a melodic, singsong tongue. The man was so startled he nearly dropped his hammer on his foot. The stranger had to repeat his query more slowly before he got a reply.

"Most unusual. White Devil speaks fluently the tongue of my home. You have traveled that far, honored sir?"

"Once or twice. I'm never for sure how many. Canton's a nice little town, though the food's a bit thin for my taste. Now, how about my question?"

The spike driver hesitated at that. Despite his size and strength, the worker seemed suddenly frightened; he looked past the visitor's horse as though someone might be watching him.

Mad Amos followed the other man's gaze and saw only tents. "Don't worry," he said reassuringly. "I won't let the one I'm after harm you or any of your friends or relatives back home. I will not allow him to disturb your ancestors. Will you trust me, friend?"

"I will," the worker decided abruptly. "The one you seek is called Wu-Ling. You will find him in the third tent down." He leaned on his hammer and pointed. "Good fortune go with you, White Devil."

"Thanks." Mad Amos chucked his horse's reins and resumed his course up the track. The men working on the line watched him intently, whispering among themselves.

Outside the indicated tent he dismounted, pausing a moment to give his horse an affectionate pat. This unique steed was part Indian pony, part Appaloosa, part Arabian, and part Shire. He was black with white patches on his rump and fetlocks and a white ring around his right eye. This eye was unable to open completely, which affected the animal with a sour squint that helped keep teasing children and casual horse thieves well away.

"Now you wait here, Worthless, and I'll be right back. I hope." He turned and called into the tent.

"Enter, useless supplicant of a thousand excuses," replied an imperious voice.

Seated on a mat inside the tent was a youthful Chinese clad in embroidered silk robes and cap. He wore soft slippers and several jade rings. There were flowers in the tent, and they combined with burning incense to keep out the disagreeable odors of the camp. The man's back was to the entrance, and he gestured with boredom toward a lacquered bowl three-quarters filled with coins.

"Place thy pitiful offering in the usual place and then get out. I am meditating with the forces of darkness. Woe to any who disturb my thoughts."

"Woe to those who meddle with forces they don't understand, progenitor of a hundred bluffs."

The genuflector whirled at the sound of English, only to find himself gaping up at a hairy, ugly, giant White Devil. It took him a moment to compose himself. Then he slipped his hands (which Mad Amos thought might be shaking just a little) back into his sleeves and bowed.

Mad Amos returned the bow and said in perfect Cantonese, "Thy ministrations seem to have exceeded thy knowledge, unomnipotent one."

A hand emerged from silk to thrust demandingly at the tent entrance. "Get out of my tent, Devil. Get out! Or I will assuredly turn thee into a lowly toad, as thy face suggests!"

Mad Amos smiled and took a step forward. "Now let's just settle down, inventor of falsehoods, or you'll be the one gets done to. I can't turn you into a toad, but when I finish with you, you'll look like a buffalo carcass a bunch o' Comanches just finished stripping."

The man hesitated but did not back down. He raised both hands and muttered an important-sounding invocation to the skies.

Mad Amos listened a while, then muttered right back at him.

The would-be sorcerer's eyes went wide. "How comes a White Devil to know the secret words of the Shao?"

"That's a long, nasty story. Course, I don't know *all* of 'em, but I know enough to know you don't know what the hell you're invoking about. I suspect that's what got you into trouble the last time. I know enough to know this is all a show to impress your hardworking kinfolk out there. You ain't no Mandarin, Wu-Ling, just as you ain't no Shao sorcerer. You're nothing but a clever amateur, a dabbler in darkness, and I think you got yourself in over your head with this dragon business."

"So that is what inflicts you upon me. That damnable beast!" He threw his cap to the floor. "May its toenails ingrow a thousand times! I knew it would bring me problems from the moment the incantation expanded beyond my ability to control the signs." He sat heavily on a cushion, no longer bold and commanding, now just a distraught young would-be lawyer whose pact with the forces of darkness had been overturned by a higher court.

Watching him thus, Mad Amos was able to conjure up a little sympathy for him, no small feat of magic in itself. "How'd you come to have to call him up, anyways?"

"I needed something with which to cow my ignorant kinsmen. There had been mutterings ... a few had begun to question my right to claim their support, saying that I was not a true sorcerer and could not threaten them as I claimed or work magic back in the homeland for their relatives and friends. I required something impressive to forestall such uncertainties once and for all."

"I see. How'd the railroad feel about your brothers supporting you in luxury while they worked their tails off?"

"The White Devil bosses care nothing for civilized behavior so long as the work is accomplished on time."

"So you finally had to produce, magically speaking, or risk going to work with your own delicate fake-Mandarin hands. That about right?"

"It is as you say." Wu-Ling turned and assumed a prideful air. "And I did produce. A dragon of whole cloth, of ancient mien and fierce disposition, did I cause to materialize within the camp one night. Since then there have been no further mutterings among my kinsmen, and my support has multiplied manyfold."

Mad Amos nodded and stroked his luxuriant beard. "Yup, you got a nice little racket going here. Course, there might be some trouble if I were to stroll outside and announce that you've got no more control over this dragon than I do over a thunderbird's eye. I think your toiling kinsfolk would be a touch unhappy."

The young man's boast quickly turned to desperate pleading. "Please, you must not tell them that, White Devil! Please ... they would linger over my killing for weeks if they once learned that I have no power over them." His gaze sank. "I confess all this to You Who Know the Words. I have no control over this dragon. I tried to make it vanish once its purpose had been accomplished. It laughed at me and flew off toward the high mountains. I have tried to call it back, to no avail. Now it does as it pleases, threatening your own people as well. I was an overanxious fool, determined to overawe my people. I should have settled for a less dramatic materialization."

Mad Amos nodded sagely. "Now you're learning, inheritor of troubles. It's always best to make sure you've put all the parts back into a disassembled gun before you go firin' it. I kinda feel sorry for you. The main thing is, the damage this dragon's already done wasn't by your direction."

"Oh, no, Honored Devil, no! As I confess before you, I have no control over it whatsoever. It does as it desires."

"Okay, then, I'll strike you a bargain. You quit dealing off the bottom of the deck with your brothers out there. Pick up a hammer and go to work alongside them. I promise it won't kill you, and you'll gain merit in their eyes by working alongside 'em when you supposedly don't have to. Tell 'em it's time for you to put aside wizardly things and exercise your body for a change. You do that and I'll keep my mouth shut."

The young man rose to his feet, hardly daring to hope. "You would do this for me? My ancestors will bless you a hundred times."

"They'd damn well better. I'll need all the help I can gather if I'm going to do anything about this dragon you cooked up, Wu-Ling."

"But you cannot! It will surely slay you!"

"Sorry. I'm bound to try. Can't just let it wander about, ravaging the countryside. Besides which, this country of mine is a young one. It ain't quite ready to cope with dragons yet. Havin' enough trouble recoverin' from the war and the devils it spawned. Now, this ain't one of those types that likes to carry off women, is it?"

"It would be in keeping with its lineage if it chose to abduct and consume a virgin or two, I am afraid."

Mad Amos grunted. "Well, even so, that ain't a worry. There ain't a virgin between here and Kansas City. That means it's just this gold affinity we got to worry about. That's a new one on me, Wu-Ling. What's it want with this gold it keeps stealin'?"

"I thought one so wise as thyself would surely know, Honored Devil. Gold is a necessary ingredient in the dragon's diet."

"It eats the stuff? Well, I'll be dogged. And all this time I thought it was doin' something normal with it, like buying up spare souls or accumulatin' a memorable hoard of riches or some such nonsense. Gulps it right down, you say?"

"Truly," Wu-Ling admitted.

"Huh! World's full of wonders. Well, gives me something to think on, anyways." He gazed sternly down at Wu-Ling. The would-be sorcerer paid close attention. A baleful look from Mad Amos Malone was something not to be ignored. "Now, you mind what I told you and quit leeching off your kinsfolk out there. They're good people, and they deserve your help, not your imaginary afflictions. It's tough enough gettin' by in a foreign land. I know; I've had to try it myself. I've ways of knowin' when someone gives me his word and then backs off, and I don't like it. I don't like it one bit. You follow me, son of importunate parents?"

"I follow you, Honored Devil."

Wu-Ling allowed himself a sigh of relief when the giant finally departed. He wondered by what method the dragon would slay him.

Mad Amos worked his way up into the heights of the Medicine Bows despite the signs that winter was arriving early that year. It would be bad if he were caught out on the slopes by a blizzard, but he'd weathered bad storms before and could do so again if compelled to.

Near a fork of the Laramie River he paused and made camp, choosing an open meadow across which the river ran free and fast. To the west the crests of the mountains already slept beneath the first heavy blanket of snow.

"Well, Worthless, I guess this is as good a spot as any. Might as well get on with it. Oughta be an interesting business, unless I've figured it all wrong. In that case, you hie yourself off somewhere and have a good time. These mountains are full of herds. Find yourself some fine mares and settle down. Bet you wouldn't be all that sad to see me go, would you?"

The horse let out a noncommittal whinny, squinted at him out
of his bad eye, and wandered off in search of a nice mud wallow to
roll in.

Mad Amos hunted until he found a willow tree of just the right
age. He cut off a green branch, shaped it, and trimmed off the leaves
and sproutings. Then he sharpened the tip with his bowie, fired it in
charcoal, and used the white-hot, smoking point to etch some
strange symbols in the earth around his kit. Some of the symbols
were Chinese ideographs, some were Tibetan, and a few were not
drawn from the lexicon of man.

Next he rummaged around in his battered old saddlebags, which
some folk whispered held things it were best not to talk about. Out
came an owl's head, a bottle of blue goo, several preserved dead
scorpions, three eagle feathers bound together with Zuni fetishes,
and similar exotica. He reached in a little farther and withdrew a
shiny metal bar. It was five pounds of enriched tumbaga, a gold alloy
made by the Quimbaya Indians of the southern continent,
composed of roughly sixty-five percent gold, twenty percent copper,
and the rest silver. This he set carefully down in the center of the
inscribed symbols.

Lastly he pulled the rifle from its fringed and painted holster.
The holster had been fashioned by one of Sacajawea's daughters.
Good gal, that Sacajawea, he mused. Someday when they were both
ruminating in the Happy Hunting Ground, he hoped to meet her
again.

The rifle had an eight-sided barrel, a black walnut stock, and a
breech large enough for a frightened cottontail to hide inside. It was
a Sharps buffalo rifle, fifty-caliber, with a sliding leaf sight adjustable
to eleven hundred yards on the back. It fired a two-and-a-half-inch-
long cartridge loaded with a hundred grains of black powder and
could drop a full-grown bull buffalo in its tracks at six hundred
yards. The bandoliers draped across Mad Amos's chest held oversized three-and-a-quarter-inch shells packed with 170 grains of
black powder.

The Sharps was a single-shot. But then, if you could fire it
proper without busting your shoulder, you only needed a single

shot. To Mad Amos's way of thinking, such built-in caution just naturally led to a man improving his marksmanship.

He loaded it with more care than usual this time, paying special attention to the cartridge itself, which he carefully chose from the assortment arrayed on his chest.

Then he settled down to wait.

The moon was setting and the sky had been temporarily swept clean of most clouds when he heard the wings coming toward him out of the west, out of the mountaintops. Soon he was able to see the source of the faint whistling, a streamlined shape dancing down fast out of the heavens, its long tail switching briskly from side to side as it sniffed out the location of the gold.

It landed between the river and the camp and strode toward the lonely man on feet clad in scales of crimson. Its neck was bright blue, its body mostly yellow and gold, its wings and face striped like the contents of a big jar stuffed with assorted candies. Moonlight marched across scimitarlike teeth, and its heritage burned back of its great eyes. "Whoa up there!" Mad Amos called out sharply in the dragon tongue, which is like no other (and which is hard to speak because it hurts the back of the throat).

The dragon halted, eyes blazing down at the human, who had one foot resting possessively on the golden bar. Its tail twitched, flattening the meadow grass and foxgloves, and the tendrils bordering its skull and jaws twisted like snakes with a peculiar life of their own. Its belly ached for the cool touch of yellow metal; its blood burned for the precious golden substance that purified and helped keep it alive.

"Oho!" it replied in its rasping voice. "A human who talks the mother tongue. Admirable is your learning, man, but it will not save you your gold. Give it here to me." It leaned forward hungrily, the smell of brimstone seeping from its garishly hued lips and parted mouth.

"I think not, Brightbodyblackheart. It ain't that I resent you the gold. Everybody's got to eat. But you scared the wits out of some good people hereabouts and killed a couple of others. And I think you're liable to kill some more afore you're sated, if your appetite's as big as your belly and your desire as sharp as your teeth. I'm not fool enough to think you'll be satisfied just with this here chunk." He nudged the bar with his foot, causing the hungry dragon to salivate smoke.

"You are right, man. My hunger is as deep as the abyssal ocean where I may not go, as vast as the sky which I make my own, and as substantial as my anger when I am denied. Give me your gold! Give it over to me now and I will spare you for your learning, for though gluttonous, I am not wasteful. Refuse me and I will eat you, too, for a dragon cannot live by gold alone."

Casually, Mad Amos shifted the rifle lying across his knees. "Now, this here's a Sharps rifle, Deathwing. I'm sure you ain't too familiar with it. There ain't the like of it where you come from, and there never will be, so I'll explain it to you. There ain't no more powerful rifle in this world or the other. I'm going to give you one chance to get back to where you come from, hungry but intact." He smiled thinly, humorlessly. "See, I ain't wasteful, neither. You git your scaly hide out of this part of the real world right now or by Nebuchadnezzar's nightshade, I'm oath-bound to put a bullet in you."

The dragon roared with amusement. Its horrible laughter cascaded off the walls of the canyon through which the Laramie runs. It trickled down the slopes and echoed through caves where hibernating animals stirred uneasily in their long sleep.

"A last gesture, last words! I claim forfeit, man, for you are not amusing! Gold *and* life must you surrender to me now, for I have not the patience to play with you longer. My belly throbs in expectation, and in my heart there is no shred of sympathy or understanding for you. I will take your gold now, man, and your life in a moment." A great clawed foot reached out to scratch contemptuously at the symbols so patiently etched in the soil. "Think you that these will stop me? You do not come near knowing the right ways or words, or the words you would have uttered by now." It took another step forward. Fire began to flame around its jaws. "Your puny steel and powder cannot harm me, worm-that-walks-upright. Fire if you wish. The insect chirps loudest just before it is squashed!"

"Remember, now, you asked for this." Quickly, Mad Amos raised the long octagonal barrel and squeezed the trigger.

There was a crash, then a longer, reverberating roar, the thunderous double *boom* that only a Sharps can produce. It almost matched the dragon's laughter.

The shot struck Brightbodyblackheart square in the chest. The monster looked down at the already healing wound, sneered, and took another step forward. Its jaws parted farther as it prepared to snap up gold and man in a single bite.

It stopped, confused. Something was happening inside it. Its eyes began to roll. Then it let out an earthshaking roar so violent that the wind of it knocked Mad Amos back off his feet. Fortunately, there was no fire in that massive exhalation.

The mountain man spit out dirt and bark and looked upward. The dragon was in the air, spinning, twisting, convulsing spasmodically, thoroughly out of control, screaming like a third-rate soprano attempting Wagner as it whirled toward the distant moon.

Mad Amos slowly picked himself off the ground, dusted off the wolf's head that served him for a hat, and watched the sky until the last scream and final bellow faded from hearing, until the tiny dot fluttering against the stars had winked out of sight and out of existence.

From his wallow near the riverbank, Worthless glanced up, squinted, and neighed.

Mad Amos squatted and gathered up the tumbaga bar. He paid no attention to the coterie of symbols he'd so laboriously scratched into the earth. They'd been put there to draw the dragon's attention, which they'd done most effectively. Oh, he'd seen Brightbodyblackheart checking them out before landing! The dragon might bellow intimidatingly, but like all its kind, it was cautious. It had taken the bait only when it was certain Mad Amos owned no magic effective against it. Mere mortal weapons like guns and bullets, of course, it had had no reason to fear.

Malone used his tongue to pop the second bullet, the one he hadn't had to use, out of his cheek and carefully took the huge cartridge apart. Out of the head drifted a pile of dust. He held it in his palm and then, careful not to inhale any of it, blew it away with one puff. The dust duplicated the contents of the bullet that had penetrated Brightbodyblackheart: mescaline concentrate, peyote of a certain rare type, distillate of the tears of a peculiar mushroom, coca leaves from South America, yopo—a cornucopia of powerful hallucinogens that an old Navajo had once concocted before Mad Amos's attentive gaze during a youthful sojourn in Canyon de Chelly many years before.

It was not quite magic, but then, it was not quite real, either. The dragon had been right: Mad Amos had not had the words to kill it, had not had the symbols. And it wasn't dead. But it no longer lived in the real world of men, either. In a month, when the aftereffects of the potent mixture had finally worn off and Brightbodyblackheart could think clearly once more, it might wish it *were* dead. Of one thing Mad Amos was reasonably certain: the dragon might hunger for gold, but it was not likely to come a-hunting it anywhere in the vicinity of Colorado.

Carefully he repacked that seemingly modest pair of saddlebags and prepared to break camp, casting an experienced eye toward the sky. It was starting to cloud over again. Soon it would snow, and when it started it again, it wouldn't stop until April.

But not for two or three days yet, surely. He still bad time to get out of the high mountains if he didn't waste it lollygaggin' and moonin' over narrow escapes.

He put his hands on his hips and shouted toward the river. "C'mon, Worthless, you lazy representative of an equine disaster! Git your tail out of that mud! North of here's that crazy steamin' land ol' Jim Bridger once told me about. I reckon it's time we had a gander at it ... and what's under it."

Reluctant but obedient, the piebald subject of these unfounded imprecations struggled to its feet and threw its master a nasty squint. Mad Amos eyed his four-legged companion with affection.

"Have t' do somethin' about that patch on his forehead," he mused. "That damn horn's startin' t' grow through again...."

I love Latin. I never studied the language, but I love the sound of it, the rhythms. Every time I encounter Latin, usually as a quote from some famous long-dead native speaker, my mind immediately flashes to the glory that was Rome. I see massive temples, the Colosseum, the Baths of Caracalla, and the Appian Way. We actually lived on a street called Appian Way. Not the Roman one. Ours ran right by the famous Santa Monica Pier in southern California. The only thing even remotely Roman about it was a nearby pizza place.

Such imaginings, of course, do nothing if transported to the Old West. There rise no grand temples to Zeus in South Dakota, reverberate no sounds of Roman legions marching on their way to battle in the Sand Hills of Nebraska. But while the Empire has vanished, the language remains. So, one day I found myself amusedly translating one of the West's most iconic symbols into that wonderful old language of Cicero and Tacitus, and with nothing else to go on, handed the result over to Amos Malone to see what he could do with it.

FERROHIPPUS

The clerk frowned as the Indian entered the hotel. Fortunately, it was late and the last of the regular guests had already gone off to bed. The nearby parlor was empty. He hurried around from behind the front desk.

"We don't allow Indians in here. Get out."

The young man was simply dressed in pants and open shirt of trade cotton. His black hair hung down to his neck and was secured by a red headband. To the clerk he appeared as one of the unclean. The visitor ignored the order and stared with undisguised curiosity at the etched bowl of the imported hurricane lamp that illuminated the entryway.

"I told you to get out," the clerk repeated, louder but not loud enough to disturb the guests. He wondered if he should wake the owner, Mrs. Hedrick, or maybe even send for the sheriff. "You understand English? Savvy?"

"I'm looking for a man," came the soft reply. "Big man."

"Listen, you, I don't care if you're looking for ..." He hesitated. "How big a man?"

"Very big. Bigger than man ought to be. Big crazy man."

Reflexively, the clerk glanced up the stairs. By an odd coincidence, someone fitting that terse description had checked in early this morning. "His name wouldn't happen to be Malone, would it?"

"That him."

"What do you want with Mr. Malone?"

"Got business with him."

"What kind of business?"

"What kind of business not your business."

"Look, heathen, I ..." But again the clerk hesitated. Something about this young savage marked him as different from the tired members of the Gila River tribe the clerk saw in the village of Phoenix during the day, trading vegetables and hides and game for simple tools and muslin from back East. He decided that it would be better not to wake Mrs. Hedrick, better still not to fetch the sheriff.

He also noticed for the first time that his visitor was very tired, as though he'd come a long way through the January night in an awful hurry. Best not to cross a man in a great hurry even if he was only an Indian.

"Up the stairs ... *quietly*. People are sleeping. Can you read?"

A single nod.

"Number six. Down the hall on your right."

"Thanks."

The clerk watched until the young man disappeared onto the upper landing. Then he quickly checked to make sure the pistol in the drawer behind the front desk was loaded, even though the Indian had entered unarmed.

As for the guest whose rest the visitor was about to disturb, that was none of the clerk's business, was it? Besides, he was more than a little certain that the occupant of room number six could take care of himself.

At the end of the hall the young man knocked on a door. A voice boomed back from within.

"Go away! Get lost! A pox on your privates, tarantulas in your boots, and ticks in your beard, and I promise you worse if you don't leave me in peace!"

The young man considered this thoughtfully, noted that he had no beard, and replied, "May I come in?"

Silence. Then, "Oh, hell, come on, then."

It was dimly lit inside. A single lamp glowed on a far wall by the window. His eyes adjusted to the weak illumination. Then he closed the door behind him. Quietly, as the nervous white man downstairs had requested.

Standing next to the lamp and blowing out a long match was a thickly bearded white man of indeterminate age. There was silver in his beard and hair, but in odd places. He reminded the young Indian more of a black bear than a man, and the profusion of visible hair did nothing to dispel the image.

In the middle of the room was a wide bed. The top sheets had been turned down, but the bottom linen was as yet undisturbed.

A quick examination of the visitor was enough to satisfy the guest that no harm was intended. So, in addition to putting down the extinguished match, he also put aside the big LeMat pistol he'd been holding in his other hand.

"Come on in, son."

"I am in."

"Well, then, come on in farther, dammit."

The visitor obeyed, staring at the stained long johns that were all that stood between the giant and nakedness of an unpredictable nature.

"What brings you to civilization, son, as the locals delude themselves into callin' it?"

"You crazy big man?"

"Haw! Guess I shouldn't laugh, though. Most folks'd agree with you. My name's Malone. Amos Malone. Or Mad Amos Malone, if you prefers the colloquial."

"I do not understand your words."

"You got company. Folks can be weird about namin' other folks. Unconventional I may be, but not the other. Leastwise, I think not."

"Amos Malone, I have trouble. My people have trouble."

"Well, now, I'm sorry t' hear that. What did you say your name was?"

"Cheshey."

"Okay, Cheshey. Now, if you'll just tell me ... Cheshey? You got a grandpappy called Ma-Hok-Naweh?"

"That is my grandfather, yes." Cheshey began to feel more secure in this small dark room with the crazy big white man.

Malone turned reflective. "Good ol' Ma-Hok-Naweh. Chief medicine man to the Papagos. Great man, your grandpappy. What brings his grandson so far north?"

"Do you know of the Big House that stands between here and the home of my people?"

"Casa Grande? Sure I do. A place full o' long memories and much magic. Spirit home."

Now Cheshey was nodding eagerly. "Crazy white men want to run the trail for their Iron Horse right next to it. Grandfather says the shaking the Iron Horse makes will make Big House fall down. If this happens, times will be made very bad for us as well as for white man."

Malone frowned and stroked his impenetrable beard. "Sure as hellfire would. I'd *heard* that the new Southern Pacific was goin' to cut north so they could make a station here in Phoenix. Goin' to lay track right alongside the Big House, huh? We'd better do somethin' about that right quick. Your grandpappy's correct."

"He waits for us at the Big House. He told me to find you here, said you would help. Would you really help us against your own people?"

"What makes you think the railroad men are my people, son? There's only two kinds of folk in this world: the good folk and the bad folk. Mine's the good folk. They come in all shapes and colors, just like the bad ones. Don't never let nobody tell you different."

"I will remember, Amos Malone," Cheshey said solemnly. "You must come quick, while there is still time. You have a horse?"

"If you can call Worthless a horse. I'm comin' as fast as I can, young feller-me-lad." As he spoke, he was dragging on his buckskins, then the goatskin boots. When at last he was ready, he paused for a final lingering glance at the still-unused bed. "Real sheets," he muttered darkly. "I almost made it. Them railroad people better listen to reason, 'cause I'm mad enough at 'em already."

Of course, they didn't.

"Let me make certain I understand you, sir. You want me to move the route of the line several miles eastward to make sure that the vibrations from passing trains won't knock over a pile of Indian rocks?"

"That's about the sum of it," Malone agreed.

The foreman took his feet off the desk, rose, and stalked over to the wall where the map was hung. The only reason he didn't laugh at his outlandish visitor outright was because he had the distinct feeling that to have done so would have been unhealthy. He would have to be satisfied with being in the right.

He ran one finger along the map.

"Look here, sir. *I* didn't buy this godforsaken territory from the Mexicans, and I wouldn't give you a mug of fresh spit for the lot of it! There's nothing here but cactus, sagebrush, mesquite that sucks the water out of the earth, and Indians too poor to spit it back again. But buy it we did, and the Southern Pacific is chartered to span it from Texas to California. I aim to see that done exactly as laid out by the company's surveyors."

"But why d'you have to pass so close to Casa Grande?"

"If you must know, I think some fool with a sextant and too much time on his hands decided the old relic might be worth a passing glance from passengers."

"Not if it falls down, it won't."

"That's not my problem; that's the Indians' problem." He walked back to his desk so he could be closer to the Colt that resided in the top compartment there. "Anyway, the decision's already been made. What's the big ruckus over an old stone tepee, anyway?"

"It's not a tepee. This ain't the Plains Country, friend. Big House is thousands o' years old."

"Sure looks it, but how do *you* know that?"

"You can taste it. The air in them old rooms reeks o' antiquity. So do the red clay pots you dig up inside sometimes. It was built by a people the local Indians call the Ancient Ones. Still the tallest building in this territory, if you don't count a few mission steeples. You go shakin' it to bits, and there'll be hell to pay."

"Are the Indians making threats, Mr. Malone? I have the authority to request Army protection, if necessary."

"No, they ain't makin' threats. I'm just relayin' to you what ol' Ma-Hok-Naweh told me last night."

"Ma-Hok ... you mean that old savage who's been living up there?" The foreman smiled. "I think we can handle any attack he might mount."

Malone leaned forward and put a big hand on the desk. The wood creaked under the rough, callused skin. There were some mighty peculiar scars in the skin between the thumb and big finger. "Listen, friend, I don't think you understand me. You're not just dealin' with one senior shaman. You're dealin' with the Ancient Ones. Now, if'n I was you, I'd make it a point to shift the line a mile or so to the east." Having had his say, he turned without a good-bye and strode out.

The foreman was glad to see him leave. It would make a good story to tell the work gangs. Mountain men were kind of rare hereabouts, and it wasn't every day you got a visit from one big as a house and crazier than a bedbug.

It was cold in the desert that night. In the Sonoran summer you prayed every day for the heat to dissipate, and then in the winter you prayed for it to return. Those who survived and prospered in such country realized early on that whatever deity was involved, it had made its decision about the land a long time ago, and constant pleading for change would get you nothing but a sore throat that no change in the weather would make any better.

At Malone's back, Casa Grande—the Big House—the place of the Ancient Ones, rose four stories toward the new moon. Windows like square black eyes gaped at the clouds milling uncertainly overhead. A big rattler slithered into a crack in the caliche, and Malone listened to the final surprised squeak of a startled kangaroo rat.

For a while he concentrated on listening to the sounds of the snake swallowing. Then he let his gaze come to rest on the figure seated across the small fire from him.

Ma-Hok-Naweh's age was unknown save to himself and a few intimate friends. A true shaman keeps his real age private, which is understandable since it's the age not of his body but of his soul. Malone held Ma-Hok-Naweh in high regard. He was a true medicine man, not an accomplished fake like Broken Water of the Ute.

A few ribbed saguaros stood sentinel behind the old man, guarding him from the night. At their bases, lines ran through the sandstone, across his face, to continue down into the stone on which they sat.

"The Ancient Ones are restless. They are restless because they are frightened for their house in this world."

As Ma-Hok-Naweh spoke, his grandson Cheshey sat cross-legged nearby, watching and listening without comment. A wise boy. Like his grandfather and like Malone, he wore only a breechcloth and the ever-present headband.

"How will the Ancient Ones make their fear known?" Malone asked.

"I cannot tell, my friend." The shaman studied the sand pictures before them, watching as the wind played with the granules stained that afternoon with fresh vegetable dyes. As the sand shifted, the earth shifted with it, for the sand is of the earth and knows its ways. "All I know is that it will take the form of the white man's own medicine, but seen through the eyes of the Ancient Ones."

"Will many die?"

Again the old eyes examined the play of wind and sand. "It may be. I am saddened. Though I argue with the white man's steel trail, I do not wish to see him die. There are many who are like well-meaning but ignorant braves, who only follow the orders of their chief, he who makes war upon the land, and question not what he says."

Now the moon was hidden by dark clouds, and the rumble of

approaching thunder rolled over the paloverde and the thorn bushes.

"Can nothing be done?"

"Not by this old one. Perhaps by you, if you would wish to try. You know the white man's ways as well as our ways. The spirits might look kindly on you as an intermediary. With help and will, you might do something."

Carefully he reached down and collected a handful of green sand and put it in a small leather sack. He did the same with a palmful of ocher grains. Malone accepted both sacks and put them aside.

"Keep them apart, for they contain both life and death," Ma-Hok-Naweh admonished him. "You know the words. Use the sand and the words together and you may turn the unrest of the Ancient Ones. Do not be startled by what you may see. Remember that it is only white man's medicine as seen through the eyes of my ancestors. And if you cannot work this thing, get out, get out quickly, my friend!"

Malone rose, his near-naked body massive against the ancient wall behind him. "Don't worry about that, old teacher. I don't aim to die fer no damn-fool railroad man. But maybe I kin save his braves in spite of themselves."

Ma-Hok-Naweh stared worriedly at the sands as his friend dressed, mounted, and rode off toward the south, toward the railhead. After a while his grandson spoke for the first time all evening, his voice a whisper as befitted the enormity of the occasion.

"Do you think he can do anything, Grandfather?"

"No, I do not think so. But he is a strange man, this Amos Malone, even for a white man. It may be that I am wrong and that he *can* do something. Also, you must always remember that he is crazy, and that is a great help in dealing with the spirits." Ma-Hok-Naweh looked to the ground. Dark spots began to appear on the dirt. "Now help me inside the Big House, grandson. It is the best place now for me to be."

The boy looked around uneasily. "Because the wrath of the Ancient Ones is upon us?"

"No, you young fool. Because it is starting to rain."

Worthless was breathing hard when Malone rode into the railhead camp. But Worthless always breathed hard, whether he'd been
ridden ten miles or ten feet. It was his form of protest at being
subjected to the indignity of having a man on his back.

The foreman had a tent all to himself, set apart from those
shared in common by the laborers. Malone strode inside, reached
into the bed, and yanked the foreman to a sitting position. The man
weighed well over two hundred pounds, but that didn't keep Malone
from shaking him like a child.

"Wake up, Dungannon! Wake up, you son of a spastic
leprechaun, or I'll leave you to die in your bed!"

"Huh? Whuzza ... You! Let go of me, you bloody trespassing
madman. I'll see you hung in Tucson if I can't have you lynched on
the spot! Let go of me, or I'll ..." He paused, and his voice changed.
"What's that?"

"What's what?" So mad was Malone, so intent was he on shaking
some sense into this fool, that he'd tuned everything else out. Now
he let his senses roam.

Sure enough, there it was. Whatever *it* was.

He let go of the foreman's nightshirt. Dungannon pulled on his
boots and in nightshirt and peaked cap followed the mountain man
toward the doorway of the tent.

Dungannon sounded confused when he spoke. "Sounds like a
train coming," he said. "Don't know why they'd be bringing in extra
supplies at night. Funny they're not sounding a whistle. Guess they
don't want to wake us.... No, there's the whistle, all right."

Malone strained his senses at the night. There was more outside
the tent than the smell and sounds of rain falling steadily, more than
the suggestion of metal coming closer. He could sense it, and it
wasn't good.

"That's no train a-comin', Dungannon, and that weren't no
whistle you heard."

"Sure and it was, you great deaf amadán. There, hear it again?"

"Listen, man!" Malone was running out of patience and he knew
they were running out of time. "That's no train whistle. That's a
whinny, though like none I ever heard before."

He knew what he knew, and so did Worthless. He'd seen his docked unicorn fight off a wounded grizzly with his front hooves and dance neatly around a whole den of jittery rattlers without bucking or getting himself bit. But now Worthless was pulling frantically at the hitching rail where he'd been tied, eyes wild like with locoweed—even the squinty one with the white circle around it—bucking and yelling hoarsely. Worthless, who was usually afraid of nothing.

The wind rose, bringing mournful thunder with it. Malone and Dungannon stepped out into the blowing rain and shielded their eyes. Finally, Malone had to put a big hand on the foreman's shoulder and spin him around.

"You're lookin' the wrong way!" the mountain man shouted against the wind.

"But the line ends here" was the reply. Already Dungannon was soaked to the skin. "It *has* to be coming up from the south. There're no rails north of here!"

"What makes you think it's coming down rails?" Malone yelled at him.

At the same time Dungannon saw it coming. His face turned pale as whitewash, and he turned and bolted. Malone let him go, stood his ground, and made sure the two leather pouches were close at hand while he fought to keep the rain out of his eyes.

Worthless was brave and loyal but no equine fool. With an astonishing heave on his bridle, he wrenched both posts out of the ground and went bounding off like blazes to the west, the hitching rail bouncing wildly along behind him.

"I'll be hornswoggled," Malone muttered as he stared northward. Ma-Hok-Naweh had been right: white man's medicine seen through Indian eyes.

Thundering down out of the scrub-covered hills came the Iron Horse. Lightning flashed on its metallic flanks. It breathed no smoke and whistled no greeting. Its eyes were the fiery orange of the wood box, and the spirits of the dead kept its engine well stoked. It rattled and banged as it ran, and there was a blind indifference about it that was more terrifying than any overt sense of purpose could have been. Looking at it, you'd think it had no more sense in its iron skull, no more care for what it was trampling under-foot, than did a train.

Big it was, bigger than any horse, iron or otherwise. It came crashing into the camp, kicking aside piles of big ties like they were toothpicks, orange eyes flaming, its massive iron hooves making pulp of wheelbarrows and buckets and storage sheds. While Malone stared, it took the most recently completed section of rail in its teeth and pulled, ripping up a hundred feet of new line as if it were toying with a worm. It turned and kicked out with both hind feet. The rail-laying locomotive parked on the siding nearby went flying, tons of steel and wood, and landed loudly in a shallow pool of rainwater.

Then it came for Malone.

The wind and lightning and rain had drowned out its approach and kept the men in their warm beds, but when a locomotive flies a hundred yards through the air and lands hard on the ground, it makes a good bit of noise. A few sleepy-eyed, tough-skinned laborers began stumbling out of their tents.

Malone could smell steel breath and squinted against the iron filings that were spit his way. Taking a deep breath, he spoke in a voice as large as any the clouds overhead could muster:

"WHOA!"

That brought the iron monster up short for just an instant, more startled than intimidated. It was long enough for Malone to take aim and fling the two handsful of colored sand he held. Somehow, in spite of the wind and rain, that sand stayed compacted long enough to strike the broad iron chest.

Without pausing to see if he'd thrown true, Malone began to recite in booming tones: *"Hey-ah-hey-hey, ah-wha-tey-ah, hey-hey-oh-ta-hoh-neh,"* and added for good, if unscholarly, measure: "Now *git!*"

A few shouts sounded dimly from those workers awake enough to see something towering over the camp there in the rain, but by the time they reached the place where Malone stood standing, hands on hips, staring off into the storm, the mountain man was all alone.

"What happened, mister?" one man yelled.

Another stuck his head into the foreman's tent. "Mr. Dungannon? Mr. Dungannon, sir!" He emerged a moment later. "He ain't here."

"Who're you?" Malone asked.

"Harold Sipes, sir. I'm tie and spike supervisor for this section of line. What the devil happened here, sir? I thought I saw something ... something impossible."

"That you did, Harold."

"Where's Mr. Dungannon?"

Malone turned back southward. He thought he could still hear a distant clanking through the wind, but he couldn't be sure. His ears were full of rainwater and iron filings. "Mr. Dungannon told me he's tired o' the railroad business and that he's gone south fer his health. Before he left, he did tell me one thing to pass on to his immediate subordinate. I guess that'd be you, Harold. He said to be sure to tell you t' move the track a couple o' miles east of here before you start northwest up toward the Salt River. Said to be sure the company stays well clear of those old ruins the Indians call the Big House."

"He did?" The supervisor wiped water from his head. "He never said nothing like that to me before."

"Mr. Dungannon took a sudden interest in the culture of the local people. It were his last wish before he left."

Sipes looked uncertain. "Well, sir, I don't know as how I have the authority to alter the recommendations of the survey."

"Harold, remember what you think you saw out here when you came stumblin' out o' your warm bed? Somethin' a mite impossible, you said?"

"Yes, I ..." He paused and found himself staring into black eyes so deep that they just went right on through into that big hirsute head, never really stopping anywhere, just fading on and on into dark nothingness. "Actually, sir, maybe I didn't see much of anything. It was awful dark. Still is. Leastwise, I don't think I'd write my missus I saw it."

"Or your superiors, either. They wouldn't take well to such a tale, I think. Be a good idea to shift that line."

"Um, maybe it would at that, sir. Now that you put it clear like you have, I expect it would be the sensible thing to do, especially seeing as how it was Mr. Dungannon's last request."

"Before he left to go south," Malone added.

"Yes, sir. Before he left to go south. I'll see to it."

"Good man, Sipes." Malone turned from him. "Now, if you'll excuse me, I've got a date with a clean bed and new linen. But first I've got to run down my fool horse." He gestured toward two holes in the ground nearby, now half-full of water. "Went and took off with the whole damn hitchin' rail, he did."

Sipes glanced at the holes and smiled. "Not arguing with you, mister, but there ain't a horse alive strong enough to pull that hitching rail out of that rock. I saw them posts set in myself. There was talk of putting a small station here someday and they were put in to last."

Malone was already wandering out of earshot, a sour expression on his face. "Then where d'you expect that rail's got to, Harold? Worthless ain't no normal horse." As the rain began to close in around him, he raised his voice. "You hear that, you good-for-nothing, four-legged, useless hunk o' coyote bait! Wait till I get my hands on you, you lily-livered, swaybacked equine coward!"

Supervisor Sipes listened until the falling rain swallowed up sight and sound of the mountain man. No, he thought, that wouldn't be no normal horse, mister. And you sure ain't no normal human being. Then he saw the torn-up section of track and wondered how the wind had done that, and then his eyes lit on the laying locomotive lying on its side like a dead mammoth a good hundred yards away, and he *knew* the wind hadn't done *that*.

Then he thought back to what he'd half maybe glimpsed through the storm and decided it would be a good time to get back into bed under the covers where it was safe. But by now there might be scorpions crawled in there to get out of the rain, and he hesitated.

Until something far way, but not far enough away, went *clank* and the supervisor decided that for the remainder of this night, anyways, it would be smarter to bed down with the scorpions....

I think that once writers have decided to put the word "witch" into a story, they should be able to go in any direction they choose and produce something of interest. My wife introduced me to the fable of the kitchen witch, who keeps watch over that part of the home. But in my mind, "benign" and "witch" are not words that play well together.

What if a kitchen witch turns out to be more witch than kitchen? Worlds might not be at stake, empires might not tremble: after all, your average kitchen witch tends to run to the diminutive. But even a characteristically small one could, if so inclined, make a lot of trouble in a household. Malone always being ready to lend a helping hand, no matter how small or seemingly insignificant the problem, I thought I'd present him with a conundrum more irritating than earthshaking.

Not much of a problem, you might say. But then, it's not your kitchen that's under siege.

WITCHEN WOES

Amos Malone was sipping at his fourth whiskey when the distraught woman wandered into the saloon. Her mere presence served to indicate the degree of her distress, for no female citizen of good repute would enter a hard-core drinking establishment unescorted unless her motivation arose from intentions indecent or insane.

Her arrival distracted several pairs of eyes from cards, drinks, and the unwholesome hostesses who were the only other non-males present that afternoon in the Piccadilly. Several hands groped for her, and her country prettiness provoked more than one lascivious proposal. She ran the gauntlet of hopeful debauchery as she searched the crowd for someone in particular, twisting out of one grasp after another, skirt and hair flying, yanking her shawl free of the grimy, rum-slick fingers that clutched at it.

One ex-miner was more persistent (or less drunk and therefore more accurate) than the rest, for he soon had her in a firm grip with both hands. "Now, don't be so contrary, little lady." He leaned close and spoke with breath that was borderline flammable. "Howsabout a little kiss?"

Her back arched as she fought to dodge his mouth and the miasma that issued from the inebriated depths beyond. "I am a married woman, sir, and a decent one. I'll thank you to let go of me!"

Laughter rose from the surrounding tables at this pious declaration. "Shore you is, missy," her captor jeered. "As to the fust, thet don't give me no trouble, and as to the second, it naturally explains whut yer doin' in a fancy hotel like this!"

More laughter—which Malone found he could not ignore though he had done so to the entire contretemps up to then. Generally he was of a mind to attend solely to his own business, but there was something in the woman's attitude and tone that led him to believe she might be as upstanding as she claimed. Anyhow, it was a slow afternoon in the sleepy town of Sacramento, and he didn't have anything better to do, so he downed the last of the amber liquid remaining in his shot glass, set the glass down slowly on the oak bar, wiped his lips, and turned. On his face was an expression that made the bartender make haste to sink out of sight.

"Pardon me, friend," Malone rumbled in a voice that sounded as if it were rising from the bottom of a mine shaft, "but it appears the lady is in some trouble and doesn't need any additional of your makin'."

"And jest whut business be it of ..." The ex-miner hesitated as he caught sight of his questioner. "... Mad Amos Malone?" he continued, his voice suddenly less than a whisper.

Mad Amos Malone stood a mite taller and spread a tad wider than most men ... and not a few bears. He was—or had been—a member of that unique breed known as the mountain man: that peculiar subspecies of *Homo sapiens* closely related to both the angel and the Neanderthal. Sane folk left such individuals alone.

The young woman wrenched around, and her eyes grew wide as she caught sight of Malone. "Sir, if you are truly the Amos Malone they call mad, then you are he whom I have been seeking."

Danged if she didn't have green eyes, Malone mused. He'd always been a sucker for green eyes. "Then that makes it personal." Malone took a step toward the ex-miner, who was no featherweight himself. "You kin understand my concern now, friend."

"Yeh. Shore I kin, mister." The other man kept his eyes focused on the mountain man as he let go of the woman and edged aside.

"Now then, ma'am," Malone said politely (such *limpid* green eyes!), "this is hardly the place to engage in genteel conversation. I suggest we step outside."

"Thank you, Mr. Malone." Pulling her shawl protectively about her shoulders, she headed for the swinging doors, Malone following in her wake.

As they reached the doors, Malone sensed the nervous whisper of retreating air behind him. Air's funny that way. It can laugh, it can cry, and it knows when to get out of the way. Air ain't no fool.

Neither was Amos Malone, who whirled and brought his hand up as he jerked to one side. Several gasps were heard, and a few cards fluttered to the floor of the saloon as he plucked the knife out of the air not three inches from the place his neck had been just seconds earlier.

The ex-miner who had thrown it let out a strangled cry and crashed through the back-alley door, pausing neither to recover his property nor to turn the lock.

Years later, a few who claimed they had been there swore that they saw the mountain man lean forward and whisper a few words to the knife before throwing it in return. One of those insisted that the knife answered back. At the time, though, none of them voiced their observations, not wishing to be thought of by their friends as unbalanced. On one account, however, all agreed. Malone threw that knife so hard an echoing thunder trailed behind it like a dog worrying a wagon. It went straight through the gap the miner had made in the course of executing his precipitate exit, then turned sharply to the right, down the alley. A minute or so passed before a distant scream reached the attentive listeners.

The piano player circumspectly resumed his off-key rendition of "I'll Wake You When the Mail Boat Comes In," and the other inhabitants of the Piccadilly Saloon returned to their poker and drinks.

"I hope you did not kill him, Mr. Malone," the young woman said as they exited into the street.

"No, ma'am. I don't cotton to killin' drunks. Most times they don't know what they're about. Just gave him a warnin' prick, so to speak, somewhere between his waist and his holster."

"I am glad to hear it. I would not want to be the cause of another man's death." She looked a little uncertain. "Am I mistaken, or did I clearly see that knife you threw make a sharp turn to the right upon leaving this establishment? Such a thing is contrary to nature ... for a knife."

Malone shrugged, his expression noncommittal. "There's not much that's contrary to nature if you just know how to sweet-talk her along a little."

"Which is precisely why I have sought you out among those ruffians, Mr. Malone. It is said among those in the know that you are familiar with many things the rest of us have no desire to be familiar with. I have desperate need of someone with such knowledge, for I am at my wit's end what to do."

She started to sob. Malone knew they were real tears, not merely tears concocted for his benefit. Real tears smell different from falsified ones, and mountain men are known for their acuity of smell.

Malone thought the tears looked faintly green.

"Now, ma'am, it's true I've been exposed to certain things they don't teach in eastern colleges, but I can't presume to help you until I know the nature of your trouble. Clearly it's affected you deeply."

"Not only me," she replied, "but my entire family as well. It's a calumny for which I blame myself."

"Family? Oh," said Malone, crestfallen (*ah, fare thee well, ocean eyes*). He drew himself up and put aside his disappointment. "I'll help if I can, of course. I was never one to turn away from a lady in distress."

"You are gallant, sir."

"No, ma'am, just stupid. What be your problem ... and your name?"

"Oh. Excuse me for not saying to start with. Mary Makepeace is my name, sir, and Hart Makepeace my husband." She dabbed at her face with a tatted handkerchief redolent of lilac. "I have a kitchen witch, Mr. Malone."

"Call me Amos. Or Mad," he chuckled, "if you prefer." Then, seriously, "A kitchen witch? You mean one of those little good-luck figures made out of paper and wood and paint and scraps of old cloth?"

"No, sir ... Amos. A real kitchen witch, and the very manifestation of horror she is, too. She won't leave me alone, and she won't bring back my poor family, and I ... and I ..." The flow of tears started again from those vitreous green orbs, and Malone found himself holding and comforting her—a not entirely unpleasant circumstance.

A derisive snort sounded nearby. Malone glanced toward the hitching rail, where a mongrelized, oversized, squint-eyed hooved quadruped was giving him the jaundiced eye. He made a face at the sarcastic creature, but he did take the hint. Reluctantly, he eased the unhappy Mrs. Makepeace an arm's length away.

"A real witch, eh? In the kitchen? I've heard of 'em before, but they're supposed to be pretty scarce hereabouts. They're the inspiration for those little doll figures you find in kitchens, but the real ones are twice as ugly and a hundred times more dangerous."

She stared up at him (*with emeralds*, he thought ... *olivine and malachite*). "You ... you mean that you believe me, sir ... *Amos?*"

"I can tell a liar as far off as a month-dead wapiti, ma'am, and 'tis plain for any fool to see that you're tellin' the truth. I'm not sure if I can be of any help, though. For its size, a witchen—for that's what you're afflicted with as sure as a djinn dry-cleans his clothes—packs a mighty powerful wallop. But I'll do what I can. Where's your place at?"

She turned and pointed eastward. "That way, a half day's ride, Amos Malone. But there's no stage going back that direction for another fortnight."

"Then we'd best get started, ma'am." He turned and mounted his horse, extended down a hand, and pulled her up behind him as though she weighed nothing at all. "Let's go, Worthless," he told his mount.

The horse turned and started eastward.

"Your pardon, Amos," said Mrs. Makepeace from her delightfully warm position immediately at his back, "but I don't believe I saw you unhitch this animal."

"That's because he wasn't hitched, ma'am." He patted the horse's neck. "Worthless don't cotton to bein' tied up. He's pretty good about staying in one place, though, so I don't insist on it no more. I only have trouble with him when there's a mare in heat around."

"That's understandable, of course," she replied gravely, putting both arms around his waist and holding tight.

At which sight the piebald steed of uncertain parentage let out a most unequine laugh....

The Makepeace farm was located beside a burbling little stream not far from the north fork of the American River. Less than twenty years before, the entire length of that river had been aswarm with thousands of immigrants in search of instant fortune, for the bed of the American River had been paved with gold. Now the gold and most of the immigrants were gone. Only the scoured-over river remained, draining farmland that was worth far more than the yellow metal that made men blind. A few, though, like Hart Makepeace, had seen the richness in the soil that had been stripped of its gold and had stayed on in the hope of making a smaller but surer fortune.

Now, however, it seemed that something small and vicious was determined to quash that dream. Malone could smell it as they trotted into the fenced yard. His suspicions were confirmed by the sound of a plate shattering somewhere inside the modest little farmhouse.

"She's still at it," Mary Makepeace said nervously, peering around the bulk of the mountain man. "I'd prayed that she'd be gone by now."

Malone shook his massive head, squinting toward the house. The evil that lay within was strong enough to make his nose wrinkle and start a pounding at the back of his neck. "Not likely, ma'am. Witchens are persistent stay-at-homes, especially if they choose to make your home theirs. They're not likely to leave voluntarily, nor put to rights the damage they're fond o' doin'."

"Then what am I to do?"

"What we can, ma'am. What we can." He dismounted and helped her down....

The kitchen had been turned into a wreck worse than that of the *Hesperus*. Only a few pieces of porcelain and crockery remained intact. Cracked china littered the wooden floor, mixed with the contents of dozens of baskets and jars. Pickles lay scattered among fruit turned rancid. Home-canned jams and preserves had made the oak planks slick as river rock. A butter churn lay forlorn and shattered across the room, below the sink pump that had been torn loose from its mounting bolts. Broom straw was everywhere, sticking to walls and floor alike.

Buzzing and soaring through the air above this culinary wreckage on a sliver of wood the size of a good cigar was the tiny figure of a wrinkled old woman. Her gray hair flowed from beneath a little scrap of a bandanna, and her skirt was stained with pepper sauce. She had a nose the size and color of a rotten grape, and her skin was the shade of old tobacco juice. On either side of that heroically ugly nose flashed tiny eyes sharp and dangerous as the business end of a black scorpion.

"Hee-hee-hee-hee!" she was cackling as she tore through the air of the ruined kitchen like a drunken dragonfly. "More's the food and more's the pity, hee-hee-hee!" *Crash!* A pot of beans went spinning to the floor.

Mary Makepeace huddled fearfully behind the imposing bulk of Amos Malone. "M-m-make her go away, Amos. Oh, please make her go away and put to rights the damage she's done!"

"Where's the rest of your family?" Malone asked her.

"Over ... there." She fell to sobbing again as she pointed.

Standing in a far corner of the kitchen, a fistful of cigars clutched in one frozen hand, was a wooden figure of startling realism. It was not made in the image of a stolid Plains Indian, though, but rather in that of a young man clad in woolen white shirt, suspenders, work boots, a pair of Mr. Levi's revolutionary new pants, and an expression that mixed bafflement with sheer terror.

"That's my husband, Hart," Mary Makepeace bawled, "and those large cookie jars at his feet are our sons, Frank and Christopher."

Malone nodded, his expression grim. "You got yourself a mean'un, for sure." He readied himself.

They waited while the witchen continued to engage in her orgy of destruction. At last the tiny evilness clad in the guise of an old woman zoomed over to hover in the air a foot in front of Malone's beard.

"Oh-ho-hee-hee," she laughed gleefully. "So, the missy of the house has come back, eh? Good! I was so busy, I missed you the first time!" She glared mischievously at the terrified Mary. "What would you like to be? A nice harp, perhaps? You'd make a good-looking harp, missy. Or maybe that's too fine for such as you, yes, too fine by half. A beer mug, maybe, for some filthy-minded man to drink from? Or how about a slop jar? Hee-hee-hee! Yes, that'd suit you, yes, yes, a green-eyed slop jar!" She whirled around in a tight circle, delighted at her own perverse inventiveness. Mary Makepeace cowered weakly behind Malone.

The witchen tried to dart around him. Each time, he blocked her path with a big, callused hand. Finally, the enraged little nastiness floated up to stare into his eyes.

"Now, what's this, what's this what interferes with my housework, eh? I think it's alive. I think it does live, I think. At first I thought it was a big sack of manure the missy had pushed ahead of her to hide behind, but now I see that it moves, it moves, hee-hee-hee. Could it be that it talks as well, could it?"

"You are, without question," Malone said studiously, "the vilest, most loathsome-looking little smidgen of bile it's ever been my displeasure to set eyes upon."

"Flattery'll get you anywhere, sonny," she cackled. Then, in a dark tone rich with menace, she added, "Perhaps if I put those eyes out for you, you wouldn't be troubled with setting them on me, eh?" When Malone didn't respond, she said, "What shall I do with you, with you? You're too big to make into a piece of furniture for this besotted kitchen. Maybe I'll turn *you* into a kitchen, yes, yes? Yes, with a nice little cook fire in your belly." Her tiny eyes blazed threateningly. "I'll bake my bread in your belly, man."

Ignoring her, Malone whispered to Mary Makepeace, "Have you and your husband been fighting lately, ma'am?"

"Of course not," she started to say. "We were happily ..." Then she recalled what Mad Amos Malone had told her about being able to smell a liar some good distance away and thought better of her response. "Yes, yes, we have been." She was shaking as she stared at the floor. "But if only I could have him back, Amos! We fought over such little, insignificant things! And the children ... I'll never yell at my dear boys like that again!"

"Most folks don't think clearly about the consequences o' strong words when they're spewin' 'em, ma'am. That's what likely brought this badness down on you. Fightin' can poison a home, and a kitchen's especially sensitive to it. If the other conditions are right —not to mention the *ether* conditions—well, you've seen what can happen."

"Please give my family back to me, Amos," she pleaded. "Please ... I'll do anything for another chance. *Anything.*"

Green eyes rich with promise fluttered at him, but Malone turned resolutely away from that beckoning gaze with a resolve a Kiowa pony would have envied. "Just stay behind me, ma'am. Just stay behind me." He turned his attention back to the waiting witchen.

"I don't think you're goin' t' turn me into no fireplace, filthfingers," he told it, "and I aim to see to it that you don't hurt this lady no more and that you undo the damage you've already done."

"Hee-hee-hee, you do, do you?" She took her little hands off the nape of the tiny broomstick and waved them at him. "Hibble-deglum, mubble-me-mock, fire and iron, kettle and stock, make of this mountain a—"

Malone didn't give her a chance to finish. He had the advantage of volume, if not timing. "Bellow and roar all you wish, balloonbeak, but you won't sunder me. I've been circled round by the five fingers of Rusal-Ratar, Queen of the Kitchens of the Earth and personal chef to Quoomander, Ruler of All the Djinn, Spirits, and Unassigned Ghosts of the Nether Regions!"

"—two-armed stove crock!" the witchen finished emphatically.

There was a flash of smoke and fire as she threw something at him. Mad Amos Malone disappeared in a cloud of green haze. From behind it, Mary Makepeace let out a despairing scream, and the witchen's "hee-hee-hee!" of triumph soared above it.

Her triumph, however, dissipated as rapidly as the haze, for within it Mad Amos Malone still stood in the kitchen doorway, unchanged, unharmed, and certainly unstoved, though a faint fragrance of unholy boiling did issue from the vicinity of his slightly scorched belt.

"Now then, wart-heart," he whispered huskily as he reached toward his waist, "how'd thee like to try riding a bowie knife for a change?"

"No, no, no, no! Not possible! It's not possible ... eeeee!" The witchen found herself dodging Malone's huge knife, twisting and spinning for her life as the mountain man sliced and cut at her agile little form.

But she was quick and experienced, and while Malone was so fast that the knife seemed but a shining in his hand, he was not used to dealing with so small a target. "Hold up there," he finally told his quarry, gasping for breath. He bent over and put his hands on his knees as he fought for wind. "I'm plumb tuckered out."

So was the witchen. Exhausted, she landed on a shelf and climbed off her broomstick, dangling withered little legs over the edge. "Fast ... so fast he is," she wheezed. "Almost too fast for old Beeblepwist, almost, almost ... but not quite, not quite." A sly grin snuck over her extraordinarily ugly face. "Should be a better way to settle this, settle this. A better way, yes."

"Don't listen to her, Amos!" Mary Makepeace shouted from her position just outside the kitchen. "She'll try to trick you and ..."

"No harm in hearin' what she has to say, ma'am." Amos took a deep breath, straightened, and was eye to eye with the sitting witchen. "I've no stomach for this constant chasin'. What have you in mind, corpse-cleaner?"

"No stomach for chasing, for chasing, eh? Have you stomach for some food? A cooking contest, yes? Yes, me and thee, hee-hee-hee?"

Malone considered the proposal carefully. He was a man of many talents. There were those who regarded him as a middlin' to clever cook. "Cookin' contest with what as its aim?" he asked guardedly.

"You win, I'll put this hovel to rights and lose myself in the Bottomless Jar. I win ... hee-hee-hee ... I win, and you become part of the decor, along with Little Miss Priss, there." She threw a short finger of fire in the direction of Mary Makepeace, who barely kept herself from swooning. "And one other thing," she said, her voice becoming less scratchy than usual, "one thing other. I keep your soul, man, your soul."

"I thought you wanted me for a stove," he said nonchalantly.

"I do, I do, but a soul's no good to a stove, and I can always find a buyer for a spare one."

Malone scratched his beard. "If you think a good stove don't need no soul, you ain't half the cook you think you are. I agree. What kind of cookin' do you propose? We ought to work similar, or there'll be no basis for comparison."

"I'm partial to spicy foods," the witchen said encouragingly. "Think you the same, the same?"

Malone nodded. "I can handle tol'able condiments in my food."

"Then something spicy it shall be," cackled the witchen, adding, unsurprisingly, a "hee-hee-*hee*!"

Soul or surcease at stake, it was determined that the spiciest dish would be declared the winner. A truce blanketed that abused kitchen then, for both mountain man and witchen needed time to gather the ingredients for their respective dishes. Mary Makepeace saw a few of her precious utensils and pots restored for the purposes of the contest.

Three days slipped by. The sky over the farm grew as dark and angry as the odors that began to issue from it. People remarked on the peculiar scents in the air as far away as San Francisco to the west and Chinaman's Bar to the east. Rabbits dug their burrows a little deeper that autumn, the birds moved their nests higher in the tree-tops, and for the first time since its founding, the citizens of Sacramento were not plagued by hordes of mosquitoes from the swamps along the Feather River—all the insects having dropped dead of unknown cause.

The heat that began to rise from two steaming kettles blistered the wood of the farmhouse on the north fork of the American River. Paint peeled off furniture hauled undamaged clear across the country from New England, and rusty iron was scoured miraculously clean. Mary Makepeace huddled on the floor just outside the kitchen, not daring to peer inside, yet she still acquired a tan so deep and permanent that from that day on people mistook her for a Mexican.

By the third night the two dishes were nearly finished. A deep yellow-orange glow illuminated the kitchen, and no bullfrogs called along the length of the American River.

From the kettle above which the witchen danced and flew rose a pink glow alive with tiny explosions of spice. It emanated from a soup the color of pahoehoe, the thick ropy lava that sometimes flows from the lips of angry volcanoes.

Mad Amos Malone stood like a russet cliff above his own pot, stirring the contents occasionally with an iron bar until the mixture was thick and sizzling and the bar had melted clean away. The glow from both kettles suffused the room with the hues of Hell. So spice-ridden were the two concoctions that the wood fires burning beneath each pot had begun to cower away from the metal bottoms, so that witchen and mountain man alike had to chide the flames back into heating them.

And when the smell and temperature were at their highest, when both courses were ready for the tasting, the witchen floated in the hot air rising from her own pot and said with great anticipation to Mad Amos Malone, "You ... go first ... hee-hee-hee."

Mad Amos somberly removed his wolf-skull cap and unbuttoned his buckskin shirt. Ceremoniously, he downed half a gallon of cold stream water from a still-intact jug. The soup ladle burnt his fingers slightly when he picked it up, but he held tight to it. Cupped in the scoop of the ladle was something that bubbled and burst into little sparks. He brought his lips to the edge of the spoon. Mary Makepeace peered fearfully around the corner of the open doorway, one hand shoved reflexively into her mouth.

Malone hesitated. "What is it?"

"Why?" the witchen challenged him. "You afraid of a little soup, hee-hee-hee?"

"Nope. Just like to know what I'm eatin'."

"It's soup," she cackled, her eyes bunting evilly. "Just plain red pepper soup, seasoned with brimstone and jellied kerosene and a few other personal spices. A delicate consommé sure to please as rugged and discerning a palate as yours, man. My own recipe ... hee-hee-hee."

Malone nodded once, his face aglow with the light rising not just from the boiling kettle but from the liquid frothing on the ladle and downed the contents in a single gulp. He smacked his lips and put the ladle back in the pot.

Water started to stream from the corners of his black eyes, to cascade down his cheeks and into his beard. The tears were so hot that the hairs of his beard curled aside to give them free passage and the hair on his head began to writhe desperately as if trying to flee his skull. Smoke began to rise from the region of his belly, and the leather there darkened ominously. The veins in his eyes swelled until there wasn't any white for all the red. A fingernail fell intact and smoking from the fourth finger of his right hand, leaving a steaming scar in its wake.

Malone opened his mouth, and a gust of fire issued forth that put to shame the roaring of the falls of the Yosemite—a great, intemperate blast of flame that turned the iron pump on the edge of the sink into a tired lump of slag. A sharp explosion shook the house as the heat of that exhalation blew out every one of the house's twelve imported windows, and Mary Makepeace held her head and screamed and screamed. Outside the kitchen, where the blast had struck, twenty-five feet of grass and brush was vaporized in a swath five feet wide.

The force of his reaction had propelled Malone into the far wall of the kitchen, cracking a support log and threatening to bring down the whole upper story along with the roof. The log creaked, but it held.

Slowly, Malone picked himself up from the floor, his eyes still watering, and rubbed at his throat as he nodded admiringly toward the aghast witchen. "Not bad. Not bad at all." The lining of his mouth had gone numb, and his tongue felt like what a match is like after it's been used. "Now," he said softly, "it's *your* turn."

"Hmph! Waste of time this now, waste of time." She flew over to float above the steaming kettle at which Malone had labored. Some of the bravado had fled from her cackle. Malone ought not to have been alive, much less offering comments on the quality of her most incendiary dish. She stuck her bulbous nose downward and sniffed contemptuously, then dropped lower and studied the simmering surface. "Maybe you survived the tasting," she said dangerously, "but you won't survive the contesting, hee-hee-hee." Using the end of an unlit match for a spoon, she dipped out a sample of the concoction and popped it into her mouth.

For a moment she chewed reflectively. Then it hit her. Her eyes bulged enormously, and her mouth dropped open, for what Malone had wrought was as feral and fey as it was flamboyantly effective. "Ohhh myyyyy!" she exclaimed sharply. Her skin turned from brown to pink to cherry red, and her tiny body ballooned up like a pig bladder. Bigger and bigger she swelled, until at last she burst in a cloud of red heat that filled the whole kitchen.

When the cloud had gone, so had the witchen. A corner of the mountain man's mouth turned up, and he gave a loud snort of satisfaction. "Hee-hee, *hee*," he growled at nothing in particular.

"Mary?" a querulous, uncertain voice murmured. "Mary?"

Malone watched enviously as Mrs. Makepeace rushed to embrace her newly restored husband and children, vowing as long as she was granted life to live in understanding and harmony with him again, to love and honor and all those other words so many people take so casually the first time around. Her only problem was that she didn't have enough arms to hug him and the children as tightly as she wished.

When the tearful reunion had settled down somewhat and the

thankful Hart Makepeace had learned what had transpired during his cellulose sojourn, Mary was able to inspect a gleaming, completely restored kitchen. Even the ruined jams and preserves had been returned to their respective jars. Only the melted sink pump remained to remind all of what had gone before.

Unexpected side benefits arose from the confrontation. For the remainder of his life Hart Makepeace would smoke neither cigar nor pipe. The two Hart children, who spent the rest of the afternoon vomiting up cookies, chocolate, oatmeal, raisins, nuts, and other baker's ingredients, were able to resist permanently the most tempting blandishments Sacramento's millers could proffer.

That night, as Amos Malone was preparing to take his leave of the farm, Mary Makepeace asked him, "What was it you prepared that affected her so, Mr. Mal ... Amos?"

"A little something I learned from Tullie Kanotay, ma'am." He cinched the saddle a little tighter, and a warning groan issued from Worthless's throat. "Tullie Kanotay's part Apache, part Irish, part somethin' not entirely human, and all Texan ... which latter often amounts to the same thing as the former. Bit o' the witch in her own right. That dish can only be made up once a year by any one individual, and then only by one who knows the proper proportions, has the touch of a master French chef and the heart of a Hindoo raj, or else the emissions might unbalance the ice which caps the head and backside of our world. Why, I can hardly eat more than a bowl or two of it myself.

"It's chimera chili, ma'am, and its effects can't be countered by any spell or magic known, because the taste changes every couple o' seconds. It had to be that dish and that one only, or your nasty visitor could've spelled her way around it. But the flavor kept shiftin' too fast for her taste buds, not t' mention her counterspells, and so the moment she sipped it she was done for." He patted the Sharps buffalo rifle slung next to the saddlebags on Worthless's back.

"The recipe itself ain't too hard to work up. Hardest part's findin' chimera meat." He gestured toward the distant, moonlit, serrated crest of the High Sierra off to the east. "Ain't too many chimeras hereabouts, but you can track one down if you know how they work their meanderings."

Mary Makepeace listened to this quietly, then glanced back toward the farmhouse, which once more smelled of cleanliness and home. Inside, her husband and sons were reveling in being once more themselves instead of sterile objects of china and wood. She looked back up at the mountain man through eyes made of lime-green glass. "Dear, kind Amos Malone, whom I shall never call Mad, I don't know how to thank you, but I ... I would offer you one last favor in return for your aid."

Malone eyed her uncertainly. "Now, ma'am, I'm not sure that I ought ..."

"Would you ... would you ... stay for dinner?"

Malone wasn't sure whether to be disappointed or relieved. He rubbed gingerly at his stomach. The heat lingered ... though it hadn't really been a bad soup at all. No, not bad at all.

"I'd be pleased to, ma'am. I don't get the chance to eat much in the way o' home cookin'. I'll stay ... so long as there's plenty of plain meat and unsalted potatoes."

"I'll lock up the pepper," she assured him, smiling delightedly, and led him back toward the house.

Worthless watched them go, then ambled off toward the nearby barn. The forehead horn that Malone kept constantly trimmed back was itching again. That meant for sure there had to be a mare nearby who, like himself, would care nothing for the antics of silly humans but only for the things that really mattered....

A good story usually comes about when two or more elements fuse together. Sometimes these may relate to one another, sometimes not. Beloved of inventive tellers of tales and maniacal taxidermists alike, the jackalope is to be found stuffed and mounted in innumerable western bars and honky-tonks, patient recipient of whiskey stains, crude jokes, and the occasional criminally misplaced dart. Yet rumors of its actual existence continue to surface, even if largely due not to scientific reports but to the rumor-mongering persistence of elderly bewhiskered gentlemen comfortably ensconced in wooden rocking chairs on creaky porches.

The critter itself is story element one. Element number two derives from the steady trickle of European aristocrats who came to visit the Old West, marvel at its landscapes, exchange greetings with the fascinating Native Americans (some bewhiskered, some not), and slaughter as much of the local wildlife as nineteenth-century munitions would allow. All the while dining on tea and crumpets and roast pheasant set out on tablecloths of Irish linen adorned with the contents of wicker baskets filled with embossed silver service. It was all very elegant, civilized, and bloody.

Bragging rights among this imported mélange of dilettante toffs usually went to whoever had killed the most game, or sometimes the most unusual game. Hence one imperial and imperious visitor's insistence on finding and blowing away the extraordinarily elusive jackalope.
Or maybe something else.

JACKALOPE

I'm sorry, gentlemen, but there is nothing left to tempt me. I've killed everything there is to be killed."

Lord Guy Ruxton extracted an imported Havana cigar from a jacket pocket, utilized an engraved Italian cutter to snip the end, and turned slightly to his left so Manners could light it for him. As he puffed it to life, there was a subtle but unmistakable shifting of bodies in the saloon as cardplayers and drinkers leaned in his direction in a vain but hopeful attempt to partake, however infinitesimally, of that expensive aromatic smoke that would forever lie beyond their modest means.

Though they shared the best table in the house with him, Ruxton's audience of Butte's leading citizens was equally admiring of the drifting fragrance, if not nearly so obvious in their appreciation. Being connoisseurs of silver, they admired the cigar cutter as much as the smoke. The town of Butte would not exist save for silver.

Ruxton was a rara avis in Montana Territory: a wide-ranging world traveler and hunter of big game. A fine orator, he held his after-dinner companions spellbound with his tales of tracking exotic animals to the far corners of the earth. Miners and bankers were enthralled by stories of stalking tiger in British India, oryx in Arabia, and all manner of dangerous game in Darkest Africa.

Ruxton was only mildly condescending to the colonials, and they responded in kind. Still, it was clear he was bored. He took a sip of the best scotch Butte had to offer.

"I think the time has come for me to pack it all in, gentlemen, and retire to my estate in Hampshire. You see, there is nothing left for me to hunt. The walls of my trophy room will see no further additions because there is nothing further to add. I lament the end of excitement!"

Silas Hooten had founded the town's first bank and watched it grow along with the production of silver. Now he smiled and put down his drink.

"If it's excitement you crave, why not have a go at hunting buffalo in Sioux territory?"

Ruxton regarded his cigar rather than the banker. "Because there is nothing to hunt in the eastern portion of your benighted territory *except* buffalo, and I have found that animal a singularly uninspiring quarry, though I have hunted it with bow and arrow in the fashion of the savages as well as with rifle. The presence of red hostiles in the vicinity does not alter the object of the hunt." He sighed tiredly.

"No, gentlemen. I have sampled the best of your cuisine, your scenery, and your women. Now I fear it is time I return permanently to England. I do not fault your bucolic hospitality. America was the only land remaining to be hunted. That I have done. Would that there were more truth and less wind to some of the tales I have heard of this country."

"Jackalope."

Ruxton frowned and peered past Hooten. "I beg your pardon, sir." His drinking companions turned to stare with him.

"Jackalope, I said. Got ears, ain'tcha?"

The mouth that had given birth to the word was hidden by a massive buckskin-clad back. The individual seated at the bar looked like a chunk of dark granite blasted from the depths of one of the town's mines, hauled in by mine trolley, and set up on a stool like some druidic monolith. A hat fashioned of the neck and head of a wolf crowned the huge head. Black curly hair lightly flecked with white tumbled in an undisciplined waterfall from beneath the incongruous headgear.

As miners and bankers and visiting nobility looked on, the man turned like an Egyptian statue come to life. Deep-sunk black eyes regarded them from beneath Assyrian brows. The hair at the back was matched in front by a dense beard that might have been forged of wrought-iron wire. Two thick, gnarled fingers supported a beer mug full of whiskey.

"I was sayin', sir, bein' unable to avoid overhearin' part o' your conversation, that it might be you've never hunted for jackalope."

"Yes. Well." Ruxton noted that his companions were now smiling and chuckling softly among themselves. He lowered his voice. "Who is this extremely large chap, and what is he nattering on about?"

"Malone." Orin Waxman ran the biggest general store in town. "Amos Malone."

"*Mad* Amos Malone." Hooten pointed a finger at the side of his head. "The man's crazier than a field of drunken prairie dogs, but it's a rare soul who'll say so to his face."

"Looking upon him, I can understand that. You say he's mad?" Several of the men nodded. "What's this 'jackalope' thing he's on about?"

Waxman shook his head, grinning. "There is no such animal. Somebody somewhere faked one up, and it's turned into a long-standing gag for foolin' Easterners. No offense, Your Lordship. Someone will shoot a jackrabbit and a small deer or antelope. They'll take both to a good taxidermist with a sense of humor, and he'll stick the deer antlers on the rabbit's head. And there's your jackalope."

"I see. It is quite imaginary? You're positive of that?"

The men eyed one another uncertainly and left it to Hooten to reply. "Of course it is, sir. The mountain man's just having a little joke at your expense."

"A good joke, is it? At my expense?" Ruxton's eyes glittered as he turned back to the bar. "Here now, my good fellow. I am intrigued by your comment. Do come and join us."

Mutters of disbelief and distress rose from Ruxton's companions, but none dared object when Malone lurched over to assume the lone empty chair at the table. Such men were not famed for their hygiene. Waxman and the others were relieved to discover that Malone, at least, seemed to have bathed sometime in the not too distant past.

Obviously enjoying himself hugely, Ruxton swept a hand toward his hosts. "These gentlemen insist vehemently that there is no such creature as the one of which you speak. I interpret that to mean they are calling you a liar, sir."

Waxman choked on his liquor, while Hooten's eyes widened in horror. Malone simply eyed them intently for a long moment, then sipped at his tenth of whiskey. The resultant sighs of relief were inaudible.

"None of 'em knows enough to call me a liar. I ain't insulted by the denials o' the ignorant."

His response delighted Ruxton. "Sir, you are a man of surprises! For the moment I intend to leave aside the matter of your sanity. As you overheard, I am something of a sportsman."

"Your claim, not mine."

Ruxton bristled slightly at that but restrained himself. "True enough. You claim I have not hunted this creature you call a jackalope. These good citizens dispute the assertion that it exists. I would put you and them to the test, sir." He made sure he met Malone's gaze evenly. "If you are game."

"I ain't, but the jackalope is."

Ruxton hesitated a moment, then burst out laughing when he was sure. "Upon my word! A rustic with wit. I like you, sir. 'Pon my word I do!" He stubbed out his half-finished cigar and tossed it over his shoulder, ignoring the near riot that followed its descending trajectory as a dozen men scrambled for possession of the butt.

"I would engage you, Mr. Malone, to direct me to the place where I might find such an animal and add it to my collection. I will pay you well, in gold, to serve as my guide in such a venture. Our bargain will be that should we find nothing except fast talk, all expenses will be borne by you."

Malone considered, seeing the doubt in the others' faces. Then he gently set down his mug. "Done. It'll be you and me alone, though. I don't like travelin' with a crowd." He glanced at Ruxton's valet. "Especially slaves."

The valet stiffened. Ruxton only smiled. "Manners is a valued member of my household staff, not a slave. However, it shall be as you wish. I will accompany you alone. Where are we going, sir, or is it to remain a mysterious secret?" He was clearly amused.

Malone turned and nodded westward. "Up thataway. Into the Bitterroots."

"The Bitterroots!" Hooten half rose out of his seat. "Lord Ruxton, I implore you to reconsider this foolishness. The veracity of this—gentleman—is to be doubted. His reputation is eccentric in the extreme. There's nothing up in those mountains except Nez Perce and Blackfeet. You'll find only trouble and danger in that range, not nonexistent game!"

"Come now, gentlemen. Are you again openly disputing the good Mr. Malone's word?"

Waxman's lower lip trembled, but like the others, he said no more.

"Then it is agreed. When do we depart, Mr. Malone?"

"Morning'd be fine with me. We'll be gone a few weeks. Take what you need, but it's best to travel light."

"As you say, sir. I understand the weather is good this time of year. I am looking forward to our excursion."

They headed northwest out of town despite the last-minute pleas of Hooten and his friends. The death of so distinguished a visitor to their territory would not be the best of publicity for a growing community, and they feared it; yes, they did. Ruxton's valet tried to reassure them.

"Lord Ruxton, gentlemen, is used to the life of the camp and the trail. He has been in difficult circumstances many times and has always emerged unscathed. He is a crack shot and an athlete, a man who relishes danger and its challenges. Your concern does him an injustice. No harm will befall him. If you must worry about someone, concern yourselves with this crude Malone person."

"Mad Amos is no genius, but he ain't dumb, neither," said one of the men who'd gathered on the porch of the hotel to bid the hunters farewell. "Ain't nobody never been able to figure him out noways."

"I assure you," Manners continued, "Lord Ruxton is more than a match for any situation this lout can place him in."

"Oh, I wasn't worried about how your boss is going to get on with Malone," said the man who'd spoken. "I was wondering how he was going to cope with the Rockies."

———————

Once they left town, they commenced a steady climb into mountains as serene and lovely as any in the world. They reminded Ruxton of the Alps without the spas and fine hotels and other amenities of that ancient region. By way of compensation, there was a freshness in the air, a newness not to be found at the watering holes of the wealthy that dotted the Continent. Ruxton's packhorse trailed behind Malone's.

"That is an unusual animal you ride, sir." He nodded at Malone's mount.

The mountain man spoke without looking at his guest. "Worthless has been called plenty of names, Lord. Most of 'em less complimentary than that."

The animal Malone called Worthless was black except for patches of white at the tail and fetlocks. A single white ring encircled one eye, giving the horse the aspect of a permanent squint. He was a cross among half a dozen breeds. For reasons Malone chose not to elaborate on, a heavy leather patch was affixed permanently to the animal's forehead.

Have to attend to that again soon, he mused. He didn't worry about it out in the backcountry, but it was just the sort of thing to provoke consternation among simple city folk.

The horse snorted, just to let the two riders know he was listening.

"Magnificent country, your West. Do you think we might encounter some Red Indians, as Mr. Hooten seemed to fear?"

"Only if they're in the mood for company. Nobody sees the Blackfeet unless they want to be seen, and sometimes the Nez Perce don't even see each other. I don't anticipate no trouble, if that's what you mean. I've an understandin' with the folks hereabouts. If we do meet up with any, you keep your mouth shut and let me do the talkin'. I ain't sure how they'd take you."

"As you wish, Mr. Malone. How long before"—he bent to hide a smile—"we stand to encounter one of your jackalopes?"

"Hard to say. They're shy critters, and there seem to be fewer of 'em each year. Seems to be as folks start movin' into this part of the world, certain critters start movin' out."

"Indeed? How inconvenient. Well, I am in no hurry. I am enjoying our excursion immensely. I took the liberty of stocking up on the finest victuals your community could provide. I shall enjoy dining *au camp* at your expense, Mr. Malone."

"Ain't my expense unless we don't git you a jackalope, Lord."

"Of course. I am remiss."

"Don't know about that, but you're sure as hell premature."

Many days went by without them encountering evidence of any other humans of any color. Malone seemed content to lead them ever deeper into the mountains. Snow-clad peaks soared ten thousand feet overhead as they picked their way across a rocky slope above a wide, white-flecked river. Ruxton marveled at Malone's ability to find a path where none was visible. The man was a fine tracker, like many of the primitives Ruxton had engaged in other lands.

He was watching his guide carefully now. Perhaps robbery had been his motive all along in agreeing to this trek. Ruxton had considered the possibility back in the saloon, but instead of deterring him, it only added spice to an expedition such as this. He lived for such excitement. If thuggery was indeed in the mountain man's plans, he was in for a surprise. Ruxton had dealt with drunken cossacks and silent-footed dacoits. Despite Malone's size, Ruxton knew that in the event of a fight, it would be an Englishman who returned to tell the tale.

He was careful to sleep on the opposite side of their campfire, Colt pistol at his side, the intricately carved pepperbox snug in its special holster inside his boot. Malone would not surprise him in the middle of the night.

So he was more than mildly shocked when he found himself being shaken awake the following morning. His hand lunged for the Colt, then paused when he saw that Malone was looking not at him but past him.

"Whisper," Malone instructed him, "and then speak softer than that."

"What is it?" Ruxton was up quickly, pulling on his jacket. "Savages?"

Malone shook his head.

"What, then?" Chilled fingers buttoned the coat. Even in late spring, dawn was cold in these mountains.

"What you come fer, Lord."

Ruxton's hands stopped. "Pardon, Mr. Malone?"

"Jackalopes, you damn idjit! You want that trophy or not?"

Ruxton gaped at him, then hurriedly resumed his dressing.

Malone led him away from camp. They crossed two small ridges before surmounting one slightly higher. The roar of the river masked their climb.

Clutching his .30-30, Ruxton peered over the crest of the ridge. There was no need for Malone to remind him to keep his voice down, because he had no words for what he was seeing.

Not one, not two, but a whole herd of the utterly impossible creatures were feeding and frolicking in a small grassy meadow. They were bigger than he would have imagined, bigger than the largest jackrabbits he'd shot in New Mexico. They nibbled contentedly at the grass or preened themselves or lay on their sides soaking up the early morning sun. Several pairs of young males were play fighting. They would eye each other intently, then drop their heads and leap like rutting rams. Heads made contact six feet above the ground. Antlers locked and clacked loudly before the combatants separated, tumbled back to earth, and gathered themselves for another charge.

"I don't believe it," he mumbled under his breath.

Malone was impatient. "I don't care whether you believe it or not, Lord, but I never did cotton to havin' my word doubted. I reckon we won't be hearin' no more o' such nonsense. You think you can shoot one, or you want me to do it fer you?"

"What? Oh, yes."

Ruxton checked his weapon. He'd come to Montana in search of trophies, had gone along with Malone for the excitement of the wager, and now found himself in the position of obtaining far more than he'd sought. This expedition would yield much more. There would be articles in *The Times*, scientific honors, perhaps a special room in the British Museum.

Oh, he would take care to acknowledge Malone as his guide to this wonder. That would be proper. But recognition as discoverer would mean nothing to such a simple soul. The honor would be wasted on him. Ruxton therefore would graciously relieve him of the burdens it would entail.

Though nervous, he knew he could not miss. Not at this range. His valet had not exaggerated his master's skill with a rifle. Ruxton settled on the biggest buck in the herd, a magnificent ten-pointer. It was squatting off to one side, grazing contentedly. *Sorry, old fellow,* he thought as he squeezed the trigger.

The gun's report echoed noisily up the canyon. The buck screamed once as it jumped convulsively. By the time it hit the ground, it was dead, shot cleanly through the heart. Like fleas exploding from an old mattress, the rest of the herd vanished in seconds.

But the dead buck jackalope did not vanish like a character from *Through the Looking-Glass*. It was real. Malone followed behind as the excited Ruxton scrambled over the rocks toward it.

He lifted it triumphantly by the antlers. It was heavy, at least twenty pounds. This was not some clever fake conceived at great expense to deceive him.

"Mr. Malone," he told the mountain man when he finally arrived, "I am sorry for doubting your word. Oh, I confess to being as skeptical as your fellow citizens. I thought I would be the one to have the good laugh. I apologize profusely."

"No need to apologize, Lord. Leastwise you had the guts t' back up your words. And there's worse things to go a-huntin' fer than a good laugh. Come on, now, and let's be gettin' away from here."

"Why the rush? I thought I might have a shot at another one."

"I promised you one trophy. You bagged it, and a big one at that." He was scanning the canyon walls as he spoke. "Now it's time you and I were makin' tracks."

Ruxton frowned and joined Malone in studying the river and the enclosing canyon. "Why? Surely we're in no danger here. Or do you fear Indians may have heard my shot?"

"Nope. Ain't worried about Indians. Ain't none in this place. They won't come down this canyon."

"Well, then, what troubles you? Pumas, perhaps, or a bear?"

"Not them, neither."

Ruxton sighed, not wishing to spoil this historic moment with an argument. "I warn you, sir, I have little patience for linguistic obfuscation."

"Tell me somethin', Lord. What kind o' critter d'you think would be fast enough and strong enough to catch somethin' like a jackalope?"

"Why, I don't know. I should imagine that the usual predators manage to—" But Malone had turned and was already taking long strides back toward camp. Ruxton followed, too elated by his kill to remain angry with his irritating guide.

Having put the incident completely out of his mind, he was furious when Malone woke him in the middle of the night. He could see the mountain man outlined by the glow of the dying campfire.

"Sir, I have no idea what your absurd intention may be in disturbing me thus, but I am accustomed to enjoying a full night's rest, and I—"

"Shut up."

"Now listen to me, my good fellow, if you—"

He went silent as the muzzle of an enormous rifle tilted toward
him. "I told you to shut up, Lord. If you do, maybe I can keep you
alive."

Ruxton had plenty more to say but forced himself to keep quiet
so that Malone could explain. That was when he noticed that his
guide was staring anxiously at the sky.

A diadem of stars flattered a half-moon that turned the granite
slopes around them the color of secondhand steel. Far below, the
unnamed river ran nervously toward the distant Missouri. Ruxton
was about to mention the possibility of marauding Indians once
again, when a man-sized mass filled his field of vision. Its eyes were
like saucers of molten lead. He let out a scream and fell backward
even as the gun in Malone's hands thundered. Something like a
Malay dirk cut his shoulder, slicing through his shirt. Then all was
still.

He lay panting as Malone rushed to reload the buffalo gun.
Putting a hand to his shoulder, Ruxton found not one but three
parallel cuts through shirt and skin. They were shallow but bloody
and were beginning to sting as his body reacted to the injury.

Wordlessly, he started to stand, only to drop to hands and knees
on Malone's terse command. He crawled over to the thing the
mountain man had shot out of the sky.

It was not intact. Malone's Sharps carried a three-inch-long
cartridge in an octagonal barrel. The nocturnal attacker had been
blown apart. But enough remained to show Ruxton it was no creature known to modern science.

"What the blazes is it, Malone?"

The mountain man continued to survey the sky, his eyes
seeming to flick from star to star as though he knew each intimately.
The horses pawed nervously at the ground, rolling their eyes and
tugging at their reins. Of the four, only Malone's mount, Worthless,
stood calmly, occasionally shaking his head and turning it sideways
to gaze sourly at the two men.

"Wolful," Malone replied curtly. He set the rifle aside and drew
his peculiar LeMat pistol.

The body was certainly that of a very large wolf. What lifted

Ruxton's hackles were not so much the powerful, now-broken wings that sprouted from just above and behind the enlarged shoulders or the grasping talons on all four feet, one of which had slashed his shoulder and just missed his throat. It was the face that was really disturbing. The familiar long wolf muzzle was curved slightly, like some furry beak. The ears were too wide and long for any member of the *Canis* genus. And the now lifeless eyes that had shone like the lamps of Hell were so swollen in size they nearly met above the bridge of the muzzle. It was a creature worthy of the imagination of a Dante.

He crawled back to the fire and began pulling on his boots. Malone grunted satisfaction.

"Good. Reckon I don't have to tell you everythin'. We got to get under some cover." He nodded upslope from their trail. "Thought I might've seen a cave on our way in. Don't much care for dark places, but it might be big enough to hide us and the horses both." He rose and holstered the rifle, then began assembling their equipment with one hand. Ruxton noted that he did not at any time let go of the LeMat.

They lost one of the horses despite their caution. Neither man rode, and the unflappable Worthless led, but Ruxton's pack mare still broke her tether and bolted for the nearest stand of tall trees. As she charged across the slope, she shed cooking pots and utensils and food and tools, the equipment making a terrible racket as it banged and bounced off the rocks. Malone and Ruxton watched her go.

"She'll be all right," Ruxton declared hopefully. "We'll track her down come morning."

Malone's expression was grim in the moonlight. "Why do you think *I* didn't head for the woods?"

As the mare approached the first trees, the entire forest canopy appeared to rise from the topmost branches. Ruxton's mouth went dry, and he shivered. But what was more natural than for nocturnal flying creatures to roost in flocks? The fleeing mare had disturbed them.

There were at least thirty of the huge wolfuls. They swooped down on the terrified animal, circling low and snapping with wolf jaws at her withers and neck. She kicked out frantically and sent one of her tormentors spinning. It yelped unnaturally.

There were too many to prevent the inevitable. A pair landed on her back, using their talons to cling to flesh and pack straps. They tore at her face and flanks. Others cut her legs out from under her, striking at the tendons until they had her hamstrung. Unable to run or kick, the mare was buried beneath an avalanche of snarling, tearing bodies. She whinnied wildly to the last.

Malone and Ruxton didn't linger for the end. Even as the mare went down, a couple of the flock were making exploratory passes at the remaining horses and men. Ruxton felt heavy feathers brush his head as he ducked. He was not ashamed to admit that he screamed. Malone's LeMat boomed several times. Once there was a deeper, sharper explosion as he fired the .410 shotgun barrel that was mounted beneath the revolver barrel. Ruxton found himself surrounded by blood and feathers. He had a brief glimpse of feral yellow eyes. Then the sky disappeared as they stumbled into the cave.

It tunneled far back into the mountain. As Malone had hoped, there was more than enough room for all of them, including the surviving horses. They secured them to boulders near the back wall of the cave.

Bored with the carcass of the rapidly dismembered mare, the flock began to gather outside the entrance, padding back and forth and flapping their wings excitedly. The cave was actually larger than Malone would have liked. There was flying room inside. A lower ceiling would have been much more comforting.

Ruxton was breathing hard, his eyes nearly as wild as those of his mount. While it had stopped bleeding, his injured shoulder was throbbing mercilessly. But he could still hold a rifle.

"I regret the loss of my large-bore," he told Malone as he checked the .30-30. "It was packed with my other supplies on the mare."

The mountain man grunted. There followed an uncomfortable silence.

"Look here, Malone," Ruxton said finally, "I'm sorry I doubted you, old chap. I've been a bit of an ass all along, and I apologize." He stuck out his hand.

Malone eyed it, then enveloped it in his own huge paw and squeezed briefly. "I like a man who can own up to his own mistakes. I just hope you'll live to regret it." He turned back to the cave entrance. "There'll still be some meat left on your mare. When they've cracked all the marrow out o' the bones, they'll work themselves up for another go at us. We have to stop 'em before they get inside or we're done."

Ruxton nodded, resting his rifle atop a boulder that had fallen from the ceiling. "I've never even heard rumors of such a creature."

"Any folks whut sees one never gets away to tell of it. The Nez Perce know about 'em. They call 'em Sha-hoo-ne-wha-teh. Spirit wolves of the air. But the Nez Perce are unusual folk. They see things the Blackfeet and even the Cheyenne miss. Course, white folks don't find their way into this particular part of the Bitterroots.

"Way I figger it, no ordinary predator's fast enough or strong enough to take down a jackalope, especially when they stand and fight together. So these here wolfuls evolved to prey on 'em. Unfortunately, they ain't real particular about their supper. You and me, we're a damn sight slower than a sick jackalope. As for the horses, well, they're regular walkin' general stores as far as these critters are concerned."

"Listen, Malone. Most of my shells were packed on that poor mare along with my big guns. If things start to look bad, I'd appreciate it if you'd save a round in that LeMat for me. I don't mean for my rifle."

"I know what you mean. We ain't somebody's supper yet, Lord. They got to get in here first. Meanwhile, why not have a go at askin' your namesake for help?"

"My namesake?"

Malone's eyes rose as he jerked a finger upward.

"Oh." Ruxton nodded somberly.

The wolfuls continued to gather outside, their massed wingbeats a vast rushing that soon drowned out the livelier, healthier babble of the river below.

"First they'll sing for courage," Malone explained. "Then they'll start circlin' as they decide which one of 'em will get the honor of goin' for our throats first. After that the rest'll come for us. Try and pick your shots. One way or the other, it'll all be over quick."

Ruxton nodded, his teeth tightly clenched as he stared at the moonlit oval that marked the entrance of their sanctuary.

When the flock began its howling, it was as if all the graves at Battersea had opened to release the long dead. The sounds were higher in pitch than normal wolf calls, a sort of moan mixed with the kind of screech an enormous vulture might make.

The horses panicked at it, kicking up dust and gravel, pawing at the unyielding stone. Foam spilled from their lips. Only Worthless stood placidly, one eye half-open, swaying on his legs as if asleep. It made Ruxton wonder. Perhaps the animal was partly deaf and blind.

The flock leader was silver across his muzzle. He came in low and then rose abruptly toward the ceiling, awful talons spread wide to grasp and rend, vast yellow eyes staring hypnotically. They froze the startled Ruxton for an instant, but not Malone. The Sharps blew the wolful in half, the huge shell tearing through flesh and bone. Ruxton had no time to appreciate the difficult shot, because the rest of the flock followed close on the heels of their dead leader.

The terrified whinnying of the horses, the howls and roars of the wolfuls, and the rapid firing of both men's guns were deafening in the enclosed space. Ruxton saw Malone put down the empty LeMat and race to reload, his thick fingers moving as precisely as those of a concert pianist. He'd drawn his big bowie knife and was using it to fend off his attackers as he worked.

Then Ruxton saw him go down, the wolf's-head hat flying as a diving wolful struck him across the forehead. The claws missed his eyes, but the impact was severe.

"Malone!" Ignoring the pain shooting through his shoulder, Ruxton rushed to the other man's side. His rifle cracked, and another wolful dropped, snapping mindlessly at its crippled wing.

The mountain man blinked dazedly up at him, bleeding from the gash in his head. It was a shallow wound. He was only stunned.

That was when the flapping and howling and gnashing of teeth ceased. So concerned was he with the guide that Ruxton didn't notice it at first. Only when he helped the much larger man to his feet did he see that the last of the wolfuls had turned tail and was fleeing the cave.

"They're leaving. We beat them, old man! Gave them a sound hiding!"

"I think not, Lord." Malone fought to penetrate the oil that seemed to be floating on his retinas. "The Sharps—gotta get the Sharps." He stumbled, blinking dizzily.

"Hang on. I'll get it. But we don't need it anymore. They've gone, you see, and—"

He stopped in midsentence, holding his breath even as he left the dazed Malone to pick up the heavy buffalo rifle. The last howling of the wolfuls had faded into the distance, but it was not silent outside. A dull booming, as of some heavy tread, was clearly audible and growing steadily louder as he listened. He forced himself to keep his hands steady as he loaded the Sharps.

The massive breathing was right outside the cave. Evidently, they were not the first creatures to make use of its shelter. The horses were too terrified to whinny. They huddled together against the back wall, trembling.

The moon went out as something immense blocked the entrance. Ruxton raised the Sharps and tried to hold it steady. Though he was a strong man, the weight of the weapon sent shivers along the muscles of his arms.

Whatever stood there had to bend to fit beneath the twenty-foot-high ceiling. Its eyes were red instead of yellow like those of the wolful. An overpowering musk assailed Ruxton's nostrils as the hairy leviathan paused to sniff loudly.

It growled, and Ruxton felt his knees go weak. Imagine a whale, growling. The growl became a snarl that revealed teeth the size of railroad ties in the blunt, dark muzzle. It was coming for them.

Ruxton pulled the trigger, and the Sharps erupted. He thought he'd prepared himself for the recoil, but he was wrong. It knocked him on his back. The echo of the gun's report was drowned by an incredible bellow of pain and anger as the monster stumbled backward.

The rifle was pulled from his numb fingers. Malone reloaded as Ruxton staggered erect. The owner of the cave was already recovering from the shock and preparing to charge again. This time it would not hesitate curiously. A second slug from the Sharps wouldn't stop it. Not this time. As well to try shooting a runaway locomotive.

Something went flying past him like black lightning: Ruxton had a glimpse of white fetlocks and flying mane. Worthless slammed headfirst into the belly of the monster like a Derby winner pounding for the finish line. The Gargantua went backward, falling head over heels down the slope.

"Dumb, stupid son of a spasmed mare!" Malone growled as he gripped Ruxton by the shoulder. "Let's git out of this damn possum trap!"

They stumbled outside. There was no need to lead the remaining horses. Freed from their tethers, they sprinted madly past the two men. Malone and Ruxton ran downslope toward the forest, which was now devoid of roosting wolfuls.

Ruxton risked a look backward. A less brave man might have fainted dead away right then and there or swallowed his tongue at the sight.

Worthless had become a darting, spinning black dervish on four legs, nipping at the ankles of the immensity that now stood on its hind feet. It swiped at the much smaller but nimbler horse with paws the size of carriages. Each time a blow capable of demolishing a house descended, Worthless would skip just out of its reach.

Only when the two men were safely in among trees too old and thick even for the leviathan to tear down did Worthless abandon his efforts. With a roar, the monster chased the horse a few yards. Then it bellowed a final defiance before dropping to all fours. Like a piece of the mountain come to life, it turned and lumbered back to reclaim its cave.

Running easily, Worthless galloped past both winded men. He turned the fleeing horses, circling them until they slowed, nuzzling Malone's pack mare until she stood quietly, spittle dribbling from her jaws. Then he snorted once, shook his head, and bent to crop the tops of some wild onions that were growing nearby.

"Mr. Malone, that is quite a remarkable animal you have there." Ruxton fought for breath as he rested his hands on his knees. "How did you ever train him to do something like that? 'Pon my word, but that was the most gallant action I have seen a horse take on behalf of its master."

"Train 'im? Gallant? The idjit bastard like to got hisself killed! I had a clean shot. Coulda stopped it."

"Stopped that behemoth?" Ruxton nodded in the direction of the cave that had initially been their refuge and had nearly ended as their grave. "Not even with that cannon you call a rifle, old chap. Your animal saved us for sure."

"Well—mebbe. But it was still a damn-fool thing to do."

Malone repeated the assertion to his mount's face, shoving his beard against that squinty-eyed visage while holding it by the neck.

"You hear me, you moronic offspring of a mule? Don't you never try nothin' like that again!"

Worthless bit him on the nose.

"What was it, anyway?" Now that they were well away from the nameless river and the canyon it had carved, Ruxton found he was able to relax a little. The sun was rising over his unsatisfied curiosity.

Malone had spent much of the morning muttering curses at his mount while occasionally feeling gingerly at the bandage Ruxton had applied to his nose. It was an incongruous slash of white above the black beard. Personally, Ruxton had felt the animal justified in its response.

"Somethin' big enough to snatch a wolful right out of the sky. Nez Perce, they call it—wal, never mind what the Nez Perce call it.

You wouldn't be able to pronounce it, anyway. Me, I call it a grizzephant. Only the second one I've ever seen. If the Good Lord wills it, I'll never see another. Reckon you could call it *Ursus loxodonta*."

"Why, Mr. Malone, sir. Latin? I do believe you are at pains to conceal a real education."

"Nope. Just don't use it much 'cause nobody around here cares one way or t' other. They don't believe half of what I try to tell 'em anyways, so I just keep my mouth shut." He leaned over to give his mount a reluctant pat on the neck. "Old Worthless here, I reckon he deserves a genus of his own. I just ain't come up with the right one yet, though I kinda lean toward *Equus idioticus*. With the emphasis on the 'cuss.'"

Ruxton leaned forward for a better look. As he did so, he noticed that the leather patch that normally covered the animal's forehead was hanging loose, having been dislodged in the fight.

"Mr. Malone, would I be remiss if I were to suggest that your horse has a horn growing from the center of his forehead?"

Malone leaned out for a look, straightened. "Drat. Got to fix that before we git to Randle's Farm. Folks in these parts don't rightly understand such things as unicorns."

Ruxton couldn't keep from staring. The horn was six inches long and looked sharp. Undoubtedly it had helped keep the grizzephant's attention last night. He could just make out the marks where Malone had kept it filed down.

"I know an elderly Chinese gentleman who will give you a million pounds sterling and six of the most attentive and beautiful women you ever set eyes upon for that horn, sir."

"No, thanks, Lord. Be happy you got your jackalope."

"Yes, my jacka—" Ruxton's eyes got very wide. "The jackalope! It was tied to the packhorse the wolfuls killed!"

Malone eyed him evenly. "Want to go back and try again?"

Ruxton turned around in his saddle. His shoulder still throbbed, but the injury was almost completely healed thanks to some strange-smelling herb powder Malone had rubbed on it while mumbling some nonsense about Tibet and Samarkand. He straightened resolutely, bringing his gaze back to the trail ahead.

"I will mount the memory in my mind," he said firmly, "and make do with that."

For the first time since they'd met, Amos Malone smiled. "I reckon mebbe you ain't as dumb as you look, then, Lord. Even if you do ride funny. Ain't that right, sweetie-dumplin'?" He caressed his mount's neck.

Worthless looked back out of his half-closed squint eye. A kind of thunder rolled across the Bitterroots one more time as the unicorn farted.

There was a time when elaborate hood ornaments on cars were as critical to signifying the status of the vehicle's owner as the rest of the road machine itself. These usually metal sculptures mounted on the front end of even cheaper models made a statement: about the car, about its owner, about the manufacturer. They varied from simple to elaborate enough to find their way into museums. Some were designed by well-known sculptors or companies such as Lalique.

Such ornamentation is pretty much gone now, thanks to a proliferation of hood ornament thieves and an ever-increasing desire on the part of manufacturers to eke out even small improvements in a car's aerodynamics. Loath to abandon its famous Spirit of Ecstasy hood decoration, Rolls-Royce has a built-in system that lowers the ornament down into the front of the car if it is tampered with.

A number of these elaborate hood decorations featured American Indians. While I generally don't like time-travel stories, the idea that sprang from this one was too much fun to pass up. That, and the alliteration.

THE CHROME COMANCHE

E sau was checking the wagon's rear axle when the dog started barking. It was the middle of the day, and it made no sense. The dog ought to be asleep somewhere back of the barn, not out front barking in the sun. In any event, it stopped soon enough. The dog was as exhausted as the rest of them.

At first he didn't even bother to look up, so absorbed was he in his study of the wagon. It had to be loaded and ready to go by this evening so that they wouldn't have to spend another night in the cabin. It wasn't much of a house, but it was a home, a beginning. Rock and sod mostly, braced with rough-cut cedar and mesquite. What milled lumber he'd been able to afford had gone into the barn. It wasn't finished, and the chicken house wasn't finished.

The only thing that was finished here on the south bank of the Red River was them, he thought.

He didn't raise his gaze until the dog came over and begin licking him.

"What the blazes ails you, hound?"

"He's scared, I think," said a deep voice. "I hope not of me."

Esau hesitated, then realized that the wagon offered little protection. Might as well crawl out and confront the speaker, whoever he might be. Were they now to have as little peace during the day as they'd found here at night?

No spirit gazed back at him, though the animal the speaker rode was unusual enough. Esau knew horses, but this particular mount appeared more jumbled than mixed. The rider was nearly as unclassifiable, though from what could be seen behind the flowing black beard, Esau was pretty sure he was white. Esau had to squint to make out individual features. The more he squinted, the more indefinable the details of that face seemed to become. Though it was as full of lines as a sloping field after a storm, it didn't hint of great age.

The man himself was immense. The pupils of his eyes were of a blackness extreme enough to spill over and stain the whites. He wore fringed boots and buckskin, his attire not so much dirty as eroded. Like the face, Esau thought. Had man put those lines there or nature? Bandoliers of huge cartridges crisscrossed his chest, fuel for the Sharps buffalo rifle slung next to the saddle. The octagonal barrel was only slightly smaller than a telegraph pole.

"You're a long ways from the mountains, friend." Esau shielded his eyes as he spoke, while the dog began to sniff around the horse's hooves. The confused-breed piebald ignored the attention. "No beaver to trap around here. Not in North Texas."

"You'd be surprised what there is to trap in Texas." The mountain man considered the little cabin. "But you're right enough. I'm jest passin' through, out o' New Orleans on my way to Colorado." He nodded in the direction of the chimney. "Saw your smoke."

A vast growl arose from the vicinity of the giant's stomach, belly thunder heralding the approach of an expansive hunger. Esau smiled slightly, relaxing.

"You're welcome here, stranger. Come in and set a spell. Be right to have company for our last meal here."

Though the giant slipped off his mount, he seemed to lose nothing in stature as he stood on his own two feet. "I thank you fer your hospitality. Your last meal, you say?"

Esau nodded gravely, indicating the wagon. "Just checking out the frame and the springs before loading her up. Never thought I'd have to do that again. We'd planned to live out our days here. This is a good place, mister. River's always running, and the grass is high. Best cattle country I ever saw." He shrugged fatalistically.

The mountain man addressed the uncomfortable silence. "Name's Malone. Amos Malone."

"Esau Weaver." The rancher's hand vanished inside the giant's gnarled grasp. "Sarah's inside fixin' dinner. You're welcome to stay for supper, too, if it suits you. We'll be out soon after. Have to be."

"It ain't in me to linger long in any one place, but I appreciate your offer, Weaver."

Esau led the visitor toward the home he was preparing to flee, unable to keep from glancing at his companion. "Didn't think there were any of you boys left. Thought the beaver had all been trapped out, and the market for 'em faded away anyways."

"There's still places in the backcountry where a feller can make a livin' if he works hard and has half a mind for figures. Only real trouble's that the country's gettin' too citified. Even Colorado's fillin' up with folks tired o' city life." He chuckled, an extraordinary sound. "So naturally, soon as they arrive, they all light out fer Denver. Folks sure are a puzzlement sometimes."

"Wish all I had to deal with were country neighbors." Esau opened the door and called to alert his wife. Malone had to duck double to clear the low doorway.

Behind them the dog concluded its inspection and disdainfully peed on the horse's rear right leg, whereupon the mountain man's mount did a most unequine thing. It raised its own leg and liked to drown that poor unsuspecting hound, sending it shaking and yapping around the back of the cabin. The horse, whose name was Worthless, let out a soft snort of satisfaction and went hunting for fodder. Malone had not tied him. Would've been useless to try.

Sarah Weaver showed the lack of sleep the family had endured recently. She wore her hair pulled straight back and secured in a small bun, a simple long-sleeved dress, and an apron decorated with fine tatting. She hardly glanced at her husband and his guest. Her son, Jeremiah, was far less inhibited. He stared unabashedly at Malone, firing questions that the mountain man answered readily until the boy's mother warned him to mind his manners.

"Heck, ma'am, he don't bother me none," Malone said with a smile so ready and wide that the tense woman relaxed. "It's good to be around young'uns. Reminds a man what the future's for."

"I then take it that you're not married, sir." She dipped stew from the black cast-iron kettle that hung in the fireplace. Once things got settled, Esau had promised her a real stove, but now ...

"Name's Malone, ma'am. As fer lockin' up, I've had the urge once or twice, but as I ain't the type to settle down, it wouldn't be fair to the woman."

"I hope you like this stew." She set the bowl in front of the visitor. "It's all we have. What's left of all I could salvage from my garden before *they* destroyed it."

Malone inhaled pointedly. "Ambrosia and nectar, ma'am. Though if you cleaned out your barn an' boiled the results, it'd still be bound to be better than my own cookin'."

She smiled thinly and sat down opposite her husband. Jeremiah took the high seat opposite Malone.

An unnatural silence settled over the table. Any slight creak or groan caused both rancher and wife to look tensely at walls or windows before resuming their meal. There eventually came a time when Malone could stand it no longer.

"Now, you folks tell me to shut my food hole if you want to, but I'm afflicted with a confusion I got to vent. Friend Esau, you told me what a fine place you had here, and havin' seen some of it, I don't find any reason to dispute. So maybe you'll sympathize with an ignorant bumpkin who sits here delightin' in your wife's fine cooking while wonderin' why you're in such an all-fired rush to leave."

Esau Weaver glanced at his wife, who said nothing. He started to resume eating, then paused as though considering whether to speak. Clearly it burned within him to share this matter with someone else.

"Spirits, Mr. Malone." The rancher broke a chunk of bread from the round loaf in the middle of the table. "Ghosts. Devils. Indian devils."

"They come upon us in the middle of the night, Mr. Malone."

Sarah Weaver had her hands on the table, the fingers twisting and twining. "Horrible sounds they make. They terrify Jeremiah. They terrify me."

"Got no heads." Weaver was chewing his bread unenthusiastically, but he needed something to do with his mouth and hands. "Thought it was just raiders at first, till I got a look at 'em during a full moon. No heads at all. That don't keep 'em from howling and yelling and tearing up the place. They want us off this land, and by God, they're going to have their way. I can't take any more of this, and neither can the woman." Love filled his eyes as he gazed across the table at his wife; love and despair. "White men or Indians I'd fight, but not things without heads."

"Esau went into town and spoke with one of the pacified Comanche medicine men," Sarah Weaver murmured. "He told Esau that this part of the country along the river was sacred to the tribe. But he couldn't say how much. He did say there could be spirits here."

"There are spirits all over this country," Malone said. "Some places don't matter so much to 'em. Others do." He sat back in his chair and it creaked alarmingly. "But you were told straight, I think. This lands reeks of medicine, old medicine. But not," he added, his face twisting in puzzlement, "this place right here."

"You know about such things, do you, Mr. Malone?" Esau's tone was sardonic.

"A mite. I sensed the medicine when I was ridin' in. But not where we're sittin'. If there's spirits about, I wouldn't see them choosin' this place for a frolic. Upstream or down, maybe, but not right here. Besides which, it ain't like spirits to drive off cattle and tear up vegetables. If they're real and they wanted you off, they'd be a sight more direct in their intentions."

"They're real enough, Mr. Malone," Sarah Weaver said. "If you don't believe us, stay and see for yourself, if you dare."

"Well, now, ma'am, I jest might do that. Been a while since I seen a gen-u-wine spirit. Oh, and that Comanche medicine man you talked to? He might've been right or he might've been wrong, but one thing's sure: he weren't pacified. You don't pacify the

Comanche. They jest got plumb tuckered out." He glanced at his host.

"Now, you say these here no-heads keep y'all awake a-yellin' and a-hollerin'. Do they sound somethin' like this?" Somewhere behind that bear thicket of a beard, lips parted as Malone began to chant.

Jeremiah's jaw dropped as he stared in awe, while his parents sat stock-still, listening. Night, not due for hours, seemed to encroach on the little cabin, and a breeze probed curiously where moments earlier the air had been as still as a bad man's eulogy.

"That about right?" Malone finally inquired.

Esau shook himself back to alertness. "Something like that but deeper, long syllables."

Malone tried again. "Closer?"

Sarah Weaver found herself nodding unwillingly. "That's it, Mr. Malone. That's it exactly."

"Interestin'. First chant was Comanche. Second was Shoshone. Now, the Comanche and the Shoshone are related, but there ain't no love lost between the tribes and there ain't no Shoshone in these parts. Too far east, too far south. Makes no sense."

"Neither do headless devils, Mr. Malone."

The mountain man nodded somberly at the rancher's wife. "That's a truth fine as frog hair, ma'am. The devils I know always keep their heads about them, if not their wits. A head's something man or spirit tends to get used to and downright lonely without.

"You said they're about to run you off this land, but all they've done is make your lives more miserable than North Texas weather?"

"Maybe you're not afraid of devils, Mr. Malone, but I have a family to protect. I'll take no chances with something I do not understand."

"I comprehend your position, Esau. You're a good man in a bad spot. Now, a fool like myself loves to take chances with what he don't understand. Mrs. Weaver, I will take you up on your offer to stay and see for myself. But I don't fancy doin' so all by my lonesome. You've stuck it out this long. Could you see your way clear to stickin' around one more night? If my suspicions are wrong, I'll be the first to up an' confess my sins."

"Another night?" Sarah Weaver's exhaustion showed in her tone and expression. "I don't know. What would be the good in it?"

"Might not be any good in it, ma'am." Malone didn't mince words with her. "Might be only understanding, and that ain't always to the good. But I've got a hunch it ain't your place the spirits here-abouts are concerned with."

Esau Weaver leaned forward. "Then you do believe there are spirits here?"

"Didn't I say that? This is old Comanche land. Lot o' coups counted here, lot of warriors' bones interred along this river. What I said was I don't see why they'd bear you folks any malice. You ain't even turnin' the soil."

"Why should you want to help us? You said you were just passing through."

"That's my life, Esau. Passin' through. The time to stop's when good people like yourselves are havin' trouble. It's what we do in the passin' that's remembered." He beamed at Sarah Weaver, and despite her exhaustion, she surprised herself by blushing. "Notwith-standin' that I owe you fer the best meal I've had since leavin' New Orleans."

Weaver was wrestling with himself. His mind had been made up for days. He would not go so far as to allow himself to hope, but this towering stranger was so damned sure of things.

He glanced one last time at his wife, who acquiesced with her eyes. Then he turned back to Malone. "You mind sleepin' in the barn with the horses?"

"Not if the horses don't object. Uh, you got any mares in heat?"

Weaver made a face. "No. Why would you ask that?"

"Don't want t' cause a ruckus." He jerked a thumb in the direc-tion of the door. "Worthless may not look like much, but he's able to do more than trot when his back's up."

"I'll find you some blankets, Mr. Malone." Sarah Weaver started to rise from the table.

"Now, never you mind me, missus. I've got my own blanket. Buffalo robe's good enough fer me. Warmer than homespun and strong enough to keep the mosquitoes away."

"Thick pile, is it?" Weaver inquired.

"Not especial. But it ain't been washed in a bit, and the smell's strong enough to mask my own."

Jeremiah gazed wide-eyed at the mountain man. "What if the headless spirits come for you, Mr. Malone? What if they come for you in the barn when you're asleep and all alone?"

That huge wrinkled face bent close. The boy could smell the plains and the mountains, the sea and suggestions of far-off places. For just an instant those black eyes seemed to shine with a light of their own, and Jeremiah Weaver was sure he could see unnameable things reflected within them.

"Why, then, son, we'll have ourselves a gen-u-wine set-to and we'll gamble for souls or answers."

Malone guessed it was around two in the morning when Worthless's cold, wet tongue slapped against his face. Grunting, the mountain man swatted at the persistent protuberance as he sat up in the darkness, hunting for his boots.

"Godforsaken miserable son of a spavined mule can't let a man get a decent sleep." Worthless snorted and turned toward his waiting saddle and blanket.

"No, you stay here." Malone hop-danced into one boot, then its mate. "Bright night like this, you'd stick out like Tom Sawyer's fence. I won't be too long. Meanwhile, you leave those two mares alone. They ain't interested in you, nohow."

As Malone traipsed out of the barn in the direction of the faint sounds, his mount stuck out his tongue at him. Then Worthless turned to begin chewing at the rope that secured the paddock gate.

There was ample moon, though Malone didn't need it. He could track *them* by their movements. They were chanting already, but softly, as if practicing. Peculiar and peculiar. Spirits didn't need rehearsals, and it was hard to imagine any Indian, real or ghostly, crashing through the brush like a runaway mine cart.

But there were spirits here. That he knew. So he continued to tread silently.

Then he could see them. There were about a dozen, advancing slowly on the cabin, crouching as they walked. They wore painted vests and leggings and, just as the Weavers had insisted, had no heads.

Maybe that explained why they were so clumsy, Malone thought. Spirits floated. Comanche floated, almost. These critters, whatever they were, bulled their way through the brush.

Only one of them was chanting louder than a whisper. Malone focused on him. There was something about the way he moved that was real. His feet caressed the earth instead of bludgeoning it, and he wore moccasins. His companion spirits wore boots. A few were equipped with spurs. Odd choice of footgear for a ghost.

The crackling anger of a thousand crickets made Malone look down and to his left. The snake was already tightly coiled. So intent had he been on observing the advancing "spirits" that he'd neglected to note the leathery one close by his feet.

The rattler's tongue flicked in Malone's direction. Malone's tongue jabbed right back. If it had any sense, the rattler would bluster a few seconds more and then slither off in the grass. Snakes, however, were notoriously short on common sense. This one struck, aiming for Malone's left leg.

The mountain man disliked killing anything without good reason, and the snake's unwarranted attack was evidence enough it was already deranged. So instead of drawing the bowie knife, Malone spit, faster and more accurately than was natural. His spit caught the snake in the eyes as its target leapt to one side.

Confused and queasy, the rattler lay silent a moment. Then it hurried off into the brush. It would not come back.

Unfortunately, it had been heard. Four headless figures surrounded Malone. All of them carried Colts, distinctly unethereal devices. The man in their midst regarded them thoughtfully.

"Didn't think you'd chance it forever on your singin' alone."

The one nearest Malone reached up and yanked at his chest. Painted fabric slid downward in his fingers, revealing a quite normal face. At the moment the expression on it was pained.

"You're a big one. Where'd you spring from?"

"The seed of an eagle and the loins of a cat—not that it's any of your business." Malone studied his captors thoughtfully as the speaker carefully removed bowie knife and LeMat pistol from the mountain man's person. Malone made no move to retain them. "What're you boys doin' out here in the middle o' the night in those getups? I didn't know the circus had made it this far west."

The speaker's expression turned sour. He was about to reply, when two other figures arrived. Those holding the Colts quickly made room for the newcomers. One of them was the loud chanter. Malone studied his features intently. Shoshone, all right. Teetering the horizontal side of half-drunk and, by the look of him, not caring much about his condition.

His companion was bigger and older, made up to look like what he wasn't. He was neither ghost nor spirit, though the scent of the Devil was surely about him. He had about him the air of one with no time to waste, clearly a man poisoned by impatience.

"Who the hell are you?" he inquired belligerently of the mountain man.

"Malone's the name. Amos Malone. Mad Amos to some."

"That I can believe. Well, Mr. Malone, I don't know what you're doing out here, but I am told that the country on the north side of the river is more hospitable to strangers. I would suggest that you betake yourself there as soon as possible. Perhaps sooner."

"Your solicitude is touching, but I like it here, Mr. ...?"

"Cleator. This is my associate, Mr. Little-Bear-Blind-in-One-Eye." He clasped the Shoshone possessively on the shoulder. It was enough to shake the other man's none-too-stable equilibrium.

Malone murmured something in Shoshone to the chanter, who promptly and unexpectedly straightened. He blinked hard, as if fighting with his own eyes, trying to focus on the man who'd spoken to him. Meanwhile, the mountain man gestured at those surrounding him.

"Kind of an obscure locale fer a theatrical performance, ain't it?"

"This is not theater, sir. This is seriously real."

"Might I inquire as to its purpose?"

Cleator gazed at him. "Why should I trouble myself to explain to a passing nonentity? Why should I not simply have you shot?"

"Because you don't want any shooting." Malone indicated the

still-sleeping cabin. "If that's what you wanted, you'd have killed all three Weavers long ago instead o' constructin' this elaborate masque."

"You are surprisingly perceptive. I am intrigued. You are, of course, quite right. I dislike killing, because dead people cannot sign legal documents. It is much better for them to sign willingly, while they are still alive."

"This show is all because you have a hankerin' fer the Weavers' land?"

"Certainly. It lies between two of my holdings. But that is not the most important reason." He paused, studying Malone, and then shrugged. "I will show you. Understanding will make you dangerous to me. Then I will have no compunctions about having you shot if you refuse to depart."

They led him to the edge of the Red. Little Bear followed but stayed as far away from Malone as possible. He was still fighting to focus his eyes.

Cleator pointed upstream, then down, and lastly at the far side of the river. "My land, Mr. Malone." He kicked dirt with his boots. "Weaver's land. Notice anything unique about it?"

Malone studied the river, the far bank and the near. "This is a narrows."

Cleator smiled, pleased. "Very good, sir. Very good, indeed. I may tell you that in fact this is the narrowest part of the Red River for many miles in either direction. Can you suspect why it is of such interest to me?"

"You need a bridge."

"Running cattle across a bridge saves the need of fording them to reach the railhead north of here. Every extra mile a steer runs costs weight and therefore money. I need this land to build my bridge."

"Why not simply lease the portion you need? I'm sure Weaver would be amenable to a fair offer. A bridge could be o' benefit to his stock as well."

"Of course it would, but I don't want to benefit his stock, Mr.

Malone. Nor do I wish the uncertainty of a lease. I want to own it all."

"You're goin' t' all this trouble fer that?"

"No trouble, Mr. Malone. I invent some mischievous spirits to frighten away the Weavers, and then I buy their land at auction."

"If you jest asked him, he might be glad t' sell out direct."

"But in this fashion I obtain a much better price."

Malone considered. "Mr. Cleator, you are an evil man."

Cleator shrugged. "I am ambitious. They are not the same."

"I find it hard to separate the two much o' the time. Joke's on you, though."

The rancher frowned. "What joke, sir?"

"You didn't have t' invent no spirits to haunt this place. The spirits are here already. Have been fer a thousand years or more." He turned sharply on Little Bear. "Ain't thet right?" And he added something in Shoshone.

As wide as the chanter's eyes got, this time they had no difficulty focusing. Little Bear began to gaze nervously around him. Ordinary rocks and bushes suddenly caused him to retreat, to stumble.

"What did you say to him?" Cleator asked curiously.

"Nothin' he don't know. The whiskey you give him kept his eyes from workin', if not his mouth. He's seein' now, takin' a good look around, and he don't much like what he sees. Always been bad blood between Shoshone and Comanche. He's feelin' dead Comanche around him now, and he don't care for it. I wouldn't, neither, were I you, Mr. Cleator."

A couple of the hired gunmen were starting to glance around uneasily. Malone had started them thinking. North Texas is a bad place for a man to be thinking with the moon glaring down at him accusingly.

"Really? And why not? Am I supposed to fear a few dead Indians?"

"I'm jest sayin' that if I were you, I wouldn't try to put no bridge over these narrows."

Cleator was grinning now, enjoying himself. "Mr. Malone, you are a caution, sir. I defy the Weavers, I defy the Comanche, and I defy their dead or anything else that attempts to slow progress on this land. Do not try to frighten me with my own intentions."

"Sometimes it's healthy to be a mite afeared o' progress, Mr. Cleator. It can jump up when you ain't lookin' an' bite you severe." He looked up suddenly at the opposite bank, his heavy brows drawing together like a small black version of the bridge Cleator proposed to build.

The gunmen jumped when Little Bear let out a cry and bolted. One of them raised his weapon, but Cleator stopped him from shooting.

"Let him go. We'll track him down later. He'll be in town, drunk."

"I wouldn't figure too near on that," Malone informed him. "I think our friend's seen the light. I reckon by tomorrow he'll be headed northwest if he can find himself a horse. You see, he saw what was waitin' fer him here and did the sensible thing by lightin' out."

One of Cleator's men stepped forward. "We're losin' the night, boss." A very large knife gleamed in his right hand. "Let me stick him, and we'll dump him in the river and get on with this."

"Very well. Now that he knows, by his own wish, he is a threat, and as previously stated, I can have no compunction about terminating a threat. Therefore, you may ..."

He broke off, gazing across the river at the spot Malone was watching. One by one the men wielding the Colts joined him in staring.

"Hell's bunghole," one of them stuttered, "what is *that?*"

It was larger than a bull buffalo, with teeth the size of an opium dream and burning yellow eyes. Even at that distance they could hear it growl as it raced toward them.

"Mr. Cleator, I wouldn't linger in this vicinity if I were you."

The rancher was shaken but otherwise unmoved. "I am not afraid of night beasts, Mr. Malone. That is no spirit. I don't know what it is, but if it is alive, it can be slain." He wrenched a rifle from the man next to him. "This will be my land, and I will build my bridge *here*. I will deal with any intruders." He glanced back and smiled. "You set this up, didn't you? You and the Weavers. Some kind of trick. It will not work. I am no gullible plainsman, sir. And you are dogmeat." He looked sharply at the man with the knife.

"Stick him or shoot him, as you please."

But the gunman was staring across the river, staring at the unbelievable thing that was coming toward them faster than a train could travel. As he stared, he kept backing up, until he prudently decided to turn and run. He was accompanied.

Cleator roared at his fleeing men. "Come back! You cowards, idiots! Can't you see it's a trick! That damn farmer will be laughing at you tomorrow!"

A couple of the men slowed to turn, but what they saw made them tremble with fear and run faster still. The monster reached the far bank of the river. It did not stop but kept coming, soaring through the night air as easily as the fabled roc of legend, as cleanly as a bad dream. They were not particularly brave, those men, and they were not being paid well enough to stay and tussle with Hell.

The scream made Cleator turn. So fast had it traversed the river gorge that it was already almost upon him. It screamed again, a cross between a bleat and a howl. Malone whirled to flee, yelling at Cleator to do the same.

Perhaps he didn't have enough time or chose to react instinctively. The rancher raised his rifle and tried to aim.

The burning yellow eyes blinded him. He flung his gun aside and tried finally to dodge.

That was when Malone saw the Indian. He was riding the monster's muzzle.

It was solid and yet spirit, a brave dressed in untraditional cladding. Small but perfect, he thought as it turned toward the stumbling, half-paralyzed rancher and loosed a single shining arrow. It struck James Cleator squarely in the right eye, penetrating all the way to the brain and killing him instantly.

Then the monster was upon him. Cleator was struck once and sent flying, his already dead broken body landing ten yards away in a crumpled heap. Malone slowed. The monster had not come after him but had vanished eastward, howling into the night.

Breathing hard, he waited until he was sure before returning to study the rancher's corpse. Nearby he found the monster's tracks. They were unlike any he'd ever seen. He knelt to examine them more closely.

A voice came anxiously from behind: "Mr. Malone! Are you all right, sir?"

The mountain man did not look up as Esau Weaver slowed to a halt beside him. The rancher was carrying a rifle, old and battered. There was nothing worn about his courage, however. He blanched when he espied Cleator's body.

"I know that man."

"Your antagonist, though you did not know it. Not spirits. Gold will buy a man much, but not truth and not the spirits of the dead. Too easy by half to defile yesterday as well as tomorrow. I believe he were done in by both." He put a comforting hand on the rancher's shoulder. "Nothin' more to be done here. Cleator was dead of heart before the rest of his body caught up with him. Let's go get some shuteye. I'll have a go at explainin' it all to you and the missus tomorrow, while I'm helpin' y'all t' unpack that wagon."

Weaver nodded wordlessly. Together they returned to the cabin, which would be disturbed no more. Around them the land and all it contained were once again at rest. Yesterday and tomorrow slept peacefully, flanking the present.

———————

"Hell of a restoration job." The attendant looked on approvingly.

"Thanks." The owner was standing before the object of the other man's admiration, examining it minutely.

"Something happened, I can see that."

"Hit something coming over the bridge last night, just this side of Childress. Might've been a coyote. Might've been a small deer."

"Lot of damage?" The attendant was sympathetic. Out here you never knew what you might run into at night.

"Not as bad as it felt. Plenty of blood, though. That'll wash off okay. Then there's this." He fingered the Packard's nose. "Bent halfway around. And there's a little arrow that went right here, see? Must've lost it in the collision." He straightened, shaking his head sadly.

"These cars from the thirties and forties, they built 'em tough, but it seems like something's always happening to the damn hood ornaments."

When one is considering potential subject matter for a fantasy tale, fruits and vegetables are usually not at the top of the list. Nor is farming. But without hordes of orcs to battle or evil sorcerers with whom to contend, one roots out story ideas in the Old West where one can.

In this tale, instead of hordes of ravening monsters to battle, we have farmers. Lots of farmers. Plain old ordinary farmer folk. Some of them intending to be farmers from the start, others forced into it because the perceived easy ways of making money that betook them to the Golden State in the first place didn't materialize (not much changes). But in a strange country, where the lay of the land is new and unknown, decisions on what to plant, where to plant, and when to plant can make or break a newcomer to the soil. The drainage in Montana is different from the dirt in Indiana. Potatoes are not tomatoes.

It's the sort of expertise that seemingly may not require a wizard's touch, but when challenged, Amos Malone is ever ready to take on all problems ... even if it means disputing the merits of broccoli.

And of course there's the capper to this tale, which started it all in my mind and from which I had to work, for quite a spell, backward scribewise.

AGRARIAN DEFORM

Y ou talk to him, Jesse."

"Not me. Look at him. It can't be the right man."

"Have to be," said George Franklin. "Can't be another human being on God's green earth looks like that. It's him fer sure."

They argued vociferously among themselves. Since no one was willing to approach their quarry alone, they had no choice but to do so in a group.

"Shoot," Deaf Jackson pointed out, "he's jest sittin' there whittlin'. Ain't like he's gnawin' on baby bones."

"Yeah," said Slim Martin, "but you ever see anybody whittlin' with a bowie knife before?"

Having finally screwed up sufficient courage to approach the giant, they found they had nothing to say.

Amos Malone pushed back the wolf head that covered his scalp and regarded the sightseers. From somewhere behind that impenetrable black beard, luxuriant enough to offer succor and shelter to any number of small unidentifiable creatures, a surprisingly balsamic voice arose to break the uncomfortable silence.

"You folks never seed a man whittlin' afore?"

As the wealthiest and largest of the six, it fell to George Franklin to reply. Also, his erstwhile friends and neighbors were doing a fine job of concealing themselves behind him.

"Are you Amos Malone?" He swallowed uneasily. "The one they call Mad Amos?"

The bowie knife sliced. Wood chips flew. Standing there on the covered porch outside the hotel, Franklin was acutely conscious of the proximity of his belly to that huge hunk of razor-sharp metal.

"Wal, 'tis Amos Malone I am, but at the moment I ain't particularly mad. Next week, now, I wouldn't vouch fer that." He paused, squinting up at Franklin. "Kin I do something fer you folks, or are y'all just wanderin' art lovers?"

Jesse Kinkaid stepped forward. "Mr. Malone, sir, we got ourselves a bit of a goin' problem. Word around is that you might be the man to help us out."

"We can pay," Franklin added hastily, grateful for the supportive voice of a neighbor.

"Ain't said I'd take the job yet." Malone sheathed the knife and scratched at the hem of his buckskin jacket with a huge, callused hand. "What makes you think I'm the feller you need?"

The men exchanged glances. Though there were six of them, they were peaceable folk, and they felt badly outnumbered. "Now, don't be takin' this as no insult, Mr. Malone," Kinkaid began cautiously, "but the word in these parts is that you're some kind of magician."

"Black magic," said Deaf Jackson much too loudly before his friends could shush him.

Malone just smiled. At least, it looked like a smile to Kinkaid and Franklin. One couldn't be sure because only the center portion of the man's mouth was visible behind his black rat's nest of a beard. You couldn't tell what the corners of his mouth were up to.

"I'm no magician, gentlemens. Jest a poor seeker after knowledge. A wanderin' scholar, you might say."

"What kind of knowledge might you be seeking, sir?" Young Hotchkiss was too wet behind the ears to know that in California Territory it was impolite at best—and potentially lethal at worst—to inquire too deeply into another man's business.

Malone took no offense, however, and smiled at the youth. Wiser men among the six heaved silent sighs of relief.

"Oh, this and that, that and this. Same thing as the poor feller Diogenes. He has his lamp, and I've got that." He gestured out into the street, indicating a massive horse of unidentifiable parentage.

Young Hotchkiss would have asked who Diogenes was ... sounded like a furriner ... but Franklin hastened to cut him off before he said too much.

"The point being, sir, that you are rumored to be in the possession of certain arcane skills." When Malone did not comment but instead waited patiently, Franklin continued. "We are farmers, sir. Simple farmers."

"I'd say that's right on both counts." Malone held his whittling up to the light, examining it carefully.

Franklin looked helplessly to his neighbors. Again it was Kinkaid who picked up the gauntlet. "Mr. Malone, sir, we got ourselves real troubles. Our land is, well, sir, it seems to be cursed."

The mountain man looked up at him. "Cursed, sir?"

Kinkaid nodded somberly. "Cursed."

"I wonder if you mightn't be a tad more specific, friend."

Emboldened, Slim Martin spoke up. "It's our crops, Mr. Malone. They get lots of water, plenty of sun. We work as hard as any folk in the Central Valley but it don't make no difference. Corn tops out at less than a foot; apples just shrivel on the tree; tomatoes never get ripe. It's a caution, sir. And it don't seem to matter none what we plant. Nothin' comes up proper."

Malone straightened in the chair, which groaned under his weight. "An' you think I kin help you?"

It was not necessary for them to reply: their desperation was plain on their sunburned faces.

"Now, I ask you, fair gentlemens: do I look like a farmer to you?"

They eyed him up and down, noting the heavy goatskin boots, the wolf's-head chapeau, the bowie knife and LeMat pistol secured at his waist, and the twin bandoliers of enormous Sharps buffalo rifle cartridges that crisscrossed his massive chest, and the truth of what he said laid them low.

A couple turned to leave, but not Kinkaid. "Sir," he pleaded desperately, "if you can help us, we'd be more than just obliged. Most of us"—he gestured at his companions—"came to this country for the gold. Well, the placer gold's all run out, and big companies have taken over most of the claims up in the high country and on the American River.

"When the big money started moving in, a lot of folks picked up and left, but some of us stayed. My people are Illinois original, and I know fine farming country when I see it. A man ought to be able to make a good living out of this earth hereabouts. Plenty of folks are: those working the valley to the east of us.

"I don't mind bein' run off by bandits, or the weather, or grizzlies or Indians, but I'm damned if I'll give up and just walk away from my spread without having a reason why."

Malone considered silently. Then he rose. Involuntarily, the little knot of farmers retreated a step. The mountain man had to bend to avoid bumping his head on the porch roof that shaded the sidewalk. "Like I said, I ain't no farmer. But I don't like to see good folks driven off their places when mebbe there's a simple straight way their troubles kin be fixed. So I will have a look-see at your country, gentlemens. Don't promise that I kin do nothin' for you, but a look-see I'll have."

"As to the matter of payment," Franklin began.

"Let me see if I kin help you folks out first," Malone told him. "If I can fix your problems, then it'll cost you, oh, a hundred dollars U.S. In gold." Franklin inhaled sharply but said nothing. "Until then, bed and vittles will do me jest fine. A bucket or two of oats for Worthless wouldn't be turned down, neither."

Across the street the enormous multicolored nag looked back at the group and whinnied.

Franklin and Kinkaid exchanged a glance, then Franklin turned back to the mountain man and nodded. "Agreed."

Buoyed by their success but simultaneously wary of the man they'd engaged, the farmers headed for their own mounts or, in the case of Franklin and Kinkaid, a fine new buckboard.

"Think he's the man?" Kinkaid asked his neighbor.

"I don't know, Jesse." Franklin glanced back up the street to where the mountain man was mounting his ridiculous animal. "Might be he's telling us the truth when he says he doesn't know a thing about farming."

Kinkaid lowered his gaze. "Well, it weren't a farmer we come to find, was it?"

"I'm not very confident about the other, either," Franklin murmured. "I don't see anything remarkable about him except his size."

Deaf Jackson swung his right leg over his saddle. "What'd you expect to find, George? Somebody with horns growin' out of their head, breathin' fire and riding a cloud?"

"No, I expect not." Franklin heaved himself up into the buckboard while Kinkaid took the reins.

Young Hotchkiss mounted alongside Slim Martin. "Funny thing, back there."

"What's that?" Martin asked him as they turned up the street that led out of San Jose.

"That odd-looking horse of his turning back to us and whinnying when we were talking about him."

"What's funny about that?"

"Malone wasn't talking that loud, and there were wagons and horses going all the time we was there. How'd that animal hear him clear across that street?"

Malone had been studying the terrain ever since they'd ridden south out of San Jose. Rolling hills that gave way to flat, grassy plains. You could smell the richness of the earth. Blessed as it was with adequate water and California sunshine, there was no reason why the soil they were traversing shouldn't produce crops as fine and healthy as any in the world.

But it was not. Something was wrong with this land, something major unpleasant, Malone decided.

The men kept their distance from him, wary and uncertain. All except young Hotchkiss, who was too green to know better. He rode alongside, keeping the stranger company and asking too many questions for his own good. But the mountain man didn't appear to mind, and the others were delighted to include among their number one fool whose chattering ignorance served to free them of the accusation of inhospitality.

"That's quite a hat you've got, sir. Did you kill the animal yourself?" The young farmer indicated the wolf's head that protected Malone's scalp.

The mountain man kept his attention on the land ahead, studying the soil, the increasingly twisted trees, and the scraggly brush. Surely it was damaged country they were entering. Sick country.

"I didn't kill it," he replied offhandedly. "It ain't dead."

Young Hotchkiss hesitated as though he hadn't heard correctly. "Begging your pardon, sir."

"It ain't dead." Reaching up, he adjusted the wolf's head over his forehead.

Hotchkiss regarded the canine skull. "I wouldn't be found calling you a liar to save my life, Mr. Malone, but if it ain't dead, then where's the rest of it?"

"In a cave a thousand feet above the Snake River. Old wolf's denned up for the winter. Since he don't need his head while he's hibernatin', he didn't see the harm in lettin' me borry it till spring. I told him I'd look out for his family in return." Malone leaned close and whispered conspiratorially. "Don't talk too loud or you're likely to wake him up. I don't know what his head's likely to do without the rest of him, but it might not be real amiable."

The wide-eyed young farmer nodded and spurred his mount to rejoin his companions up ahead. As soon as he'd gone, Worthless cocked his head back to peer up out of his good eye at the man on his back.

"What're you squintin' at, you useless offspring of a spavined mule? The boy was gettin' to be somethin' of an irritation."

The Percheron-*cum*-Appaloosa-*cum*-Arabian-*cum*-unicorn snorted with great deliberation, compelling his rider to wipe his left boot while visiting additional imprecations upon his mount, which plodded on, thoroughly unimpressed.

The town wasn't much: schoolhouse, church, smithy, barber-shop, two general stores, a small hotel. It was the spittin' image of a thousand similar farming communities all across the country.

A woman with two kids was coming out of the general store. When she saw the riders approach, she ran back inside. Several men emerged to greet the tired arrivals.

"Well, we're back!" Deaf Jackson declared loudly as he dismounted.

"Yep. This is Malone," Kinkaid said. "The man we heard about."

The two men standing on the store porch looked uncomfort-able. Franklin eased himself down from the buckboard and mounted the steps to confront them.

"Josiah, Andrew, what's going on here? This isn't the greeting we expected. What is our friend Mr. Malone going to think?"

The storekeeper picked at his apron. "You're late, George."

Franklin frowned. "What's that got to do with anything? It took considerable time to find our man."

"Well, George," said the storekeeper's companion, "it's just that you all were gone so long, and then this other gentleman rode into town...."

Franklin's eyebrows rose. "Other gentleman?"

"Me."

All eyes went to the general store's entrance. The man who stood there was as thin as Slim Martin but taller. He had pale blue eyes and undisciplined blond hair and rather more lines in his face than he ought to have had. He wore a brightly checked, long-sleeved flannel shirt over a new pair of Mr. Levi's best pants and was masticating a chaw of the store's best tobacco.

"And who might you be, sir?" Jesse Kinkaid inquired.

"Sam. Folks just call me Sam. You can call me Sam, too." His gaze rose to the silent, contemplative mountain man. "So can you, friend. That's me, just plain Sam. The farmer's best friend."

Malone touched the nose of his unusual headgear with the tip of one finger.

Franklin, Kinkaid, and the rest gathered around the two men from the store. Intense whispering ensued.

"Andrew, how could you go an' hire somebody when you knew we were lookin' for this Malone fella?"

"Well, George, he just wandered in, and we all got to talking, and he said he was sure he could help us. Before we go an' do something dumb, let's think this thing through. How much is that Malone gonna cost us?"

"Hundred dollars," Kinkaid murmured.

The storekeeper looked triumphant. "This Sam fella says he'll fix all our troubles for fifty."

"Fifty?" Slim Martin said eagerly.

"Now listen here," young Hotchkiss began, "we've as much as hired this gentleman Malone. He's rode all the way down from San Jose with us, expecting to be employed on our behalf, and—"

"Shut up, boy," Franklin snapped. "Pay attention to your betters. Fifty, hmmm?" The two men from the store nodded.

Franklin turned and put on his best smile, simultaneously checking to make certain that no one stood between him and the open doorway.

"Mr. Malone, sir, I don't quite know what to say. I'm afraid we've got ourselves a situation here."

The mountain man regarded him unblinkingly. "Situation?"

"Yes, sir." Franklin shaded his eyes against the March sun. "It seems that unbeknownst to the rest of us, our friends here have gone and hired this other gentleman to assist with our difficulties. I'm sure you understand that since he was engaged first, the conditions of his employment take precedence over yours."

Malone glanced at the tall, thin individual standing on the porch chewing tobacco, then looked back down at the big farmer.

"No problem, friend."

Franklin's heart, which had commenced to beating as if in expectation of the Final Judgment, resumed a more natural rhythm. "It's only business, sir. Perhaps we can make use of your services another time."

"Perhaps." Malone glanced down the narrow street. "I'll just find

Worthless a stall for the night, and tomorrow I'll be on my way."
Again a finger rose to touch the lip of the wolf's head.

He heard the footsteps approaching. It was pitch dark in the stable.
In the stall across the way, Worthless slept soundly, for a change not
snoring. Two stalls farther up, a mare shuffled against her straw.

Will Hotchkiss quietly approached the recumbent bulk of the
mountain man. No one had seen him enter the barn. He reached
out to shake the man's shoulder.

Less than a second later Will was lying on his back in the straw, a
knife blade more than an inch wide so close to his Adam's apple he
could feel the chill from the steel. An immense shape loomed over
him, and for an instant he thought the eyes glaring down at him
were glowing with an internal light of their own, though whether
they belonged to the man atop him or to the wolf-skull headpiece in
the corner, he could not say.

"Hotchkiss." Malone sat back on his haunches, a mountainous
shape in the dim light. The massive blade withdrew.

The young farmer sat up slowly, unconsciously caressing his
throat. "You're mighty fast for a man your size, Mr. Malone, sir."

"And you're mighty stupid even fer one so young." The mountain
man sheathed his blade. "Don't you know better than to sneak up
on a man in the middle o' the night? Your head could've ended up a
play-pretty for my wolf friend's cubs."

"Sorry, but I had to come get you without my neighbors
knowing what I was about."

"Did you, now?"

"Mr. Malone, sir, it weren't right how my neighbors treated you
today. It just weren't right. And I think they're wrong about that
Sam fella. Something about him rubs me the wrong way.

"I'd like for you to come out to my place, sir, and see if you can't
do something for my land. I'll pay you myself. I've got a little money
put aside. I'd rather have you working for me than that Sam fella."

"What, now? In the middle of the night?"

"If you would, sir. That way my neighbors won't be disturbed by my doing this behind their backs, as it were. It's them I've got to live with after both you and this Sam fella are gone."

Malone rose, grinning in the darkness. "And if I turn out to be the biggest fraud since Munchausen, I won't embarrass you in front o' your peers, is that it?" He waved off Hotchkiss's incipient protest. "No, never you mind, son. This ain't a bad way to go about it. I don't like bein' embarrassed any more than you do. So if'n I can't extricate you from your troubles, why, this way there won't be none others t' see me fail."

Hotchkiss waited nervously until the mountain man had saddled his complaining, grumbling mount. The animal's spirits picked up considerably once outside the stable, however. Hotchkiss had come into town on a wagon pulled by two mares, one of which was near coming into her time.

Nor had the young farmer come by himself. Seated on the wagon, holding the reins and bundled against the evening chill, was a vision of pure country grace.

"Mr. Malone, this is my wife, Emma."

"Mr. Malone." She eyed him about the way Worthless was eyeing the nearest mare. Malone pursed his lips.

"Ma'am."

She kept up a steady stream of chatter all the way out of town, laughing and giggling and batting her eyes at him like an advertisement for a minstrel show, all physical innuendo and sly music. Hotchkiss guided his animals, his attention on the road ahead, oblivious to nocturnal flirting so blatant that it would have put a blush on a bachelor jackrabbit.

Nor did it cease when they reached the neat wood-and-stone farmhouse. Sweet Emma Hotchkiss managed to bump up against Malone once outside and once on the way in, where she made a grand production of removing her cloak and bending toothsomely to stir the sleeping fire. Malone eyed her speculatively. She was a bumptious, simmering three-ring circus barely restrained by tight gingham and lace, and no ringmaster in sight.

Nor was she the only surprise awaiting him.

As Hotchkiss led him into the sitting room, a lanky shape uncoiled from the couch to greet him with a smile. "Malone, ain't it?" A hand extended toward him. "Ought to be an interesting evening."

Malone did not take the proffered hand but turned instead to his host. "What is this?"

Hotchkiss looked uncomfortable. "I said that I felt my neighbors had treated you unfairly, Mr. Malone, and I hold to that. But they're thinking of the money in their pockets instead of their futures, and I'm not. I don't care who helps us so long as someone does, right quick. Otherwise, everyone in this part of the country is going to go under before the next harvest. So I thought the only fair thing would be for me to hire the both of you for one night to see what each of you can do."

Malone stroked his beard as he eyed his host. "Reckon I were wrong about you, son. You're only half-stupid."

Emma Hotchkiss turned gaily from the fire, which wasn't smoldering half so much as she, and eyed each of her visitors in turn.

"I think Will was ever so clever for thinking of this. He's such a clever boy. And if both of you gentlemen can help us, why, then we'll be twice as well off, won't we? I'll be ever so happy to thank the best man with a nice kiss on the cheek."

Sure she would, Malone thought, watching her warily. The way Venus wanted to kiss Tannhäuser in that German feller's opera.

Hotchkiss seemed oblivious to it all, his mind on his crops when he ought to have been paying more attention to his field. "How long after you've finished your work will it take to show results? A month? Two?"

"Shoot, no, neighbor," said Sam the farmer's friend. "I can't speak for Mr. Malone, but as for myself, I think we can prove something right here tonight." He smiled up at the mountain man. "What about it, friend?"

"I don't like contests," Malone rumbled.

The lanky stranger shrugged. "Don't matter one way or the other to me. The other good folks hereabouts seem pretty convinced of my skills already. I don't mind accepting a forfeit."

Malone was being truthful. He didn't like contests, and he didn't like the way he'd been rousted out of a sound sleep on false pretenses. But he also didn't like the way this blond stranger was eyeing his host's young wife. Not that she wasn't encouraging him, along with probably every other human male west of the Sierras, but it wasn't very tactful of him to respond so readily.

"I don't like forfeits, either. Might be harmful to my reputation."

"And do you have a reputation, friend?" Sam asked him tauntingly.

"Here and there. Not always good. How about you?"

"Me? Why I'm Sam, just plain Sam. The farmer's friend." He winked at Emma Hotchkiss. Her husband didn't see it, but Malone did. She responded by licking her upper lip. From what Malone could see, it didn't look chapped.

"What say we have a look at these fine folks' uncooperative land, Mr. Malone."

The mountain man nodded. "I think that'd be a right sound place to begin."

Hotchkiss provided lanterns to complement the light of the full moon. The four of them walked outside, the young farmer and his wife leading the way toward the nearest field. The stranger toted a large canvas satchel, his eyes eagerly following Emma Hotchkiss as he envisioned the bonus he imagined would be his before the night was over. Malone carried a small pouch he'd extracted from one of his saddlebags and with unvoiced disapproval watched the stranger watching Emma.

The sound of wood striking ground drew their attention. Everyone looked toward the corral as two shapes bolted into the moonlight.

"I tried to tell you, Will, that your mare was coming into heat," Emma Hotchkiss said accusingly.

"Don't worry none, son." Malone followed the galloping, rollicking pair of steeds with his eyes as they disappeared over the nearest hill. "Worthless won't hurt her. They'll have themselves their run, and he'll bring 'er back."

Hotchkiss looked uncertain. "Can't you call him in?"

Malone shook his head. "Worthless pretty much does as he pleases. I reckon they'll have themselves a tour of most o' your property before he feels winded enough to amble on back."

"Hard to believe that a man who can't control his horse can do much with the earth," the stranger observed insinuatingly.

The mountain man looked down at him. "Tryin' to control Worthless would be about like tryin' to control the earth. Myself, I'd rather have a friend for a mount than a slave."

The neatly turned field stretched eastward, bathed in pale moonlight. Ryegrass whispered warningly beneath their feet. A single silhouetted tree stood leafless, lonely, and bruised amid a mound of broken yellow rock. There was no wind, no clouds: it was a place where a man could smell silence.

A deep creek ran between the two sloping halves of the field. Malone studied it thoughtfully, then bent to examine the soil. Lifting a pinch of dirt to his nose, he inhaled deeply, then tasted of the soil. He straightened.

"Sour," he declared brusquely as he brushed his hands together to clean them.

The stranger nodded, eyeing the mountain man with new respect. "That was my thought as well. You do know something about the earth, friend."

Malone eyed him evenly. "This and that."

The stranger hesitated a moment longer. "Well, then, this looks like as good a place to begin as any." Reaching into his satchel, he fumbled around until he found a pinch of seed. He flicked it earthward and waited, eyes glittering.

"Father Joseph!" Will Hotchkiss whispered, gazing in disbelief at the ground.

Where the seed had landed, tiny pools of light appeared in the sterile furrow. They spread, trickling together within the soil, a pale green glowing effulgence staining the dark loam.

As the four looked on, tiny stems broke the surface. Vines first, climbing toward the moon like umber snakes. Three feet high they were when they halted. Like soap bubbles emerging from a child's toy pipe, bright red fruit began to appear beneath the green leaves, swollen and red-ripe as the lips of a succubus. The stranger turned proudly to the farming couple. His words were directed at both of them, but his eyes were intent on Emma Hotchkiss.

"Well, now, that wasn't so difficult, was it?"

"Tomatoes," Hotchkiss was muttering. "Finest damn tomatoes I ever seen. In March." He eyed the stranger warily. "This ain't farming, sir. It's witchcraft."

"Not at all, friend, not at all," the stranger replied, smooth as cream. "Merely the application of sound agrarian principles." He glanced at the mountain man. "Wouldn't you agree, sir?"

"Too soon to say." Malone grunted and reached into the bag he carried. Choosing another furrow, he scattered seeds of his own.

The earth did not glow where they landed. Instead, it rumbled softly like an old man's belly. Emma Hotchkiss put her palms to her face as she stared. Even the stranger backed away.

Not vines this time, but entire trees emerged from the ground. Fruit appeared on thickening branches, bright and bursting with tart juice. At Malone's urging, Will Hotchkiss tentatively plucked one from a lower branch and rotated it with his fingers.

"Oranges." His gaze shifted between the modest tomato bushes and the full-blown orchard, and he did not have to give voice to how he felt.

Frowning, the stranger selected and spread another handful of seed. This time the vines that arose with unnatural rapidity from the earth were shorter but thicker than those that had preceded them. With a grandiose wave of his hand, he beckoned the young farmer close.

Will Hotchkiss knelt to examine the thumb-sized dark fruit. "Grapes," he exclaimed. "And already ripe!"

"Sam, that's fabulously clever," said Emma Hotchkiss, throwing her arms around the stranger and bussing him not anywhere near his cheek. He responded without hesitation, both of them ignoring her husband, who was wholly intent on the miraculous grapes.

Malone surveyed the scene and shook his head. Then he sighed and carefully dusted a nearby mound with seed. This time it was as if the earth itself coughed rather than rumbled, as if uncertainly trying to digest the unexpected fodder. New vines emerged with astonishing speed: to everyone's surprise except Malone's, they looked no different from those the stranger had just called forth.

"Well." Will Hotchkiss sounded slightly disappointed. "A tie."

"Things ain't always as they seem, son. Taste one," Malone suggested.

The young farmer did so, and as the grape squinched between his teeth, his eyes widened. He stared wonderingly up at the mountain man.

"Already turned to wine ... on the vine!"

"Mr. Malone!" his wife exclaimed. "How wonderful!" But her attempt to explore her other guest was doomed to defeat, as Malone was too tall for her to reach, even on tiptoe, and he declined to bend. She settled for favoring him with a look that despite his moral resolve raised his body temperature half a degree.

"I don't know how you did that." The stranger's disposition had passed from mild upset to middlin' anger. "But fruit isn't all that this land will produce if coaxed by someone who knows truly the ways of the soil."

He whirled and flung a handful of seeds in a wide arc. Where they struck, a section of earth the size of Hotchkiss's corral began to burn with cold green fire. Clods and clumps of earth were tossed aside as trunks two feet thick erupted from the ground. No fruit hung bounteous and ready to pick from the gnarled, newly formed branches. Hotchkiss searched a black extrusion until he found the first of the small oval clusters that were as wooden-dark as the branch itself.

"Walnuts," he exclaimed, picking one. "Ripe and full-meated."

"Oh, yes," his wife murmured huskily.

The stranger eyed Malone challengingly.

"That's quite a feat," Malone said. He held up his pouch. "Don't carry near that much seed with me. So I reckon one'll have to do." Digging into the much smaller second sack, he removed a single seed.

The stranger smirked. "That's all you got left, friend? My bag's still near full."

"I don't much like to travel heavy." Carefully, Malone pushed the single seed into the soil, using one callused thumb to shove it deep. Then he stepped back and waited.

The tree that blossomed forth was no larger than any one of the dozen walnut trees that now blocked the stream from view. As soon as it reached its full growth, Hotchkiss approached to pick from a lower branch.

"Walnuts," he declared disappointedly as he cracked the shell with the butt of his knife. With the point of the blade, he pried out the contents, popped them into his mouth, and chewed reflectively. "No worse, but no better."

"Pick another," Malone suggested.

Hotchkiss looked at him funny but complied. It seemed that his eyes couldn't get any bigger than before, but they did. "Pecans." He stared wonderingly at Malone. "On the same tree?"

"Thought you'd be the kind who'd appreciate good nuts," Malone told him. "Why stop now?"

The young farmer picked some more. His delighted wife joined him. Together they sampled the tree's bounty.

"Peanuts ... on a tree!"

"Chestnuts," his wife exclaimed. She displayed the rest of her pickings to the mountain man. "What are these, Mr. Malone?"

He examined the contents of her perfect hands. "The big curved ones are Brazil nuts. Little curved ones are cashews."

"What are cashews?" Hotchkiss asked.

"They don't come from around here, but they're good to eat," Malone told him. "Those big round ones are macadamias, from Australia." He peered up into the tree. "I reckon there's some up in there I don't rightly know myself."

The stranger walked right up to his taller opponent to search his face. "You're a very clever man, friend. Very clever indeed. But you're no farmer's friend. And whatever you be, I swear you can't match this."

He stepped back and took a seed the size of a peanut from his sack. It pulsed with a faint inner light of its own, as though a tiny heart were beating inside the hard outer covering. Instead of scattering it carelessly as he had the others, he planted this one very carefully. Malone thought the stranger whispered some words over it as he ground it into the soil with the heel of his boot. Then he stepped back.

From a red refulgent patch of earth another tree emerged, its branches sagging under the mass of multihued fruit they carried. The trunk of the tree seemed permeated with that pale red glow, which did not diminish when the tree ceased growing. There were apples and oranges, lemons and limes and soursops, jackfruits and star fruits and litchis and rambutans—fruits that never should have grown in that dirt, in that country. It was a cornucopia of fruit sprung from a single unsuspecting square of soil.

Even Malone was impressed and said so.

"Go on," the stranger said proudly, "taste some of it. Taste any of it."

The mountain man carefully scrutinized one of the groaning branches. He picked a couple of rambutans and began to peel them, the sugary white centers emerging from behind the spiny red outer husks. The stranger looked on intently as Malone put one fruit to his lips. Then he hesitated.

"You must be gettin' a mite hungry yourself after so much hard work." He held out the other rambutan.

The stranger waved him off. "No, thank you, but I enjoyed a fine supper and am quite content."

"Oh, go on," Malone urged him. "I dislike eatin' by meself."

Hotchkiss frowned at the stranger. "Is something wrong with the fruit?"

"No, of course not." The blond man hesitated, then took the proffered fruit. Eyes locked, the two men ate simultaneously.

"Can I have some, too?" Emma Hotchkiss asked coyly. "I'm not full at all. In fact, I'm just ever so positively empty inside."

Malone smiled at her. "Maybe later, ma'am. We need to make sure it's truly ripe."

"Oh, I think it is." She smiled up at him. "But if you're not sure, then I'll wait until you are."

"Pretty good," Malone said, tossing aside the nut that lay at the center of the fruit. He wiped his lips with the back of a huge, hairy hand. "You know your crops, Sam the farmer's friend, but I ain't so sure you know your soil. This hereabouts is soured fer sure, and not all the fruits and vegetables and grains that you or I could grow on it in a night will cure that."

The stranger did not hear. His face had acquired a faintly green glow itself. A hand went to his stomach as he turned to Hotchkiss.

"Are you all right, sir?" the young farmer inquired, alarmed.

"I am. Just a mite too much of my own bounty, I fear. Might your fine little community be home to a competent physician?"

Hotchkiss nodded. "Dr. Heinmann. Travels between towns hereabouts. He's at the hotel for another day, I think, but should be leaving tomorrow."

"Then I'd best hurry." Suddenly the stranger was running back toward the farmhouse, exhibiting more energy than at any time that night.

"What happened to him?" Hotchkiss asked. Malone followed the stranger with his eyes as the man reached the house, mounted his steed, and urged it into a mad gallop toward town. Retching sounds drifted wistfully back over the fields toward them.

"I reckon he got too full of himself. He has a lot of knowledge but ain't quite sure how to control it. Your land hereabouts is soured. With his kind of help it'd grow you one fine crop this year and probably fail the next, mebbe forever. By which time the likes of Sam the farmer's friend would have harvested whatever he desired from this part of the world and moved on." He glanced in Emma Hotchkiss's direction, but rather than mark his point, she only gazed back at him invitingly, ignoring such inconveniences as admonitory implications.

Hotchkiss was crestfallen. "You're saying that the trouble's still in the ground and that it can't be fixed? That all our efforts here are doomed to failure?"

"Oh, no, I didn't say nothin' like that, Will. The problem can be rectified by the application of an appropriate nitrogen-fixin' substance, not by seein' how many outrageous fruits and vegetables one man can grow in a night by trickery and deception."

"Nitro fix ...?" Hotchkiss frowned up at him. "What kind of talk is that?"

"Science, my young friend. The same science that makes the telegraph work and steam engines turn wheels. There's all kinds o' science stalking about the world, even among vegetables."

"Where do we get this kind of substance?"

"Wal, now, it might take some time to gather what you need from certain islands I know, like the Galapagos, or certain holes in the ground, like in New Mexico, but seein' as how you folks have already had such a bad time of it and are so far down the road o' discouragement, I thought it best to attend to the problem as quickly as possible. So while we've been out here playin' farmer, your difficulties have already been attended to."

"Already? You mean the ground is fixed?"

"Yep," said Malone. "Won't grow you no already-wined grapes or many-nut trees, but you'll do right well hereabouts with regular walnuts and grapes, wheat if you need it, and a bunch of other stuff I don't reckon you know much about yet. Like artichokes." He stroked his beard. "I reckon I'd try the oranges a mite farther south, though."

"But the soil—how did you put it right?"

Malone put a fatherly hand on the young farmer's shoulder. "Now, don't you worry yourself none about the hows here, son. Sometimes it's jest better to accept things than to question everything."

They walked back to the house, which seemed already to have taken on a cheerier, happier air. As they did so, Malone glanced toward the corral. Worthless and the mare had returned. It was difficult to tell which was worse winded, but it was plain to see that the stallion had been attending to business. No doubt he'd sprayed most of young Hotchkiss's property in addition to his mare.

How could Malone tell his host that a little unicorn seed invigorated everything it touched?

Emma Hotchkiss could certainly cook, he had to admit. She had changed and wore a smile and a dress that revealed at least two rings of that three-ring circus whose presence he'd remarked on earlier. Several of the acts repeatedly bumped up against Malone as she leaned over the table to serve the men. As always, her husband did not notice. He was too delighted, too thrilled by the knowledge that his farm had been saved, to note that his field was in danger.

After she slipped off to bed, leaving in her wake a trail of perfume and promise, the two men shared conversation and tobacco in front of the crackling fire.

"I can't thank you enough, Mr. Malone. My neighbors won't believe it."

"They will when your crops come up, son. I promise you that."

Hotchkiss regarded him curiously. "For a man who's fulfilled every promise he made and vanquished the opposition to boot, you don't sound very content."

"I'm troubled, my young friend. Course, I'm always troubled, but I reckon that's my destiny. I'm not talkin' about those kinds of troubles, though. Jest the local ones.

"Fer example, if'n I were you, I wouldn't be entirely convinced that this was such a fine place to put down roots."

"But I thought you set the earth here to rights."

"Oh, she's unsoured, that's certain, but whatever cursed this ground in the first place I ain't sure is entirely cured. It might cause problems somewhere down the line. I'm not sayin' it will fer you, understand, but it might fer your children and your children's children. When you've put a few good years in, you might consider sellin' this property at a good profit and movin' farther down into the valley, mebbe somewheres along the San Joaquin. Better water there, anyways."

Hotchkiss was silent. "Well, sir, I cannot but take your advice, having seen what you've done here this night. I will certainly keep your words in mind."

"Thet's not the only thing. There's more cursed hereabouts than jest your land."

"More than the land? I'm afraid I don't follow you, Mr. Malone."

The mountain man nodded in the direction of the bedroom, the firelight deepening the shadows that were his face. "It's your Emma."

Hotchkiss gaped at him, then jerked around to follow his gaze. "Emma, cursed? Good God, Mr. Malone. By what? She seems well and healthy."

"She is that. But she's also tormented by the worst curse than can afflict any woman, Will. That of boredom."

Hotchkiss frowned. "Boredom? But how could she be bored, Mr. Malone? There's so much to keep a woman busy on a farm: caring for the garden, washing, feeding the chickens and hogs, cooking, mending...."

Malone coughed delicately into a closed fist the size and consistency of a small anvil. "I don't think you quite follow my reasoning, son. There's activity, and then there's boredom, and the two ain't necessarily mutually exclusive." He leaned forward, his eyes intent on those of the younger man, as if he were trying to communicate much more than mere words.

"She needs a change, Will. She ain't the stay-on-the-farm-all-year type. You're a hardworkin' young feller, and I kin see that you're gonna do yourself proud with your farmin', make yourself some good money. Spend some of it on her. Don't just tell her you love her. Show her. Take her up to Frisco for a while. Tell her how beautiful she is. Give her little gifts and presents, and not jest for her birthday and holidays. The best time to give a woman something is when she ain't expectin' anything." He rose from the chair.

"Where are you going?" Hotchkiss asked numbly.

"Out to the stable. You'll be wantin' the house to yourself."

"But I promised you ..."

"Never you mind what you promised me, son. Most beds are too soft for me, anyhow. I'll sleep fine in the stable." He glanced toward the front door. "Need to keep an eye on Worthless anyways. Come springtime he don't always know how to slow himself down." He grinned. "Thinks he's still a colt."

"Wait!" Hotchkiss said suddenly. "What kind of presents should I give Emma? What kinds of gifts?"

"Don't need to be big things. Lots of times little'uns mean more to a woman." He donned his wolf's head, and Hotchkiss thought he saw tiny lights flare briefly in the headgear's eye sockets again, though more likely it was the glow from the fire. "You might start with this."

He reached into a pocket and extracted an object that he handed to the young farmer. It was a small wooden sculpture, exquisitely detailed, of a man and a woman holding each other close, staring into each other's eyes. Some of the detail looked too fine to have been fashioned by human hands.

With a start, Hotchkiss recognized the piece of whittling Malone had been working on outside the hotel in San Jose when he and his fellow farmers had confronted him.

"I can't take this, sir."

Malone stood in the doorway, bending low to clear the jamb. "Sure you can, son. I jest gave it to you. Go on. She'll like it." Before Hotchkiss could protest further, Malone closed the door behind him.

The young farmer stood there, unnerved by the gift. Then he shrugged and carefully put out the fire, retiring to the bedroom. In the dim light he failed to notice that the man and woman depicted in the sculpture were in the exact likeness of himself and his precious Emma.

The following morning Emma Hotchkiss made Malone the best breakfast he'd enjoyed in some months: grits, toast, biscuits and gravy, bacon and eggs, and homemade jam and sausage. She hovered close to her husband, the two of them exchanging little kisses and touches, and both wore expressions of great contentment and affection. The circus, Malone noted with satisfaction, had folded its tents, pulled up stakes, and left town.

Hotchkiss escorted him back into the settlement, the two men chatting like old friends in the morning sunlight. Worthless all but trotted the entire distance. Malone gave him a couple of knowing kicks, which with great dignity he studiously ignored.

They walked into the general store, to find a meeting already in

progress. Faces turned in their direction as they entered, only to
look quickly away.

Seated in the center of the group was the blond stranger. He was
smiling. Evidently the good Dr. Heinmann's ministrations had
mollified his internal confusions.

"What is this?" Will no longer sounded young and insecure.
"What's going on here?"

"Well, Will," George Franklin said as he slowly turned in his
chair, "we were just finalizing our agreement with Sam here."

"But you can't do that." Hotchkiss started forward, only to be
restrained by his much larger companion. "I mean," he said more
quietly, "Mr. Malone here fixed my problems by himself last night.
Now he's ready to do the same for the rest of you."

"We're sorry, Will." Kinkaid was apologetic. "But we did have a
prior agreement with Sam here. Whatever your Mr. Malone did last
night was between you and him. The rest of us have made another
arrangement."

The blond stranger held up a paper. "This here is a signed
contract, all legal and irrevocable. Fifty dollars for fixing these fine
folks' land. Which I will do."

"Pretty underhanded, running back here to have that drawn up
when you knew Mr. Malone was tied up with his work out at my
place," the young farmer exclaimed heatedly.

"Easy there, Will." Malone gazed silently at the nervous faces of
the farmers. "This how you folks want it?" No one had the guts to
speak. The mountain man nodded knowingly. "All right, then. But
I'm warnin' you to keep an eye on this feller. Some things he knows
how to do; other things I ain't so sure. T' other night his own handiwork made him sick. If you ain't careful, it might make you sick,
too. Might make your land even sicker than it already is. I just want
you to know that anything happens after I leave, any problems you
have, 'tain't my fault. It's his."

Kincaid and Franklin exchanged a look. "We are prepared to
deal with any adverse consequences, Mr. Malone, though we are
confident there will be none. We are mature men, and we know
what we are doing."

"Saving yourselves fifty dollars. That's what you're doing," Will Hotchkiss muttered angrily.

"It's all right, son," Malone told him back out on the street. "Jest remember what I told you about considerin' that move."

"What did you mean when you said in there that he might make the land sicker?"

Malone lifted his gaze to the sunburned hills and fields that surrounded the town like a grassy sea. "I don't rightly know myself, Will. That Sam's a right clever feller, but I think mebbe too clever by half. A little knowledge is a good thing, but a lot ... well, you better know what you're doin' when you start playin' around with the earth." He clapped the young farmer on the shoulder, a friendly good-bye.

"You take care o' yourself, young feller, and your good woman, too. Come later this summer, I think you're gonna come into a foal that might act a mite peculiar, but it'll be a good work animal for you if you can learn to tolerate its eccentricities."

"I will bear that in mind, Mr. Malone, sir. And thank you." Searching a pocket, he found the double eagle he'd been carrying with him since yesterday. "It's only a part of what you're properly owed, but ..."

"Thank you, Will." Malone accepted the twenty dollars. "Fair payment for services rendered." He mounted the four-legged massif that was his steed. "Give artichokes a try."

"I will, sir," Hotchkiss shouted after him as Malone rode south out of town, even as he wondered anew what the devil an artichoke was.

Inside the general store, the stranger was holding court, promising the small-minded, shortsighted men around him bounteous crops and enormous profits. He knew a lot, he did, but less than he thought.

"You heard what the mountain man said," Kinkaid told him.

The stranger smiled: relaxed, supremely self-assured. "Sure, I heard, and it don't worry me none. Shouldn't worry none of you, neither. I know what I'm doin'. When I finish my work, your farms will be more prosperous than you've ever imagined. Course, there might be a slight recharge fee each planting season, but nothin' none of you won't be able to afford. A trifle compared to what you'll be making.

"As for any problems that come up, why, I'll gladly take the blame for them. You think, if I didn't have confidence in my skills, that I'd stick around? I know my responsibilities, gentlemen, and am prepared to discharge them to the fullest. So, if anything untoward should occur hereabouts, let it be deemed my fault. My fault, gentlemen, or my name ain't Sam Andreas. Sam the farmer's friend."

It stands to reason that a traveler like Amos Malone would tend to find his way back to regions of especial interest, particularly those that feature the unusual and the exceptional. The Yellowstone region would certainly qualify. Furthermore, as a man of letters, Malone is someone who is fond of language. Despite his impressive size, he is actually quite a mild-mannered chap. This does not keep terrified folk from fleeing from his presence. But once you get to know him and settle down for a drink and a casual conversation and can ignore a certain lack of personal hygiene, you might find yourself privy to marvels big and small. All rendered through language, of course. Malone has nothing to prove by putting a massive fist through a wall. If confronted, he'd much rather unleash a cornucopia of interesting verbs and adjectives.

Though there are times when those can prove even more powerful than that gnarled, scarred fist.

HAVING WORDS

W e would like to go up into that country. There are many animals there. Good hunting and fine places to camp." Bending toward the fire, Grass-in-Hair cut a choice piece of dog with his knife and passed it to his guest, who accepted the morsel with a grunt of thanks.

Amos Malone hunched closer to the tepee's central heat and chewed thoughtfully. When he'd ridden into the encampment early that morning, his imposing bulk had frightened the children, but now Grass-in-Hair's youngest son slept peacefully on the mountain man's legs like a rabbit nestled in a bear's lap.

"Then why don't y'all just do it?"

Two-Feathers-Falling sniffed and repositioned the heavy robe that lay across his shoulders. It was late, and cold despite the fire. He would rather have been lying with First Woman, but Grass-in-Hair had insisted he be present. As far as Two-Feathers-Falling was concerned, the meeting was at best a polite waste of time. Half as big as a bull buffalo the white man might be, but in this matter he could do nothing.

"Do you not think we would if we could?" he snapped.

The mountain man took no umbrage at the medicine man's tone. "What's stoppin' you?"

Two-Feathers-Falling shifted uncomfortably. He was no coward, but neither was he a fool. Grass-in-Hair let the silence lie as long as was decent, then saw that he was going to have to do the explaining himself.

"Tongue Kills lives there. He has claimed all that fine land for himself and will let no one else in. Not to camp, not to hunt. He is a greedy, evil person."

Malone swallowed the last scrap of dog, extracted his pipe from a pocket, and commenced to chew on the rose-hued stem that protruded incongruously from the otherwise impenetrable black-wire mass of his beard. "How big's his tribe?"

"He has no tribe, no family. He is alone."

Malone's gaze narrowed. "Mean to say one warrior's been starin' down the whole Cheyenne nation?"

Two-Feathers-Falling spoke bitterly. "Tongue Kills is not a warrior. He is a medicine man. Like myself. But his medicine is too strong for me. And not just for us. No one dares to challenge him. Those who go into his country do not come out again."

"Except for One-Who-Carries-Stone-Behind-His-Head," said Grass-in-Hair. "He was a war chief of the Crow who announced to his people that he would kill the medicine man so they could move into his land. He did come out. But he lived only a few minutes after returning to his village." The old chief was solemn. "We heard the story when we were trading with the Crow up on the big river last autumn. Those who told it to us are known to be truthful men."

Malone tamped some brown dried substance into the bowl of his pipe. "What happened to him?"

"The warriors said that he was burned all over." The chief's tone was hushed. "As if he had been in a great fire. His pony had been burned, too. It lived two days longer. Since then the Crow, like us, have stopped trying to go into that country." Grass-in-Hair looked wistful. "But we would still like to. I should like very much to hunt there. It is more land than any one man needs. Even one as strong in medicine as Tongue Kills." He went silent, expectant.

The fire crackled. Along with silence, the tepee was permeated by the pungent rankness of cooked meat and unwashed men. Finally Malone said, "What makes you think I kin help you?"

Grass-in-Hair looked up at his visitor. "I have met a few of the other white men who have passed through this country. Some spoke of you. They said you could do strange things."

Malone laughed as he lit his pipe with a blazing splinter from the fire. "They probably meant to say that I *was* strange."

"They also said you were crazy. Here." The disgruntled Two-Feathers-Falling meaningfully tapped the side of his head.

"Might be as they were right."

"Only a crazy man would challenge Tongue Kills."

Malone chose not to comment.

"If you will try to help us in this," said Grass-in-Hair, "I will give you my eldest daughter. She is a fine woman and will bear many children."

"Wal, now, that's a swell offer, sir, but I fear I must decline. I ain't quite ready yet to start in on a family."

Grass-in-Hair nodded, disappointed but understanding. "What, then, could we give you?"

"Your friendship ... and mebbe that knife. I've kind o' taken a fancy to that knife of yours."

Grass-in-Hair held up the blade he'd used to partition the dog. It was a good knife made of the kind of shiny black stone that always held its edge. But it was not irreplaceable.

"I would give it to you gladly. But I must tell you that I do not think it is worth risking one's life for." He gestured toward the visitor's belt. "You already have a knife of metal, one that is better."

Malone shook his head. "Not necessarily better. Just different. Somethin' about your knife calls out to me, Grass-in-Hair. And when somethin' calls to me, I make it my business to listen."

"Then I make you a gift of it. Will you use it to slay Tongue Kills?" he asked curiously as he handed it over.

Malone took the knife, admiring the way the light from the fire shone through the carefully honed edges. "Hope not. After all, y'all don't necessarily want him made dead. Just agreeable." He slid the knife into his belt alongside its steel cousin and leaned forward.

"Now, then. What makes this Tongue Kills's medicine so strong? What songs does he use? What powders? What is his animal? Badger, bear, eagle?"

Two-Feathers-Falling replied tiredly, knowing it would make no difference. "He uses no songs, no powders. He has no animal."

"Then how the devil does he make medicine?"

"With words," Two-Feathers-Falling explained. "Only with words."

Malone nodded as if this meant something, took a couple of puffs, then removed his pipe and passed it to the old chief, who inhaled experimentally.

"Good tobacco," he said as he handed the pipe back.

"Thanks," Malone told him. He grinned at Two-Feathers-Falling. "I kin tell you don't think I've much of a chance against this feller Tongue Kills, but don't count me out till you see me down. I know a few words of my own."

The sleepy Cheyenne medicine man started. For an instant the mountain man's eyes seemed to have disappeared, the whites and the dark blackness to have vanished completely, leaving only dark pits beneath heavy brows. For an instant, within those twin voids could be seen stars and music, tenderness and power, indifference and compassion. Wide awake, Two-Feathers-Falling blinked.

But there was only a very large white man sitting there opposite him. One with real eyes. The rest, he decided, had been a trick of the fire.

———

"What do you think?" Grass-in-Hair asked the next morning as they watched the white man ride westward out of camp. "Of course he must be as mad as the other white men say, else he would not try this for us. But that is not necessarily a bad thing."

Two-Feathers-Falling held his buffalo robe snug against his body. Though it was warming up as the sun rose, stars still lingered in the bluing sky, pieces of ice the morning was slow to melt. "I think you

have lost a good knife," he muttered as he shuffled off in the direction of his tepee.

It truly was beautiful country, Malone mused as he nudged Worthless to his right. Green and heavily forested. While his mount
usually could be left to his own devices to find the easiest path
down a slope, sometimes his bad right eye played him false and
Malone had to help out.

Plenty of forage, good water. Excellent country. Elk and deer in
abundance and a host of lesser animals. Grizzlies, too, of course, but
they didn't bother Malone. Those possessed of a cantankerous
disposition usually sought alternative routes as soon as they set eyes
on him.

He settled in by the side of a meandering stream lined with new
spring growth. There were trees nearby from which he'd soon raised
a fine lean-to against a smooth outcropping of granite. Upstream he
found beaver and remarked the location for future visitation.

He was preparing to put a door on the lean-to one afternoon,
when he heard footsteps approaching. He tensed as he turned, alert
but in no way particularly concerned. His rifle lay close at hand,
within convenient reach. In wild country a man always kept his rifle
closer to him than anything else, including his woman.

His visitor's attire was simple and traditional, except perhaps for
an unusual breastplate that was decorated with feathers from a bird
Malone couldn't identify. They were orange tending to yellow at the
tips. The man wore much red paint on his face and clothing. His
braids were long and, despite his apparent age, black as soot. He
carried no weapons. Worthless spared him a glance, snorted, and
returned to cropping the fresh new grass behind the lean-to.

The visitor was shorter than Malone, but then, so was most of
the human race. He stopped to study the mountain man. Malone
waited for a while, then shrugged and returned to his work.

As the day wore on, the visitor maintained his silent inspection,
eventually taking a seat on a small rock that protruded from the

bank of the stream. Malone finished the door, peeled two large poles, and used them to brace the roof by jamming them into holes he'd dug earlier. Then he fished three good-sized trout from the stream, gutted and filleted them, and set about building a cookfire. Not one word had passed between the two men.

When evening arrived, Malone put the spitted fish on the fire, crossed his legs, and sat down to wait for them to cook. "For someone who's supposed to be master of a lot o' words, you're downright stingy with 'em, friend."

"You know who I am." Tongue Kills did not have a voice. He was possessed of an instrument, nay, an entire orchestra. Strings and brass, woodwinds and percussion, all were present and active, vibrating and resonant within his throat. Each word that fell from his lips was of itself a self-contained speech, a declamation, an oration of conciseness and import admirable. It was a thing wondrous and beautiful to behold.

"I expect so," Malone told him.

"Then you must know, white man, that you are a trespasser on my land."

Malone gestured expansively. "Plenty o' land here. Why are you so reluctant to share it?"

Tongue Kills sat a little straighter. "It is my wish. I have taken this place for my own."

"Your brothers think you greedy."

"They are not my brothers, and I do not care what they think. I do not care what you think. Like them, you must leave."

Malone arched his back, stretching. "Shucks, I was jest gettin' comfortable here. Reckon I might stay awhile."

Tongue Kills leaned forward. Light danced in his eyes like individual flames skating on sheets of mica. "I say that you will leave. If you try to stay, I will make it bad for you."

"With what? Some words? Mister, I've been around. I've seen a lot and heard a lot. Why, you're lookin' at the original lover o' words. I know all the words of my own people as well as those of the Crow and Shoshone. Not to mention the Assiniboin and Kwaki-utl, the Zuni and Arapaho, the Choctaw and the Seminole and

Sioux. I know words in languages you ain't never heard of: Chinee and Nippon, Tamil and Urdu, Basque and Romany and pidgin. I know words in languages that was, like Assyrian and Maya, and words in languages that ain't been born yet.

"Better to share the plenty you got with your fellows. That's the proper way for one to live."

Tongue Kills smiled unpleasantly. "You speak of many strange things, but I see no signs of power. It matters not the kind of words but how they are used. I, too, know of other languages and other words. I have made the knowing of them my business." His tone deepened ever so slightly. "You do not want to know of them, white man."

Malone plucked a sprig of grass between thumb and forefinger and stuck it between his teeth. "Shoot, I'm always willin' to learn. And since I ain't goin' nowhere, why don't you take the time to enlighten me?"

Tongue Kills's expression darkened. He nodded once, cleared his throat with a rumble, then spoke afresh. That extraordinary booming, reverberant voice spoke out, rustling the grass, its tone and emphasis sending birds fleeing from their nests and insects rushing to burrow deeper into the ground as the ominous speaker dropped one turgid obloquy after another into the previously calm pool of reality.

"Man, your spirit cannot escape the cradle of dung in which it was originally nurtured, a place shunned by the lowest living things, a birthplace so vile that it is avoided even by the beetles that seek to feed in such holes. The odor of the misbegotten clings to you and can never be washed off, so that the stink of your ever-putrefying soul turns others from you no matter whither you may seek to flee."

As Tongue Kills spoke, Malone felt himself growing distinctly hot under the collar and, somewhat surprisingly, not only there. Looking down, he saw that the fringe of his deerskin leggings was beginning to curl slightly at the tips. Wisps of smoke emerged from several as if they were not strips of cured leather but rather thick, sweat-sodden matches. He began to perspire and, despite the chill of approaching evening, experienced an unexpected desire to be rid of attire that had become suddenly suffocatingly warm. It was clear that Tongue Kills played for keeps.

Not that Malone was about to take those words lying down or even standing up. He'd picked up a turn of phrase or two in his travels, damned if he hadn't: the rapierlike accusations of cotton auctioneers in Savannah, the seasoned dressings-down of unyielding Prussian drill instructors. The lamentations of Calcut merchants and the withering complaints of the camel traders of old Araby. Lisboa's fisherwomen had shared their best and most scatological insults with him, and once, severely in need of a trim, he'd had his scalp professionally singed by the singsong calumnies of a famed Canton trader in opium.

Why, subsequent to one pleasant evening's drinking and concomitant commentary on Washington politics, none other than Dan'l Webster himself had ventured admiringly that when properly inspired, Amos Malone's palate was truly an anvil of imprecations on which the mountain man's tongue could hammer out insult after admirable insult, a river of inventive invective as grandiosely appalling as New York City's sewer system after a major summer storm.

"I might tolerate that," he replied carefully, "if it didn't come from someone so ugly that mere sight of 'im would shock the feathers off a constipated buzzard, the taste of whom would induce in a flock o' starvin' mosquitoes permanent indigestion soon as they discovered that their quarry had urine for blood. Why, your countenance'd drive a dozen o' the world's homeliest women to sworn celibacy an' turn the Medusa herself to stone."

As he listened to this, Tongue Kills's expression did indeed begin to harden, if not actually to fossilize. His skin began to redden noticeably until, in the gathering darkness, he was actually glowing slightly. Currents of agitated air streamed upward from his head and shoulders like heat waves rising from a paved road on a blistering July noon.

"Your mother," the medicine man retorted, his voice crackling like a newly set bonfire of Georgia fatwood, "must have mated with a snail, for it is clear that slime was the sole offspring of that union.

You reek of man's civilization, of noxious hypocrisy and embalming greed, of the air you have infected and the water you have poisoned. The soil itself recoils from beneath your feet, and the air screams as it is tortured by your lungs. The fecal matter that emerges from your body is the only pure thing you give back to the suffering earth, on which you are the foulest of parasites, in which even other parasites refuse to dwell."

Malone was forced to remove his heavy jacket, from which dense smoke was beginning to billow. He threw it down and began jumping madly on it to stomp out the flames that were trying to spurt from the sleeves. His exposed forearms, big around as aspen trunks, began to blister, and the sweat pouring from his forehead threatened to blind him. Even his teeth felt hot.

But he who listens learns. It struck Malone as more than slightly significant that Tongue Kills had spoken not of white man's civilizations but of man's. As they continued to trade dysphemisms of greater and greater heat, it set him to wondering as to just exactly whom he might be contending with by the shore of the wandering stream.

Not only the palaverers but the atmosphere surrounding them grew hotter as their calefacting conversation sent the very molecules of the air into an agitated frenzy. They tried to flee, crashing into one other and raising the temperature near the campsite to nearly tropical levels. Malone's overheated pants and leggings joined his well-pounded jacket underfoot as he was forced to expand the range of his frantic dance. Even the mountain man's hair was beginning to sizzle.

Meanwhile, Tongue Kills's smile grew forced, and though he did not give off any smoke, be looked more than a mite disconcerted. Heat continued to pour off him in waves, and he glowed like the big lantern that hung outside the Three Whalers' Tavern in Boston's High Street.

When an uneasy Worthless whinnied, Malone realized he'd better do something quick. A mere glance from his mount was suggestive of something seriously askew, but when he whinnied, it was time for a man to give serious consideration to proximate possibilities. It meant ordinary folk had better clear out fast, and the commonly fearful seek cover.

From the beginning there had been a glow in Tongue Kills's eyes, a particular glow that made Malone suddenly squint with recognition. He realized that he'd seen that exact thing before in another place, far off in the southern seas. It wasn't a glow that belonged in a man's eyes, which led him to a corollary that was as revelatory as it was inescapable.

"You win," he gasped, his throat scalded, the skin on the back of his neck beginning to curl from the heat. "I can't match you fury for fury, hot word for hot word. You've beat me."

Tongue Kills's triumphant expression twisted into a sneer. "It is good that you realize this, but it will not save you. I warned you, and you did not heed but chose instead to challenge. You will die, as will all who try to come to this place."

Malone was down to his long johns now, and only the fact that they hadn't had any contact with soap or water for an inexcusable length of time kept him from being spontaneously combusted right then and there by Tongue Kills's unceasing cataract of execration.

"What'll happen to me, I don't know, but there's just one thing more I have to say about you," he rasped out. "It's a durn shame that your mastery of heated language happens to be inversely proportional to your humanity."

Tongue Kills gave a start, then a cry of outraged realization as the paradox wrapped him in its inescapable grip. His fury imploded, inescapably self-contained. Malone shielded his face with an arm as heat, the by-product of all that anger, rushed outward in waves from his antagonist. Frustration, volatile as black powder, erupted. Somewhere behind him Worthless was whinnying loudly while trying to simultaneously keep all four feet off ground grown suddenly intolerably warm.

"You vile apparition, you imposition that walks on two legs; your existence outrages the world!"

"Yeah, well," Malone bellowed in response as he continued to shield his face, "you ain't no rose o' creation yourself!"

Tongue Kills's skin began to ripple and run like taffy, his flesh to sag. Malone had been witness to that phenomenon before, too, in the same places where he had seen the unholy glow, both in the Sandwich Islands and in the still-farther, distant Land of the Long White Cloud.

Even as he continued to shower fulminations on the mountain man, Tongue Kills was melting, unable to deny the uncontrollable fury and anger that were reducing him to his natural state. The vibrant red and orange and yellow of him spread out upon the ground, racing to take possession of the fertile valley. Where his colors, like his words, ran hot, the ground split like stale pudding and belched forth fresh fury, the earth itself melting and bubbling, until the entire region seemed to be seething and echoing the maledictions of its master.

"Enough of words!" screamed the column of molten contumeliousness that had been Tongue Kills. It towered higher than the tops of the pines, bathing the lean-to in hellish yellow light, twisting like a pillar of coiled sulfur. Malone prepared to defend himself against something stronger than fiery language.

"That weapon will not protect you!" the quivering pillar snarled. "Nothing made of man can affect me!" A pseudopod of orange fire reached for the nearly naked Malone, intent on securing him in its grasp and crushing him to a crisp.

The mountain man crouched and parried, flicking the flaming tendril aside. A moan of frustration emerged from the unstable column. Its cohesion spent, it promptly began to shrink and collapse in on itself.

Somehow Malone's voice carried above the dispersing hell that confronted him. He gripped tightly the knife Grass-in-Hair had given him. "This here blade's good traditional obsidian, and it ain't of man. It's of *you*."

"Excretion of carbon!" the disintegrating pillar shrieked. "Boil upon the earth's buttocks! You *cannot* take this place for your own. You cannot drive me from it. Here I have been, and here I will remain, to shout the words that will keep you from this place! Where I am now, no grass shall grow, no animals live! The land will be denied you, and the very water itself I will season so sharply that it kills! I will remain forever, deny burbleiss shussh ...!"

Tongue Kills continued his epithetic diatribe without pause, but having been reduced by Malone's carefully applied paradox to his true self, he could speak now only in the language of the earth from which he'd sprung. Malone could comprehend that speech as few others could but protected himself from it not with magic but by the simple expedient of stuffing his ears with bits of duck down extracted from his bedroll. As the mountain man gathered up his scorched but still-intact clothing, Tongue Kills continued to rage all around him. He had indeed managed to render much of the fertile region useless but had also been compelled to leave many places untouched. Malone had neither triumphed nor been defeated. He had half won and was lucky to have managed that.

Only when they were well clear of the valley and beyond earshot of Tongue Kills's pursuing screams did man and mount pause gratefully at a clean, untrammeled pool to cool their blistered feet. Thus assuaged, a chastened but relatively pleased Malone sought additional absolution in the mountain man's ultimate sacrifice. He undertook to have a bath.

"Ah-weh," Grass-in-Hair muttered understandingly. "It is no wonder, then, none could outtalk him, for he was not a man but a spirit." The chief frowned slightly. "What happened to your face?"

Malone gingerly felt of his scorched pinnacle of a proboscis. "As it progressed, our exchange grew heated. In my face you see the result."

"You say he is still there?" Two-Feathers-Falling said uncertainly.

Malone nodded. "Still there, still a-screamin' and a-hollerin'. But the words he shouts now can't hurt y'all because you won't understand 'em proper unless you get too close to him. So stay clear o' the places where he's doin' his insultin' and complainin', and you'll be okay. There's still plenty o' game about and water he ain't poisoned with his anger."

Grass-in-Hair replied thankfully. "You have helped us much, and we are grateful. We will move camp in three days."

"Suit yourselves. Me, I think I'm gonna head on south. Seen all o' this Yellowstone country I want to for a spell." He leaned back against a heaping pile of buffalo robes.

"I mean it, though, when I say you need to keep your kinfolks away from the places Tongue Kills has kept for himself. His words may not be able to hurt you no more, but I'll be damned if he can't still spit."

It's hard writing stories to order. Well, to request, anyway. I love writing short stories. I'd write a lot more if this was the 1930s or 1940s and the heyday of the pulps. But yo, you know, I don't make enough to pay Stephen King's tax bill (but then, neither does Mozambique). To stay alive as a writer, you have to write novels, which fortunately I also enjoy doing.

Which brings us to Amos Malone's saddlebags. What's in them, nobody knows. Not even Malone, I think. They're big, and floppy, and full of compartments, and generally speaking not a real smart place to go rooting around in without permission.

It's dark in there.

WHAT YOU SEE ...

"... Bunions, lumbago, bad back, consumption, whooping cough, dysentery, yellow fever, heart problems, liver trouble, infertility! Afflictions of the eye, the ear, the nose, and the throat! Broken bones, sprains, strains, disfigurations of the skin, and suppuration of all kinds!"

Now, the blacksmith, he had a disposition not dissimilar to that of the mules he frequently shod, but so suave and convincing was the stranger's pitch that the square-brick man with the arms like railroad ties stepped to the front of the milling crowd and squinted up at the platform.

"Thet leetle bottle, it can cure all thet?"

From the back of the garishly decorated wagon, Dr. Mohet Ramses gazed down benevolently at the first (and hopefully not the last) of the warm afternoon's potential supplicants.

"Sir, I would not claim it were it not true." He held up the compact, winsome black bottle, letting the sunlight fall flush on the florid label. "All that and more can the Elixir of the Pharaohs cure."

"Then you best take some yourself," shouted someone from the back of the crowd. "Maybe it'll keep you from runnin' off at the mouth!"

Dr. Ramses was undaunted by the scattered laughter this rude sally brought forth. He drew himself up to his full height, which though just over six feet seemed greater because of his parsimonious construction, and glared haughtily at the cloddish locutor.

"For twenty years I have endured the slurs of disbelievers, and yet fate finds me still plying my trade. Why is that? I ask you. It is because the Elixir of the Pharaohs works, my friends!"

The blacksmith scratched dubiously at his bewhiskered chin. "A dollar a bottle seems awful high, Doc."

Ramses leaned low, bringing his voice down with him. "Not when compared to what it can buy, my friend. How much is your health worth? How much another year of life, or two, or ten? For you see," he said, straightening and raising aloft the inimitable, the peerless black bottle, "this venerable elixir not only cures, not only prevents, but actually *extends* the life of the user!

"Unlike the traveling charlatans you good people have doubtless encountered before, I do not claim that my wondrous tonic cures every ailment, every time. Only most ailments, most of the time. I have records of hundreds of exhaustively documented cases from across this great country and from the Continent itself in which the elixir has proved itself time and time again. I speak only the truth when I say that it can add to your life, actually make you live longer."

"How much longer?" wondered a woman in the front row on whose cheeks the blush of youth had grown stale.

"A year per bottle, madam. One year of life, of good and vigorous and healthy existence, for each bottle you ingest according to instructions. One dollar for three hundred sixty-four days of continued subsistence on this good green earth. Is that not worth a little sweat of the brow?"

"A dollar a bottle's too high," said a farmer angrily. "At them rates we can't afford to try it."

Dr. Mohet Ramses smiled compassionately. "Ah, my good sir, all things are granted freely in heaven, but in this world, sad it is to say, nothing comes without cost. You should not think that you can't afford to purchase the Elixir of the Pharaohs but rather that you can't not afford to buy it."

Near the front a middle-aged lady looked at her husband. She hadn't been feeling well lately, had if the truth be known been in fact doing poorly. A dollar was a lot of money, but ... if it did only a tenth of what the doctor claimed ...

She struggled with her purse and dug out a handful of coins, holding them up toward the wagon. "I'll buy a bottle, Doctor. What have I got to lose?"

"A dollar," her husband muttered under his breath.

She glared at him. "See if I give you any, William."

Dr. Ramses's smile widened as he exchanged brimming black bottles for coins. When one well-dressed citizen eagerly pressed a quarter eagle into the erstwhile physician's perfumed palm, he positively beamed.

Bit by bit the crowd thinned, clutching the precious bottles tightly to shirt or bodice. Eventually there was but a single old woman left. She was so small and insignificant, Dr. Ramses hardly noticed her as he contentedly tallied his take for the day. Time it was to move on. Other towns waited just over the horizon; other needful communities beckoned. All needed his services; all doted on his presentation as eagerly as they did on his marvelous solution.

The elixir really was a wondrous concoction, he knew. Versatile as well, depending as it did for the bulk of its constituency on whatever creek he happened to cut across whenever his stock was running low.

He very rarely had trouble because, unlike that of so many traveling snake-oil salesmen, his pitch was different. Contrary to the rest of his silver-tongued brethren, he promised not merely cures but hope. For when his purchasers passed on, it was invariably with the conviction that the Elixir of the Pharaohs had truly extended their lives. He smiled to himself. A difficult assertion to disprove when the principal complainants against him were all dead.

Only then did he notice the woman. His initial reaction was to ignore her, but he hesitated. She had remained throughout his talk and remained still after all the others had departed. Her dress was simple patched homespun, and the bonnet she wore to shield herself from the sun was fraying. No fine Irish lace decorated the hem of her dress; no clever tatting softened the edge of her cuffs. Still, he owed it to her to repeat the offer one last time. Mohet Ramses was nothing if not magnanimous.

He knelt on the platform. "Can I be of assistance, madam?"

The woman hesitated. On her face could be seen the aftereffects of a long lonely life of hard work and toil. It was clear she was not used to speaking to anyone more educated than the town schoolmaster or the local parson. Her expression was a mournful mix of hope and despair. She managed a hesitant reply.

"It ain't fer me, Doctor, sir. It's Emmitt. My husband."

Doctor Ramses smiled tolerantly. "So I assumed, madam."

"He's in the wagon, Doctor." She pointed, and Ramses noted a gutted buckboard and team tied to a rail outside the nearby general store. "Emmitt, he's gettin' on to still be herdin', but he just tells me to shut up ... he don't mean nothin' by it ... and gits on with his work.

"It happened yesterday. Got the last of our twenty head in the corral; time to market 'em, don't you know, and that cursed old nag of his spooked. Still don't know what done it, but Emmitt, he went a-flyin'. Panicked the cattle, one kicked him, and, well, I'd be beholden if you'd come an' see for yourself, Doctor."

Ramses hesitated. It really was time to pack up the store and get a move on. There was invariably some local who would ignore the finely printed instructions and chug an entire bottle of the noxious brew in hopes of quickly curing some bumptious black eye, or constipation, or some other mundane ill, only to have his hopes dashed. Whereupon, fierce of eye and palpitating of heart, he would set out in search of the good doctor's whereabouts. As a purely prophylactic measure, Ramses historically had found it prudent not to linger in the vicinity of prior sales.

As the streets were presently devoid of any more potential customers, however, this was an internal debate easily resolved.

"Tell me, madam, do you have a dollar?"

She nodded slowly. "'Bout all I do have right now, sir. See, when the cattle git sold, that's the only time all year Emmitt and me have any real money. I was goin' to pay the regular doctor with it, but he don't come to town but once a week, and this bein' Friday, I don't expect him for another four days." She sniffed, and the leathery skin twitched. "My man's a tough one, but he took that kick right hard." She rubbed the back of one hand under her nose. "I ain't sure he can last another four days."

Dr. Ramses reached down to take the woman's hand comfortingly in his own. "Fear not, good woman. Your husband is about to receive a dose of the most efficacious medication known to nineteenth-century man. Lead the way, and I shall accompany you."

"God bless you, Doctor!"

"There, now," he said as he hopped off the back of the floridly painted wagon, "control yourself, madam. It is only my Hippocritical duty I am doing."

He winced at the sight of the battered, lanky old man lying in the rear of the wagon. He lay on his back atop a dirty, bloodied quilt, a feather pillow jammed beneath his head. His eyes were closed, and his thin brown hair had long since passed retreating to the region above the temples. Several veins had ruptured in his nose, which reminded Ramses of a map he'd once sold that purported to depict in some detail the delta of the Mississippi.

A crude bandage had slipped from the left side of the old man's head. A glance revealed that the force of the blow he had received had caved in the bone. Dried blood had run and caked everywhere: on the pillow, on his weathered skull, on the floor of the buckboard. His mouth hung half-open, and his sallow chest heaved with pained reluctance. As they looked on, the aged unfortunate raised a trembling hand toward the woman. It fell back, and Ramses had to fight to maintain the smile on his face. Turning away from the disagreeable scene, he held out to the anxious woman a small black bottle.

"One dollar, madam. One dollar to extend your husband's life. A worthy trifle, I am sure you will agree."

She fumbled with her purse, and Ramses, eager to be away from this rustic municipality, waited impatiently while she counted out the money in pennies and nickels. Only when the count had reached one hundred U.S. cents did he pass to her the precious container. She accepted it with trembling fingers.

"You're sure this'll work, Doctor?"

"My good woman, it has never been known to fail. Ten years." He thrust high a declamatory finger. "Ten years did I live among the multitudes of heathen Aegypt, perusing the primordial scrolls, learning all there was to learn, acquiring great knowledge, until at last I understood the mystic formula of the great and wise pharaohs. Trust in me, and all will be well."

In point of fact, Dr. Mohet Ramses had never been to Aegypt. But he had been to Cairo. Cairo, Illinois, where he had practiced a number of trades, none of which were remotely related to medicine, until the furious father of an outraged daughter had gone searching for him with gun in hand. At which point Dr. Mohet Ramses, alias Dickie Beals of Baltimore, Maryland, had sought and found expediency in a life on the road. A most profitable life.

The sun was going down, the town's two saloons were lighting up, and the venerable doctor was anxious to be on his way.

"Good luck to you, good woman, and to your husband, who should begin soon to exhibit a salubrious response to the most noteworthy liquid. Give him a spoonful a day followed by a piece of bread and you will find yourself gazing in wonder upon the medical miracle of the age. And now if you will excuse me, there are others who have need of my services, access to which I am sure you would not wish to deny them."

"No, sir, no! And thank you, Doctor, thank you!" She clutched his hand and, much to his disgust, began to kiss it effusively. He drew it back with as much decorum as he could muster.

"A woman ought to consider carefully what she's kissin'."

The deep voice boomed out of the shadows, and a man rode into view from behind Ramses's wagon. He was enormous, as was the preposterous mongrel of a steed he bestrode. For an instant Ramses panicked. Then he saw that the man was an utter stranger to him, and he relaxed.

The rider wore thick buckskins and showed salty black hair that hung to his shoulders. An incipient conflagration in his beard would've died for lack of oxygen, so thick were the bristles. His eyes were the color of obsidian and darker than a moonless night.

He dismounted from the ridiculous stallion and lumbered over. A huge hand reached toward the woman, and she flinched instinctively.

"May I see that, ma'am?" His voice turned gentle as a cooing babe's.

"What ... what for, sir?"

"I am by nature an inquisitive man, mother. I'd have a look to satisfy my curiosity." He squinted at Dr. Ramses. "Surely, sir, as a man of learning, you've no objection."

Ramses hesitated, then stiffened. "I, sir? Why should I have any objection? But you delay this poor soul's treatment." He indicated the wagon and its pitiful human cargo.

"Not fer long, I reckon." He reached out and plucked the bottle from the woman's uncertain fingers.

Ramses had to repress a grin. If this stranger had been the aforementioned local physician, there might have been trouble, but there was nothing to fear from a gargantuan bumpkin like this. He watched amusedly as the giant opened the bottle and sniffed at the contents.

His smile vanished when the mountain man swallowed the oily contents in a single gulp.

The old woman let out a cry and, astonishingly, threw herself at the giant. She hardly came up to his waist, but that didn't stop her from flailing away at him with her tiny fists. She might as well have been trying to reduce Gibraltar to dust.

Gently the giant settled her. A thick finger wiped at her tears. "Easy, mother." He tossed the empty bottle to Ramses, who caught it reflexively. "There weren't nothin' in that bottle that could've helped your man."

"Now, sir," declared Ramses, a fount of mock outrage, "I really must protest! If you were a man of science, I might accept—"

The huge form turned to him. "Listen well, 'Doctor.' I am Mad Amos Malone, and I am a man of many things. But what is in any event called fer here ain't science." He jabbed a huge forefinger toward the buckboard. "That man there is dying, and he needs somethin' rather stronger than what you're offerin' him. He wants to live, and I aim to help him."

"You, sir?" It was growing dark rapidly. Night fell quickly on the open plains. "How might you intend to do that?"

"By helpin' these folks t' help themselves." He smiled reassuringly at the old woman, white teeth gleaming from within the depths of the beard. "You just calm yourself, mother, and we'll see what we can do."

Ramses thought to depart. There was nothing for him here but a distraught old woman and a man crazy from too much time in the wilderness. But Ramses was curious, and he already had the woman's dollar. Maybe the mountain man was some sort of competitor. If he had something worthy to sell, they might, as any two men engaged in the same trade were occasionally wont to do, strike a bargain. The doctor was ever ready and willing to improve his inventory.

To his disappointment, the mountain man returned from fumbling with his saddlebags with nothing but an old wooden cup. It was scratched and chipped and appeared to have been carved out of a single piece of some light-colored hardwood. It had a thick brim and was in appearance nothing remarkable.

He offered it to the old woman, whose tears were drying on her cheeks. "Here, mother. Use this to give your man a drink of water." He gestured toward the town pump, which sat in a small Spanish-style square in the center of the street.

"Water?" She blinked in bewilderment. "What good will water do my Emmitt? He needs doctorin'. He needs this man's medicine." She indicated Ramses, who smiled condescendingly.

Malone spoke solemnly. "Let him drink from that old cup, mother, and if it don't help your husband, I'll buy you another bottle of this gentleman's brew myself." Whereupon he produced from a pocket a shiny gold piece. Not U.S. issue but a disk slick with age and worn by time. Ramses's eyes widened as he recognized the ornate cross and Spanish lettering on the visible side. In his whole life he'd seen only a single piece of eight. It had belonged to a New Orleans gambler. What the mountain man flashed was worth rather more than a dollar. Ramses was glad he'd trusted his instincts and stayed.

"Sir, you are as noble as you are curious."

The giant's eyes seemed to disappear beneath overhanging thick black brows that drew down like a miniature portcullis. "Don't be too sure o' that, friend." It was not a threat, but neither did the big man's tone inspire Ramses to move nearer the speaker.

Unsteady and bewildered, the woman shuffled to the well. The men heard the pump handle creak, heard the attendant splash of water. She made her slow way back to them and, after eyeing the giant blankly, climbed with surprising agility into the back of the wagon. There she dubiously but lovingly tipped the wooden lip of the cup to her husband's parted lips.

"Here now, darlin'. You got to drink, even if it is just water. You got to, so's this man'll buy us another bottle of the doctor's medicine."

The dying old man wheezed and tried but failed to lift his head. Some kind of unvoiced communication passed between them, as it can only between two people who have been married so long that the two have become one. She spilled the water into his mouth, and he gagged, choking, the liquid running out over his parted, chapped lips and down his furrowed cheek. Ramses suppressed a smile. A pitiful exhibition but one that, given the circumstances, he was quite willing to endure. In the giant's fingers the piece of eight shimmered in the fading light.

The old rancher coughed again. A second time. Then he sat up. Not bolt upright, as if hit by lightning, or shakily, as if at any moment he might collapse again. Just steady and confident-like. His wife's eyes grew wide, while Ramses's arguably exceeded them in diameter.

With profound deliberation the old man turned to his wife and put his arms around her. The tears streaming down his face started to dissolve the coagulated blood. "Sorry, woman," he was mumbling. "Sorry to make you worry like thet."

"Oh, Emmitt, Emmitt!" She sat back from him, crying and

smiling and half laughing all at once. "You gonna listen to me now and git yourself a hand to do the heavy work?"

"Reckon I ain't got much choice." The rancher climbed effortlessly to his feet and extended a hand down toward the beaming giant and the flabbergasted Ramses. "Mighty grateful to you, mister."

The mountain man nodded as he shook the proffered hand. "Glad to be o' service, sir. I could sense you were a good man, and I could see how serious you wanted to live."

"It weren't fer myself. Heck, I done had a decent life. But the woman, it would've gone hard on her. This way I got a little time to make some better plans."

"It's good fer a man to have plans, Emmitt," the giant said.

Leaping lithely from the buckboard, the rancher loosened the reins from the hitching rail, climbed back aboard, and lifted his startled wife into the seat alongside him. She almost forgot to hand the cup back to Malone, following which her husband chucked the reins. Jerking forward, the buckboard rattled up the dirt road that led out of town, kicking up dust as it passed the seeping pump.

Ramses had forgotten all about the piece of eight. His attention was now riveted on the old wooden cup. "Might I have a look at that vessel, sir?"

"Don't see why not." The giant handed it over. Ramses scrutinized it as minutely as he'd ever inspected a suspect coin, turning it over and over in his fingers, feeling the scars in the old wood, lifting it to smell of the interior. It reeked of old rooms, and dampness, and something he couldn't quite place. Some fragrance of a faraway land and perhaps also a distant time.

With utmost reluctance he passed it back. "What potion did you have in that, sir, that brought that man back from the dead? For the country of the dead was surely where he was headed. I saw his skull. It was well stove in, and his brains were glistening in the sunlight."

"'Tweren't no potion." The mountain man walked back to his lunatic steed and casually returned the cup to the unsecured saddlebag whence it had come. "That man wanted to live. Out o' love for another. That right there's a mighty powerful medicine. Mighty powerful. Didn't need but a little nudge to help it along."

"Yes, of course." Then it was no potion, Ramses thought furiously, but the cup itself, the cup! "Might I ask where you acquired that vessel?"

"What, the grail? Won it off the Shemad Bey, pasha of Tripoli, durin' a game o' chess we played anon my last sojourn along the Barbary Coast. After he'd turned it over, the old pasha confessed to me that it had been stolen many times afore comin' his way. So, I didn't see the harm in relievin' him of its possession. I reckon it's better off in my care than his, anyways." He pulled the straps of the saddlebag through both buckles and notched them tight.

"Your pardon, sir," said Ramses, "but did you say 'grail'?"

"That's right. Belonged long time ago to a feller name of Emmanuel. Took his last swallow from it, I believe."

"You are jesting with me, sir."

"Nope." The giant walked down the street, his mount trailing alongside with a notable air of equine indifference. "When I jest, I laugh, and when I laugh, rivers bubble and mountains shake. You don't see no rivers bubblin' or mountains shakin' hereabouts now, do you?"

"Sir, we stand in the plains of the Missouri. There are no mountains hereabouts, and the nearest river is the Meramec, some twenty miles to the south."

"Why, 'tis right you are. I reckon you'll just have to take my word for it, then."

"Sir, would you consider selling that gr—that drinking vessel? I will make you a fine offer for it, in gold."

"'Tain't fer sale, friend. Fer one thing, I got plenty o' gold. Fer t' other, it wouldn't work for you nohows."

"And why not?"

"The grail, see, it don't do nothin' by itself. It's just a cup, an ordinary drinkin' cup. It's what's in the heart and the soul of whomever's drinkin' from it that makes a difference. Most times it don't make no difference. Sometimes it do. I was glad it did tonight, but you kin never be sure." He halted, and Ramses saw they were standing outside the blacksmith shop and stable.

"Now, if you'll excuse me, friend, I've been three days and nights on the back of this lamentable alibi of a horse, and I've a might o' sleepin' to catch up on." With that he turned and entered the stable. Emerging a few minutes later, he strode off down the street toward the town's single hotel, from whose attached saloon could imprecisely be heard the brittle jollities of a banjo player in shifty voice.

Ramses was left standing solitaire in the starlight, thinking hard. The giant would be a bad man to cross, he ruminated. He'd seen the heavy Sharps rifle protruding from its scabbard on the side of the saddle. But the Promethean rustic had neglected even to lock the stable! And Ramses had taken careful notice of the fact that there were no locks on the saddlebags, not even a knot. Just a couple of straps on each one.

But Ramses was no simpleton. He returned to his wagon and mounted the seat, chucking the reins and making as much noise as possible on his ostentatious way out of town. The mountain man had refused to sell him the cup, and that was that, and like the honest soul that he was, he was moving placidly on.

A mile out of town he set up a hasty camp by the bank of a running stream, tethering one of his horses to a convenient cottonwood while hoping there were no acquisitive Indians or white men about. He made and drank some strong coffee, considered the night sounds and the stars, and round about three a.m. saddled up his other animal and rode quietly back into town.

The wooden buildings were shadowy now, the two saloons as silent as the distant church that dominated the far end of the main street. Dismounting outside the stable, he kept a wary eye on the distant hotel. The door hardly creaked as he edged it aside just enough to slip through. His excitement rose as through the dim light he saw that the mountain man's animal stood where he'd left it in the farthest stall.

Ramses could move fast when he needed to, whether running from irate fathers or from authorized representatives of the law. He moved fast now, the straw hissing under his feet as he hurried to the far end of the building. The dozing horses and one mule ignored him.

Lifting the stall door as he opened it so the hinges wouldn't creak, he stepped inside. Facing him, the improbably large quadruped filled the smelly enclosure from wall to wall. At the back of the stall, the saddlebags lay draped across a pile composed of saddle and tack.

Turning sideways, he attempted to slip between the animal's mass and the unyielding stall panels.

"C'mon there, boy. Give us a little room. Move on over just a bit, won't you?"

Swinging its mottled face to cast a skewed eye at him, the ludicrous creature emitted a soft snort and promptly lowered its head to begin cropping at the straw underhoof.

"Come on, damn you!" Ramses put both hands on the animal's flank and shoved, bracing himself against the wall and putting all his weight into the effort. He might as well have been trying to convert a reluctant Jesuit.

Breathing hard, Ramses deposed on the four-legged barricade to his intent a few choice nonmedical terms. He bent and passed through the slats of the stall wall into the vacant stall next to it, then carefully slipped in again near the rear, taking care to keep an eye on the horse's oversized rear hooves. It continued to ignore him, wholly intent on the available fodder.

The saddlebag's straps yielded easily to his deft fingers. He'd filch the cup and be clean out of the county before morning.

Lifting the nap, he dug around inside until his hand closed over the unyielding wooden cylinder. Extracting his prize, he held it up to the available light. In the moonlight it was outstanding in its ordinariness, and for an instant he wondered if there were more than one of the vessels. That was absurd, he knew. There was only one of what he sought. Only one in all the world, and now it was his, his!

He turned it in his fingers, letting the moonlight play across the bowl and rim. So plain, he mused. So utterly unremarkable. It was slightly bigger than he remembered it, but then, his first and only previous view had been clouded by astonishment and the realization of inherent possibilities.

His gaze narrowed. There was a hint of movement within the vessel. Lingering water or possibly some more viscous liquid.

Something crept out of the bowl to wrap itself around his left wrist.

Startled, he inhaled sharply. At the sound of his soft gasp, the horse looked back wearily. Then it delivered itself of a decidedly disinterested whinny and returned to its browsing.

A panicked Ramses tried to shake loose of the cup. He flung his hand about wildly and banged the vessel against the back of the stall. But the old wood was tough, and the sinuous band around his wrist was like a steel cable. It was gray in hue and ichorous and glacier-wet. As Ramses fought to extricate himself, it began to snake farther up his arm. With his free hand he fumbled frantically for the derringer he kept always in his right shirt pocket. While he did so, he made rapid breathing sounds, like a dog after a long run, as he struggled to scream but failed.

Before his wide, disbelieving eyes a second serpentine coil emerged from the interior of the cup to wrap itself around his head, blocking one of his eyes. It was cold and slick, cold as ice. The tip forced itself past his clamped lips and down his throat. He started to gag.

Tilted toward him, the depths of the cup revealed a pair of eyes. They were about the size and shape of a sparrow's eggs, bright red with little black pupils centered on fiery crimson. Of any face they might front there was no sign. As he goggled madly two more emerged below the first pair.

Then he saw that all four were part of the same countenance, which he finally got a good look at. He did scream then, but the sound was muffled by the tentacle swelling inside his throat, and no one heard.

In the stalls across the way two dray animals, a mare and a gelding, looked on motionlessly. Well, they were not quite motionless. Both were trembling violently, and sweat was pouring down their withers.

The mountain man's steed munched straw while ignoring the flailing, thrashing man who occasionally bounced off his hindquarters and legs.

More tentacles erupted from the abyssal depths of the cup, far more than it should have been able to hold. They lashed and bound the softly screaming, utterly desperate Mohet Ramses before they began to retract, dragging the unfortunate doctor with them. As he didn't fit inside the bowl of the vessel nearly as efficiently, there ensued a great many cracking and rending noises as he was pulled in, until only his spasmodically kicking legs were visible protruding beyond the smooth rim. Finally, they, too, vanished, and lastly his fine handmade shoes, and then he was all gone.

It was quiet again in the stable. Across from the silent stall the dray pair gradually ceased their shivering.

———

Amos Malone rose early and, as the other guests looked on in fascination, ate breakfast enough for any three men. Then he made his way outside. A few other pedestrians were about. They glanced occasionally in his direction, but not always. Unusual men frequented the frontier, and Malone was larger but not necessarily more unusual than some the townsfolk had seen previously.

At the smithy he chatted awhile with the owner, then paid him his fee and entered the stable next door.

"Well, Worthless," he informed his steed as he set blanket and saddle on the broad back, "I promise you some oats first decent-sized town we hit. You look like you had an uneventful night." The stallion snorted at Malone as he cinched the saddle tight, shaking its head and mane.

The mountain man hefted the bulky saddlebags and prepared to secure them behind the heavy saddle. As he did so, he noticed the cup lying on its side in the dirt. Plonking the awkward load astride Worthless's butt, he bent to pick up the stray vessel, considering it thoughtfully in the morning light. The old jet-black wood drew in the sunshine like a vampire sucking blood. With a sigh he moved to place it back in its container.

"Warned him," he muttered. "That ain't the way it works. A smart man doesn't go foolin' around in another feller's kit." Reaching inside the near saddlebag, he pulled out a second cup and held it up to the light. The morning rays turned the burnished cedar the color of Solomon's gold, pure and radiant.

"Course, it didn't help him that he got ahold o' the wrong grail."

Roy Rogers had Trigger. The Lone Ranger had Silver. Hopalong Cassidy had ... c'mon now, western trivia buffs. All the great western heroes had great western horses.

When I was a kid, it made me sick.

I mean, come on, now. Who wants to watch a film or TV show where the horse is obviously smarter than the hero? Not to mention braver and better-looking. The giants of animation recognized this contradiction and jumped on it with all four pencils. In Robert Clampett's Buckaroo Bugs *the horse can barely stand his idiot master. Tex Avery (as one would expect) frequently gave the horse as many lines as the other protagonists in his western-theme cartoons. Chuck Jones satirized the western horse in "Drip-Along Daffy," even allowing two of them their own shootout on Main Street.*

And the inimitable Jay Ward gave us a heroine in the Dudley Do-Right *cartoons who quite sensibly (and with just a hint of borderline bestiality) preferred horse to hero.*

No, sir, pardner. If I'm expected to survive in the real Old West, I don't want no gussified, slicked-up, pommaded palomino between my legs. I want a horse that'll kick and spit and bite and go all day on a diet of sagebrush and tumbleweed. That's to match me. One to match Amos Malone would be something.

Might not even be a horse, strictly speakin'.

NEITHER A BORROWER BE ...

For three days it had snowed hard enough to freeze a preacher's sermon to his pulpit. Now it had let up some, but while Mother Nature had become less profligate with her precipitation, sporadic flakes still spiraled to earth fat and flat, heavy with moisture, while a blindingly blue sky flirted with the fast-moving clouds as intermittently as a Swedish dancer.

The little brown box of a cabin was two-thirds blanketed and buried. Smoke curled fitfully from the stone chimney, winkling its laborious way skyward, cutting a sinuous path through the drifting snow. The rough-hewn unpeeled logs of which the modest structure was fashioned differed in appearance from the surrounding pines and firs only in their spatial orientation. The living trees towered above shelter and snowpack alike, their branches slack and burdened with hermetic whiteness. They dominated the surrounding mountain slopes, clawing toward the barren, rocky tree line.

A bit away from the building, the crest of a split-rail fence barely showed above the snow. It enclosed a partially cleared oval of bare ground. Accepting of the deceptive moderation, the scraggly grass thus revealed thrust bravely toward a bright sun and a false spring.

The clearing fronted a crude lean-to beneath which clustered three horses. A chestnut mare stood nose to tail with a roan gelding. Slightly off to one side, the third member of the equine contingent leaned against the rear of the shelter. It was a stallion of indeterminate lineage, being mostly black with white markings on rump and fetlocks and a distinctive white ring around its right eye. Thin straps secured a leather patch to its forehead. Part Shire, it loomed over its more svelte cousins. While they browsed on the newly sprung grass, quick-frozen exhalations emerging from their nostrils like the signatures of miniature steam engines, it chose to doze contentedly in the shade.

A slight noise from the nearby forest caused the massive animal to straighten. Lifting its muzzle, the stallion sampled the air and peered into the dense woods with its good eye, the one that was white-ringed being half-shut in a perpetual squint. It stood thus for a long moment. Then it snorted a small cloud and relaxed again.

When the heavy horse huffed, Fifth John froze. Only after it had turned away from where he stood crouched in the snow did he move, turning and hurrying back to where his companions waited anxiously by the little stream that flowed clear and free beneath sheets of clinging ice.

Having mocked the warnings of wiser, more experienced men, they'd sure enough found themselves caught out unprepared by the early spring storm. With hopes and bravado dashed in equal measure, their thoughts had been only of making it safely back to the lowlands with nothing to show for their recklessness. Until now.

His wide-brimmed, floppy hat slumped down over his face, and Fifth John cursed improvidently as he angrily shoved it back. It was nearly as filthy as the rest of his outfit, but then, he'd never been one much for personal hygiene. It wasn't his mother's fault, either, though his name was. A poor, simple woman gifted with minimal powers of cogitation, she and her dour husband between them had possessed just enough skills to feed themselves and about as much imagination as a Denver omelet.

They'd had ("raised" being too genteel a term) five children, all of the male persuasion. The father's name being John, they'd named the first boy John. And the second, and the third, and so on unto

Fifth John, whose handle anyone could rapidly discern related no more to that portion of the good book than did its ornery namesake.

He was the de facto leader of the importunate trio by virtue of determination and sheer meanness rather than any inherent talent, his skills consisting pretty much of humble expertise with a sharp knife and the ability to lie like a Tennessee lawyer.

"There's smoke comin' from the cabin, but no movement. Couldn't smell nothin' cooking. I reckon they must all be asleep."

"Any pickin's?" asked Great Knox, chewing on a finger. It was a wonder the huge mule skinner had any left. He always had a well-gnawed digit between his brown and yellow tobacco-stained teeth. John had seen him chew on his toes, too, the bulky Yankee displaying unexpected dexterity. It was good that he was comfortable in his habits, because he wasn't apt to be invited to any local cotillions. He wore a hat too small for his head, a narrow brown beard that traced the lower curve of his face from ear to ear, and an old tobacco-juice-stained vest over his heavy winter clothes.

Halfweed crouched nearby and listened. Though he was quite capable of speech, he chose not to say much, which was fine with his companions. Wiry and ruddy-hued, with a thin, down-arcing mustachio, he was good with both animals and a gun on the rare occasions when his brain and eyes managed to act in concert. His name descended not from his scrambled ancestry but from an addiction to peyote, which he'd acquired in the course of an extended jail stay down in Santa Fe.

These three solid representatives of the republic squatted in the snow by the creek and contemplated larceny.

"Three horses." Despite their cover and the distance from the cabin, Fifth John was careful to keep his voice down. "All of 'em healthy and well rested, though one's kinda weird-lookin'."

"What d'you mean weird-lookin'?" Great Knox pursed badly chapped, swollen baby lips.

"I ain't sure." John scratched under his left arm. "Just weird. Big, though. Biggest damn animal I ever seen." Beneath the brim of the battered hat, iniquitous eyes glittered. "Great for packin'. Bet he'll fetch twenty, maybe thirty dollar in town."

Knox nodded. "We're wastin' time sittin' here talking about it, then."

John agreed curtly. "You stay with the horses. Halfweed and I'll do it." The half-breed broke out into a wide, gap-toothed grin as he rose.

Knox watched them go, pleased that their ill-conceived journey into the mountains wouldn't turn out profitless, after all. He wondered idly whose animals they were stealing, hoping he hadn't at some time in the past made their acquaintance.

Leaving a man stuck in these mountains without a horse was not too different from shooting him in the back. Just slower.

Caiben was preparing to clean the previous night's dishes when he noticed the empty makeshift corral. As he straightened, his gaze instantly swept the surrounding forest, but there was no sign of movement. Setting the laden bucket aside, he dashed over to the fence line, ignoring the powdery snow that clung to his faded long johns and slid with icy slyness down into his boots. He yelled even as he was checking the gate and the double set of footprints nearby.

In response to his shouts, two men emerged from the cabin. One had to bend low to clear the lintel. His companion replied, his words as sharp in the chilly afternoon air as if they'd been chiseled from granite and hung in the sky to read.

"What's happened, Caiben?"

Caiben rejoined them, looking grim. "Bad doin's, friends. Horses are gone. Two men. Whites, not Indians." He shaded his eyes against the snow glare as he looked back and nodded toward the trees. "Reckon they got about a two-, three-hour start."

"Damnation." The other man spit into the snow, making a tiny stained crater. "What you think, Amos?"

The giant who stood next to him gazed phlegmatically at the

forest, an incongruous sight in his bright red, custom-sewn over-sized long johns. As he considered the situation, he slowly stroked the impenetrable tangle of black wire that was his beard. There were some folks who thought strange small critters lived within that ebon briar patch, but none ever had courage enough (or the reach) to examine the confusion for themselves. Beneath heavy brows, star-tlingly black eyes examined the distant line of tracks in the snow.

"Never catch 'em in this." He kicked absently at the deep powder. "Not on foot." His expression was unreadable. "I don't know about you two, but first off I'm gonna fix me some breakfast. Then I think I'll go back to bed." He squinted skyward. "Not much point in checkin' the traplines while it's still snowin'."

His companions exchanged a glance. "Is that wise, Amos?" the man next to him wondered.

The giant peered down at him. "That depends, now, Jim, on whether or not you think I am."

Caiben shook his head slowly as he eyed the forest. "I dunno. They get more'n a day ahead of us, we'll never find 'em even if this starts to melt."

"Don't reckon we'll need to." Malone had turned toward the doorway. "Cold out here. I'll put some wood on." He bent to clear the opening and glanced back at his companions. "Y'all comin'?"

They hesitated briefly. Then Jim Bridger sighed. "Hell, I remember once Amos told me we could make it from New Orleans to St. Louis in half the regular time, and we did. Never did tell me how he'd knowed that the Mississip was gonna reverse her course that day. Danged if she didn't." He followed the giant into the cabin.

The third mountain man gazed longingly at the woods, then shrugged. The snow that had fallen into the bottom of his boots was starting to melt, a condition sufficiently incommodious to decide the immediate course of action for any man.

The three thieves allowed themselves to hoot and holler freely once they were certain they were well clear of any immediate pursuit.

Their plunder followed meekly behind Halfweed's mount, each animal tethered securely to the one trudging on before it, with the unclassifiable prodigy bringing up the rear.

"Hell's fire if'n I wouldn't give a dollar to see their faces when they wake up and find their animals gone!" Great Knox chortled and slapped his leg gleefully, his hand returning immediately thereafter to his mouth, regular as a homing pigeon.

Fifth John rose in his stirrups and turned to peer back the way they'd come, their trail as definitive in the deep snow as if it had been bashed out by a six-team wagon. He could see almost to the top of the ridge they'd just traversed, and his little piggish eyes were sharp. He allowed himself to relax. There was no sign of any pursuit.

Damned if they hadn't brought it off, he thought with satisfaction. Tough for those marooned in the valley behind them, but it was their own damn fault for leaving good horses unguarded. Served 'em right. Fifth John sure enough knew all about life's lessons. If only he hadn't failed so many of them.

"Me, I'm gonna get me some whiskey with my share." Knox salivated around the finger he was masticating. "Not that cheap shit. Real drinkin' whiskey. And a *woman*. I'm gonna have me a pretty woman. A *big* woman. With red hair. All night, on a real bed, with sheets."

Fifth John struggled to avoid mental contemplation of such an invidious collusion. Great Knox was a useful associate, a good man to have in front of you in a fight but was afflicted with constipation of the brain. Whereas Halfweed's hypothesized higher functions were much diluted by his daily intake of peyote, above the neck Great Knox was simply ill-endowed.

Which was just as well. Fifth John was suspicious of anyone smarter than himself, which meant that suspicion was the country in which he most habitually dwelt.

"Get drunk," Halfweed mumbled as he swayed atop his mount. "Stay drunk a week. Maybe a month." He grinned like a tubercular cherub.

"They ain't followin' us, that's fer sure." Fifth John was mightily well pleased with himself. He'd take three good horses over a stack of beaver and otter pelts any day. "Thought we might have to ride on through the night, but looks like we can have a camp, somethin' to eat. You boys done good." Knox tried to smile in reply but was reluctant to remove his finger from his mouth. Halfweed was always smiling.

They found a good spot near the base of a steep slope, largely clear of snow and not particularly muddy. After making certain all six animals were secured, Fifth John broke out the jerky while Knox and Halfweed worked to start a fire. They lucked into a stack of dead dry wood that had accumulated in the hollow of an old light- ning-blasted fir and by the time night fell had a crackling good blaze going atop stones gathered from the hillside.

Halfweed was making a last check of the tethers. Two of the horses they'd absconded with snorted and shied uncertainly at his approach, but the big stallion just stood motionless, watching him out of its good eye. Halfweed studied it intently.

"Me, I know horseflesh pretty good, *seguridad*. But I never seen nothin' quite like you, *grande*. What's this for, huh?" Reaching up, the half-breed took hold of the patch over the animal's forehead and tugged sharply. On the third pull it came away in his hands. His gaze narrowed in confusion.

"Hey! I think maybe this big one got something wrong with him."

Fifth John looked up from the fire. "What, fer instance?"

"I dunno." Halfweed reached up to gingerly feel of the two-inch-high conical bump that protruded from the animal's skull. "He got some kind of risin' or somethin' on his head. But it ain't soft like a risin'. It's hard. Like bone."

"So he's got a funny head. Nothin' wrong with his teeth or his back an' legs, an' that's all what matters. We'll cover it up agin afore we sell 'im. Meanwhile, leave that piece o' leather off. Maybe the air'll help the spot heal."

Halfweed nodded to himself, turned to rejoin his companions, and found himself glancing back over his shoulder. He could've sworn that, just for an instant, the big stallion had been grinning at him. That was crazy. Horses occasionally smiled. They didn't never, ever grin.

Especially not like that.

Fifth John lit the stuffing in his pipe and leaned back on his bedroll, much gratified with the way things had turned out. It was not a sensation he'd been able to experience often.

Unfortunately, it did not last long.

The howl made Knox sit up fast. Then he smiled a trifle warily and lay back down again. The fire continued to sputter, and he tossed another broken branch in the middle of it. Embers flew up like escaping moths.

"Wolf," he mumbled.

"Yeah." Fifth John turned in his bedroll. "Shet up and go back to sleep."

Knox nodded and closed his eyes. He ignored the howl when it was repeated. When it was picked up by a second animal, he ignored that, too, and tried to cover his ears when the nocturnal choir was joined by a third.

The fourth howl, however, made them all sit up quick.

"Madre de Cristo." Eyes wide in the firelight, Halfweed sat erect in his dirty roll and stared into the night.

"What in hell ...?" Fifth John squinted hard. Twitching skittishly, their mounts were pawing the ground where they'd been tethered. Two of the stolen horses were also moving, though less restively.

Sitting back on its haunches, its long head thrown back, lips parted and teeth white in the firelight, the outlandish heavy horse was baying at the moon. Its howl was perfectly indistinguishable from that of the unseen carnivores, melding with and simultaneously inspiring the chilling moonlight chorus.

Great Knox was shaking his head slowly. He was so stunned, both hands hung at his sides. "That ain't no horse. No horse never made a noise like that."

Fifth John hesitated, then deliberately lay back down in his roll. "Course it's a horse, you dang fool. Looks like a horse, walks like a horse, smells like a horse. A mighty big horse, true, but a horse nonetheless."

"Don' sound like no horse." Halfweed's voice had dropped to a whisper, and he was looking around uneasily, as if the night itself were watching him.

John glanced up irritably. "An' you don't sound like no normal man, neither, but I still ride with you. But that'll come to quittin' if you don't shut your food hole and go to sleep."

The horse continued to howl. John tried, but with the woods by now resounding to what seemed like the concerted wailing of a hundred wolves, it was impossible for any man to rest. Frustrated, he rose to realign his sleeping kit, when he heard something else. Something different.

"You hear that?" he asked no one in particular.

Knox blinked sleepily. Somehow the great oaf had managed to fall asleep. "Hear what?"

"I hear it." Halfweed rose and stood trembling in his long johns, looking around edgily. "I hear it, yes."

As the two men listened intently, the suggestion became a whisper, then a rumble. Then a thunder that woke even Great Knox.

"Hey, Fifth. What's makin' thet …?"

John's eyes became as wide as Halfweed's. "Run! It's the Devil's own signature! Run for your lives!" Still half-asleep but waking up fast, Great Knox struggled with his bedroll. It had become all twisted around him in his sleep and was reluctant to release his legs. The horses whinnied and shied, rolling their eyes. All except for the big black, which continued to sit and howl.

Fifth John's chest heaved until he thought it would burst as he raced down the mountainside in the darkness. He could feel the snow catching up to him, teasing him, toying with his backside. He slid, fell, and came up scraped and bleeding but still running, leaping over fallen logs, sliding down talus crumbly as stale johnnycake. When he could run no more, he scrambled desperately behind the biggest tree he could find and closed his eyes tight.

It was like being swallowed by an express train. The tree shook, quivered, even bent a mite, but stayed put. As quickly as it had gathered strength, the avalanche began to spend itself, spreading out like white butter across the land. Only when it was done did

Fifth John allow himself to leave the shelter of the tree and begin the long, difficult slog back uphill.

Of their camp there was no trace. Kettle, pan, bedrolls, clothing ... everything gone, swept downslope and entombed beneath tons of snow. Only the horses remained. Apparently the angle of the cliff beneath which they'd been tethered had caused the bulk of the avalanche to just miss them. It infuriated Fifth John to realize that had he kept his wits about him instead of panicking, he could have survived alongside the horses and completely avoided the dangerous downhill flight.

Halfweed joined him a few moments later as John was dragging his insufficient but nonetheless welcome spare clothing from the saddlebags they had providentially left near the horses. The skinny half-breed was terrified but otherwise unhurt. He looked around, blinking in the moonlight.

"Where's Knox?"

John continued to dig at the saddlebags. His good buffalo coat was gone, and he'd have to put on every stitch of clothing he had left in the world if he expected to keep from freezing. "Dunno. He ain't with you?"

"No, man." Shivering, Halfweed crossed his arms over his sallow chest. "I thought he'd be here."

"Well, he ain't, so I guess it's done for him." Fifth John grunted. "More for us. Split the money from the horses two ways."

"Yeah. Hey, yeah, that's right." Halfweed relaxed a little, his smile returning. It didn't stay long. "Hey, Fifth, you notice somethin'?"

"No, what?" the other man replied testily.

Halfweed was looking around again, jerkily scanning the woods. "It's quiet. Howlin's stopped."

Fifth John eyed the night sky and the treetops, then returned to his digging. "Yeah? What of it? Avalanche scared 'em off."

"Yeah, that's right."

"Check the animals."

Halfweed nodded, glad to have something to do to take his mind off the misfortune that had just struck their camp and taken the life of their beloved friend. Friend, anyway. Well, maybe casual companion.

The horses, at least, had survived unharmed. The way east out of the mountains was clear, and their four-footed booty was intact. He was about to rejoin John when something made him squint into the moonlight. The stallion stood munching a green branch it had pulled from a nearby tree. Once again it stood placidly and allowed him to approach. Halfweed reached for the broad forehead, ignoring the bad right eye, which swiveled up to watch him.

"Uh, hey, Fifth?"

"What now?" Fifth John did not look up as he wrestled a ragged shirt over the upper half of his long johns.

"That bump I told you 'bout? On the front of the big one's head? Pork me for a nervous nun if it ain't got larger."

John shoved his head through the reluctant shirt, wondering what his companion was babbling about. "What's that?"

"Come look for yourself." The half-breed stepped back.

Fifth John slogged over and frowned. The broad-backed stallion regarded him expressionlessly. Fingering his goatee, John ran his fingers the length of the bony protrusion, then gripped it hard and pulled. The animal's head didn't move, nor did it otherwise react.

"*Cabra del diablo.*" Halfweed tried to cross himself, nearly stuck his finger up his nose, tried again. He was more or less successful the third time, but by then he entertained serious doubts that the Virgin Mother was still paying attention.

"Naw, it ain't the Devil's goat," John groused, "though I grant you it's passin' strange. You're right about t' other, though. It is bigger. 'Bout six inches long now, I reckon. Grows fast, whatever it is." He shrugged, secure in his ignorance. "Don't matter none so long's the rest of the animal is sound. We'll cut it off before we sell." He turned away, grumbling to himself. "Now, where the blazes did I put those old coveralls?"

By morning his good mood had returned. Too bad for Great Knox but better for him, and Halfweed. 'Tis not an ill wind that gives the other man pneumonia, he mused. There was still no sign of any pursuit, and by evening even Halfweed had mellowed. The half-breed didn't have sense enough to stay upset or unhappy for very long. Truth be told, he didn't have sense enough to find his ass with both hands.

As the sun scurried for cover behind the mountains, it started to snow again, just hard enough to be indifferent. Fifth John was thinking of fashioning a lean-to when he spotted the opening in the hillside.

Halfweed took one look at the shadowy fissure and shook his head violently. "I ain't goin' in there, man."

"What's the matter, toad *cojones?* You frightened?" John dismounted. The rifle that had providentially been secured to the back of his horse in one hand, he hunted up the precious box of matches and fashioned a torch of reasonably dry pine needles and twigs. Burning taper in hand, he was able to enter the spacious cave standing up.

Halfweed held on to his reins and waited nervously, his face turned skyward, on the lookout for the tentative moon. A deep moan from within the cave made him sit bolt upright in his saddle.

He'd half turned to flee when John reemerged, smiling maliciously. "Scared you, didn't I? Damn fool crazy half-breed." He gestured curtly at him with his rifle. "There ain't nothin' in there. Ain't been for some time. It's dry an' warm, plenty of room for both of us to stand and walk around, even."

Halfweed slid out of his saddle, as much relieved as angry. "Dumb sumbitch. You didn't have to do that."

"Yeah, I know. But it was fun. Shoulda seen the look on your face. For a moment you was even dumber-lookin' than usual." John started to remove the saddlebags from his mount. "Let's get a fire goin'. Rate we're travelin', I figger by tomorrow this time we'll be well on our way to startin' out of these damn mountains. Then it's over the trail back to town and the high life."

"Right." Halfweed perked up at the thought.

They built the fire near the entrance so it wouldn't smoke up the cave. In such snug quarters even the tired old jerky tasted good.

"Got to take a piss." John rose and headed toward the outside. Halfweed didn't bother to look up, concentrating on his jerky.

Something close by went *snuf*.

"Hey, man, no more jokes, okay?" The half-breed flailed absently behind him. Much to his irritation, the sound was repeated. Smiling to himself, he deliberately extracted his revolver from the gun belt lying nearby.

"Okay. I ain't afraid o' no *duende*. Since you won't answer, I guess you some kinda animal now and I got to defend myself, *verdad*?"

"Defend yourself ag'inst what, you loco freak?" Fifth John stood framed in the entrance to the cave, fastening his pants.

"Fifth?" Halfweed fumbled for a flaming brand from the fire as he cocked his pistol. He tossed the burning stick toward the unexplored recesses at the back of the cave.

Something monumental rose up in the light. Primeval fire glinted from black eyes and off teeth the length of a man's hand. The bear raised forepaws equipped with claws like bent railroad spikes. It was ten feet tall—no, fifteen—with silver hairs shimmering among the brown. The Great Bear of the Arapaho, the bear overwhelming: the ur-bear.

"*Jesus!*" An openmouthed Fifth John stumbled backward, fumbling with his belt. In the confines of the cave, the bear's roar was Vesuvius and typhoon and the Port Royal earthquake all rolled into one. It shook the ground underfoot and shattered rock from the walls.

"*Oh, Gawd, John, help me!*" Adding to the frantic pandemonium as the bear lumbered forward, Halfweed fired his Colt repeatedly, six times in all. All this did was make the brute mad, a tactical decision not dissimilar to Napoleon's decision to invade Russia.

Between the earthshaking roars of the bear, Halfweed's Colt going off, and its owner's terrifying screams as the monster dismembered him one limb at a time, it was a choice cut of purgatory.

"*John, John, it's eating me, it's killin' me, oh Gawd, help me!*"

Fifth John had not survived an upbringing among four tormenting elder brothers each as mean and ornery as himself without becoming pretty good at sizing up his chances in a fight. It was deuced clear to him that poor Halfweed was already as good as finished and that even with rifle in hand he didn't stand much of a chance against a grizzly from Hell, and what would be the point, anyways?

Too bad, Halfweed, he thought sorrowfully as he swung into his saddle. Unlike Great Knox, who'd been tolerated, he'd genuinely liked the greasy, addled dimwit. The bellowing from the cave followed him down the mountainside as he struggled to lead five horses behind him. They were all understandably skittish and edgy. All except for the big black-and-white, who brought up the rear docile as an old hound.

He thought of the money he was going to make selling the five and how Providence had decreed he was going to have to spend it all by himself, and it did help to drown out the memory of Halfweed's final piteous shrieks.

When he was confident he was safely beyond the attentions of the monster bear should it have felt any unsociable inclination toward his person, he stopped and tied his animals. Then he passed methodically among them, speaking to each in a reassuring voice, rubbing its muzzle and neck until it calmed down. Only when that was done did he think to give a care to himself.

"I saw that!" He whirled, simultaneously drawing his gun. "You wuz grinnin' at me, you gawddamned big-butted squint-eyed sumbitch!"

Easy, Fifth, he told himself. *Horses don't grin. They dang well can't grin. You're jest tired an' upset. And no wonder, what with the past couple days' goin's-on.*

Mighty peculiar goin's-on at that.

Funny thing how that avalanche come up on that howlin' horse. He'd about forgotten that, but it came back to him now, sharp an' clear. That big old animal a-howlin' like a wolf, and then the snow crashin' down on them and buryin' poor Great Knox and somehow just missin' all the horses. Then that bear. Biggest gawddamn bear ever was. But he'd checked that cave himself and woulda swore it was cleaner than the inside of a crinoline skirt.

Down the mountain then, all the animals a-frothin' and a-rollin' their eyes until he could quiet 'em. All except this one, this over-sized, overfed, great ugly four-legged bad-eyed bastard of a horse with a lump growin' out of its head. He blinked in confusion. Damn thing was more'n a foot long now, and pointed at the end, an' all twisty-curly round like a stick of store-bought peppermint candy.

Impossible or no, he'd have bet a quarter eagle then and there that it had winked at him.

"What are you, anyways?" He approached with caution. It raised its head from where it had been cropping the grass that poked green threads through the snow, and gazed back at him blankly, innocently. Just another dumb animal.

Fifth John wasn't afraid, but he kept the muzzle of his pistol aimed straight at the creature's forehead, just below the ivory-colored spiral spear.

"You cursed? Thet what it is? You a bad-luck beastie? I heard tell o' such down in New Orleans. Island people come up and put curses on chickens an' such. Or maybe you're jest bad luck. I kill you, I still got t' other four to sell. You worth the trouble? I wonder." He was within arm's length now. As before, the animal just stood patiently and gazed back at him out of bland equine eyes.

Reaching out, he stroked the spear that grew from the creature's forehead. It was smooth and warm to the touch. Fifth John lowered his pistol. "You're different, that's fer sure. Reckon you might be worth a passel to the right buyer. Maybe you *are* worth the trouble. But from here on I'm gonna be watchin' you as well as my step, hear?"

Carefully but with increasing confidence, he began to circle the animal, patting it on its flanks, inspecting its withers. It was sure enough an odd-lookin' concoction: a blind Quaker could've told that. But all muscle underneath that peculiar back. No, he wouldn't kill it. Too much money to be made, and he'd already put up with enough trouble to make it worth keepin' him.

He smiled and nodded at nothing in particular. "Guess you're all right, big'un. Somebody pay plenty to have you hitched in their team." A hot, wet sensation made him glance down at his boots.

The horse was pissing on his right leg.

"The hell with it, you damn four-legged play-actor! I *knewed* you wuz grinnin' at me!" Irate beyond common sense, he raised the pistol.

The big animal swung its head around to regard him thought-fully. As John leveled his gun at his impassive target, he noticed that something else was different about it. Something new.

Lit from beneath, from inside, the white circle around the bad eye was glowing intensely. And that eye weren't squinting now, weren't more'n half-shut. It was full open, open all the way wide. And staring straight ... at ... him.

Mesmerized, Fifth John looked deep into that eye and let out a meager, completely involuntary moan. His whole body started to shake. That wasn't surprising because in an instant his mind had become as unhinged as his body. At the end of his arm, his gun was waving up and down like a semaphore flag in the grip of a high gale. The precarious moan rose up in his throat as if trying to escape.

The animal was *growling* at him. That was crazy. Horses didn't growl. The growl became a snarl. Crazier still. Horses didn't snarl. Tremendous unsuspected muscles rippled and tensed in its back legs, its hindquarters, its neck, as it prepared to spring. That was madness. Horses didn't spr—

"I'll be hornswoggled and hog-tied." Caiben turned and yelled back toward the cabin. "Amos, Jim! Git out here and have a look at this!" Clutching the water bucket and heedless of the cold, he splashed through the stream back toward the cabin.

Amos Malone and Jim Bridger emerged, Malone with skillet in hand. It was his turn to do the cooking. Bridger specialized in rabbit, while Caiben wasn't good with anything more than beans. They didn't much understand what Malone was talking about when he served them medallions of elk béarnaise au poivre or trout almondine with new potatoes and asparagus hollandaise or even how he came by the fixin's. Smart men that they were, they didn't push the question too hard.

Ignoring the icy water dripping from his deerskin leggings,

Caiben joined his trapping companions as they watched the six horses, with Malone's in the lead, wander solemnly back into the crude corral from which three of them had been abducted. Once within, they dispersed amiably and began to nibble at the greening grass.

No small man himself, Caiben got a crick in his neck looking up at Malone. "Well, you were right, Amos. Danged if you weren't right. They come back."

"Wonder what happened to the thieves," Bridger murmured.

"Reckon they had enough." Malone started toward the corral. His companions followed.

"What's that thing on your animal's head?" Caiben asked. "Looks like he got somethin' stuck in it."

"Just a growth," Malone murmured. "'Tain't hurtful. I'll take care of it."

They entered the corral. Each man saw to his own mount and then collectively to the three they'd apparently acquired. Malone patted the stallion on the neck. It snorted as if bored by the attention.

"Well, Worthless, they give you a hard time? Other way round, I reckon. Some folks are just dumber'n dirt, thinkin' they could horsenap a unicorn."

"A what?" Bridger had come up behind him and overheard. "I know what that is. A mythical creature. Somethin' out of stories, that don't exist." The two mountain men regarded each other silently for a long moment. Then Bridger broke out into a wide smile. "Kind o' like you, Malone."

Malone smiled, too. *Have to replace that restrainin' patch quick, he mused.* "I reckon so, Jim. Tell me: you ever had crawfish étouffée on saffron rice?"

"Huh-uh. Sounds like Frenchie food."

"Sort of. With lemon chiffon cake for dessert."

Bridger eyed him sideways. "Now, where you gonna git lemons up here, Amos? In late winter, no less."

"Leave that to me, Jim." Malone gestured with a nod. "Better get cleaned up. Looks to me like you might've had an accident."

Bridger glanced around and down at his stained backside, thoroughly baffled. "Now, when'd I do that? I don't recall ..."

Malone put an arm around the other man's shoulders. "Let's eat, Jim. Caiben, you ready for dinner?"

"Ain't I always?" The third trapper joined his companions as they sloughed back toward the cabin.

Behind them Worthless shifted his phenomenally flexible anatomy and turned to thoughtfully eye the nearest mare.

Espying his intention, she gave a startled snort and bolted twelve feet.

A lot of folks don't know it, but part of the Old West just skipped over the Great Basin region and the West Coast to land full bore in the Sandwich Islands. Different natives (same treatment) and even cowboys. The cowboys, in fact, are still there, hanging around Makawao and Wailea, discussing weather and cattle and posing for the tourists.

But a different group of indigenous folks were there first, with a very different and equally rich culture. Not that it would make a difference to Amos Malone.

The man is, after all, all business. Just what kind of business is sometimes hard to figure.

THE PURL OF THE PACIFIC

S hark!"

Amos Malone glanced back over his left shoulder. The men on the whaler *Pernod*, out of Nantucket, were running along the rail, shouting and gesticulating wildly. One native harpooner was actually hanging off the bowsprit as he did his level best to draw the mountain man's attention to something in the water midway between himself and the ship.

Malone dropped his gaze and squinted. Sure enough, there it was: a dark, sickle-shaped fin cutting the water directly toward him. A couple of the whaler's crewmen had rifles out and were frantically trying to load and aim. Malone hoped they'd take their time. They were as likely to hit him as the fish.

Tiger shark, by the look of it, Malone decided thoughtfully. Fourteen, maybe fifteen feet. It was still a ways off, uncertain what to make of this unprecedented intrusion into its home waters. In its piscine bafflement it had been preceded by company both common and illustrious, for Mad Amos Malone constituted something of an intrusion no matter where he went.

Leaning to his left, he peered into his mount's eye. It rolled upward to regard him, its owner's dyspeptic temperament much in evidence.

"Shark over there, Worthless." He casually jabbed a thumb in the direction of the oncoming fin. "Just thought you'd like to know."

Beneath him the enormous stocky steed of mightily confused parentage snorted once, whether by way of acknowledging the warning or indicating its contempt for their present mode of travel, one had no way of knowing. Transporting them both, the stallion was swimming easily for shore, Malone having decided not to wait for the first boat to be lowered. He was anxious to see this new cattle country, even if it was as hot as the Brazos Valley in July and twice as humid.

The water above the reef was refreshing, though, and the island lay close at hand. The bustling whaling town of Merciless Sun lay before him, cloud-swathed green mountains rising sharply behind it. A brilliant rainbow arched over the heavily eroded gullies that flayed the slopes, looking for all the world like a gigantic advertising sign raised by elves. Or in this instance, Malone reminded himself, Menehunes. Dozens of vessels, mostly whalers like the *Pernod*, swayed at anchor in the Lahaina roads behind him, their masts representing entire forests transported to the open sea.

They looked hot, too, Malone reflected. Everything hereabouts looked hot.

The *Pernod*'s captain had sympathized with his passenger's desire to get ashore but was dead set against any attempt to do so without the use of a boat.

"Most of these ships stink of whale oil, Mr. Malone, sir, and the great-toothed fish that ply these waters are always ready for a handout in the most literal sense of the word. Furthermore, if you will not be insulted by my saying so, no matter how well your animal may have weathered the journey from San Francisco, it is no seal, sir, to easily swim this distance to shore. Especially with a rider so large as yourself seated astride its back."

Malone had smiled down through his great, unfurled nimbus of a beard. "Now, don't you go worryin' about ol' Worthless, Captain. He's a right fine swimmer and takes to the water like a fish."

In point of fact, Malone's unclassifiable steed had once swum Lake Superior from the American side to the Canadian at the height of a ferocious autumn storm. The captain would not have believed that, either, unless he happened to be familiar with a unicorn's extraordinary powers of endurance, which he was not. With his horn kept cut down and filed flat, Worthless's true lineage remained a necessary mystery to all who encountered the exceptional, if ill-dispositioned, creature.

The shark was quite close now, not even bothering to circle. The men on the boat were frantic.

Worthless turned his head, located the shark, and kicked out all in one swift motion. A portion of the lagoon foamed. His left hoof caught the fish beneath its jaw and knocked it clean out of the water. It lay there belly up, floating and dazed. The frenzy aboard the ship was instantly transformed into stunned silence. A dozen or so sharp, pointed teeth, forcibly ejected from their intimidating loci, spiraled lazily down through the crystal-clear water and came to rest on the sandy bottom, but not before being thoroughly investigated by half a dozen spotted butterfly fish, a couple of Moorish idols, and one *humuhumunukunukuapua'a* (one *humuhumunukunukua-pua'a* being more than enough).

The silence was replaced by several startled but enthusiastic cheers from the crew. Malone leaned forward and whispered in his mount's ear.

"Don't get no swelled head, now, horse. It were only a dang fish." Beneath him Worthless blew bubbles in the salt water. Perhaps recognizing a kindred spirit if not species, several sea horses had attached themselves to his tail.

The town of Merciless Sun (or Lahaina, as it was called in the native tongue) certainly lived up to its name. Emerging from the water alongside the short stone jetty, Malone carefully unpacked his kit and removed his mount's tack, spreading it all out in the sun to dry. Handling it as gently as a baby, he unwrapped his Sharps rifle from its waterproof oilskin holder. Not much use for a buffalo gun on an island with no buffalo, he knew, but the Sharps was as much a part of him as his beard or underwear. Or for that matter the great, white-dappled, jet-black, misogynistic stallion that stood nearby, nibbling at the exquisite tropical flowers that grew wild where the jetty met the land.

Not everyone glanced in Amos Malone's direction when he passed, but most did. At six foot ten and a slice of homemade chocolate cake over three hundred pounds, he tended to draw the eye no matter where he went. Nor was the attire of a mountain man common garb in a seaport town situated in the middle of the great Pacific.

He'd come to this island as a favor to John Cochran, Esq., of Fort Worth, Texas. Père Cochran had been advised of the excellent prospects to be realized by raising cattle in the islands for export by ship to California, where there was an exploding market for beef thanks to the recent discovery in that territory of large quantities of a certain yellow metal. Never having visited this particular island and owing Cochran a favor, Malone had agreed to evaluate the possibilities in return for passage and expenses.

Certainly, the town of Lahaina was booming. Among its statistics the 1846 census had listed 3,445 natives, 112 foreigners, 600 seamen, 155 adobe houses, 822 grass houses, 59 stone and wooden houses, and 528 dogs, among other items. But not much in the way of cattle, though Cochran had assured Malone that other entrepreneurs had started to run them elsewhere on the island, using *españoles*, imported Latin cowboys, known to the locals as *paniolos*.

Well, he figured to see for himself. Repacking his now-dry kit and securing it to Worthless's broad back, he set out to find lodging for the evening.

As it turned out, lodging wasn't the problem. It was finding a place where a man could sleep. Used to spending the night out in the wilderness beneath the open and silent bowl of the sky, Malone had been forced to endure for weeks the unending rustle of sailors and ship. Looking forward to a little terrestrial peace and quiet, he discovered he'd made landfall in one of the noisiest towns in creation. Whaler and sailor alike started partying early and in earnest, the magnitude of their merrymaking only intensifying with the lateness of the hour.

Giggling, laughing native men and women as well as hopefully hymning missionaries contributed to the boisterous ballyhoo, and it was about two a.m. when a restless Malone recovered Worthless from his stable and set off in search of a piece of ground where the stars could serve as silent company for the remainder of the night.

The shore south of Lahaina was rocky and difficult, but the trail that led to the central part of the island was well maintained from much use. When at last he came down out of the hills onto the flat, semiarid peninsula that divided the two mountainous halves of the island, he turned to his right and soon came to a beach of fine white sand. Slipping easily out of the saddle, he started forward in search of a quiet place among the *kiawe* trees in which to spend the balance of the night.

Not expecting to see any buildings, he was therefore much surprised when he found himself confronted by a six-foot-high wall of finely worked rock. Atop the solid stone platform stood a long, simple structure of wood posts and poles roofed with thatch. A small fire was burning at the near end, silhouetting the figure of a native seated cross-legged before it.

Malone examined the sky. Among the millions of visible stars were a few clouds. Rain, he had been told, fell in biblical quantities on the eastern side of the island but far less frequently in the west. Still, he had experienced one aqueous immersion already this morning and had no desire to spend the night saturated by another.

"Aloha, y'all," he said, addressing the native. The man jumped to his feet as if shot. Malone immediately saw that he was clad in the simplest of raiment instead of the contemporary European fashion favored in comparatively sophisticated Lahaina by so many of the locals. The woven tapa around his waist was complemented by a simple yet well-made headdress. In his right hand he brandished a formidable club carved of koa wood studded on two sides with sharks' teeth.

He started yelling in the local tongue until he saw by the light of the stars and his fire that his nocturnal visitor was neither demon nor commoner but something in between.

"*Parlez-vous français?*"

"I'd prefer English. I'm an American. Malone's the name. Amos Malone."

The man, who was quite large and well-muscled but small compared to Malone (as was, for that matter, the great majority of the human race), stepped to the edge of the platform to confront his caller. After appraising the indifferent Worthless with a critical eye, he crouched low to study the animal's rider.

"Malone," he repeated. "I know English good. Learned in missionary school." He gestured sharply with the club. "You come from Lahaina?" Malone nodded. "You must go away from here. This *heiau* is *kapu*."

"Sorry." Malone was properly apologetic. "Didn't know. You reckon there's a place hereabouts where a man could get a night's sleep without bein' disturbed by more hollerin' and howlin' than a pack o' coyotes fightin' over a dead buffalo?"

The man frowned. He possessed the exceptionally fine complexion of his people, and his eyes flashed alertly in the flickering light.

"Coyote? Buffalo?"

"Never mind." Malone turned to leave. "I'll just find another place."

There was silence for a moment. Then the solitary supplicant called out to his visitor. "You do not like the sounds of Lahaina?"

Malone turned back. "Fine fer partyin'. Not so good fer sleeping." He tilted his head back. "I prefer the company o' stars to men."

"Ah." The local had a penetrating, piercing stare Malone had encountered before, but not frequently. "Come closer, haole." Malone complied and met the other's gaze evenly.

After several moments during which the only sound was the crackle of fire and the cry of a few insomniac seabirds, the man nodded to himself. "Yes, I can see it. You are a kahuna. A teacher, a sorcerer. But what kind?"

Malone scratched through his beard. "Depends on the moment. There's folks think I'm a fairly versatile fella. You a kahuna, too, Mr. ...?"

The native straightened, his coppery body glowing in the fire-light. "I am ... you could not pronounce my name. Call me Hau. In your English, that means 'Iron.'"

Malone extended a hand, which the other grasped firmly. "Pleased to make your acquaintance. Hau you doin'?"

"Hau ...?" It brought a slow smile to the other's face. "You are not afraid? Many haoles find the *heiaus* frightening." He gestured at the temple behind him.

Malone gazed past his host to study the wooden structure and its imposing platform. "Places of power and reverence only frighten the ignorant. Or those with something to hide."

Hau nodded solemnly and turned aside. "Please. Come and share the fire with me. If you are truly a kahuna, or perhaps even a *kupua*, you are more than welcome here. It is the help of just such a one that I seek."

With a hop and a jump, Malone was soon standing, and then sitting, across the fire from Hau. The native glanced in Worthless's direction. "You do not tie your animal?"

"Tie Worthless? That'll be the day. Don't worry, he'll stick around. Ain't nobody else would tolerate him, anyways." The unicorn glanced up and with great deliberation and malice afore-thought turned its head and sneezed directly onto Malone's saddlebags.

"What's a *kupua*?"

"The child of a god. You can recognize them by their great strength and beauty. Or by their great ugliness and the terror they inspire in others." Hau studied Malone's face. "Possibly one can be both strong and ugly."

Malone grinned. "Thanks fer the compliment. I think."

"I am an *ali'i*, a noble." Hau sat straighter. "I will always tell the truth."

"And what is the truth tonight, Hau?" Malone picked up an unburned stick and casually toyed with the fire.

Hau leaned closer. "What do you know of Lahaina?"

Malone considered. "It's hotter than the hinges o' Hell, the whalers 'ave made it the liveliest port in the Pacific, and they're always going at it hammer an' tong with the missionaries. On t' other hand, I understand there's a real school above the town."

"Lahainaluna, yes. A copy of your New England schools and almost twenty years old now. A very good school that teaches both haole and local children modern ways." His voice dropped. "That is why Kanaloaiki hates it."

"Somebody hates a school? Thet ain't right."

"Not only the school," Hau continued. "He hates everything about Lahaina and what it has done to the people. Since King Kamehameha III moved the kingdom's capital to Honolulu, Kanaloaiki's ire has only increased."

Malone nodded. "Tell your friend things'll settle down. There's fewer whales this year than last, and so fewer whalers. There'll be fewer still next year and the year after that. But the school should stay. It's a good school, I hear, and a good school is a good thing."

"Not to Kanaloaiki. He has vowed to destroy it, and all of Lahaina, and all who share in its life. He makes no distinctions. All are to die: haoles, missionaries, and local people alike. The town will be razed to the ground. Not even a breadfruit tree is to be left standing."

"I see." Malone considered the stars. "This Kanaloaiki, he's a powerful chief with a lot o' warriors who'll follow him?"

"Worse." Hau shook his head. "He is a *kahuna 'ana'ana*, a sorcerer who practices black magic. For more than a year now he has been gathering the materials for a great spell that he plans to cast on a certain mountain." The *ali'i* pointed into the darkness. "*That* mountain."

Turning, Malone could just make out the dark ridgeline of a nearly six-thousand-foot-high peak.

"That is Pu'u Kukui. It has been asleep for as long as we can remember. But the island is not. Less than seventy years ago there was a modest eruption far to the south of here, on the slopes of the House of the Sun." He smiled. "I know this because I have been to the school. I know it did not happen because Pele was angry. It was geology."

"Don't be so sure," Malone murmured. "This Kanaloaiki, he thinks he can reawaken the old volcano?"

Hau nodded solemnly. "Lahaina lies at its foot. The town will die, buried beneath fast-flowing superhot *aa*. Nothing will remain. The school, too, will be buried, and the ships offshore will go away and not come back. So Kanaloaiki intends. Thousands of people will die."

"You can't stop him?"

"Nothing can stop the spell. Not now." Hau brooded over the fire. "Kanaloaiki began last week. Once begun, it can only be countered after it has started."

"What about your local kahunas? Do they all support Kanaloaiki?"

Hau looked up. "No. Most are against what he is trying to do. But they are all afraid of him. His power is very great. But *you* are not afraid of him, haole kahuna."

Malone shrugged. "Haven't met the old boy. Don't see offhand what I kin do, though. How d'you counter a spell that can't be countered until after it's begun?"

"I have been told there is a way. There is a tool. A special tool. The wisest kahunas say it still exists, but none believe them."

"Except you."

Hau nodded. "I would use it if I could to stop what Kanaloaiki intends. But while I am *ali'i*, I am not a kahuna. I do not have the power to use such a thing. If it exists. But another, one not afraid of Kanaloaiki or under his sway, might do so." He looked searchingly at Malone.

"Whoa, now. I'm just here t' look over the cattle-raisin' prospects fer a friend o' mine. Course, I don't much like the idea o' standing by while a few thousand innocent folk get burned and buried alive. Never much did. I just ain't sure I kin do anything about it."

Hau considered. "If I show you the best land for cattle, will you consider helping?"

"It's sure enough a good cause. All right, I'll see what I kin do. Now, where's this here good grazin' land you're talking about?"

"It's very interesting, but the place you are talking about and the place I am talking about are in fact the same place."

Malone grunted. "Don't say? And whut place might thet be?"

Hau turned and nodded to his right. "You will see tomorrow, Amos Malone. Tonight it sleeps beneath the blanket of night. Tomorrow I will take you to the House of the Sun."

The House of the Sun, or Haleakala, as the natives called it, rose to a height of more than ten thousand feet, completely dominating the entire island. It wasn't its height that impressed Malone, who had seen far taller mountains elsewhere. It wasn't even its breadth, which allowed for a slope so gradual as to be almost imperceptible.

No, it was the weight of the mountain, which plunged another twenty-seven thousand feet to the ocean floor. Composed almost entirely of cementlike solidified *aa*, the mountain was massive enough to dimple the earth's crust beneath it. Unlike many mountains, which were simply magnificently decorative, this one had a presence you could feel. Malone sensed it as the light broke over the distant summit, and commented on it to Hau.

"It is the House of the Sun," the native replied simply. "No one may go there save *ali'i*, and none may live upon its upper reaches but kahuna. You can go there. I cannot."

Malone reined in Worthless. Hau had been walking alongside the entire way, refusing to ride behind Malone or even alternate in the saddle with him. He was, he assured Malone, quite comfortable walking.

As they ascended, villagers came to gawk at the huge haole and his companion *ali'i*. The two travelers were offered food and deference in equal quantities, and the locals marveled at Malone's appetite. A few of the children, grinning and giggling, tried to play with Worthless. The great black steed generally ignored them, even when they swung from his tail or tugged on his mane. He munched fruit in quantity and reacted only once to the juvenile attention.

One of the older youngsters stood directly in front of the stallion and reached for the patch on its forehead, intending to pull it loose and see what it concealed. The next moment he was running and crying for his mother, who was unable to determine exactly how he had been struck in the eye by a flying mango pit.

As the two men climbed, the air grew steadily cooler. About three degrees for every thousand feet, Malone reckoned. More than adequately protected in his buckskins and boots, he marveled at the nearly naked Hau's ability to withstand the increasing chill.

At four thousand feet Hau pointed out excellent high grassland suitable for grazing cattle. At six thousand they entered and passed through a solid layer of cloud. At ten thousand they encountered isolated patches of icy snow.

Then Malone found himself gazing down into a black-streaked, rust-brown crater big enough to hold all of Manhattan Island.

Hau pointed to a distant cinder cone within the crater. "Down there, my friend, there is said to be a cave. In the depths of the cave is a tool. Only the truest of kahuna can recover it. Others have tried; none have succeeded. Whether anyone can even make use of it I do not know. I know only what the kahunas here tell me: that it is the only tool with which Kanaloaiki's terrible plan can be foiled."

Malone nodded. "Maybe it's a big hammer that I kin whack him on the head with." So saying, he flicked Worthless's reins, and together man and unicorn started down into the barren, nearly lifeless crater.

Silversword grew in isolated bunches, thrusting their highly specialized leaves into a pristine pale blue sky. Exotic carmine, yellow, and emerald-hued birds fluttered in and out of the crater on air currents that rose from the volcano's rain-forested eastern slopes, each exotic flyer more brilliantly colored than the next. They reminded Malone of a rainbow's tears. Occasionally a *pueo*, the native owl, would dart low as Worthless's hooves disturbed a mouse.

The browns and blacks and russets and rusts of the crater seemed endless, but eventually Malone found himself approaching the cinder cone that had been singled out by Hau. Trotting around its base, he skirted the edge of an undistinguished depression in the crater floor. According to what Hau had been told, the cave was to be found on the far side of the cone.

A few cinders slid away beneath Worthless's hooves, tumbling toward the center of the depression. Each step sent a few more skittering downward. Before long the slide had become continuous. Just to be on the safe side, Malone urged his mount higher up the slope they were traversing.

But instead of ascending, Worthless, too, began to slide.

As steed and rider fought for stability, Malone saw that the sliding cinders were flowing rapidly toward the center of the depression, and not just from beneath Worthless's feet but from all sides. It reminded him of something he'd seen before.

Despite the unicorn's heroic efforts, they continued to slip. Finally, Malone saw something else, something that at last brought back to him the memory of what they had encountered previously. This was very much identical, only on a larger scale.

A much larger scale.

Two projecting, curving, sharp-edged, sicklelike hooks, each taller than a man, clashed and clacked together expectantly in the exact center of the depression. The owner of those jaws would have been instantly familiar to anyone who had ever run across them in sandy, dry soils. They belonged to an ant lion.

An ant lion that, to judge by the size of the depression and its now-visible jaws, must be as big as an elephant.

What it subsisted on here in this barren crater Malone couldn't imagine, but he understood now why courageous but foolhardy travelers who defied the old *kapu* to visit this sacred place never returned to their homes, and why even kahunas avoided the crater floor.

His first thought was to unlimber the Sharps, but even its fifty-caliber bullets would not be likely to have much of an effect on the slow-paced nervous system of the gigantic insect. Instead, as Worthless continued to slip and slide toward those expectant, waiting jaws, Malone began undoing one of his saddlebags. Fingering various vials and containers within, he sought hurriedly for the right one.

Those jaws, large and powerful enough to crack the bones of a man's skeleton like twigs, were much too near when he finally found the vial he'd been searching for. Unscrewing the lid, he tossed the entire open container into the center of the depression, only to see it swallowed immediately.

For a few moments nothing happened, and they continued to slide lower and lower. Then the descent ceased. With Malone whispering in his ear, Worthless kicked and scrambled frantically to gain height.

The ground behind them began to tremble. It was an eruption, but not of Haleakala. With a violent, concussive roar the cinders and air behind them vomited skyward, forming a temporary but spectacular fountain. Malone held on to his wolf's-head cap, his saddle, and his dignity as best he could as the wild rush sent man and mount flying out of the depression.

It had been, he reflected as he and Worthless picked themselves up and continued on their way, one hell of a sneeze. But then, the open vial that he had thrown into the pit and that had found its way into the ant lion's mouth had contained absolute essence of cayenne, a substance useful in numerous spells and Tex-Mex cooking and not ineffective when employed strictly in its purest form.

In contrast to the encounter with the crater dweller, the cave in the cinder cone was very much an anticlimax, starkly unimpressive. Within, Malone found a few handfuls of bone tools, some old pots and desiccated baskets, and a frayed sleeping mat. Nothing more. Certainly nothing that on the face of it was potent enough to use against a formidable sorcerer.

Nevertheless, he knew from long experience that even the simplest object could be imbued with considerable power. Gathering up everything he saw, he secured it to one saddlebag and started back toward the crater's rim, this time employing a different route. Being completely out of essence of cayenne, he had no wish to tempt the gargantuan ant lion's energy and appetite a second time.

What was worse, he mused as he rode, was that now he was going to have to have his evening meal inadequately seasoned.

Hau could hardly believe it when Malone rejoined him just below and outside the crater rim. "You have survived!" the *ali'i* exclaimed. "No one has been to that place in living memory and returned to tell of it."

"I reckon I know why." Slipping down out of the saddle, Malone unpacked the artifacts he had accumulated. "Now, this 'ere basket, what's it fer?" He passed a finely woven container to the *ali'i*.

Hau's demeanor was less than reverent as he turned the object over in his hands. "Gathering fruit, I would imagine. It is a simple basket. What did you think it was?"

Malone grunted. "Never mind. How about this?" They went through every item in the mountain man's perilously acquired inventory, Hau discarding one after another with nary a word. Malone was growing not just discouraged but angry, wondering if he'd risked his life only to recover some long-dead kahuna's household goods.

So it was that when Hau's eyes grew wide and his hands began to shake as he held up an ordinary-looking fishhook, Malone hardly knew what to make of it.

"You must have much mana, Amos Malone, to bring this out of the House of the Sun."

"So I've been told in other ways." Malone squinted dubiously at the hook, unable to discern anything remarkable about it. "What do we do now? Go fishin'?"

Hau cradled the object piously in both upturned palms. "Of course you cannot know what this is. But by its shape, which I recognize, and its design, which I well remember from the old tales, and by the picture writing on both sides, I know it for what it is."

Malone was hungry. Behind him, Worthless whinnied impatiently. "A means fer catchin' our lunch?" he asked hopefully.

Hau handed the artifact to his haole friend. "This, Amos Malone, is the *Manai ikalani*, the sacred fishhook which one of the god Maui's ancestresses fashioned at his request from her own jawbone. Using it, Maui raised from the depths of the sea all the land that became the islands of my people and those of their ancestors. When Maui caught the sun here atop Haleakala, the fishhook fell from where it was tied at his waist. It has lain here ever since."

Without waiting to see if Malone would follow, he turned and started down the mountain.

"Come, my friend. With this even we may be able to stop Kanaloaiki from destroying Lahaina."

Malone swung himself up into the saddle and followed. "How? By bribing him with fish?"

Hau looked up and smiled. "You do not fool me, kahuna. I know that when the time comes, you will know what to do. Now that we have a hook, we must find a line to attach to it. The strongest line imaginable. There is good rope in Lahaina, fashioned to sell to the whalers. We will find the toughest there is and buy, borrow, or steal what is needed."

Malone considered. "That may not be necessary. You say we need a sturdy line?"

"The strongest that can be woven."

"Will that little hook hold a big line?"

Hau looked back and said in all sincerity, "It once raised from the bottom of the sea all the islands of Polynesia."

"Okay, I take your meaning. But I think I know where I kin find us an even stronger line than you have in mind."

"Excellent. But we must hurry, Amos Malone. See that light on the far slope of Pu'u Kukui?" In the distance, on the upper slopes of the West Maui Mountains, Malone could just make out a fitful, flashing light. "Kanaloaiki has begun his evil work. We have little time."

Malone sighed heavily. "In the wizardry business it seems like a man hardly ever does."

———

"What on earth d'you plan t' do with this ashore, Malone?" George Wilfong indicated the length of material Malone had sought to buy.

"You needn't know, George. Better you don't." Seated next to the whaler, Malone pulled hard on his oar. Around them lights flickered from murderous ships riding innocently at anchor.

"That's all well and good, I suppose. All I knows is that you'd better give me payment enough to satisfy the captain, as you promised, or there'll be hell to pay."

"There'll be hell to pay this night anyway. Rest assured the captain will be satisfied with the trade I have in mind."

Wilfong frowned. "He had better be, or he'll have me keelhauled right here in the Roads. Malone, I don't know what you're up to this night, but one thing I am sure of: you owe me as well as the captain for this."

"Fair enough, George." Malone considered the looming bulk of the island and the tiny but intense light that was now clearly visible just below the shaft of the highest crag. "I hear tell you're thinking of giving up whaling."

"How'd you know that?" Wilfong looked startled.

"Sometimes a man thinks loudly, and I reckon myself a good listener. This is a sweet favor you're doin' me, so I expect it's only just and fair that I slip you a sweet notion in return. The *far* side o' this island is wet as any in the world, and the soil there is rich. Right now there's a hunger for all kinds o' seasonings in California and gold to pay fer them. Myself, I'm here to see to the possibilities o' raising more cattle in this country, beef cattle t' feed hungry miners. Someone's needed t' see to other items. It's a known fact that prospectors are most all afflicted with the sweet tooth."

"What are you saying, Malone?" Wilfong pulled steadily on his oar.

"Sugarcane, George. I've a thought that it would do well here. Why not try some on the well-watered side o' the island?"

"Sugarcane?" Wilfong's brows drew together in thought. "I've seen how it's done in the Caribbean. But what would I use here to boil the juice? There's no manufacturing in these islands, and I couldn't afford to bring heavy gear over from the mainland."

"Use some of the big blubber pots off any whaler," Malone suggested.

Wilfong brightened. "Blubber pots. Now, that's a fine idea, Mr. Malone, a fine idea. It just might work, and Lord knows I've experience enough boiling things down. Sugarcane; yes, by God. I'll give it a try, I think, and thankee."

"Welcome."

"But there's still the matter of the captain's payment."

They were very close to shore now. Easing off on his oar while Wilfong did the same, Malone dug deep in a pocket and handed his companion a triangular-shaped object that seemed to glow from within with a supernal whiteness. On both sides were etched in black finely wrought scenes of whales, whalers, and whaling men.

"'Tis the biggest sperm whale tooth I've ever seen," Wilfong admitted, "and the scrimshaw is excellent, but scrimshaw to a whaling man is like ice to an Esquimau. I'm not sure the captain will account it a fair trade."

Malone's tone was somber. "Tell him that so long as this sleeps in his sea chest, he need never fear that any ship he commands will come to harm. This 'ere were given to me by a fella name of Herman after I rescued him from the natives down in the Marquesas." The mountain man chuckled. "Been writin' about it ever since, he has.

"The scrimshaw on this tooth was done by a Maori fella called Quehquoag, who pried it from the hull of a capsized lugger out o' the Fijis. Came from a white whale, he told my friend. Last I heard, Herman was still workin' on a book about thet." Malone turned thoughtful. "Ought to be out in a year or two, I reckon."

Wilfong was still doubtful but willing to be convinced. "All seamen are superstitious, captains no less so than common sailors. The size of it ..." He hefted the enormous white tooth in both bands. "It's warm to the touch, as if still connected to the lower jaw of its owner." He nodded to himself. "I think the captain will accept it. You must be badly in need of this"—he gestured at the cargo they towed behind them—"to part with so powerful a talisman."

Once more Malone's gaze turned to the mountain. "The world's full of talismans, George, but short on good people and shorter still on good schools."

Hau led the way up the western slope of Pu'u Kukui, which was steeper and brushier than that of Haleakala. They were guided by the baleful light of Kanaloaiki's work, which pierced the darkness like a malevolent eye.

"There!" The *ali'i* pointed, and Malone found he could see clearly.

The old man was as wrinkled and bent as an old *ohia* tree, but his voice was unbowed. The fire into which he was casting ingredients and words blazed higher with each successive addition. Kanaloaiki took those from a pile off to his right, a pile that was growing smaller by the minute.

"See here," Malone suggested, "why don't I just ride on over and have a word with the old gent."

"He is protected." Hau was looking around worriedly.

"By what?" Malone searched the *kahuna 'ana'ana's* immediate vicinity. "I don't see anything."

"If you do, you will die."

"Pretty good protection," the mountain man agreed solemnly. "How do we deal with guardians if we can't look for 'em?"

"They will declare themselves. Listen for their presence. Listen for the chanting. The old chanting." They continued to approach. Once Malone thought he saw Kanaloaiki glance in their direction and smile evilly before returning to his work, but he couldn't be certain.

What he could be sure of as they drew very near indeed was the rise of a distinctive moaning, the echo of a dirge signifying the proximity of doom incarnate, and the smell of death drifting like black floss on the wind.

Hau shut his eyes tight and turned his back to the sorcerer's position. "That is it; that is the sound of which I spoke! The Marchers of the Night! To look upon them is to die."

Unperturbed, Malone spit to his right. A small spot on the ground sizzled. "Marchers of the Night, eh? What sort o' outriders might they be?"

"The souls of dead *ali'i*. Only a *kahuna 'ana'ana* can control them, because his withered soul is given over to evil. Somehow we must get close enough to Kanaloaiki to break the spell the instant it has begun, but we must do so without looking directly upon him."

"Kind o' like workin' in Washington." Fumbling in a saddlebag, Malone removed a scratched, chipped, but still serviceable mirror. Pulling hard on the reins, he turned Worthless about. Using the mirror to scope their route, they resumed their ascent, Worthless following Malone's guiding tugs on his reins while methodically advancing hind end first.

"A clever trick." Hau kept pace by the simple expedient of walking backward alongside Worthless. "What made you think of it?"

"Old acquaintance o' mine name of Perseus had to deal with a similar dilemma once. Involved a woman." He adjusted the mirror. "Works better with a bronze shield, but it's danged hard t' fit one o' those in a saddlebag."

"Ah," Hau murmured. The moaning rose louder around them. "It will still be difficult to get close to Kanaloaiki with so many Marchers about."

"Actually, I had kind o' another notion for dealin' with them." So saying, he extracted not from the capacious saddlebags but from a pocket a small tubular instrument. Placing it in his mouth and using the fingers of one hand to manipulate the notes, he began to tootle a winsome tune.

Hau winced. "A strange music but somehow attractive." Malone could only nod a response, his mouth being full of instrument.

The moaning grew shrill and strident. Then, astonishingly, it began to mellow, harmonizing with and eventually chanting in counterpoint to the tune Malone was playing. Still backing Worthless up the mountainside, he played on until he had all the dead *ali'i* moaning in perfect time to his music. Gradually they drifted away, sighing softly and, Malone was convinced, contentedly. Only when the last of them had vanished into the all-absorbing night did he remove the instrument from his mouth.

"Reckon we kin turn about now. I expect they're gone."

"How did you do that?" Hau asked. Ahead of them Kanaloaiki saw that his protective spirits had departed and worked furiously to finish his spell.

"Friend o' mine named Louie Gottschalk composed that little tune. It's a cakewalk; they're pretty much irresistible. This variation incorporates a little voodoo. Louie's from New Orleans, and he doesn't publish everything he composes. I figured an enchanted cakewalk was bound to work on any bunch o' spirits called the Marchers. Jest weren't completely sure it'd sound good enough on a kazoo. But they all seem to have cleared out right promptly."

"Powerful magic!" Hau exclaimed.

"But not powerful enough," declared old Kanaloaiki with a sneer, overhearing them. Stepping back and raising his arms, he pronounced the final words of the spell. As the earth began to tremble, the old *kahuna 'ana'ana* started to laugh. "Say farewell to all the evil that is Lahaina, for the earth is soon to take her back! Sprite of Pele, heed my call!"

For the first time since Malone could remember, Worthless lost his footing. The mountain man was thrown to the ground. Recovering quickly, he staggered to the unicorn's side as the earth heaved and buckled beneath them. Hau didn't even try to rise. Sprawled helplessly on his side, the *ali'i* looked on in horror.

In front of old Kanaloaiki the ground split asunder. An unholy refulgence bolted from the depths as a hellish yellow-red glow illuminated the sky. Slick and viscous, *aa* lava could be seen rising within the dilating cleft, bubbling and boiling, ready to pour down the mountainside and roar through Lahaina, incinerating and inevitably burying everything in its path.

"The *Manai ikalani*!" Hau shouted. "Quickly, Amos Malone!"

"I've got 'er!" Malone was fumbling with the saddlebags.

"The line," the *ali'i* yelled, "what about the line? Do you think it will be strong enough?"

"I reckon!" Malone hollered back. "Figured since you said we were liable to be dealin' with some serious heat, we'd want something that wouldn't burn too easy!"

A mountain man must be self-reliant in everything, must know how to cook as well as shoot, repair leather as well as hunt, even has to know how to fix his own clothing when there's nary a tailor within a thousand miles. So Malone had no trouble threading the line through the fishhook, though drawing one of the iron links through his teeth in order to make it thin enough to fit through the hook's eye did set his mouth on edge a trifle.

With the hook securely fastened to the line, he began to twirl one end of it over his head, the sacred *Manai* thundering through the air like a hog-tied earthquake. What he was about to try was not unlike roping steers down in Texas, except that his target this time was at once larger and more difficult to hold down and the line itself was just a tad heavier than your ordinary lariat.

Not knowing if he'd have an opportunity for a second chance, he did his best to fling the hook straight and true. It soared across the expanding seam in the ground, trailing the spare anchor chain from the *Pernod* behind it. The iron links clanked above the roar of the superheated earth as they landed on the far side of the widening chasm.

The fishhook struck the earth ... and stuck. With a sharp tug Malone set the hook. Making sure the other end was secured to the pommel of Worthless's saddle, he swung himself up and slapped his mount on the side of his scruffy neck.

"Ready there, Worthless? Back, boy! Back er up now!"

As Hau looked on in awe and Kanaloaiki in aghast fury, the muscular quadruped slowly began to back to the south, digging his hooves into the ground and pulling the anchor chain with him. The crack stopped expanding and began to contract as Malone drew it shut, binding up the wound in the earth as neat and clean as any surgeon would stitch up a wound. A few dollops of lava boiled out of the ground before the rift was closed completely. By the time Malone called a halt, the lava near the top of the vent had cooled sufficiently to seal the opening.

No ordinary horse could have managed it, or even an ordinary unicorn, but Worthless, for all his equine peccadilloes, was special indeed.

"Attaboy. Now stand!" Malone patted his steed on its neck as he dismounted. Worthless snorted and fell to cropping the nearest bush, breathing no harder than if he'd just pulled a wagon from a shallow muddy-bottomed creek.

Avoiding the site of the vent, where the ground was still too hot to walk on, Malone joined Hau in approaching the stymied sorcerer. The frustrated *kahuna 'ana'ana* did not try to contest their approach, did not even lift an arm to defend himself as Hau raised his formidable club.

Malone put out an arm to forestall the blow. "Easy there, Hau."

The *ali'i* looked at him. "But if we let him live, he may try again."

Malone shook his head. "I don't think so. Take a good look at him. Can't you see he's done for?"

It was clear that the excruciating effort had used up the old sorcerer utterly. As he lay back, his breath came in increasingly difficult gasps. A grim-faced Hau stepped aside, satisfied.

"Summonin' evil kin be exhausting," Malone murmured.

At that the frustrated sorcerer turned to face him. "You are a great kahuna. I did not know there was such among the haoles."

"Not many," Malone told him. "Say, how come you can speak good English?"

"I, too, went to the haole school." With obvious difficulty, the old man sucked air. "It is not haole learning I was trying to kill. Only haole culture. It overruns the land like a big wave. It is overrunning *this* land."

Hau stepped forward. "I do not know about that, old man, but I do know that it is wrong to kill innocent people. I will have a *kapu* put on this spot so that none will come here and see what you have tried to do. No one will disturb the metal rope, and this ground will stay peaceful."

"You will see," the old man wheezed. "One day you will see. Or your children will." His head fell back as he gazed into the star-flecked black crystal of night. "I hear the Marchers. They could not protect me, and now they come for me. Life is never just; death always is."

With that he went away, eyes open to the darkness and unfulfilled.

"Reckon that's that." Malone began to secure both ends of the anchor chain, choosing volcanic spurs that were firmly a part of the solid rock of the mountainside. Hau tried his best to help, but though he was accounted a strong man among his own people, he could not move any part of the heavy chain, which Malone handled with apparent ease.

"You have done a good thing this night, Amos Malone. Give me the *Manai*." Without word or objection, Malone removed it from the chain and handed it over.

"What'll you do with that?"

"It is too dangerous to keep where others might find it. I will take paddlers and a canoe far south of here, to the southeast even of the big island, where the sea is very deep. There I will throw it into the ocean. It will fall to the depths and not raise any more land until it is safe." A sudden thought made him look closely at the massive haole. "What will you tell your friend about our cattle lands?"

"That he'd better get here fast if he's interested before these *españoles* already working the slopes buy up all the good grazing. And I reckon you might try to buy some fer yourself as well now that the king's allowed as how private folks kin own their own plots. Me, I'd recommend acquirin' thet beach where we met up."

"Beach?" Hau made a face. "What would a man want with empty beach? You cannot grow anything on it or raise any animals. There is no good water there. Such places are worthless." The unicorn pricked up its ears, whinnied querulously, and then returned to its cropping.

"Mebbe they are now." Malone swung himself up into the saddle. "But take my word on it. Your grandchildren'll thank you." So saying, he started downslope toward the flickering lights of Lahaina, its raucous inhabitants blissfully unaware of the fiery death they had barely avoided.

Hau followed at his own pace, thinking hard as he descended the slope. Beach? What would any man want to own beach for? He decided that his new haole kahuna friend was joking with him. There was beach all around the island, most of it even more desolate, white, and sunstruck than the place where they had met. No one owned it because it was not worth a single American dollar.

And surely never would be.

Yellowstone is a wild fantasy landscape all by itself. As it exists, it needs no embellishment. Viewing the place, one imagines all manner of possibilities. Imps in the hot rivers, ethereal beings rising from the innumerable steam vents, all manner of illusory beings gamboling among the hot springs and geysers. Arthur Rackham would've loved it.

Given the excessive thermal nature of the region it is only natural for one to envision the possibility of its being home to less than benevolent beings. Since the earth itself seems downright angry most of the time, there's no reason to expect that any elemental abiding therein would be of an agreeable nature. Dyspeptic, more likely. Quick to take offense and prone to easy aggravation. Full of fire and brimstone and hot spittle.

Just the sort of personality to rub Amos Malone the wrong way.

VENTING

Y ou're going where?" the clerk exclaimed, gaping at his
customer. He exclaimed because of what the customer had
just told him. He gaped because the individual looming over the
service counter was not just a mountain man, but a mountain of
a man.

Mad Amos Malone had that effect on people.

It wasn't just his height—a couple of inches short of seven feet.
It wasn't just his size—bigger than most men and not a few bears. A
lot had to do with his attitude: as if he'd already seen and done most
everything and weren't ashamed to admit to it. Attitude, and maybe
his eyes. They seemed to go in and out of focus, like the lens of a
telescope, as if one moment the crazy giant was looking right at
you, and the next, at some far-off distant land ordinary mortals
knew nothing of and wouldn't dare visit even if offered the chance
for an escorted tour.

"Yellowstone." Methodically, Malone fingered out coins from a
leather pouch to pay for his goods. Salt pork and sugar, coffee and
beans, tobacco, bacon, salt, pepper, bullets. Really big bullets, each
one three and a half inches long. For buffalo, the clerk assumed. For
other things, though Malone did not tell him what.

The clerk, who was young, and skinny, and red-haired, and full of the cocky confidence of a youth too handsome and insufficiently wise, shook his head in disbelief. "Hard to believe they just made a park out of it. Who'd want to take a vacation trip to Hell?"

"Folks who git cold easy." The mountain man's massive arms enveloped his supplies and he turned to leave.

"Why you going there?" When Malone turned with a frown, the clerk (who while not wise was not entirely stupid) hastened to add, "If you don't mind my asking?"

Malone smacked his lips, two leathery lumps of flesh just visible in the depths of his black beard. The clerk thought he saw something else moving in there, but was chary of staring too long.

"Guvmint agent asked me t' check out a certain part o' the new park. Somethin' 'bout some trailbreakers tryin' to chart a new course into the backcountry. Course, the whole park is new country. Fer most folks."

The clerk was unable to keep himself from probing just a little further. "What about them trailbreakers?"

"Seems they didn't come out again."

The young man had another question or two tingling his tongue. He decided not to ask them, looking on as the giant ducked his head to clear the general store's front doorway and turned sideways to squeeze through. After allowing a discreet few moments to pass, however, he ambled outside. Doc Jensen was there, too, on the plank sidewalk, and Millicent Lawrence, the wife of Samuel Lawrence, the owner of the hardware store. The three of them stared in unison as the huge visitor rode out of town. As the extraordinary figure trotted past them, other townsfolk also stopped to gawp. But not for too long, lest their gawping be repaid in kind.

"Now, what do you make of that?" Mrs. Lawrence's voice was a blend of emotions. "I declare, that is the largest human being I have ever set eyes on. And also the strangest. Almost as strange as that odd creature he is riding. I think it must be a horse, but of what breed I cannot for the life of me say."

"Told me he was going into the Yellowstone." Her marital status notwithstanding, the red-haired clerk had on occasion entertained impure thoughts regarding the attractive Mrs. Lawrence, and was pleased at the opportunity, however brief, to show off his knowledge of things passing strange.

Doc Jensen nodded sagely and adjusted his spectacles. "I should say an entirely appropriate destination, from the look of him."

Worthless complained most of the time it took to reach the borders of the proud young nation's first national park. He continued complaining as they entered and proceeded to progress beyond the limits of the first tentative, hesitantly marked trails, pushing into mountainous backcountry that was unknown and unsurveyed. It was possible that beneath the camouflaging leather patch on his forehead, the unicorn's trimmed-down horn was irritating him again. The next time they stopped, Malone would put some of that special ointment on it, the golden goo he had bought in a bazaar in Jaisalmer some considerable time ago, when crossing the Thar Desert.

It certainly was an outlandish place, this new park. In parts down low between the mountains, the ground steamed and hissed and suppurated, so that in the chill of autumn, clouds rose upward to air-wrestle with those descending. The result was a climatological confusion that often left him squinting to see through the resultant heavy fog. The surveyors and soldiers who had forced fitful penetration into this isolated pocket of the country feared stepping into concealed pools of water hot enough to fry man and mount alike, or being swallowed by steaming mud that would boil off a man's boots before he could reach stable ground. Such concerns didn't worry Malone. Even with one eye locked in a permanent squint, Worthless could sense and avoid dangerous earth long before he put his hoof in it, so to speak.

Days had passed since Malone had seen another human being. Bears and elk, yes. Fox and beaver, in plenty. Even wolves, who came close, perhaps drawn by the prospect of prey, perhaps by the wolf's-skull cap that adorned Malone's head. When that cap winked back at them, the paralleling pack hesitated. When it threw back its half head and howled, they took off running so fast they left more than one unintentional longitudinal marker behind them in the shallow snow.

It wasn't yet deep. Too early in the season for that. But if the party Malone had been deputed to find didn't get out quick, they'd be trapped by some of the coldest, snowiest weather on the continent. That was what Malone had been hired to do: find 'em and bring them out. Difficult work, given the first snow and the absence of much in the way of trail spoor. If anyone could do it, he and Worthless could. The unicorn was not pleased with the undertaking. This time of year, he much preferred the company of a warm stable and compliant mares. Or, not being particularly particular, t' other way around.

The faint tracks of those who had preceded them eventually led man and mount down into a valley furiously alive with the Earth's breath. Intermittent geysers spewed hissing whale spouts of water into the crystal-clear air of morning. Noxious gases vented from fumaroles while mud pits bubbled and stewed like the paint pots of the maddest of damned artists. Lush evergreens blanketed the surrounding mountainsides. High overhead, an eagle screamed. Searching diligently for prey, it saw only a lone rider on horseback: too big to carry off, too big to ignore.

Sympathetic to the plight of any creature whose daily foraging amounted to endless searching for moving needles in a geologic haystack, Malone threw back his head and screamed a reply. This so startled the eagle that it banked in midair sharply enough to shed a feather. In the way of eagles and hawks, their consequent conversation was shorter than Hawthorne or Melville would have countenanced.

Eagle: Seen any vermin?

Malone: Nope.

Eagle: Bye.

Malone continued on, moving ever deeper into the valley of mist and ground-hugging fog. The trail of the party he was tracking grew fainter and fainter, until even he had trouble telling the difference between particles of soil that had been disturbed by man and horse and those that had simply been roiled by the unsettled Earth. It was when he was turning back, with an eye toward retracing part of the trail already traversed, that a noise most peculiar made him pause and look to his right.

Worthless was plodding gingerly around the fringe of a vast bubbling and popping mud pit. Nothing out of the locally ordinary there. It was only when a portion of the pit studdenly rose up and assumed human shape to confront Malone that he took serious notice.

The mountain man thought he was more than middling familiar with the general panoply of demonic manifestations, but this was the first time he had ever seen a mudunculus. Point of fact, he'd never even *heard* of a mudunculus. But that surely was one looming there before him, its feet sunk deep in the bubbling gunk and its distorted, lopsided, coffee-hued head flashing fangs at him from the midst of a mouth of muck. It had heavy, muscular mud arms that reached all the way to the ground, a tapering, wickedly whiplike tail, a bald, slick skull, long ears that drooped like those of a bloodhound from the sides of its head, penetrating eyes of blazing brown, and a nose that was as pointed as its glare. It grinned down at Malone from a very great height indeed. Strong men would have panicked at the sight, and women fainted.

Not Mad Amos Malone. He'd done seen quite a bit.

The mudunculus was certainly impressive. Steam rose and curled from its huge body, which, though quite naked, was covered in thick searing sludge that contributed a thankful modesty.

"Oho!" it burbled delightedly. "Another surveyor. And just in time for breakfast."

"Don't mind if I do." Sliding down out of the saddle, Malone commenced to rummaging in one of the hefty saddlebacks that was slung across Worthless's back. As the creature of the depths stared, the mountain man unlimbered skillet, spoon, and fixin's.

Instant insanity the demon expected. Insouciance was not a reaction to which it was accustomed.

"You pathetic human, I was not issuing an invitation. *You* are to be breakfast! You, and that toothsome-looking nag you rode in on.'"

Busy setting up his skillet and accoutrements, Malone glanced idly in his mount's direction, then back at the mudunculus. "I've heard Worthless called a sight many things. I've called him more names than most, myself. But I reckon 'toothsome' is a new one." Using kit from his saddlebags, he carefully began to build a fire under the skillet, making a cooking pit of stones to contain it. "I believe I rightly heard you call me 'another' surveyor. By that I'm supposin' you have some knowledge o' them that come here afore me?"

The mountain man's curiosity restored the demon's grin. "Truthfully, I do. They were not welcome." Dripping mud of different colors and extreme temperature, enormous arms spread wide, as if to encompass all that man and demon alike could see. "This is my home. None may come here without my permission. All who trespass are doomed to meet the same end." One long, thick finger pointed meaningfully toward a nearby geyser mound. "Behold the fate that is to be yours, master of some small courage."

Leaning slightly forward as he crouched by his skillet, Malone was just able to see around the edge of the built-up mound of sulfates and silicates and such. It shaded a pile of bones. Human bones, roughly disarticulated and bleached white as chalk. At least three skulls stared back at him. There might have been more. He nodded slowly to himself.

He had found the missing party of surveyors.

Showing foot-long fangs, the mudunculus leaned forward. "Do you not tremble at the sight? Are you not melting with fear? You have but a moment longer to live before your flesh is boiled from your living bones, as was theirs!"

Having stood, Malone returned to hunting through a saddlebag. "Y'know," he declared absently, "there's a real trick t' transportin' eggs on horseback." One hand full of henfruit, he headed back to the skillet. "Takes jest the right kind o' packin', and the right kind o' horse."

"Unworthy one! You have no respect. I think perhaps you are

already mad." A great sucking sound ensued as the demon took a giant step forward. Not toward Malone, but past him, to his left. "Watch then, as I consume first your beloved animal, so that you may see what is in store for your own body!"

Eggs sizzling in the cast-iron skillet, Malone glanced up. "Wouldn't try thet if I were you."

The progeny of the pit ignored him. Leaning forward, mouth agape, it brought its jaws down hard on Worthless's hindquarters. Turning its head, the horse looked back and, as usual, squinted.

There was a snapping, crunching sound. But it came not from Worthless's legs or pelvis, nor from his spine. Rather the sound was of one fang snapping. Letting out a cry of hurt and surprise, the demon drew back sharply. One massive hand felt of its upper jaw. A great tooth had broken in half, and its orthodontic companions were throbbing painfully.

"What manner of monstrous beast is this?"

Malone eyed Worthless, who had gone back to nibbling at the ground. "A tough one." His gaze shifted to the still-stunned demon. "I reckon y'would have figured that out if you'd taken the time t' notice thet he's croppin' calcite, not grass." Eggs well on their way to cooking in the skillet, he added bacon. "Settles his stomach, it does." His gaze narrowed. When Amos Malone's gaze narrowed, anything in the vicinity that had an ounce of sense turned and fled. It did not speak well for the demon that it remained where it was.

Malone continued. "Now you harken to me, Mr. Mud-Face. This here piece o' ground has been declared the first national park o' this young country by none other than President Grant himself. It's to be open to all." With one powerful, callused hand, he gestured at the seething, steaming landscape spread out before him. "Myself, I don't have no problem with you keepin' your house here. I pride myself on gettin' along with every sort o' critter, no matter how disagreeable their personal habits. But this here consumin' o' visitors, that's gonna have t' stop."

Used to being feared, the mudunculus was so furious at the mountain man's words that he forgot the loss of his half a fang.

"Miserable little human! Worthless worm that burrows in dung!

You dare to dictate to Nagaroth, Lord of Heat and Fire? I have changed my mind. I will not boil you alive. I will melt the meat from your bones, slowly, leaving your vitals for last, and begin consuming them while you are still alive!" Reaching down into the swirling stew of boiling earth and water at his feet, he dragged up a handful of blazing, glowing dust. "The flesh of your face will be first to burn!" Drawing back its arm, it flung the handful straight at Malone.

Putting up a fair-sized hand of his own, the mountain man caught the flaming dust before it could strike him. Carefully, he deposited a pinch or two in his skillet before dumping the rest aside. Smoke rose briefly from his thick-skinned palm.

"Thankee fer the brimstone. 'Tain't good Mexican spice, but it'll do. I like a little zest in my eggs."

Eyes bulging with barely controlled fury, the demon took a long, deep breath. Then it pursed its ugly lips, and spat. A stream of boiling water shot right for Malone. Though the spray was hot enough to sear the paint off the front of an unlicensed saloon, he leaned only slightly to his left.

The water struck him face on. For a moment, he was completely obscured by the resulting gush of steam. Nagaroth's grin, which had been absent for a number of minutes, now returned as he waited to see the results of his scalding aqueous assault. When the steam cleared, his face fell in full-featured flabbergastment—fell literally and almost to his chest, in fact, as it oozed downward.

Malone sat, intact and sturdy, behind his skillet. Steam rose from his fringed leather jacket, from his pants, from his boots, and from his face. Turning his head to his right, he sniffed one underarm before looking back at the astonished demon.

"Thanks, there. First time in a month this outfit's been proper clean, and that I've had a decent bath." Leaning forward, he squinted down at the top of one boot. "Even killed the lice, I do believe."

It was at that point that the demon Nagaroth went slightly berserk, thrashing the mud in which its feet were immersed, howling at the sky, beating its broad chest, and causing huge bubbles of mud to rise and burst all around it. Geysers erupted and fumaroles belched, while the very earth underfoot quivered fit to echo the great Missouri quake of 1811.

The demon threw fire at Malone. It only made his bacon cook faster. He threw hot stones. The mountain man effortlessly dodged them, save one nicely shaped one he grabbed to employ as a seat. Only then did the thwarted, frustrated fiend do something so horrific, so terrible, that it finally drew Amos Malone's undivided attention.

Leaning far forward and reaching out, it roughly slapped the skillet to one side.

Worthless looked up immediately. Normally utterly unflappable, the half-horse, half-unicorn's eyes grew wide. It began backing up, away from the scene of the tragedy. High above, a certain eagle looked down sharply, took notice of something singularly unpleasant, and hightailed it for the biggest tree it could find.

His gaze fixed on his ruined breakfast, Malone slowly rose. Not as high as the demon, but high enough. He eyed the ruins of the nearly crisp bacon and the almost ready eggs for a long moment. Then he turned his attention wholly to the one who had committed the unforgivable sin.

You can shoot a mountain man, more than once. You can cut him with a knife, or filch his goods, or impune his ancestry, or question his manhood. But you do not, not ever, mess with his breakfast.

"That," Malone declared in a low tone of voice that similarly caused the earth underfoot to tremble slightly, "was a dang near impolite thing to do."

"Suffer!" Pleased (and perhaps a mite relieved) to have finally unsettled his unexpectedly unimpressed victim, Nagaroth shook a fist in the mountain man's direction. "Soon you too will be part of the soil, and no more."

"Now you lookee here, my overheated unhygienic friend. Because I were raised polite, I'm givin' you one last chance t' agree to the requirement I've laid down. Otherwise, it's banishment forever from this valley, and to a place where I guarantee you'll get no rest."

Nagaroth shook his head slowly. "You are a fit opponent, I avow. Yet you are but mortal, while I am one with the eternal elements. You will die here, as will all who come after you: man, woman, or child." The demon raised both arms skyward. "I will build terraces of their bones."

"Have it your way, then." It was Malone's turn to shake *his* head. "I swan, but demons are stubborn folk." As the mountain man lifted one foot high, Nagaroth prepared to parry what it expected to be a blow of feeble and futile mortal strength.

But Malone did not kick out. Instead, he brought his foot down hard; once, twice, several times in succession. Rattled, the earth shook underfoot, and the resulting concussion knocked bewildered squirrels out of their trees for a mile around.

Six times Malone stamped the ground, then six times again. By the third set of six, Nagaroth was sensing the imminency of his coming triumph. If kicking dirt was the best this insolent human could muster by way of a defense, then their confrontation was nearing an end before it had even begun. Lifting first one leg out of the mud, then the other, he started forward, great hands outstretched. No slow boiling for this one, he decided. He would smother it, fill its impudent mouth with hot mud, until it choked.

A fountain of flame erupted between Malone and the oncoming demon. So hot was it that the very rocks themselves seemed to draw back in fear. A blast of sulfur corrupted the clean mountain air. Worthless looked on a moment, then dropped his head and went back to nibbling calcite.

Out of the fire and the heat and the flame stepped a singular figure. It was impeccably garbed in the oufit of a professional gambler, and a successful one at that. Ruffled white shirt with neatly looped black string tie, gleaming black vest beneath black jacket, black pants and boots, all shone as if just lifted from the haberdasher's shelf. The narrow, vulturine face featured a small, perfectly pointed goatee complemented by a thin mustache, the end curls of which defied logic as well as gravity. The teeth were pointed, as was the switching, ever-moving tail that protruded from the seat of the black pants, and the two small horns on its head punched neatly through the custom-tailored, wide-brimmed black hat. As it approached the mountain man, smiling a smile of immaculate, eternal evil, it extended a hand.

Malone did not shake it. Instead, he nodded a curt greeting.

"Mornin', Nick."

"Good morning, Mr. Malone. Good to see you again."

"Wish I could say the same. You remember that little scrape I got you out of not long these many years ago?"

"Ah yes." The figure in the gambler's outfit murmured softly. "I never forget such things. Could have been most personally embarrassing."

"Well, I'm callin' in that card today." Lifting his gaze, he nodded at the still figure of the demon Nagaroth, who had been shocked into immobility. "This 'ere property is now a park. It's plenty big, with room enough fer all manner o' critters—but the nature o' the real estate notwithstandin', I reckon there jest ain't no room fer bone-scourin' demonics." He smiled thinly. "His is a presence that might have a tendency to dissuade folks who might otherwise be inclined t' come a-visitin'."

The gambler turned to confront the demon, who quailed visibly.

"Sire, I was only being myself. By all the sacrosanct laws that govern—"

"Shut up." Eyes no ordinary human could meet and survive locked on the now-quaking demon. Their owner sighed. "This is what comes of giving the immortal impious a measure of individual independence. They invariably overreach themselves." He raised a hand, the nails of which, while pointed and sharp as knives, were exquisitely manicured.

"*Sire, no,* I beg of you, I ...!"

Thunder, dark and nasty, rolled across the valley. By the time it had died away, so had the formerly invincible demon Nagaroth. Using both hands to give a little tug-down on the hem of his fine vest, the gambler turned back to the one who had summoned him forth.

"You're a piece of work, you are, Amos Malone." Eyes flashed. "I now consider my old debt to you to be repaid. The next time we meet ..." His expression, which had begun to darken, was once more replaced by a smile of suave iniquity. "I look forward to the day when our respective positions of strength are reversed, and I can summon *you*—for a visit to my place of dwelling."

Malone snorted. "Good thing you're immortal, 'cause I reckon that's about how long you'll have t' wait. And even when that time cometh, I plan on plantin' my backside elsewhere." He glanced skyward. "Still, it's a fine morning, if a bit chilly. Would be ill-mannered o' me not t' offer to share breakfast with a fellow travel-er's acquaintance, however mean and rotten be his immortal self." He indicated the overturned skillet. "Have to start all over agin, though. Your minion made a mess o' things."

Taking a seat on the ground, the gambler indicated his accep-tance. "I'm *always* chilly, up thisaway. I like my bacon and eggs well done, if you please, and my toast—"

"—burnt. I know." Malone started back for his saddlebags. As he did so, the Devil called after him.

"It is no small matter for one to summon me, much less to readily cancel so powerful an obligation." He looked back to the place that had formerly been the home of the now banished and disgraced demon Nagaroth. "Something of considerable conse-quence must have ensued for you to do so."

Returning with eggs and bacon and bread, Malone whispered a few words to the upended skillet, causing it to tumble and bounce its way across the ground until it was once more comfortably situ-ated above the circle of rocks that surrounded the cooking fire. Occasionally, a flicker of flame would burst forth from beneath the heavy cast iron to caress one of old Nick's boots, like a cat licking its master.

"Why, I should think it would be obvious, in a place like this." Tossing the bacon onto the skillet, Malone watched as it started to sizzle. He began cracking eggs. "Your former underling, why, he got me good and steamed."

Combining science and magic is always a tough proposition. Even more so somewhere like the Old West, where science is apt to extend about as far as discussing the ingredients in lye soap. But when confronted with a problem that involves both, you have to employ both to solve it.

Stubbornness is a quality that can be found in equal measure in scientists and magicians. So is avarice. These human characteristics are present regardless of the profession to which one belongs. Dealing with them means dealing with both, understanding both, and being able to call upon both.

The science of puns being somewhat simpler, and absent of magic, I feel comfortable employing it.

FREE ELECTIONS

I'm terribly sorry, sir, but we have no water, and I fear that you will have to drink your whiskey straight."

Though the young bartender was as tough and wiry as the hard-scrabble land on which the drinking establishment in which he was currently employed had been raised, his voice trembled slightly as he explained. It was possible (indeed, it was most likely) that his current uneasy disposition was due to the presence of the customer to whom he was compelled to deliver the apology.

Mad Amos Malone had that effect on folks.

The mountain man did not so much rest at the bar as threaten to swallow it. Indeed, his colossal bulk seemed to fill a good portion of the entire Double Eagle Saloon. Standing slightly over or slightly under seven feet tall, depending on how long it had been since he had last made the acquaintance of a bath, and weighing in the neighborhood (a most inhospitable one, the bartender was certain) of three hundred pounds, give or take when he had last trimmed his enormous black beard, Amos Malone was not a man to be denied. It was therefore with considerable relief that the bartender accepted his gargantuan customer's reply.

Raising his glass, the mountain man nudged back the wolf's head that covered his scalp. One of the wolf's eyes blinked. His gaze attending elsewhere, the bartender missed this particular canine impossibility. "I didn't know thet Heaven lay this near south o' Denver," Malone declared solemnly. Draining the shot in a single gulp, he placed the leaded glass back down on the counter with surprising delicacy. "Another, if you please."

The bartender hesitated, grinned, wondered if it was wise to be grinning, consequently got his mouth all twisted up like a Baptist preacher caught out on a matter of Scripture by a twelve-year-old in Sunday school, and settled for doing as the stranger requested. This time, Malone sipped the amber liquid instead of inhaling it.

"Not my business, but as a matter o' curiosity, how come you to be out of something as basic as water, son?"

The bartender nervously stroked his own beard. It was reddish blond, washed, neatly trimmed, and a pale imitation of the facial forest that clung to the mountain man's face like a gray-flecked thundercloud.

"It's not just the saloons. Whole town's out of water. Havin' to haul it from the Carlos River just so's the kids will have something to drink." He shook his head sadly. "Poor womenfolk hereabouts ain't had a bath in weeks. There've been fistfights."

Malone nodded understandingly. "This 'ere is dryish country, fer sure. Rough geology fer findin' a well."

The bartender did not blink in surprise, nor otherwise. In Colorado, a country that had been raised up on mines and mining, one heard the word "geology" and its related terms often enough. It was the current source that the mixologist found surprising.

"Can't drill for water hereabouts, mister. Anybody tries to get a well in comes up dry. But the town's got a natural spring. A great spring she is, too. Strong flow, water sweet and clear, no arsenic or mercury. The spring's pretty much the reason the town is here, in what you rightly call rough country for a well." His expression darkened. "Trouble is, we haven't been able to draw from it for weeks now."

Brows hard and sharp as Vermont granite drew together, and the barkeep could've sworn he heard a grinding noise. "Mind my askin' why not?"

The younger man sighed. "There's someone sittin' on it. Funny old coot rode his wagon into town weeks ago. Did no harm at first. Even ate here once or twice. Then one day he unlimbered this old chair he had tied to his wagon, dragged it through town, set himself down atop the spring cap, closed the main valve, and wouldn't move. Can't no one get past his feet or that chair to open it back up."

Malone considered. "This," he murmured, "strikes me as passing strange."

"Ain't the half of it." The bartender refilled the mountain man's empty glass without having to be asked. "We tried polite at first. He wouldn't budge. So a couple of our local miners decided to take matters into their own hands, so to speak. Tried to pull him out of his chair. Went easy, at first. Then hard. Big fellers, they both were, but they couldn't shift the old fart an inch. Got some more help, until there were altogether five of them workin' on him. Still wouldn't move." He shook his head at the memory of it.

"Tied chains to the legs of that chair and hooked 'em to a team. Four dray mares, big and strong from hauling mining equipment. Those horses did strain until I thought they would fall over, mister, and through it all that chair and that old man did not so much as give out with a creak. Pretty much exasperated by then, the sheriff, he pulled out his Colt and pointed it at the old man and said—I heard him for myself—he said, 'You git your sorry skinny trespassin' old ass off the town water source right now or by the rights invested in me by the State of Colorado and in full sight of the Good Lord himself, I will put a bullet in you, sir, right where you squat!'"

Malone's face was impassive. "What happened?"

The bartender took a deep breath. "Well, mister, that old man, he just looked up at the sheriff with this funny glint in his eye and said, 'If it's all the same to you, I think I'll just continue to set a spell.' So the sheriff, he fired once.Nothing happened. The old man, he stayed a-sittin'. And that bullet, near as anyone can reckon, it traveled about two feet, stopped deader than an Apache confronted by a naked Norwegian, and fell to the ground." He nodded to his left, in the direction of the swinging doors. "Far as I know, it's still there. Ain't nobody in town dared to touch it."

"The sheriff?" Malone inquired.

"Ain't nobody seen him since. Still runnin', I reckon. His eyes got as big as an owl's, they did. Pretty much everybody else who was around at the time took off and ran, too. Can't say as I blame 'em. So that's why we ain't got no water in town. Old man says he'll move hisself and his damn chair off the spring valve for a thousand dollars. In gold. The mayor and the town's leading business folk, they're talkin' about it. Drillin' sideways into the spring to bypass the existing underground plumbing might work. Miners contend it might also ruin the natural flow permanent-like. But a thousand dollars ..." His voice trailed away as he shook his head sadly. "He doesn't get up to eat, doesn't get up to drink, doesn't get up for anything. Just sits there and rocks, back and forth, back and forth, smilin' at nothing in particular."

Silence lay middlin' in the saloon for several minutes. This was due to a combination of the solemnity that had infected the town like typhoid, a current dearth of patrons, and the fact that those customers who were present found themselves uncharacteristically subdued in the presence of the human mountain ensconced at the bar.

Eventually Malone leaned forward slightly. To his credit the bartender did not shy from this increased proximity, not to mention the actual eclipse, though the bouquet that emanated from the well-traveled mountain man did cause the young man's nostrils to clench involuntarily.

"Now then, son, what I'm about to ask you is pretty important. This old coot o' yours: Did he say, 'I think I'll just continue to *set* a spell'? Or did he say, 'I think I'll just continue to set a *spell*?'"

The barkeep frowned. "Don't rightly know. I wasn't close enough to hear what he actually said. Was repeated to me by them that were."

Malone straightened. Across the room, a quartet of hardened miners abruptly abandoned their card game and departed the premises as expeditiously as possible.

"Got some time afore dinner. Reckon I'll go have a chat with this mulish visitant o' yours. Might be I can persuade him t' set himself somewhere else and forgo the gold he's attemptin' to wrest from you folks."

"You can try all you want, mister. Lord knows you're the biggest thing I've seen this side of Pikes Peak, but I guarantee even you can't pull him out of that old chair of his."

Halfway to the door, Malone looked back. Eyes black as a six-year-old's pudding-induced nightmare regarded the bartender. "Who said anythin' about pulling?"

Outside the Double Eagle, a man was standing in the street just off the raised boardwalk and screaming. Or maybe he was crying. Probably both, Malone reflected as he paused to take in the scene. Certainly, the second man lying on the ground and clutching himself was crying. Most likely, the prone one did not have the wherewithal remaining to scream. There was also a boy of about ten, who was standing on the boardwalk quietly observing the prospect before him. Malone leaned toward him. Unlike the denizens of the saloon, the lad was too young to exhibit the instinctive fear that someone of Malone's size and appearance usually engendered.

"What happened here, son?"

The boy considered the man-mountain. "This here your horse, mister?"

"It be. His name's Worthless."

The youth turned back to squint at Malone's mount. Worthless squinted back out of the eye located within a circular white patch. A leather bandage covered the stallion's forehead. Beneath the leather, something indeterminate bulged intriguingly.

"Never seen a horse like this, mister."

"He's part Shire, part Appaloosa, part mistral, part—"

"What a 'mistral'?"

Malone grinned slightly. "French breed." He nodded toward the man who was screaming and crying.

"For God's sake, make him move! Git 'im *off* me!"

Malone ignored the man's pleas. "These two fellers been both-erin' Worthless?"

"I think they were trying to steal him, mister."

The mountain man nodded. "That would explain why he's standin' on that poor feller's right foot. Wouldn't want Worthless standin' on my foot, that's fer sure." He nodded at the man lying on the ground who was holding himself and moaning. "What happened to thet one?"

"I think he was trying to pull off your saddlebags when your horse kicked him. Right in the collywobbles." The boy looked confused. "I swear, sir, your horse, he kicked out straight sideways. But cain't no horse do that. A horse's leg just goes pretty much forward and back. Ain't never heard of a horse that could kick out straight sideways. Kinda surprised me."

Malone nodded at the man on the ground. "Not as much as it must've surprised this feller." Straightening, he stepped off the boardwalk, put his leather-clad left foot in a hanging stirrup, and mounted up. The added weight only caused the man whose right foot was pinned beneath Worthless's left front hoof to scream all the louder.

"OH GAWD, I'M DYING, LORD SAVE ME!"

Malone chucked the reins. The stallion looked back up at him.

"C'mon, you useless lump o' coyote bait. I got to see a man about a settin'. Or a spell. Reckon it might be a bit o' both."

It was only when rider and mount turned away from the saloon and started up the town's main street that the boy noticed the horse had never been tied to the saloon's railing. As for the would-be horse thief whose foot had been trapped, he promptly clutched at his lower leg and fell to the dirt alongside his equally incapacitated companion. Both foot and boot, the youth noted with interest, had been squashed flat as a potato pancake.

The stranger's horse had been big, and heavy—but *that* heavy? Why, to crush a man's boot and foot so purely flat, it seemed to the boy that the peculiar stallion would had to have been made out of solid iron.

The town spring was located uphill and off to one side of the main street. The miners who had plumbed it had made a good job of the work, finishing it off with aged hardwood banded with iron.

The life-giving rattle of running water was absent from the feeder pipe that emerged from the control cap. Eyeing the valve that normally controlled the volume, Malone wondered where the spring's natural flow was going now that the pipe designed to convey it into town had been closed off.

Might be that the old man seated in the battered rocking chair directly in front of the currently inaccessible steel wheel would know.

He was at least as weathered as his chair. While the latter was adorned with lingering flecks of red and green paint, the oldster wore faded Levi's and a pale plaid shirt open at the collar. A ring on one finger had been pounded out of a single nugget. His hair flowed gray around his shoulders, while his beard was as long, snake-slender, and white as that of an entire line of Amish patriarchs. The hat on his head was stained with the tears of eons. Or possibly cheap bourbon. Sometimes, Malone reflected, the two were hard to tell apart.

Dismounting, he left Worthless standing by himself and approached the spring source. The old man looked up at his approach. And up, and up, until one withered hand finally had to push back the age-worn hat to allow its owner a proper and complete viewing.

"Well now, if you ain't the biggest pile I ever done seen—and I done seen some fairly big ones in my time."

"I reckon you're a bit o' a pile yourself, denyin' these good folks water."

The old man chuckled. Half his teeth were gold, too. They alternated precisely with the remaining natural enamel: one gold, one white, one gold, one white.

"Business, my enormous friend, jest business."

"I find extortion the business equivalent o' what eventually results from a feller eatin' a whole sack o' unsalted beans."

"Hmph! These drylanders send you up here to try and get my goat?" He grinned. "Or to move me, or try to reach under my chair? You kin try if you want, ox-brother, but won't do you no good. You'll only strain your back, and mebbe your brain." One hand slapped down hard on a wooden arm of the chair. "When Versus Wrathwell decides to set a spell, ain't nothin' on Heaven or Earth moves him!"

Malone was silent for a moment. Then he nodded. "Reckon you must be right, though I expect Worthless there might shift you an inch or three. Once had him drag off a lightning-downed sequoia that were blockin' our way. He don't much care for pullin', though. Says he ain't no mule, to be hooked up to a load. So guess ain't nobody gonna pull you off that spot, or that chair."

"Damned right!" Wrathwell huffed. "Guess you got more sense hidin' behind that face wire o' yours than I first thought." He pointed down toward the town. The boy who had witnessed the ill-fated attempt to steal the mountain man's horse was standing in the street, looking up toward the site of the spring. Several townsfolk had joined him in staring. One well-dressed man had bent over and was talking softly to the lad.

When Malone continued to stare, the oldster made a face at him. "Well, you gonna stand there till the stink gits tired and rolls off you, or you gonna do somethin' useful and tell them sorry-ass no-hopers to pay me what I asked?"

"Neither one, grandpa." As Malone started toward him, the old man's expression tensed and he gripped the arms of his chair with long, bony fingers. But Malone didn't touch him, did not try to move him. Instead, he sat down as close as he could get to the paint-peeling piece of furniture, crossed legs the size of tree trunks, and rested his enormous, gnarled hands on his leather-clad knees.

Wrathwell's gaze narrowed. "Jest whut d'you think you're doin'?"

Malone shrugged. "It's a free country. Thought I might just set a spell."

The oldster's eyes widened. Then he began to laugh; a raucous, otherworldly cackle that boded no good. "Right then, I gits it! You think you kin outset me! Is thet it?" When the mountain man didn't reply, Wrathwell's crowing subsided to mere amusement. "So be it. Set till you get tired, old sod. Set still till the sun starts to burn your brow, till the Colorado night ices your liver. Set till hunger claws at your insides like you've swallowed a pepper-haired cat and thirst grates your throat like a carrot peeler. Ain't nobody ever outset

Versus Wrathwell, and I kin assure you thet no iggorant bucket o' beef escaped from a Chicago slaughterhouse will be the first!"

And so saying, he sat back in his birch chair, turned his gaze toward the distant clouds, and began to rock.

Malone sat still as the stone beneath his backside, and stared. Slightly downslope, a singular amalgamation of equine complexity observed this tableau for about five minutes before snorting loudly, turning, and trotting back into town, there to regard an empty trough before nuzzling up against the tired, thirsty mare tied beside it. In less than a minute she was rolling her eyes and looking decidedly stinkweed.

The mountain man was still there the next day, seated cross-legged beside the adamant intruder, staring fixedly at him and not moving a muscle. Occasionally Wrathwell would glance in his direction and snicker. Gathering their courage, more and more citizens emerged from their waterless abodes to ascend the slight hill from which in normal times the town spring sprang. Much conversation ensued. Unencumbered by the cares and concerns of their worried elders, children began to run around both rocker and sitter, laughing and making jokes. One stick-wielding older boy of fifteen attempted to poke the poker-faced mountain man with a long stick, only to find himself knocked to the ground by a gob of spittle the size of a hen's egg, which slammed into his left cheek with the force of a soggy, beslimed washrag. As Malone had not moved and the spit stank of horse, suspicion eventually fell on the mountain man's mount. Except that Worthless was hundreds of yards away, in town, standing alongside a newly destabilized mare whose recently acquired expression both puzzled and alarmed its owner.

As the end of the week drew near, word of the confrontation had spread to nearby towns, bringing curious visitors (with their welcome jugs of water) to view the standoff—or rather, the sit-off. As near as anyone could tell, while Wrathwell continued to rock, his hirsute audience had not budged. Not to eat, drink, defecate, curse, cry, sniffle, cough, or otherwise suggest he was actually formulated of anything other than the solid rock on which he sat. It was as if he had been transformed into one of those local, mysterious, human-shaped granite formations sometimes worshipped or feared by the local Ute.

For his part, Wrathwell appeared to be growing increasingly uneasy. By the second week he would sometimes turn to the staring, unmoving, unblinking mountain man and let loose a stream of curses that would cause the women in the ever-growing audience to turn away and blush, or hastily emplace their hands over the ears of wide-eyed children.

"Nobody outsets Versus Wrathwell, do you hear me! Why don't you *move*, you chunk of monkey meat? Why don't you say something, offspring of a whore and a water horse?" Suddenly, he leaned sharply to his right. At this first non-rocking motion, several in the crowd of onlookers gasped and strong men stepped back.

"So it's a settin' contest you want, is it? Well and done, then, well and done. Nobody outsets me, and nobody outstills, and by the tip of my beard, I'll see you move first and surrender, I will! I'll have your soul for an earring to hang on my own, and you'll die there dry and desiccated with your black damned eyes wide open!"

At that, Versus Wrathwell stopped rocking.

Gleaming black eyes met rheumy blue. Lids froze high and never blinked. The children who had run and laughed suddenly found reason to return to the safety of home and school. Muttering to themselves, mothers and saloon hookers alike soon followed, until only the strongest of strong men were left in audience.

And still the stares of the two men were locked, hard and unmoving as crossed swords, locked in combat as deadly. Clouds began to gather overhead, and the promise of rain that might refill empty storage barrels and tanks drew still more onlookers away from the confrontation. But while the sky grew dark and lightning began to crackle and wind gusted strong enough to stir beard black and beard white, no rain fell. It was as if such unrelenting stubbornness on the part of the seated pair angered the heavens themselves, and they responded with sizzle and flash, thunder and ground-searing bolt.

"By the scar on my sainted grandmother's neck," one man breathed the following morning as he returned to resume gazing upon the unnatural square-off, "the mountain man—he ain't breathing!"

It was true. Amos Malone's immense chest had grown still. No air was sucked in through dirty nostrils nor hissed from between slightly parted lips. He was sitting stiller than anyone could set. Across from him, ensconced tightly in his chair, Versus Wrathwell looked momentarily startled. Then, white and gold teeth clenched, he too ceased breathing. Neither man breathing, but neither man dead.

This, the remaining onlookers agreed, was settin' with a vengeance.

It was a sight so disturbing that it sent all but two friends, among the toughest of all the miners in southern Colorado, fleeing townward.

Malone stared at Wrathwell. Wrathwell glared at Malone. Then the mountain man did something neither miner could quite understand, though they understood it clear. He stopped moving at all.

He stopped moving inside.

Asa Green didn't quite comprehend what he was experiencing, but his friend Hiram confirmed it. It was as if they could see *through* parts of the mountain man. As they stared, Malone's left hand started to detach from his wrist. Fluttering like a flesh-colored butterfly, one ear commenced to shimmy and drift away from the side of his head. When Malone's right eye began to emerge from its socket, quivering like an orphaned cue ball, Hiram Hopkins let out a tremulous moan and fled. Of the curious, only Asa Green still remained as witness to what followed.

The face of the old man cracked wide in an alternating gold and white smirk. He began to laugh. "Told yez! Told yez, told yez, told yez! *Nobody* outsets Versus Wrathwell! Nobody! I once blocked a clipper from leaving Boston Harbor. They paid me. Another time was the door to the safe in Philadelphia's main bank. They paid me. So will these miserable would-be gold-leachers! They'll pay me. *Everybody* pays Versus Wrathwell. And you, you'll pay, big as you are. You'll pay with ... with ... what the hell this side of Constantinople is happening?"

Versus Wrathwell was also coming apart. As Green, no longer brave but too terrified to run, looked on, the old man's eyes drifted out of his head. Then they began to rotate around his skull. They were soon joined by his ears. Then his fingers detached, one by one, from his hands, and commenced to swing moonlike around his jerky-tough body. Above and all around, dark clouds swirled like overcooked chili. Thunder bellowed. Through the flashes of lightning, Asa Green saw more and more of the old man's body float free, until every digit and external protrusion was orbiting his skinny frame.

Eyes and ears, fingers and toes, nose and hair—all swam circuslike about him. When his torso came apart and his organs began to form a crack-the-whip around the oldster's now empty center, the miner nearly fainted. That he retained consciousness and memory of the event was due more to the shock that prevented him from passing out than to any innate audacity.

"No!" Detached from his mouth and from the rest of him, Wrathwell's lips were shouting feebly even as they too began to reduce themselves to their component parts. "It can't be! This cannot be! Nobody outstills Versus Wrathwell! No—body ..."

Flying farther and farther apart, growing smaller and smaller as they did so, the constituent bits and pieces of the curious old man eventually lost all contact with one another, until one by one the individual submicroscopic specks of ugliness that had been Versus Wrathwell let out a crackle and a pop before being sucked up by the swirling, roaring clouds.

Gradually the arid storm began to subside, the clouds to turn first brown and then golden and finally white, until, exhausted, they were much relieved to abdicate their agitation in favor of blue sky and bright sunshine.

Meanwhile Amos Malone's eye floated back to reinsert itself neatly into its empty socket, massive fingers fastened themselves firmly back to his hand, and he was full restored. Only then, for the first time in nearly two weeks, did he blink.

Something touched the back of Asa Green's neck. Nudged out of the paralysis into which he had fallen, the hardy, toughened

miner screamed once. Whipping around and looking back two
sneezes short of a heart attack, he saw that it was only the muzzle
of the mountain man's horse. A great relief wheezed out of him. As
he rose shakily to his feet, Malone was doing likewise. The mountain man eyed his mount.

"Yeah, I'm hungry, too. Let's go get something to eat." He
squinted at the still-trembling Asa Green, then nodded in the direction of the steel control wheel behind the empty chair. "Town's
thirsty. 'Bout time t' remedy that, wouldn't you say?"

Fighting to control his shaking, Green cautiously approached
the empty rocking chair. There was no sign, anywhere, of the old
man who had occupied it so long and so obstinately. Gingerly, the
miner reached down. His hands moved freely. Taking hold of the
arms of the chair, he pulled. It shifted without resistance. Pulling
harder, he lifted the heretofore unapproachable piece of furniture
off the ground. It rose without resistance. Then, mindful of the
crying children and dry-throated women and his own burning thirst
this past unpleasant month, he spun right around and heaved it as
far as he could. Describing a high arc, the aged birch struck the
surrounding rocks and shattered into kindling.

Turning thankfully back to the stolid, silent mountain man, Asa
Green nodded, bent, and began to turn the control wheel. It rotated
easily, almost gratefully, in his callused hands. The gush of water as
the formerly restrained spring once more filled the pipe with life
was like the sound children make when school lets out for summer.
From the town below, cries of surprise and then shouts of joy filled
the air. It was September in southern Colorado, it was hot, but for
the town at the base of the hill it was Christmas come early.

Straightening, the miner stared at the mountain man. "I don't
know what you did, sir, and I don't know what I saw, but speakin'
for myself I am eternal grateful." He gestured at the community
below. "My friends and neighbors are assuredly also, and forever
will be."

Malone nodded once, then walked over to and swung himself up
on his peculiar horse. The animal grunted and proceeded to utter
what Green would later swear was possibly the absolute worst, most

insulting single word in the entire English language, stretching all the way back to the Saxon, and ambled forward.

"Wait! Sir, if you wouldn't mind—if you don't mind—what exactly happened here?"

Malone did not pull back on the reins he was holding, but Worthless stopped nonetheless. "Why, feller-me-lad, 'twas all a matter of settin'. Of seeing which man could sit the most still. I've done such myself before, in other lands and days, and thought I could do so well enough here on the fringe o' your parched reality. See, now and then I like t' set a spell myself.

"What finally happened was all about what goes to make up a man. And mebbe pretty much everything else. We all of us seem to ourselves to be still when we set, but in truth we're not. Though we cannot see them, the parts of which we are made are always in motion. Look at yourself. What d'you see? Movement, or stillness?"

Green looked down at himself, then back up at the mountain man. "Not to stand here in dispute with you, sir, but I must confess that I look still and unmoving to me."

Malone smiled broadly, which action had the remarkable effect of transforming his appearance from that of a two-legged incarnation of imminent Doom to something approaching a sooty Saint Nick.

"A common illusion, friend. I assure you thet the tiniest parts of us are always in motion, though far too small to see. When I was at the Sorbonne, I discoursed much on the phenomenon with a charming young lady named Maria. Maria Skłodowska. Old Greek feller name o' Democritus was also mentioned, I recall, and other learned gentlemen of antiquity. I've come t' believe that each of us is at base composed of particles thet *choose* to comprise us. I conclude it is all a matter o' electivity, this life and existence. We choose t' hold together, therefore we are. I therefore have decided to call these tiny bits o' which we are made 'elections,' as they elect to keep things together, much as we do with our country." Raising his gaze, he focused on a part of the now-cerulean sky.

"But stay too still, fer too long, and the elections o' which we are composed kin no longer hold together. They begin t' fly apart. It is the same, I think, with everything. Rocks and trees, water and clouds, stars and sun. All and everything is made up o' these tiny, unseen elections. The late unpleasantness who called himself Versus Wrathwell sat too still and too long and too tight, until his bits could no longer elect t' remain together. Could no longer hold to their little orbits, as it were, and became free to fly off in whatever and whichever direction they wished."

Asa Green found his own gaze turning to the same portion of sky at which the mountain man was staring. "So they flew apart. D'you think they kin come together again?" Blinking at the restored sunshine, he lowered his sight until it was once more fixed on the huge man sitting straight and sure on the decidedly peculiar horse. "To make that hideous old feller whole afresh?"

"I doubt it." This time Malone did chuck the reins. Muttering under his breath, the stallion moved off toward town. "Once set free, I don't think elections can bind together easy again. Leastwise, not in a way that would result in producing something like Versus Wrathwell."

"Where you goin'?" Green called after the butt end of the stallion that was as unidentifiable as it was massive.

"Town, o' course. I'm hungry, and I'm thirsty, and I've a mighty powerful urge to pay an extended visit to the nearest long drop."

"There's water now. Water aplenty." Asa Green raised his voice as the mountain man rode slowly down the hill. "Thanks to you, Mr. Malone sir, there's all the water you can drink!"

Turning slightly in the saddle, Amos Malone slapped firmly at something that was scuttling about within one of his saddlebags. It promptly went still, though a small puff of irritated gray smoke emerged from where the opening was not quite sealed.

"Water! Why, feller-me-lad, d'you think I'm *mad?*"

Not just Native Americans but many traditional cultures believe that every manifestation of Nature is possessed of a spirit. It doesn't matter if it's a tree, a rock, a river, or a cricket, the lowest meadow or the highest mountain. In these mythologies everything is alive in some fashion and therefore deserving of respect and perhaps, depending on its nature, propitiation. The Makonde, a tribe of modest dimension in East Africa, not only have a name for such spirits (shetani), but their best artisans turn blackwood into spirit sculptures of exquisitely terrifying proportions.

Many such communities believe in an "ill wind" far more deeply than our casual saying is meant to imply. But imagine: If an ill wind is a spirit, then what is the spirit of the spirit? If a tree has a soul, what lies beyond that?

And would we want to encounter it ...?

GHOST WIND

I'm not going in there."

Barker's manicured fingers rolled and twisted like a nervous baker kneading invisible dough. "But you got to, Doc. The man's plain ill. Ain't there an oath or somethin' about how you got to take care of a body when they're sick?"

"A human being, yes." A wizened Doc Stanton kept his distance from the door that either led to room 12 of Bales Barker's hotel or to Hell. "I'm just not sure that the thing reposing within is human."

Outside, the mournful breeze that had been blowing all morning had picked up, sending papers and other debris whipping down Main Street.

"He's human enough." Both men turned to look at Hearts Doland, who had emerged from bed considerably earlier than was the professional gambler's wont. Whip-thin of body, mien, and mustache, he calmly returned the questioning stares of the doctor and the owner of the venerable establishment. "Two days ago Addie the Well spent the night with him. That not-so-good woman lies resting still in her bed, sleeping off the aftereffects of what I am told was a profitable but wearying encounter. I had occasion to speak to her about the evening in question as she was dragging her way up the stairs. It is plain from the brief words we had that she would testify to his humanness, exceptional though it might be."

Still wringing his hands, a pleading Barker turned back to the town physician. "You see, Doc? You're obligated to treat him. You got to make him well. It's your sacred duty. It's the right thing to do. The poor man is suffering, Doc!"

Stanton's gaze narrowed behind his wire-rim glasses. "You want him out of your hotel really badly, don't you?"

Barker met the older man's stare. "Please, Doc. You gotta help him. You gotta help *me*. When he sleeps, he snores, and when he snores, the vibration starts to workin' the nails out o' the walls and the floor beams. If he coughs, the sound wakes every guest in the place and the horses in the stable next door try to bolt. And if he blows his nose if blows his nose ..." The hotel owner shuddered. "You don't wanna know, Doc."

Stanton straightened his trim, elderly frame. "I am a trained physician, my good man. Cum laude Boston University of Medicine. A description of mere nasal expectoration, however extreme, would not intimidate me."

Barker nodded toward the closed door to room 12. "Then for the love of mercy, Doc, go in there and see to the poor traveler before he brings my place down around my ears! I've had four transit customers left already this week because of his roaring and snuffling."

The doctor's lips tightened. "Very well then." He took a deep breath. "I expect you are right: an oath is an oath." He faced the door, then glanced back. "I would be beholden to both you gentlemen if you would accompany me. To, um, bear witness to, um, whatever treatment it may be required that I apply."

The others hesitated. Then Bales shrugged. "It's my hotel. I reckon I've no option in the matter." Beside him, Doland blew a puff of imaginary cigar smoke.

"My life is all a gamble anyway. I will have your back, Doc."

The door to room 12 was not locked. There was neither reason nor need why it should be. No one in their right or even their wrong mind who knew anything of its present occupant would have thought to enter with malice in mind.

Mad Amos Malone lay sprawled across two iron-frame beds that, though pushed together, were still insufficient to accommodate his considerable bulk. Emerging from the prodigious eruption of gray-peppered black hirsuteness lying at the head of the two beds, a thunderous great concatenation of torso, arms, and legs sprawled across the pair of groaning mattresses. The prone mountain man was clad in rough red long johns that had been deeply stained by use, experience, and a plethora of fluids best left unidentified. Twin columns of callused flesh, his bare feet hung well over the bottom of the beds.

On an end table to the right of the recumbent figure stood a flowery ceramic water pitcher, a tall glass, a bottle of Dr. Vanhoffer's Viennese laudanum, and half a cigar. A few personal accoutrements, including a Sharps rifle, lay in a corner. While not overpowering, the general vapors in the room were less than salutary. Conscious of his professional oath, Stanton held tight to his medical bag as he approached the foot of the bed. Following directly, Doland and Barker were mindful of the door that had been left open to the hallway.

Leaning toward the conjoined beds, the doctor adjusted his glasses. "He's asleep." Having rendered this verdict, he turned to go.

From deep within a chest cavity of awesome dimension, a voice rumbled, as if from the farthest reaches of Mammoth Cave, "No I ain't."

Compelled to halt, Stanton cleared his throat. "I am Dr. Elias John Stanton. Howhow are you feeling today, Mr. Malone?"

Bushy brows drew back, and eyes fixed on the solicitous physician. "Like I been glued to a teat suckin' tar instead o' milk, Doc. What you got fer thet?"

"Um, a dilute solution of appropriate spirits might help to alleviate your discomfort, sir, by acting to thin the mucus that presently—"

"*Spirits!*" the giant mountain man bellowed, sitting up with such alacrity that Stanton threw up an arm to shield himself while stum-

bling backward. From the hallway to which they had precipitously
withdrawn, the hotel owner and the town's resident professional
gambler looked on apprehensively.

"I *knew* somethin' was preyin' on me. Spirits!"

To Stanton's credit he had not joined his companions in hasty
flight. He did, however, edge aside as the room's enormous occupant sat up, stood up (having to bend to ensure that his head would
not damage the ceiling), and hurried to peer out the nearest
window.

"I knew I heerd it! I knew!" Looking back and down, he locked
eyes with the doctor. "Don't you hear it, too, noble member of the
Asklepiades?"

Stanton held his ground. "Hear what, sir?"

"Why, the wind! The wind, friend!"

The doctor glanced back toward the open doorway. Barker and
Doland exchanged a glance, then shrugged. "Yes, Mr. Malone,"
Stanton avowed, "we all, um, hear the wind." Displaying bravery
comparable to that exhibited by the men of Pickett's Charge, he
moved close enough to place a reassuring hand on the center of the
giant's lower back. The rough material of the wool long johns
seemed to prickle against the doctor's open palm. "Mr. Malone, sir,
it may be that your illness is affecting your judgment. If you would
lie back down again, I shall endeavor to—"

"No time, no time!" Snorting through the noble promontory
centered on his bearded face, Malone bounded across the room and
began pulling on his buckskins. "Thet wind: you hear it but you
don't hear it. You feel it but you don't understand it. It's got to be
stopped, and stopped right quick, or it'll shred this town like a blind
pig goin' through a reaper."

More concerned now than ever about his incipient patient's
state of mind, Stanton tried to reassure the giant as shirt followed
pants. "Mr. Malone, sir, it is only the wind. Nothing to get alarmed
about. Here south of Denver on the east front of the Rockies, wind
is a feature of daily life. We are quite used to it even if you are not,
and being used to it, we are hardly alarmed by its occurrence."

Malone looked up from pulling on a boot. "Well, you ought to be. This ain't no ordinary wind that's comin', friend." Eyes like black diamonds flashed. "'Used to wind'? Why, let me tell you, Doc. I know the wind. I've done felt the Bayamo blowing hard off the coast of Cuba, and suffered the Harmattan while stuck atop a complainin' camel. I've sailed through the Levant round the Canaries and shouted insults at the Mistral for delayin' me in Marseille. I've fought the Ostria on behalf of the Turk, sucked up the Sirocco off of Tripoli, and stood arms akimbo while I let the Squamish scour my pits right close to where Vancouver first set his stick. I *know* the wind." Cupping a hand, he coughed into it.

"And even though I'm feelin' poorly, I aim to take a stand on behalf o' this town against the wind what's comin'." His gaze swept past the confused physician and wandered to the hallway beyond. "If fer naught else, on behalf o' a certain lady who done more than her duty by me."

"That's very thoughtful of you, Mr. Malone, I'm sure." Stanton had his bag open and was hunting among the contents. If he could just load his needle ... "For whatever reason. But I say again it is only the wind, and in my professional opinion you are somewhat unsettled in mind. If you will let me, I will ..."

Fully dressed now in skin and cotton, leather and wool, Malone was at the doctor's side in two strides. Stanton was distressed that the mountain man now stood between him and the doorway, but he bore the discomfort manfully.

"Doc, you familiar with the expression 'The wind is dying'?"

Stanton blinked. "Well, certainly, sir. Even a child knows the phrase. It is a common thing."

Malone nodded, and the wolf's-head cap he wore seemed to nod agreement on its own. "What d'you think happens, then, to the wind when it dies?"

The doctor's reaction indicated that this was a line of thought to which he had not devoted much in the way of prior contemplation. "I must confess that I fail to follow your reasoning, sir."

"The wind." Malone's voice was low and intense. "When it dies. What happens to it?"

Striving to help (from the safety of the hallway), Hearts Doland spoke up. "Why, it simply fades away, sir. One moment there is a breeze, and the next there is none. Nothing remains but a stillness of the aether."

Malone turned in the gambler's direction. "Most times, thet is the way of it, yes. Most times, but not all. There are rare occasions, scarce times, when conditions are just right, when it is with the wind the same as it is with people. Times when something remains. Some small fragmentation of former existence. Some semblance of the previous. You've probably felt it yourself. That moment when something unseen tips your hat but naught is to be felt. When a woman's petticoats are bestirred above her ankle sufficient to draw the eye but nothing else is moved. It is no more than a flicker of movement, a whisper of the cosmos, a breath of the Earth. Here and then gone." He drew himself up, banged his head lightly against the ceiling, and winced.

"But there are times when the spirit of such things, instead of going away, lingers in a kind of limbo that is neither of reality nor of nonexistence, between life and death. 'Tis true of aspects o' Nature as well as man, and more so of the wind than rock or cloud. Thus trapped twixt the Here and the Not, between the Going and the Coming or the Actual and the Imagined, such spirits become frustrated, angry, and at the final, furious. Settling score with such angry manifestations and pacifying them is the job o' certain exorcists, diviners, seers, and witchery folk."

Stanton harrumphed. "Are you claiming, Mr. Malone, sir, to count yourself among such practitioners of the fictional arts in this modern era of science and learning?" He was still trying to extract his needle from the depths of the bag. "I must remind you that it is the nineteenth century, and those of us with a claim to learning have no truck with such superstitious nonsense."

Malone nodded, sniffled massively, and headed for the doorway, where the owner of the hotel and the gambler with whom he shared less than ethical earnings made haste to remove themselves from his path.

"Then you won't mind, son of Hygeia, if I attempt to preserve your town from that which you insist cannot exist."

It was not hard to follow the mountain man at a distance, as the sound of his descending the stairs from the hotel's second floor to the ground below echoed with the booming of his passage. They would have followed him out onto the street as well, had not the breeze that had been blowing outside all morning risen to such force as to leave them to believe that a tempest of biblical propor-tions had suddenly and inexplicably descended on the town.

Huddled just inside the hotel's entrance, the three men had no difficulty peering without, since the rising gale had ripped the door from its hinges. Their curiosity as to the mountain man's intentions notwithstanding, they were careful to remain within sturdy wooden walls that had begun to rattle and shake. Off to their right, windows brought by wagon from Denver blew out with a musical crackle. Unable to turn away quite in time, Doland winced as a flying shard scored his right cheek. Automatically, Doc Stanton proceeded to treat the resulting trickle of blood, leaving Barker to report on what could be seen outside. The hotel owner's observations were not encouraging.

"Sounds like a tornado!" He had to shout to make himself heard above the rising gusts. "But I don't see no funnel cloud!"

Tending to the injured gambler, Stanton yelled without turning from his ministrations. "What do you see, Bales?"

Squinting into the howling, blowing grit that was now streaming down the street parallel to the ground, Barker allowed as how the clanging and banging they were currently hearing was due to the windmill from the Spencer place being blown straight down Main Street. This was soon followed by the Spencer place itself, intact and complete down to front porch and back barn. Leaning out farther and shielding his eyes as best he was able, the hotel owner could see that the street was cleared and vacant. As soon as the storm had struck, anyone with an ounce of common sense had retreated to the shelter of the nearest solid structure. Upper Main Street, the lifeline of the town, was completely deserted.

Looking in the other direction, with the wind now at his back, Barker saw that this was not entirely so.

All other mounts having fled or been driven away, a single horse remained on the street. He recognized it immediately as the one belonging to the mountain man. From the time Malone had rode up on his singular mount, its ancestry had been the subject of some discussion among those who had passed it by. Of dimensions proportionate to its owner, it was theorized to be part Percheron and part Appaloosa, with the rest derivative of an equine bloodline that remained resolutely indeterminate even among those townsfolk who considered themselves a good judge of such matters. There was also considerable discussion of the leather patch that was affixed to its forehead, as this appeared to cover a tumor or protruding bone the true identity of which curious onlookers were unable to discern from casual observation.

"Name's Worthless," the mountain man had announced while positioning the animal in front of the hitching rail. "Keep away from him. He can spit hard enough to knock a man down."

Though where this claim was concerned general dubiousness reigned, no one availed themselves of the opportunity to put it to the test. Now, as a wide-eyed Barker looked on, the horse slowly shifted its stance until it was facing away from the bellowing wind. By exposing only its hindquarters to the shrieking gale, it assured protection for its face and minimized its exposure to the flying dirt and sand. In his time Barker had seen many a horse's ass, not all of which were running for Congress, and as the walls of his hotel shuddered and trembled around him he had to admit that in the annals of equine butts the one that was presented to him now was of genuinely monumental proportions. It was an epic backside, a truly prodigious rear endone might even go far as to say Gibraltarian. And it defied the wind that had swept all else before it. All else except the horse and its owner.

Displaying a boldness that bordered on recklessness, Malone had stumbled out into the street. As an astonished Barker beckoned for his companions, one with forehead bandaged and the other clutching his medical bag, to join him, the mountain man turned deliberately to face directly into the wind. It seemed certain that if naught else, the wolf's-head cap he wore must surely be blown off and carried toward Pikes Peak, but nothing of the sort happened.

Perhaps because, though difficult to make out through the blowing dust and grit, it looked as if the drooping legs of the wolfskin had clamped down on the head and neck of their owner in order to hold on tight.

Facing down the tempest, Malone staggered a couple of times, coughed once, wiped his nose with the back of a treelike forearm, and inhaled. Continued to inhale. Sucked in air so that his chest, already barrel-like, expanded until it seemed to double in size. An openmouthed Doc Stanton avowed as how such an expansion was physically impossible. Unaware of the nearby physician's lightning-quick evaluation of his prodigious lung capacity, Malone proceeded to exhale directly into the teeth of the wind.

The hurricane that was blowing down the center of Main Street halted. It just stopped plum dead, as Doland pointed out. For a moment all was calm, quiet, peaceful as a Sunday morning on a September day. Malone horked up something unspeakable and spat it out, started to turn back to the hoteland flinched visibly as the wind resumed its assault. It had backed off, yes, but it had not gone away. It had not been defused or defeated. The mountain man's blow had sent it spinning, but not to eternity. Boreas still infused it, still drove it, still maintained it. It swirled, broke apart, regrouped, and bore down once more on the center of the helpless town.

Again Malone drew in an impossible quantity of air and again he exhaled right into the center of the gale. For a second time there was quiet, and for a second time the wind collated and re-formed itself to blast down the middle of the street. For a third time the indefatigable mountain man began to suck in an impossible breath preparatory to confronting the wind on its own terms. Only this time he managed but a partial volume before he broke down in a spasm of coughing. Giant though he was, he was a sick man, and the minor but still undeniable affliction from which he was suffering conspired to prevent him from mustering the full respiratory resolution of which he would ordinarily have been capable.

Lifting the defiant, coughing hulk off his booted feet, the full force of the enraged wind raised him into the air and blew him backward. Watching from the hotel doorway, a terrified Barker thought he could hear among the screaming gale an inhuman howl not unlike that of triumph.

Flung into the air and backward, Malone was forced to a last desperate tack. Stretching out one massive arm, he managed to catch hold of the reins dangling from his mount's bridle. As it took up the weight, Worthless's head snapped forward. Responding to the pull, the horse issued a slight, irritated snort from his nostrils. Otherwise he did not react, neither did he move. All four pillarlike legs seemed as firmly rooted to the earth as the iron footings of Mr. Eiffel's tower. Clutching the reins with one hand, the massive stretched-out form of Amos Malone whipped up and down above the ground like a flag over Montauk on the Fourth of July.

The frustrated, infuriated tempest tore at him, clawing at his body. But no matter how hard it blew, it could not dislodge his vise-like grip on his mount's reins. Neither could it so much as budge an indifferent Worthless from his casual stance. Bellowing wind continued to flow over and around a sprawling rump that was as solid and immobile as if it had been hewn from a block of Vermont granite.

Climbing horizontally into the wind, Malone pulled himself hand over hand toward his horse until he was once more able to stand on his own beside it. With his right fist gripping the pommel of the saddle, he steadied himself. Grim of mien, he was preparing to inhale and blow into the heart of the storm for yet a fourth time when the most peculiar expression crossed his face. His nose wrinkled up, his cheeks swelled, and his eyes began to water. His lower jaw dropped, rose, dropped again. As recognition dawned on the watching Barker, the hotel owner's own expression contorted. Throwing himself away from the now-doorless entrance, he scrambled crablike on hands and knees in the direction of the heavy walnut counter.

"Move!" he screeched above the roar of the wind and the dangerously loud rattle of barely standing walls. "If you value your life and future, take cover, take cover!"

An unquestioning Doc Stanton hurried to follow, not forgetting to bring along his precious medical bag as he scurried across the floor in the hotel owner's wake. Only a frowning Hearts Doland remained at the doorway, neither seeing nor understanding any rationale sufficient to inspire such panic and haste among his companions.

"Why?" he shouted at the rapidly retreating Barker. "What's changed that necessitates ...?"

He never finished his query. Or perhaps he did. It was impossible to tell, because his words and every other sound in the world were drowned out by the concussive force of Amos Malone's sneeze.

The mountain man's mind-boggling chuff erupted directly into the face of the onrushing wind and tore it to pieces. Stunned zephyrs whipped back and forth, too damaged to reconvene. Traumatized drafts wafted to and fro, seeking shelter of their own in crevices and alleyways until they too could dissipate privately into nothingness. Shattered, shaken, and shafted, the ghosts of winds past that had arrived in search of satisfaction and destruction vanished, elementally and totally banished to the realm of the Aeolian memories that had given them birth.

When he could hear again, when he could think again, a trembling Bales Barker rose to his feet from where he had taken shelter behind the hotel counter. Slightly steadier on his feet, a shaken Doc Stanton rose beside him. Together the two men stumbled slowly to the entrance of the building and peered tentatively outside.

Every window in every building in town was gone, blown in. Rolled up like balls of string, the carefully laid wooden slat sidewalks had all piled up like so many giant tumbleweeds in front of Mordecai Smith's Stable and Smithy at the far end of town. All the hitching posts were gone, as were the watering troughs. But the rest of the town appeared to have survived more or less intact.

Of Hearts Doland there was no sign. Having failed at the last to heed the hotel owner's warning, he had played a final gamble and lost.

Staggering outside, Barker was at once astonished and relieved to see that save for the loss of every window and a considerable quantity of decorative architectural bric-a-brac, the bulk of his establishment remained intact. All up and down the street, shaken citizens were emerging in ones and twos to take stock of their own establishments. In keeping with the general inexplicableness of the shocking occurrence, the church steeple was intact but the heavy iron bell that had come all the way from New England was missing, borne away as lightly as a leaf on an intruding breeze.

It was not many minutes thereafter that the two men encountered a face they did not recognize. This surprised them, as while sizable for one of its type, the population of the town was not so vast as to preclude knowledge of all its citizenry by each and every responsible inhabitant.

"That were something, weren't it?" Barker inquired conversationally of the unknown gentleman. "Never seen a wind like that. Never hope to again."

From the back of his horse, the man frowned. "What wind?"

The hotel owner and the doctor exchanged a look. "What do you mean, 'what wind?' sir? Can it be possible that someone was too soundly abed to have not been rudely jostled awake by the recent local apocalypse?"

The rider made a face. "Damned if I know what you two are on about. Are you daft? Been peaceable calm hereabouts nigh on a week now."

Stanton stepped forward. "Sir, I account myself a physician of some competence. Enough to know when I am awake and when I am drowsing in the grip of a dream. Setting even that knowledge aside, I and my friend can declare with the same certainty as should you that at this time of year this part of Colorado is never 'peaceable calm.'"

The other man drew back. "Now I know you two are daft." He looked around, squinting. "Or maybe you're right and I am too. Been through this part of Nebraska a dozen times before and never come upon this community. Don't know how I could've missed it."

With that he chucked the reins he was holding and, patently unsettled, continued on down the street. Barker and Stanton looked at each other. Of one mind, they commenced to search for a certain exceptionally large recent resident of the hotel owner's establishment in the hopes that worthy might could shed some light, or perhaps fresh air, on the unexpected conundrum with which they had suddenly been presented. Regrettably, they never again encountered him or his mount.

Both giant horse and giant rider were gone. Gone with the ghost wind.

As I've said, there is nothing, absolutely nothing, I like better than to pull together seemingly disparate elements into a cohesive story. For example: Mad Amos Malone, the California gold rush, a couple of tough Irish miners, Scandinavian gold-mining immigrants, and a real place and name. Oh yes, and a certain city in a distant state famed for its own gold discovery.

What made this tale so much fun to write was the collision of two different immigrant cultures, Scandinavian and Irish, with Malone acting, for a change, as not the protagonist but the intermediary. Settling conflicting miners' claims was a full-time job for some authorities during the gold rush. Who better to utilize his skills to prevent open warfare between such groups than Amos Malone?

Aside from the irritable Scandinavians and Amos himself, everyone else in the story is real and everything really did happen this way. There's just no mention of the, um, Scandinavians in the history books.

Heck, even Old Pancake was real.

CLAIM BLAME

This be *our* mountain and *our* mine and nobody digs here without *our* permission!"

Peter O'Riley turned beard and body to his partner, the mightily mustachioed Patrick McLaughlin, and then looked back down at the quartet of angry gnomes.

"Now, now, little friends, maybe we can work something out. What if we agreed to mine the strike for shares? Now, wouldn't that be lovely?"

"No shares. Not lovely." Norvalst, chieftain of the gnomes, wore suspendered pants, work boots, a long-sleeved white shirt woven of some coarse eldritch material, and a brown cap. His eyebrows were as white and heavy as his shirt, his mien uncompromising and foreboding, and his nose Herculean. His chest was broad, and downsized muscles bulged beneath the sleeves of his shirt.

O'Riley tried another tack. "We'll take just a quarter of the diggin's."

"No quarter. We give none and take none." A second gnome, stockier and even more muscular than his chief, stepped forward. He held a miniature iron pick, threateningly. "No shares. Our mountain, our mines."

"We'll throw in whiskey." O'Riley leaned over as far as he could go, until his lean jeaned form was all but face-to-face with the gnomic headman. "Lots of whiskey."

Tiny eyes nearly vanished beneath enormous ivory brows. "No whiskey!" His tone softened ever so slightly. "If you had some real *brännvin*, now ... No! No shares! Now *get off our mountain!*"

And with that he brought the flat of his small but surprisingly heavy shovel down square and hard on Peter O'Riley's right foot.

The miner stumbled back and howled as he grabbed at his insulted toes, but his yelp of pain wasn't half as loud as that of the battle cry of the gang of tetchy little men who now surged forward, swinging picks and hammers and shovels while shouting insults in several languages, a number of which had no honest counterpart among the nations of humankind. McLaughlin running and O'Riley hopping, the two men beat a hasty retreat down the rocky, scrub-covered slope. The enraged gnomes chased them past their diggings, through their unprepossessing camp, and halfway to the river before their anger finally subsided. At that point they broke off the pursuit and, picks and shovels a blur, seemed to melt back into the very ground itself.

His heart hammering against his ribs, McLaughlin bent over and fought to catch his breath. "Well, that's torn it. The little whoresons don't seem half-inclined to negotiation."

A gasping O'Riley nodded agreement. "'Tis mightily unreasonable they are bein', Pat. I say we toast their refusal with a few cans o' black powder and leave the sortin' out to the Almighty."

"Aye. But that might damage the pit. More work for us. And there be no guarantee it would loosen their grip. Or their determination to hold on to this piece of rock." He took a deep breath and considered the dry, uninhabited landscape. "Maybe we should try and hire us some help."

Still breathing hard, O'Riley stretched. Joints crackled like popcorn. His expression was grim, his tone washed with bitterroot. "Sure and now that's a fine idea, Pat. We'll just find ourselves a few of the locals and tell 'em we need their help drivin' a tribe o' tiny devils off our claim." Bending over, he held one hand palm facing downward until it was a foot off the hard ground. "This high they are, an' miners like ourselves. 'Tis naught but a wee inconvenience that we need help with." He straightened again. "We'd be laughed out o' the Sierras."

McLaughlin continued to gaze down the mountainside. "That be true enough, Peter. Though ... the last time we went into town for supplies, I heard tell of a gentleman lingering hereabouts who, if the whispers and tales about him are half to be believed, might be inclined to take the reality of our difficulties to heart and without scorn."

O'Riley sniffed. "One man? Did you not see the size of the little monsters' army? We need many guns to fight them, Pat. Guns aplenty, and men with no fear o' the unnatural to hold them back from using them. For this be no ordinary bit o' intervention we're dealin' with."

Still looking down the raw, rugged mountainside, McLaughlin stroked his mustache, the twin points of which drooped to below his chin. "Strange as it seems, Peter, I heard somewhat the same about this particular fellow."

"Well, good sor, we got gnomes, sor."

Sitting by the side of the creek that hemmed the little valley as prettily as a blue ribbon around the brim of a young girl's bonnet, the giant in the buckskins and leather puffed thoughtfully on his meerschaum as he contemplated both the stream and his visitors' problem. A wolf's-head cap covered but could not constrain the mad dash of black and gray hair that spilled out behind and to the sides. While McLaughlin waited patiently and O'Riley wondered if confronting this brooding accretion of undisciplined humanity was such a good idea, Amos Malone silently pondered water, greenery, rock, and infinity.

Eventually he turned and rose. And rose, and rose, until Peter O'Riley was convinced he and his partner had made a bad decision indeed. With a smile that materialized amid a vast flush of beard, Malone put them at ease.

"What kind o' gnomes?"

The supplicants exchanged a glance. McLaughlin spoke up. "Well now, Mr. Malone, sor, we don't rightly know, the classification of supernatural folk not bein' among our general store o' expertise."

"They're miners, sor," O'Riley put in. "Sittin' on our claim, they are, and won't get off. We offered them free shares in all our takings, we did, and they outright refused, resortin' to hostilities to force us off what's rightly ours."

Malone tapped the bowl of his pipe on a rock, checked the interior, then consigned it carefully to the depths of a pocket in his enormous shirt. McLaughlin could have sworn he heard the pale graven face on the pipe let out a small cough.

"Rightly yours?"

O'Riley didn't hesitate. "That be God's honest truth, sor. Worked that claim for weeks now, we have. Got the proper papers an' all. Had weak luck we did until Mother Fate took pity on us and all our hard work." He grinned, showing a miner's typical assortment of damaged orthodonture. "About to give up on the place, we was. Abandon the claim, as it were, when wouldn't you know we discovered that the bottom of the pit that we'd sunk merely to collect water for our rockers was layered with gold."

McLaughlin nodded confirmation. "Enough to make us rich right quick, it is. Or was, until these little men showed up an' drove us off our land. Off our own claim!"

"Talk like foreigners, too," O'Riley added darkly, conveniently discounting his own transatlantic origins.

"I see." Malone was walking toward his horse as he spoke, compelling the miners to follow. The mountain man's mount, McLaughlin observed, was of dimensions in keeping with that of Malone himself, though for the life of him the miner could not identify the elephantine breed. "And what is it exactly you fellers want of me?"

Once again the partners made eye talk. "There's whispering around these parts," McLaughlin began hesitantly, "that you, sor, are conversant with certain branches and aspects of knowledge that are denied the average man. Given our distressed circumstances, it

would seem that you would be the only one hereabouts in possession of sufficient education in such matters to cope with our unique
difficulty."

Malone looked back at the miner. As he did so, McLaughlin
could have sworn that the mountain man's wolf's cap peered down
at him as well.

"Gnomes." A far-off look came into Malone's eyes. "Don't much
care for 'em myself." His voice grew faint with reminiscence. "There
was thet time in Trondheim ..." Towering over the two men, he
nodded curtly. "Right, then. I reckon we can go and have a chat
with your gnomish interlopers. Ain't no harm in a friendly powwow,
even with gnomes. Beyond that I make no promises."

"That'd be fine, sor, that'd be just fine of you!" McLaughlin was
beaming, his partner still wary. "Now then, Mr. Malone, sor, if you
wish to discuss the matter of payment for your services ...? In truth
we're just poor hardscrabblers, but I swear we'll do our best to make
this right by you."

Again Malone flashed the broad smile that showed his teeth
were, if naught else, at least as impressive as the rest of him. "Let's
first see what it is exactly we're dealin' with here, gentlemen, and
then we'll speak to the doing o' good by it." Without another word
and displaying a surprising litheness of movement, he swung himself
up into the massive saddle. At this his mount looked back at him,
let out a disgusted snort, spat something at the ground that for just
the barest fraction of an instant lay smoking, and started off into
the hills. It occurred to O'Riley that though he had not seen
Malone pull on the reins, the horse had headed in the correct direction. A fluke, he thought as he and McLaughlin hurried to where
they had secured their own horses to a nearby tree. And no doubt
typical of Malone himself. The man seemed a collection of flukes,
not all of them necessarily benign.

Which, given the current situation he and his partner were
facing, might not be entirely a bad thing.

It was a late afternoon when they finally arrived back at their
diggings. To the miners' great relief, nothing appeared to have been
disturbed. Their tent still stood, and the rest of their meager

belongings and supplies remained where they had been left. As for the pit itself, that sainted glory-hole-to-be, as near as they could tell it had not been filled in or otherwise damaged. Except for some scattered brush, the slope where they had been working so hard was still barren and unappealing. It mattered not. That which was truly worthwhile lay below ground and out of sight. But not, hopefully, for long.

Dismounting, Malone studied his immediate surroundings. The slope was crusted with gravel and broken rock, like crumbs on a coffee cake. Of the miners' tiny tormentors there was no sign, a fact which he immediately pointed out to his anxious hosts.

"No need to concern yourself on that score, Mr. Malone, sor." McLaughlin was solemn in the face of expectation. "We know how to summon them forth."

With that he and his partner set to work, using bucket and winch to draw water as well as gravel and sand from the pit, dumping it in the big rocker and working it through, cursing all the while. As soon as they finished they presented the rocked batch for Malone's inspection.

"See the gold, sor!" O'Riley did not try to hide his excitement and enthusiasm. "Almost washes itself out if not for all the blue-black glar that surrounds it. Clogs the rocker that muck does, and just makes for more work."

Malone nodded sagely. "Gold it is, my friend. You two have struck it fair."

"Nothing fair about it!" The voice that interrupted was high-pitched but insistent.

The mountain man turned. Where a moment earlier had been only scrub-laden hillside there now stood a mass of small menfolk. Armed with the tools of their trade, they glared ominously at the intruders. Before Malone could respond, O'Riley was replyingwhile being careful to remain behind the bigger man and keeping his feet well out of shovel range.

"Sure an' we're back, you little bugger-mothers! You say this is your mountain. Well, we've brought a mountain of our own!"

The leader of the gnomes tilted his head back to gaze up at the hireling. And back, and back, until his small thick neck could abide no further inclination. Malone reacted by kneeling before him. Though appreciative of this courtesy, the chief let out a small but distinct grunt of disapproval.

"Matters not how big you be, sir. There are many of us, and should you choose to interfere in this private matter, we will cut you down to size as quickly as we can dig and shore a cross-tunnel."

"Now then, *hövding*, there be no need for threatening here." Malone gestured back to where the two miners stood watching, at once fascinated and fearful. "Let's talk this out in the manner of a proper *stämma* and see if we can't come to a conclusion that leaves all parties equally satisfied and content."

The chief's enormous eyebrows rose in surprise. "You know a little of the truespeak! What manner of man be you?"

"A mannered one, I reckon. These fellers say this 'ere mine is theirs. I don't expect they need the whole mountain t' satisfy their claim." He squinted upslope. "Seems to me there's plenty o' room fer all of you. They say they've filed right and proper papers to this place."

"That's right!" Coming forward, O'Riley pulled from his shirt pocket a sheet of paper that he proceeded to unfold and thrust first at the gnome, then at Malone. "All registered correct, as any fool can plainly see. No matter his size."

The mountain man smiled thinly. "Perhaps best not to inject matters o' size into this discussion, Mr. O'Riley."

"Pagh!" Turning, the gnome made a short, sharp gesture. One of his tribe promptly scurried forth. Slighter in build than the majority of his fellows, he wore a red cap with a bent peak and thick glasses. From within a multitude of pockets in his oversized jacket, he drew forth a scroll. This he proceeded to unroll until it stretched from his ink-stained fingers past his chief, past Malone, past the two startled miners, past the assembled horses, and another ten yards down the mountainside before the end finally came to rest against a creosote bush.

The chieftain of the gnomes punctuated this presentation with a derisive sniff. "*Our* claim deed."

"Now wait a minute ...!" McLaughlin began. But Malone had already begun to read the extensive document.

How he could discern the tiny print, much less make sense of the lines of gibberish that to O'Riley looked like nothing more than chicken scratches, neither miner could imagine. With a speed that astonished even the gnomes, the mountain man had soon scanned the entire lengthy document. Having concluded his unnaturally swift perusal, he handed the mass of paper back to the care of the gnomish clerk, who, muttering under his breath, entered into the arduous task of rerolling it.

"Their deed," he informed the two restless miners, "appears to be in order."

Barely restraining his outrage, O'Riley shook their own deed at the diminutive chieftain. "Sure an' 'tis enough o' this! Where's it registered, huh? Ours comes right and true from the territorial agency in Genoa! Where's *his* registered?"

The chief folded his stubby but powerful arms and replied defiantly. "Asgard."

McLaughlin sniffed disdainfully. "Ain't never heard o' no Asgard, Nevada Territory."

"Nonetheless," Malone told him, "they have a legitimate claim." He looked back at the chieftain and his assembled prickly tribe. They were just itching for a fight. You could smell it. Nor were they put off by Malone's size. Such a reaction was to be expected, he knew, of folk who spent their considerable lives underground while hewing their way through solid rock. Rising from his crouch, he turned and headed in the direction of his mount. Equally anxious, the two miners followed close on his heels, clinging to him like remoras to a shark.

"Sor! Mr. Malone, sor," McLaughlin exclaimed, "you're not leavin' us now, are you? You promised to help."

Checking the straps on his saddlebags, Malone looked down at him. "I said I'd come and have a look-see at your problem. That I have done. I did not know that your rival claimants also had a deed. It would appear to me, fellers, that you have a situation here. One that is on your hands, not mine."

"But what are we to do?" O'Riley was wringing his hands. "We'd fight them, but though they be small there be many of them." A throbbing in his right big toe brought uncomfortable remembrance to the fore. "They have weapons."

Malone seemed to hesitate. Then he stopped what he was doing and turned back to the two men. Behind him, his mount rolled its eyes and neighed disgustedly.

"I'll not get in the middle of a fight where both sides have a claim to right, wrong, and gold. But though I'll not engage in any fighting, I did say I would help if I could, and so it shall be." Removing a round, fist-sized green bottle from one saddlebag, he began to retrace his steps toward the diggings. Gleeful as schoolboys, the miners followed. Desperate to maintain the flow of conversation, McLaughlin gestured at the bottle.

"As pretty a piece of crystal as a lady's perfume container, sor. Where be the cut glass from? New York? Paris?"

"No place whose name you'd know," Malone informed him. "And 'tis not glass. It's an emerald."

The miner expressed surprise. "Do you mean to say, sor, that that there bottle is made of emeralds?"

"No. I said it *is* an emerald."

In front of them on the far side of the camp, the gnomish throng still waited. At the return of the miners and the mountain man, small, callused hands tightened determinedly on the hardwood shafts of picks and shovels. Hard rock chisels were drawn from belts and readied to be used as knives. Shovels were pointed sharp edge outward toward the three approaching humans.

Malone halted well short of the impending confrontation. Having seen the hexagonal-barreled Sharps slung across the back of Malone's mount, O'Riley was surprised the mountain man had not brought the enormous gun with him. Perhaps, he thought, the giant was intending to do battle solely with the LeMat pistol holstered at his belt. In truth, Malone had no intention of employing either weapon. He turned to confront the uneasy miners.

"Now then, you happy sons of the Auld Sod, I'm goin' t' need a smidgen of your blood." Subsequent to which declaration of intent he removed from his belt a bowie knife that in size would not have been out of place among the flailing swords at Agincourt. Noting the untrammeled shock on the faces of the two men, Malone hesitated a moment, realized his mistake, and smiled sheepishly.

"Sorry, fellers. I was fer a moment distracted." To the great relief of the miners, he replaced the enormous blade in its sheath and fumbled in several pockets before withdrawing a pencil-sized length of steel that gleamed in the setting sun. "This here's a mite better fer the purpose, I reckon. Not to mention fer your constitution."

Stepping forward, he placed the business edge of the scalpel against O'Riley's thumb and drew back the blade with a precision and delicacy of touch that would have drawn the admiration of Boston's finest surgeons. Anticipating the cut, the miner grimaced but did not cry out. Turning to the nervous McLaughlin, Malone repeated the action. Then he stepped back.

"Hold out your thumbs and let the blood fall upon the land you claim as your own. *Do it now!*"

The booming command was enough to focus the miners' attention and they hastened to comply. Bright red blood dripped from the twin cuts to stain the dry earth. Removing the stopper from the bottle he had brought with him, Malone poured the green contents onto the ground, where it mixed with the miners' blood. A glutinous mist began to form. Taking a tentative sniff, McLaughlin was surprised to find that the fog smelled of clover. Raising his other enormous arm over his head, Malone seemed to strike the darkening sky as he thundered.

"Talamh seo éileamh againn, is é seo óir linne, deirimid an fhóid Auld!"

The strange words meant nothing to McLaughlin, but O'Riley's eyes grew wide. He hadn't heard the original language of his people spoken since as a child he had come to the New World with his parents. The liquid vowels sang in his ears as the mountain man's invocation echoed off the stony hillsides. The mass of gnomes drew back a step or two, but they did not flee.

A low, ominous cloudbank was coalescing, taking shape between them and the miners. It was damp and ichorous and shot through with green lightning. Behind the men the miners' horses stamped, whinnied, and rolled their eyes as they fought to stampede. Meanwhile Malone's mount mustered a single squint-eyed glance in the direction of the crackling, boiling cloud, shook his head, and returned to placidly cropping the sparse ground cover as if nothing was amiss with the world.

When at last the furious lightning ceased flashing and the final echo of thunder rolled into the distance, the cloudbank dissipated to reveal ... a second host of small men. But their beards, which were varied and profuse and in general more thoroughly combed, tended to blond and black rather than gnomish white. Instead of attire suitable for digging, their garments tended to the loose and colorful. This fashion extended to their hats, which were equally as diverse as their facial hair, but not to their boots, which were universally black.

McLaughlin might not have remembered the Gaelic of his family, but for anyone who hailed from the old country there was no mistaking the identity of the multitude of newcomers.

"Sure and beggora," he declared breathily, "but they cannot be anything but leprechauns!"

"Leprechauns." Standing beside his partner, O'Riley was no less dazed by the manifestation. "No, it cannot be." Whereupon one standing in the forefront of the diminutive newcomers turned, strode directly toward the two men, and promptly whacked the hesitant miner's right foot with the stout and finely carved shillelagh he carried.

"Who cannot be, ye daft mental malingerer!" Whirling to find himself confronted by Malone, the pint-sized combatant raised black eyebrows that terminated in neatly coiffed points. "Mother Macrie, 'tis the giant who built the causeway!" Taking a deep whiff of the mountain man, he wrinkled up a considerable nose. "And with a pong to match the rest o' him!"

"Bear grease." Malone was apologetic. "Good for healin' cracked heels."

"Gah!" Retreating several steps, the taoiseach of the leprechauns pointedly waved a hand back and forth in front of his face. "For what mysterious end have ye have drawn us unwilling and in haste to this godforsaken place, monster?"

Malone nodded toward the staring, openmouthed miners. "Two o' your ex-countrymen need your help in a matter o' land use."

"Land use, 'tis it?" Forcing himself to ignore the piquant fragrance rising from the vicinity of the mountain man's feet, the stocky green-clad figure tapped his open palm with the shillelagh. "A problem with the English again?"

"Not exactly." Turning, Malone indicated the throng of watching gnomes. "Your relations have a small mine on this here land. These knäckebröd-eating immigrants from the northeast likewise claim it as their own and are uncommon insistent on keepin' it all fer themselves."

"Are they now? A mine, you say?" Malone nodded. "And why should me and the rest of the boyos get ourselves involved in a dispute between manoffspring o' Erin though they beand mice?"

"Say there now, stranger ..." began the chief of the gnomes. But the rest of his words were drowned out by a desperate McLaughlin.

"We'll pay you!" The miner spoke without hesitation. "We knowI rememberthat your kind is fond of gold. We have gold. In *our* mine." Raising a hand, he pointed toward the pit.

"Gold now, is it?" The dark eyes of the leprechaun taoiseach glittered. "'Tis hardly fair to tempt a leprechaun with gold. But in this instance we'll let it pass." He straightened as much as his foot-high body would allow. "Sure an' we'll help you then, boyos. We'll save your claim for you and leave with nothing but a fair share of the shiny stuff, no more than is needed to fill a few kettles."

O'Riley found himself suddenly reluctant, but the two miners conversed and came to an agreement, for, as McLaughlin pointed out, what choice did they have? Having taken stock of the matter, the giant mountain man was clearly inclined to wash his hands of it. They would have to engage supernatural help from the old country or none at all.

"It's a bargain, then." McLaughlin stuck out his hand and O'Riley matched him a second later, but by that time the *Taoiseach* of the green-clad visitants had already raised his shillelagh high above his head and was leading a raucous charge in the direction of the waiting gnomes.

What a fabulous confusion there thence ensued! What a furor, a fight, what a conflagration of physical confrontation! The hills were alive with the sound of cursing, in Gaelic and Norse and half a dozen other tongues not utilized in such scandalous fashion since the old gods fled the noisome proximity of a fecund humanity for the peace and contentment of an otherworldly retirement among the clouds. Sticks and shovels clashed, knees were raised, heads were butted, and butts were kicked. There was punching and screaming and biting and insulting on a scale all out of proportion to the size of those doing the wielding, and more than once 'twas the words and not the weapons that inflicted the deepest damage.

Keeping well clear of the downsized but decidedly ferocious mayhem that was taking a steady toll on small arms, legs, faces, torsos, and groins, Peter O'Riley and Patrick McLaughlin looked on with trepidation lest the fury on the mountainside expand to include and overwhelm the boulder behind which they had taken precipitous refuge. Meanwhile an estimably nonchalant Amos Malone built a fire and made supper.

The fighting surged back and forth past sunset and on into the night with neither side being able to gain an advantage. There was a fair amount of blood, a lot of bruising and contusing, but no deaths among the hardy and determined combatants. It was only when the upper half of a shattered shillelagh smashed into his campfire and upset his coffeepot, thus causing the pungent contents to spill out upon the surrounding rocks, where they dissolved several chunks of quartz-laden granite, that Malone finally had enough.

"Sure an' he's up!"

"Whawhat?" O'Riley blinked tiredly, having fallen asleep despite the noise of the boisterous conflict.

"The mountain man. He's up." McLaughlin pointed. "Maybe he's finally goin' to do something."

The other miner rubbed at his eyes. "Don't see why he didn't in the first place. Big as he is, I expect if he wanted to he could flatten the lot of 'em, both sides."

McLaughlin was nodding agreement. "I dunno what stopped 'im. Scruples or somethin'."

Ignoring the blizzard of flying wood and mining implements, Malone waded into the thick of the fighting. From time to time an addled leprechaun or disoriented gnome would mistakenly take a swing at him. Shilleleghs bounced off ironlike legs and set their owners to vibrating helplessly, as did shovels and hammers. One swarthy gnome who did his best to drive the point of his pickaxe into a gargantuan thigh found the tip bent in half by long-worn leather so infused with sweat, animal fat, and impregnated meteoric dust that the pants were as stiff and hard as Galahad's armor.

"NOW LOOK HERE!"

It was a command that rumbled and reverberated across the battleground, raced avalanchelike down the slope, and sufficiently unsettled a pair of wandering grizzlies so badly that they fell all over themselves in their haste to flee the immediate neighborhood. Fighting halted immediately as each and every undersized combatant turned to look in the direction from whence the bellowing had arisen.

Malone's voice dropped from the apocalyptic to the merely stentorian. "It's plain clear that this ain't goin' nowhere and it's gettin' there fast. I said I wouldn't take no sides in this here fracas and I intend to keep true to my words. But there's been enough bashin' and thrashin' this night fit to unsettle half a dozen worlds, and it's time 'twas settled." Searching the battlefield, he sought out and found the *hövding* of the gnomes.

"I've a proposition for you and your tribe, sir, if you'll lend me an ear."

"Well ..." His chubby face dirty and streaked and a deep bruise showing on one arm, the gnome chieftain gripped his left ear and began to bring up the cold chisel he held in his other hand.

"No, no," Malone said quickly. "Just heave to and give a listen." The chief lowered the chisel.

"Now then," the mountain man began, "at heart this is all about gold...."

"Sure and ain't it always." Having come up behind him, the leader of the leprechauns was paying close attention.

"What if," Malone continued, still addressing himself to the gnomish chieftain, "I promised to send you and your fellows to a place where there's more gold than is to be found on your claim here? A place where folks like these"—and with a gesture he indicated the two distant but not disinterested miners—"won't bother you fer a while, at least. A place where you can mine away t' your mean-spirited little hearts' content?"

The chief considered. It was a bold and generous offer, to be sure. That was, if in truth it was more than just a promise. He studied the hulking mountain man closely.

"And if we should accept, who be you, sir, to carry out such an audacious enterprise?"

"I am Amos Malone."

The chief of the gnomes started visibly. "I've heard of you. Even down in the deep dirt, that name ..."

"Rings fondly?" Malone opined.

"Nay. Sets off alarms." White brows drew together. "It's said even in Nifelheim that you are quite mad."

"I occasionally get upset, 'tis true." Malone wished for the pleasure of his pipe, but now was not the time to break away for a smoke. "But I hold to my word. Will you and yours break off this futile conniption and accept my proposal?"

The chief paused, then turned and moved to rejoin the mass of his fellows. There followed a good deal of gnomish disputation, at the conclusion of which the chieftain returned to the waiting Malone and stuck out a thickly callused hand.

"'Tis a bargain then. *If* you can deliver your side of it."

"A bargain set." Malone straightened. Tilting back his head, he studied the sky, inhaled deeply of the air, felt carefully of the ground with his booted feet. He was *here*. They needed to be *there*. The projected transposition had to be voluntary on the part of those being sent, otherwise he could have tried it earlier. But he disliked involving himself in mass transplantations. They tended to induce colic.

Stepping clear of the assembled little people, he once again raised an arm: the left one this time. As he declaimed he waved his hand toward the mob of watching gnomes. The result was to dust them with a sprinkling of clotted bear fat and jerked deer meat with a pinch of eagle feather added for thaumaturgic seasoning. Whether one happened to be conversant with transcendental auguries or not, this would not have struck a casual onlooker as a particularly efficacious combination.

"Gnome långt hemifrån, flyga till guld, tid att ströva."

A white cloud appeared. Broad and capacious, it descended slowly to cover the assembled gnomes until at last it reached the ground. The last thing O'Riley and McLaughlin saw of their gnomish tormentors was the chief, glaring at them and threatening murder and dismemberment if Malone failed to follow through on his promise. Then the cloud, like a prime San Francisco fog, lifted and was gone. With it went the gnomes, down to the last sharpened pick and pointed cap.

"You did it!" McLaughlin sprinted to the mountain man's side. "They're gone. They're really gone."

"Wouldn't have believed it if I hadn't seen it with me own two eyes." O'Riley would have broken out in a jig but he was too emotionally and physically exhausted.

"And now, sirs, if 'tis all right with you, we will be collectin' our pay for doin' the fightin' that led to this happy conclusion." With that the Taoiseach of the leprechauns was off to give orders to his green-clad troops. The lot of them were soon busy bustling over the miners' pit.

Ögrad stood beside his chief, his eyes wild with anger.

"He's cheated us! The great lumbering smelly man has cheated us!" With one short, thick arm he gestured at the wild ocean before them. "This is no new habitation, but home!"

"Nay, stand and consider a moment." Novalst, the chief, gestured at the white-capped sea beside which he and his tribe had been deposited. "This is not our ancient coast. Smell. Drink deep of it. It is not the same. The land is similar, the climate familiar, the sea alike, yet all are different."

Reluctantly, his second-in-command complied. As he did so, some, but not all, of his initial fury faded. "So. I concede the point. Another sea it is. But of gold I smell naught."

"It is here. It is here." Novalst turned a slow circle. "I can feel it."

At that moment several of their companions came running toward them. In their cupped hands they held sand taken from the nearby beach. Among the particles of quartz and feldspar were flecks and nodules of ... gold.

Novalst looked upon this wonder and was pleased. Even Ögrad experienced a deeply felt change of heart. "I am ashamed. The giant was not merely true to his word: he bested it. Who could think of such a thing? A beach full of gold!" Turning, he surveyed the frozen, barren landscape that was so like that of their ancestral home. "This will make a fine place to live. And no humans."

"No." Kneeling, Novalst picked up some of the gold-rich sand that had been deposited there and let it trickle free between his fingers. "But they will come. Sooner or later they will come here. Humans always find such places. Yet this I predict: The first of them will be men who know and respect us, and so will not interfere with our dwelling underground in this land. Others will follow and settle here, and though they know us not will call it after us." Rising, he spread his arms wide, ignoring the chill Arctic wind that was whipping his shirt around him.

"This place will be known as the City of the Gnome!"

As black kettle after black kettle was lifted from the pit, the unsettling sensation that had started in the pits of the miners' stomachs grew progressively more discomfiting.

"A lot of gold they're taking out." A patently unhappy O'Riley was chewing on his lower lip as he followed the procedure.

"An awful lot," agreed his partner edgily.

"Their 'fair share.'" Having relit his pipe, Malone gazed down at the two men. "You agreed. Unless both of you wish a shillelagh up your respective fundaments, I wouldn't interfere. Also, I've seen the blight an' sickness these folk can inflict on those who cross 'em."

"What?" McLaughlin could not help himself. "What happens to those who do?"

"Why, they find themselves transformed, forever to dwell ill and afflicted among those whom they have tried to cheat." The tiny fires of Hell bristled in the bowl of his pipe. "They become leperchauns."

The late-rising moon was still in ascent when the last of the enchanted little people from the old country paid their farewells. Tired and sore but demonstrably content, the Taoiseach confronted Malone where he was seated by his campfire.

"'Twas an experience as unique as it was unexpected to be called hither by you, Amos Malone. *A rud is annamh is iontach.*"

Malone smiled pleasantly. "I quite agree. 'That which is strange is wonderful.'"

"One would almost think you had a bit o' the green in you yourself. "

"I am a reservoir to all shades of magick," the mountain man told him. "When I ain't skinnin' beaver, that is." He nodded toward the other side of the fire, which blazed no less bright than the lights at the bottom of his jet-black eyes. "Best to tell your people over there thet Worthless ain't fer stealin'. Couple o' your boyos already tried when I was busy seein' off your northlander counterparts."

The leprechaun was mightily offended. "Sir, you accuse my men of attempted theft? I withdraw my compliment, sir!"

Malone shrugged. "As you will. While you're at it, you might withdraw the last o' your innocents from Worthless's immediate environs. I'm afraid not all o' them escaped his attentions."

Uncertain, the leprechaun leader beckoned for several of his followers to join him. None offered an apology, but when the enormous equine lifted his right front foot off the ground and revealed what was stuck to the bottom of his hoof, they set to work scraping off the greenish remains with uncommon alacrity.

The last of them had vanished when a cry rang out from the vicinity of the mine pit. Peter O'Riley's anguished wail rose above the crackle of Malone's fire and the sounds of the night.

"Gone! It's all gone! They've taken everything!" Then he was charging down the hillside toward Malone. McLaughlin tried but was unable to stop his partner from getting right up in the mountain man's face, the smell notwithstanding.

"You son of a bitch! You let them take all our gold! All that trouble and fighting, for nothing! We'd have been better off dealing with the gnomes ourselves. We could've given them ninety percent share and still been better off than this! *Go hlfreann leat!*"

Throughout the full length of the miner's diatribe, Malone had continued staring at the fire. Now he lifted his gaze. What the irate miner saw there made him draw back behind his fury.

"I'd calm down if I were you, friend. It's said that too much anger can be bad fer a man's health. As fer your suggestion, I've already been to Hell and back, thank you very much."

McLaughlin was pulling his friend away now, to one side of the fire, and trying desperately to settle him down. Realizing he had no real hope of taking out his frustration on the giant mountain man and that it didn't matter anyway now that the gold was gone, O'Riley fell to sobbing.

"Gone. All gone. Spirited back to the old country in a damn lot o' kitchen pots, no less. And us that set it all in motion left with nothing."

"I wouldn't say that." Malone rose. "You still have your claim. I reckon there's still some gold in it."

Pushing away his partner's attempts at comfort, an unashamed O'Riley wiped at his eyes. "All the easy gold's gone. Taken by that lot o' unscrupulous green midgets. Nuggets an' dust just lyin' there in the water at the bottom o' the pit, waitin' t' be scooped up, an' they surely did the scoopin'. What's left, if anything, is for hard rock mining, for them that has the resources."

"Or the will." Malone had walked over to his horse and was making preparations to depart. McLaughlin could have sworn the empty coffeepot hopped up into an open saddlebag all by itselfbut then, it was dark now. "You two can do it, if you've the backbone. Get a loan, hire help, do the work. The difficult work." His tone hardened. "Instead o' tryin' t' bring out gold with buckets and wishes."

"Oh, sure an' 'tis easy for you to say." Though not as impetuous, McLaughlin was no less upset than his partner. "Do you know what hard rock mining entails, Mr. Malone?"

"Tough work. Dedication. Drive." The mountain man paused. "Or I reckon you could sell out t' someone who has those qualities you seem to find so elusive."

"Right." A despondent O'Riley laughed. "Who'd be fool enough to buy a claim from which the easy gold has been taken and the rest o' which is a mess of rocker-ruining blue-black muck? He'd have to be half-crazy."

"Got just the man for you." Malone mounted up. "Old Pancake."

McLaughlin frowned. "T.P.? You're right, he is half crazy." He shook his head. "Buy out this gutted claim? What a load!"

"Couldn't've put it better myself, Mr. McLaughlin. Work it yourself or sell out. 'Tis up to you, as life is to any man. Meanwhile you might have a closer look at your blue-black glar."

"Huh!" O'Riley spat. But sideways, careful to lead with the liquid well away from the mountain man. "Reckon we might as well entertain offers, if anyone's loony enough to actually be interested."

"A man's life teeters on such choices." Once again Malone did nothing to the reins yet his animal began to move as if he had been clearly instructed. Or perhaps had decided to start off on his own. The two miners watched as the enigmatic mountain man disappeared over a ridge, his departure silhouetted by the moon as he passed in front of it. Or maybe over it.

To the end of their days they could never decide which.

Here's another tall tale about an immigrant to the American West. A story that also takes place in a real town, in a real building. Not a farmer, this particular immigrant, nor a hardscrabble miner, nor a railroad worker, nor a thief. An individual you'd probably greet warmly, just as you yourself would be greeted. Made to feel welcome, you would be. Made to feel important, and powerful, and sky-screamingly triumphant. From this immigrant you would sense the power of something special at work.

Just be sure you understand who you're dealing with. And if things don't go well, you'd best retain enough of your wits about you so that you can explain, as much as you're able, what transpired. That is, if you're not too embarrassed to do so. Or too weakened. Or too dead.

As in "Claim Blame," a fair number of the locations and personalities in this story actually existed, as did the problems described herein. Just not always in the way the history texts relate them. Where history is concerned, certain details always seem to get left out of the final telling. Perhaps because, sometimes, they don't seem sufficiently real to qualify as fact. Not unlike Amos Malone himself.

It's true Malone had a distinctive manner of speech and that sometimes he scrambled his language. But at least he didn't suffer a scrambling like the poor fella in this story.

HOLY JINGLE

San Francisco was beautiful in the spring, Malone reflected as he and his horse, Worthless, ambled toward town. Unfortunately, the town was Carson City, Nevada. Wild, seductive San Francisco still lay many days' ride to the west, over the imposing crest of the Sierra Nevada. Malone didn't brood over the time required, however. He would get there soon enough. He always got there, wherever *there* happened to be.

Heading down the last bit of forested hill into the city proper, they were closely watched by a pack of gray wolves. Lying in wait for something small, opportune, and filling, the wolves instead glimpsed Malone and Worthless and, so glimpsing, held their peace. Wolves are intelligent critters, and this pack no less so than the average. Or maybe it was the wolf's-head cap that Malone wore that caused them to shy off, or the fact that the cap turned to look at them with glowing eyes. Instead of the howls of outrage that might have been expected to resound from the pack upon encountering such a sight, there arose from the cluster of predators little more than a few intimidated whimpers. Also, one or two peed themselves.

It had to be admitted that there wasn't much *there* to Carson City, but its civilized surrounds were a considerable improvement over the vast desert wilderness Malone had just crossed. He was tired and thirsty and hungry and thirsty and sleepy and thirsty. Leaning forward, he gave his mount an encouraging pat on the side of its massive neck.

"Oats a-comin', Worthless. Oats and a soft straw bed. Enough o' the former so's you won't be tempted t' eat the latter, like you did that time in St. Louis."

As the steed of impressive size and indecipherable breed turned its head to look back at Malone, the mountain man noted that the leather strap across the animal's snout was bulging again. *Have to attend to that,* he told himself. Wouldn't do to get the locals gossipin'.

Room and stable stall arranged, Malone repaired to the bar in the front of the hotel, sequestering his odiferous enormity at the dimly lit far end of the counter so as not to unduly panic the other patrons. The husky mustachioed bartender with the wide impressionist apron waited upon him with good cheer, which the mountain man downed steadily and in copious quantities.

That was where Hank Monk found him. The stagecoach driver noted the impressive number of empty bottles arrayed like so many tenpins on the wooden bar in front of the slumped-over giant, carefully appraised the looming imbiber's degree of sobriety, and determined to embark on the potentially risky business of conversation. While the whip was somewhat smaller than the average man and Malone a bit larger than the average bear, the driver was possessed of the surety of someone who made his living guiding rickety, rattling coaches pell-mell down ungraded mountainsides. He was cautious but not intimidated as he cleared his throat.

"Have I the pleasure of addressing Mr. Amos Malone?"

Thundercloud brows drew together and eyes like mouths of Dahlgren cannons swiveled round to regard the supplicant. "Don't know as how many folks regard it as a pleasure, but unless there be another hereabouts sportin' the same nameplate, I'm him."

Monk smiled politely. "I have heard it tell that you are a bit mad." The man seemed fully prepared to chuckle or bolt for the front door, depending on the response.

The giant shrugged, the action jostling his expansive salt-and-pepper beard. "So have I."

"But not to your face." Monk stroked his own, far more neatly trimmed, beard. "It would take a brave man to say that."

"More usual-like they're addled. I ignore all thet they say. Actually, the entire species is crazy. Mr. Darwin failed to note that observation in his book. I called him on it but have yet to receive the courtesy of a reply."

This response, like the name Darwin, held no especial meaning to the stage driver, so Monk continued with his petition. "I would beg your assistance in a small matter of considerable urgency, Mr. Malone."

Turning away, the mountain man picked up a bottle with a particularly garish label rich with Spanish words of false promise, and proceeded to down the remaining quarter liter. This explained, Monk now understood, the absence of glasses on the bar.

"I don't much cotton to beggin'."

Monk pursed his lips thoughtfully. "Well then, I'll pay you."

Malone set down the empty bottle. "Better."

"I'm presently a bit low on ready cash." Monk dug into a vest pocket. "But I'll give you this."

Intrigued, Malone turned sideways and leaned forward to inspect the pocket watch. It was beautifully engraved and chased with raised images of horses and a coach. "A fine example o' the timekeeper's art, Mr. Monk. Real gold, too."

Monk looked proud. "Was given to me by Mr. Horace Greeley of New York, for getting him on time to a meeting in Placerville everyone said he couldn't make. I'll give it to you in return for your help." He nodded at the timepiece. "Worth five or six hundred dollars, I'm told."

Malone examined the watch a moment longer before handing it back. "I reckon you've used that watch as collateral in more than one dealing, Mr. Monk, and I expect there'll come a time you'll need it again. What need is so desperate, then, that you'd be willin' to hand it over to a stranger like myself with no guarantee o' receiving its worth in return?"

"I've a shipment to deliver to California and gold to bring back. The only man in either state who I trust to ride shotgun messenger on such a trip is John Barrel. He has been rendered indisposed by an affliction for which I am unable to find a cure. From what I've heard whispered and rumored, Amos Malone might be the one man with the wherewithal to bring him back to his duties."

"I see." Half-hidden beneath the lower lip of the wolf's-head cap, furrows appeared in the granitic prominence of the mountain man's forehead. "And would there be a name fer the nature o' this affliction?"

Monk nodded curtly. "Love. Or more properly in this instance, infatuation. One so fast and unbreakable that poor John appears unable to move from the proximity of the woman who has caught him fast." The driver's expression darkened. "A woman of the East, no less."

"New York?" Malone mused aloud. "Chicago? Dare I say Boston?"

Monk shook his head sharply. "Would that it were so, Mr. Malone, would that it were so. The East to which I refer is at once less and more civilized than those fine upstanding American cities. There are over a thousand Chinee in Carson City, sir, and this woman is of that country that supplies to us both labor and mystery. She has enchanted my friend, Mr. Malone. Bewitched him from the blond curls of his young forehead to the accumulated fungus between his toes. No argument, no logic, no reason or threat or promise of wealth has proven sufficient to bestir him from her quarters. I am not the only one who finds it more than passing strange. If there is not more to this than the straightforward draw of the loins, sir, I'll gnaw the hindquarters off a northbound polecat!"

Malone considered. "If your need be so urgent, and the attraction so unambiguous, why not go with a few armed companions and drag him out by the heels?"

"I thought to do just that, sir, but this woman has friends and a respected employer. Somehow, she commands others with words as

well as with movement, to the point that those who might help find
themselves dissuaded in her company and depart her presence
wondering what became of their senses. I have felt a touch of it
myself. The sensation is akin to drunkenness, but without the
vomiting. Also, it smells strongly of jasmine."

The mountain man sighed and turned back to his drinking.
Monk looked on anxiously. As the whip teetered on the cusp of
certainty that his appeal had failed, Malone turned back to him
once more and rose. He had been slumping on his bar stool in a
courteous attempt to somewhat mute his mass, and, now, standing,
his head nearly scraped the ceiling. Conversation in the room grew
quiet, as though an unearthly presence had suddenly made itself
known.

The djinn was out of the bottle, Monk realized. Or rather, out of
the bottles. There was no backing down now. It occurred to the
driver only briefly to flee. He was a brave man, having in the course
of his employment faced down everything from starving cata-
mounts to desperate bandits. All these paled, however, in the
shadow of the immense and ripely unwashed simian shape that now
stood, swaying ever so slightly from having ingested a truly phenom-
enal quantity of liquor, before him.

"Let's go and see if we kin speak some sense t' your pal, Mr.
Monk. I make no promises. Of all the drugs that befuddle a man's
senses, love is by far the strongest."

"Stronger even than, dare I say, sex?" Monk inquired as the room
cleared precipitously before them.

Malone stared solemnly down at the driver. "We have yet to
ascertain under which particular affliction your friend reposes. Does
he say nothing of his circumstances?"

"I've not seen him in weeks, sir, and despite my most sincere
efforts have succeeded in drawing no closer than the door to the
rooms where he now resides. I did not see him, and could hear him
shouting but one thing over and over before I was summarily
ejected. 'Holy jingle!' he kept bawling. 'Holy jingle!'"

"Interesting," declared Malone as the two men, one traveling in the umbra of the other, exited the bar. "If naught else, we can believe that whatever has inveigled him is nothing if not costly."

The building to which Monk brought him in the open buckboard was one of the more substantial structures in Carson City. Several stories tall, it was fashioned of local stone and boasted fine glass windows imported from San Francisco.

San Francisco. It called to Malone. For a scion of the mountains and the plains, he was inordinately fond of the occasional draft of salt air. Soon enough, he promised himself. Tilting back his head, he let his eyes rove the numerous windows, eventually settling on one on the topmost floor. Light from oil lamps within, the hue of soft butter, lit the rectangular opening. He nodded knowingly.

"That one. There."

Mouth agape, Monk stared up at him. "Now, how could you know that, Mr. Malone? You've never been here before."

Nearly buried beneath an incautious bramble of rabid, unkempt whiskers, a prodigious nose contorted. "I kin smell jasmine. And lotus essence, sandalwood, and other emollients most foreign to this part o' the world."

Frowning, the driver inhaled deeply. "All I can smell is street muck and night soil."

Malone grinned. "I once spent some time in Paris sojournin' with a master parfumerie and have retained a bit o' that knowledge." He started forward.

Monk contemplated the swaying, rolling gait of the giant before him and tried to imagine a connection between the mountain man and the tiny crystal bottles of mostly floral scent he had occasionally seen in rooms occupied by ladies of the evening. Failing quite thoroughly in the attempt, he set the unresolved contradiction aside and followed grimly in the big man's wake.

Not all the way, though. He was stopped inside by the redoubtable Bigfoot Terry, the madam of the house, who was quick

to inquire as to their purpose in visiting. The question was rhetori-
cal, as her establishment dispensed one class of goods and one kind
only. "The best in Nevada," as the hefty owner was oft heard to
declare. She glanced only briefly at Monk, her attention immediately
drawn to his companion, her Carolina accent as thick as her thighs.

"Ah declare, suh, you strike me as a man in need of some serious
service." Blue eyes twinkled amusedly. "The question is, can a
sizable but rough-hewn bumpkin like yourself afford the finery for
which my establishment is famed?"

Malone was not looking at her, his gaze drawn instead to the
wide walnut stairway that cleaved the back of the parlor as opposed
to cleavage of a more neighboring but no less sturdy kind. Brushing
past her without a word, he headed directly for the stairs.

Startled by his indifference, the proprietress seemed about to
summon forth the men of unpleasant mien whom she kept on
retainer to cope with just such discourtesy. Monk hastened to forestall her.

"I will pay for my friend. Despite your assessment, it is hoped
his visit will be brief, and accounted accordingly."

Adjusting the feathers that encircled her shoulders and neck
like the boa for which the adornment was named, the madam
calmed herself. Her attention turned to the smaller and more
voluble visitor. "Fair enough." She proceeded to name the figure for
a standard visit. Monk nodded his understanding and reached into
a pocket.

"I am at present a mite short of coin, but I have this watch...."

The chamber was at the end of the hall on the top floor. As he
passed the intervening rooms, Malone listened for the sounds of
commerce. There were none to be heard. Did Madam Terry reserve
this entire floor for one employee because she was special? he
wondered. Or could it be that her fellow courtesans were fearful of
working in the stranger's vicinity? Did they perhaps shun her
because she was Chinese? He already suspected that there were

things at work here that transcended love and sex, and that was saying something.

To any other inhabitant of Carson City, the smells that emerged from beneath the solid wooden door would have reeked of exoticism. Malone, however, was familiar with them, being as he was rather more widely traveled than anyone save his horse suspected. Inhaling their familiarity, he identified one fragrance after another. Shanghai and Hong Kong, Kuching and Singapore, Calcutta and even Lhasa. No wonder this woman had so thoroughly enchanted the man called John Barrel. She had taste. She had reach.

It was time to find out what else she had.

He knocked. Softly at first and then, when ignored, harder. A voice from the other side mewed, "Come in—it is not locked." Turning the knob, he pushed against the wood and entered Paradise.

Or so it would have seemed to the unsophisticated, uninitiated miners and drovers and businessmen likely to frequent such an establishment. Heavy carpets on the floor were cartographies of interwoven patterns: lanterns and birds, dragons and Chinese characters, all rendered in finely wrought wool. Tables sculpted from dark wood supported oil-filled lamps and incense burners. In one corner, a pair of ceramic Ming lions glared ferociously. A rainbow waterfall of glass beads separated one room from another. Densely arrayed on the walls were paintings rendered in pale watercolor, in fine ink, in bird feathers and butterfly wings. The room was aswirl with luxury.

There was movement behind the beaded curtain. The shape of a woman eased into the room, the smoke parting around her like a diaphanous veil. Malone had seen much in his time, but the sight made him draw in his breath.

This was not going to be easy.

Glistening black hair was drawn tightly back into a single braid. Her face was as blemish-free and pure as a bowl of cream, save for the double crimson slash of her lips, which were as red as the wound from a cavalryman's saber. Packed into the glittering sequined cheongsam she wore were breasts more substantial than might have been anticipated, a narrow waist, and hips whose curves would have troubled Newton. When she smiled, the whole room seemed to sigh.

"What have we here?" She approached him. He held his ground as one hand reached out to stroke his arm. "I sense need bottled as tight as hundred-year-old brandy, and just as hot. Relax to me and I will release it."

He swallowed. Safer to be facing a troll in the Arctic or a shark in the sea, he thought. Monk was right to be worried about his friend.

At that moment, a moan came from a back room. It was weak, yet not an expression of pain. Back there, out of sight, a man was dying slowly. But not painfully. Malone nodded in its direction.

"You are entertainin', if thet's the right word, a guest name o' John Barrel. He has been here a long time. Too long. You speak o' need. Well, his friend needs him ... now and right quick."

A second hand reached out to slip between the mountain man's right arm and his waist. Fingers dug in hard, clutching, trying to penetrate the thick buckskin. The lacquered nails did not break.

"But I need him, too. I need him *more*."

Malone frowned. "His friend needs him to ride shotgun. What d'you need him to ride?"

The irresistible lips parted, eyelids fluttered, and there came a whisper that was part pure physicality and entirely feral. "He is a fine young man, healthy and strong. Being Occidental, you will not understand, but I need what moves him. Call it a life-force. Say it is an Oriental obsession."

Malone shook his head to clear it. The room, the incense, the nearness of his hostess were making him dizzy. Hips were moving against him with a strength that would have impressed the Krupps. Resistance was not futile, but it was becoming increasingly difficult. He struggled to keep his senses about him.

"I thought you only worked fer money. Life-force is a demonic obsession that spans all continents. 'Tis something far from exclusively Asian."

A growl escaped her throat as she stepped back from him. He

was quite certain it was a growl—low but not heavy. "Who are you, to speak of such things, far less to know of them?"

"A traveler. One with needs less immorally acquisitive than your own."

"Do not judge me, master of stinks!" Regaining her poise, she replayed her smile. "You want to free the youth? Very well. I will trade you."

The mountain man hesitated. "What could I possibly have that you would want?"

When she smiled this time, sharp points seemed to flash briefly from the tips of her teeth. "You. I will trade John Barrel's life-force for yours. Come and lie with me and I will take what I need. You will feel no pain." As she turned to walk away from him, the oceanic roll of her backside caused his eyes to water as if they had been doused with pepper. She looked back over her shoulder, her inviting smile at once coquettish and carnivorous. "Come, big handsome devil. Are you afraid?"

"Let Barrel go first."

She shrugged. "Will you then run out on me? I think not." Obsidian eyes flashed. "You are intrigued. Of course you are. Having set eyes on me, you have no choice."

———

It took Hank Monk plus one of Bigfoot Terry's men to get John Barrel out of the building. Monk was shocked when he saw his friend. Normally stout and muscular, the shotgun rider had been reduced to a shrunken shell of himself. It was as if someone had stuck a straw into his body and sucked out half the juice.

"A steak." Monk spoke worriedly as the madam's man helped load Barrel into the back of the buckboard. "Two steaks. With potatoes, and bread, and ale. We'll have you fixed up right quick, John. Be back on your feet in a day or two." Climbing up onto the front of the buckboard, Monk took up the reins and set it in motion. Lying in the open bed behind him, his companion moaned, his voice barely audible.

"Holy ... jingle ..."

"No need to worry about money now, John. Don't let such things worry you. We'll soon have you right."

As they passed the far end of the building, Monk glanced upward. The light from a window on the top floor was flickering oddly. He chucked the reins a little harder, urging the team to a faster pace.

If the greeting room was overflowing with objets d'art and seductive smells, the bedroom into which Malone found himself escorted redefined opulence. A beveled mirror on the ceiling reflected a rumpled bed that had been made up with sheets of French silk trimmed with Irish lace. Embroidered pillows rode the plush mattress like manatees on a rippled silver sea. Lamps glimmered while cherubs sculpted of wood and gilt parasitized the walls. Everywhere was crystal and smoke.

Then his hostess dropped her cheongsam, and everything else vanished from view.

"Too late now," she murmured. In her perfect nakedness, she turned and waved a hand, whispering something in Chinese so ancient only a few of the most eminent scholars of the Forbidden City would have understood.

Aromatic smoke swirled and danced. An unsourced sigh at once cosmetic and cosmic filled the bedchamber. Whisked away by a zephyr, the bedsheets were replaced by new and fresh ones that smelled of roses newly plucked. As she moved toward the bed, the walls rippled around Malone. Unbidden, he found himself starting to remove his own clothes. Given the number of layers and the quantity of grease and other dried fluids they had absorbed, this was a considerable process.

She did not so much lie down on the silk sheets as spread herself across them like honey on lavash. Utterly unabashed, she turned to face him. One hand gestured and he found himself drawn toward her. He did not remember walking, just floating an inch or so above the floor. Wisps of incense-laden smoke massaged his body as he traveled, cleansing him more thoroughly than any bath, perfuming him as the Aztecs would a particularly important sacrifice.

"You will sustain me far longer than that youngster John Barrel," she murmured. "You will renew me for many months, perhaps even years, until all has been used up. And you will enjoy every moment of it."

He felt himself rising up over the bed, over her. Then he was sinking, the great mass of him descending as gently as an autumn leaf, until he became one with her.

She howled.

———

Blocks away, the door of a stable stall shattered when its occupant burst through the barrier as if it were made of cardboard. The nightwatch stableboy barely managed to fling himself aside as Worthless turned the main doors to kindling. Pounding through the streets, the fiery-eyed runaway scattered late night drunks and sober pedestrians alike.

Very soon, the stallion found himself outside a singular stone structure from whose topmost floor lamplight danced and twitched as if imbued with a life of its own. Whinnying and rearing, sending ordinary horses stampeding in panic from where they had been tied, Worthless stomped back and forth in front of the building. When two men managed to get a lariat around him, one twitch of the muscular neck sent both of them flying into a nearby water trough. Raising a rifle, a third prepared to bring the maddened mount down. One look from his intended target caused the visiting rancher to drop his weapon and sprint for the nearest available doorway.

In front of the furiously pacing horse, men and women were spilling from the building's main entrance. Though some wore few articles of clothing and others none at all, their nakedness was not of as much concern as escaping a heretofore solid structure that seemed on the verge of collapsing. Indeed, as they gathered themselves in the street, a few turned to marvel at the quivering multi-story building. Given the range of motion in which the outer walls were presently engaged, it struck all as impossible that they were not crumbling before their stunned eyes. Yet though it shivered and shook like a gelatin mold placed atop a steam engine, the building did not collapse.

Despite the grinding and rumbling of shaken stone, another sound could be heard. It was a roaring, a shrieking, a howling scree as if a pack of demons was being tormented in ways unimaginable to mere human beings. It was the sound of an evil spirit being hoisted by its own petard.

Or in this case, that of Amos Malone.

The bed, with its luscious silks and enveloping pillows and hand-wrought steel springs, was slowly disintegrating beneath its present occupants. The room was, quite literally, heaving in time to their synchronized movements. Locked against each other, they were unaware of their physical surroundings. Engaged in oneness, they became the universe while the real one disappeared. It was the totality of tao.

Beneath the immensity of Malone, the courtesan's eyes widened.

"Not possible! It is not possible! How can you ...?"

He moved suddenly, a certain way, and her eyes closed. Her nails dug at his back, much as those of an animal might dig at the ground searching for prey. She whined, she whimpered, she threw back her head and bayed. As she did so, her mouth opened wide. Determined, resolute, Malone kept moving even as an ethereal redness began to emerge from between her lips.

"I know the way," he muttered even as he strove to maintain the effort. "I know the places to touch, the moves to make. You are done in this time and place, vixen. Be off with you, says I! Take yourself elsewhere and find another to feed upon. I'm Amos Malone, and I'm afraid I got to hang onto all the life-force I've got. Might need it later." With that he thrust his hips forward as hard as he could, in a most distinctive, ancient, and thrice-forgotten manner.

"Holy jingle," Barrel had kept mumbling, over and over. Not being conversant with old Mandarin, the driver's enunciation had been only an approximation. But from the man's semi-coherent sputtering Malone had been able to divine the correct pronunciatio-nand its true meaning.

"Huli jing!" poor Barrel had been trying to say. It was not an exclamation, but a warning.

The courtesan's mouth opened wider still. Wider than humanly possible. Around them, the overheated air shuddered as the Huli jing spirit was expelled from the human woman's body. Hovering in the air by the head of the bed, the nine-tailed fox-shaped apparition spun and whirled helplessly, bereft now of its human host. It snapped at him once, barking half in anger, half in amusement, almost biting his nose. In the far corner of the room, atop his pile of discarded clothes, Malone's wolf's-head cap snarled, and its eyes glowed red with fury at the sight of its hereditary enemy.

The Huli jing growled a last time, whipped its nine tails once across Malone's face, and was gone.

Malone collapsed.

The air in the room grew still. Walls ceased their shaking and behaved once more with the discipline of stone. Crystal ceased singing and the flames in the oil lamps calmed themselves. Outside on the street, a manic horse quieted, huffed, and ambled over to a recently vacated water trough to drink long, heavy, and noisily. Beneath an utterly exhausted Malone, black eyes flickered, focused, and gazed up at him in wonder.

"Who ... who are you, sir? What has happened here?" Raising her head, the woman regarded her elegant if unsettled surroundings. "I remember last being sold and being put on a ship. I remember a place, a port...."

Worn as he was, Malone still managed to muster a thoughtful response. "That would not, by any chance, be San Francisco?"

"Yes!" A small trill of excitement underlined her words. "San Francisco, yes. I remember being delivered and then ... nothing."

Her gaze returned to him, searching his features. "You have a dangerous face but kind eyes, sir. What will you do with me?"

Letting out a groan that shook the foundations of the building one final time, he rolled off her. There was silence in the room for a long minute. Her expression expectant, she eyed the mountain of man beside her but forbore from interrupting his recovery. Then he exhaled heavily, sat up, clasped hands around knees the size of small boulders, and looked down at her.

"If it's all the same to you, ma'm, I'll take you back to San Francisco. There are good folk there o' your own kind, folks who will find a decent place fer someone like yourself. One where you won't have to worry about bein' possessed. Because that's what you were, ma'm." The great sweep of his beard framed a surprisingly reassuring smile.

She looked away, neither demure nor embarrassed by her nakedness. "You call me 'ma'am.' My name is Meifeng."

Malone nodded approvingly. Outside the closed window, a horse could be heard whinnying insistently. He started to rise. A hand, strong but graceful, reached out to restrain him.

"Before you leave to prepare for our journey, sir, I would show you my thanks for saving me, though I have but small and inadequate means of doing so."

"I really ought ... ," he began. But she was insistent, and begged him, and her dark eyes were now filled with the kind of earnest soulfulness it had always been his misfortune to be unable to refuse. Besides, despite all he had endured, he was always a fool for knowledge.

After all, Meifeng does mean "beautiful wind."

In some parts, Amos Malone's tendency to show up just in time to lend a helping hand to folks in need is almost as famed as his unsettling familiarity with arcane affairs. It's borderline uncanny how he manages to wander into a situation where his presence ultimately proves useful to ordinary folks in desperate straits. That doesn't mean he always just jumps right in to offer assistance. But despite harboring the traditional mountain man's love of privacy, Malone retains a soft spot for those who are put upon by evil. That evil might take the form of a demon, a dragon, a demoiselle, or, to destroy the alliteration, a simple piece of paper. A piece of paper's capacity for embodying pure evil is frequently underrated.

There was a time in the American West when a simple piece of paper was just that. Then "civilization" moved in, replete with its accountants, lawyers, and politicians. To this day, dealing with them often requires resorting to methods distinctive and unorthodox.

Myself, I'd rather take my chances with the demons. At least brimstone is clean.

A TREEFOLD PROBLEM

The children were wailing, his wife was sobbing, and that pitiless sliver of scum that walked like a man and called himself Potter Scunsthorpe (the individual with whom Owen was arguing fruitlessly) remained as merciless as a bull fixated on chewing three days' worth of unmasticated cud. To add to the human cacophony at the forest's edge, a pair of ravens flew past overhead, cackling like a pair of perambulating witches intent solely on taunting Owen Hargrave in his present misery.

Scunsthorpe let the farmer stem-wind for several minutes longer before raising a commanding hand for silence. He had the look of a successful undertaker, did Scunsthorpe, coupled to the unctuous mannerisms of a banker who could squeeze an orange in one hand, a nickel in the other, and get juice out of both. Slender as a reed, his skin the color of wild rice, he was clad in a finely tailored black suit entirely out of keeping with the present woodland surroundings. A black top hat one size too small clung to his white-fringed scalp with grim determination. The single red silk ribbon that protruded from the hatband was the color of blood. From the front of his immaculate white shirt, a gold watch chain dribbled into a bulging pocket. Only his scuffed and dirty boots marked him as a citizen of far Wisconsin and not more civilized New York or Philadelphia. His two troll-like lackeys flanked him, disinterested and anxious to be away.

The subject of the animated and decidedly inequitable discussion between the two men was an inundation of unbroken verdure, a veritable mantle of virgin forest that stretched as far to the west as one could see. White and red pine stabbed at the heavens, interspersed with stout woodland guardians of northern and red oak, red and sugar maple. Here and there a solitary basswood made an appearance, and where sunlight was sufficient, dense thickets of blueberry, wintergreen, and partridgeberry burst forth in energetic tangles.

All this green glory the Hargrave family owned, as part and parcel of their deeded land. It was coveted in turn by Scunsthorpe. The paper he now held out before Owen Hargrave might as well have been signed and stamped by the Devil himself. It was the mortgage to the Hargrave property. As is the way of those who lurk, wormlike, just below the surface of decent society, Scunsthorpe had bought it up on the sly. Now the final, balloon payment was due. Based on their existing equity, a Milwaukee banker would likely have extended credit to the family. Scunsthorpe was no banker. He was brother to the ravens who had just cawed past overhead, and like them, a soulless scavenger.

"The timber is mine by rights of this deed." It was an evident struggle for Scunsthorpe to speak the words while masking his enjoyment of them. He kissed each vowel with a perverse joy. "That, and the land upon which it stands, and the adjoining farm as well. Together with any buildings, wells, fences, barns, and other physical improvements you may have made thereon." Unable to restrain himself any longer, he nodded toward the untouched forest. His prominent Adam's apple bobbed as he spoke. "The law says it is so if you have not cleared this land. I see no evidence of it."

Hargrave glanced over at his wife, who was trying to ease the crying of their youngest, held in her arms, before once more confronting his tormentor.

"I have explained and explained, sir. It was a difficult winter. I meant fully to hire a crew to at least commence the requisite clearing of the timber, but all our efforts had to be bent to preserving our livestock and thence getting in the spring planting. I had no time left for tree felling."

Scunsthorpe straightened, which made him loom even higher over the stocky farmer. "My concern is not with the vagaries of the local climate, sir, nor with your petty domestic matters. The law is the law, fixed and immutable." He swept a scythelike arm to the west. "You have not, as specified, made use of the forest. Therefore it, and all else included in this deed, is now mine by right."

Unable to contain herself any longer, Hargrave's wife spoke up, her pleading carrying above the sobs of the children. Only ten-year-old Eli, who gazed at Scunsthorpe with undying hatred, was not bawling uncontrollably.

"But, sir, I beseech you, what are we to do? I would take a job and work myself to pay you something of the cash money you are owed, but with the farm and the children I have little enough time to sleep."

Scunsthorpe's mouth drew tight in a line as closed as that of his purse. "Then at least, madam, you will very soon have time to sleep, as the arduous burden of caring for a farm will be lifted from you."

All of them would have ignored the newcomer save that he could not be ignored. He appeared on the trail that led over the slight rise that hid the farmstead from the discussion, his mount ambling at a leisurely pace along the barely foot-wide pathway. Scunsthorpe certainly would have ignored him had not Hargrave turned to stare, but one cannot continue to denigrate a suddenly indifferent subject. Louisa Hargrave went silent as well, and even the children stifled their sniffling. Ten-year-old Eli simply gaped.

Not a great deal smaller than Forge, the Hargrave's breeding bull, and considerably hairier, the traveler emitted an odor not altogether different. Attired in abraded buckskins crossed by a double bandolier of huge cartridges, he wore a wolf's-head cap that gleamed as gray as the cloudy Wisconsin sky. His beard, long hair, and wooly eyebrows were jet black flecked with white, and his equally black eyes peered out from beneath brows that appeared to have been chiseled from granite instead of bone. His mount, a proportionately enormous beast, was likewise black as night save for flashes of ivory at tail, fetlocks, and one circle that surrounded a squinting eye. A patch on its forehead concealed an odd bulge. It pawed once at the ground and snorted derisively as its rider brought it to a stop.

"With all this 'ere yellin'," the mountain man opined, "a feller can't hardly hear the forest think."

"With all goodwill, let it be said that this is a private matter, sir, and it be none of your business. It is advised that you continue on your chosen path, whereupon the silence of the woods will soon once more envelop you." Irritated at having the pleasure of taking possession thus interrupted, Scunsthorpe was in no mood for digression, especially when it was propounded by a total stranger.

Making no move to secure the reins, the giant slid with surprising litheness off his mount and came forward. His approach woke Scunsthorpe's minions from their torpor. Both tensed. The one on Scunsthorpe's left, a thickly constructed gentleman of the colored persuasion who looked as if he had been run over by one of the Wisconsin Central's trains and then backed over again to finish the job, commenced a slow slide of his right hand toward the holstered pistol at his waist. As he did so, the visitor met his gaze. Not a word passed between the two men, but the descending fingers stopped advancing and their owner found sudden reason to look elsewhere.

The other scalawag was bigger and stronger, with the face of a dyspeptic baby. Turning his head to his right, he elevated a copious glob of spittle toward an inoffensive stand of broomweed. The stranger promptly matched the prodigious expectoration, with somewhat different results. The weed upon which he chose to spit swiftly shriveled and curled in upon itself, in the process venting a slight but perceptible twist of smoke. Eyes widened in the under-ling's baby face and his lips parted in surprise.

This did-you-see-it-or-did-you-not moment in time was suffi-cient to persuade Scunsthorpe, at least for the moment, to caution restraint on the part of both himself and his suddenly wary associates.

"I repeat myself, sir." Despite his own not inconsiderable height, Scunsthorpe found himself having to tilt back his head in order to meet the newcomer's gaze. "With all goodwill—"

"One can't offer what one don't possess," the stranger interrupted him. "Leavin' aside fer the nonce the matter o' what limited quantity of goodwill you might or might not enjoy, I do now find myself takin' a sudden interest in the proceedin's."

Bold as the suspenders that held up his pants, Eli Hargrave stepped forward. "He's trying to take our timber, sir! Our timber and our farm!"

"Hush now, Eli!" Cradling the baby in one arm, an alarmed Louisa Hargrave hastily drew her son away from the menfolk. "Get back here and be quiet!"

From within the depths of the stranger's mighty face mattress, a smile surfaced, as unexpectedly white among the black curls as a beluga in a lake of coal slurry. Its unanticipated brilliance dimmed as its owner regarded the boy's father.

"Is what the boy says true, Mr. ...?"

"Hargrave. Owen Hargrave."

The stranger extended a hand. At first glance Hargrave thought it similarly clad in buckskin, but closer inspection revealed it to be ungloved, if extraordinarily weathered. The fingers completely enveloped his own.

"Malone. Amos Malone."

As he guardedly shook the newcomer's paw, Hargrave reflected that he'd heard locomotives whose voices were higher pitched.

"And I," the gangly ringmaster of the discussion declaimed, not to be left out of this sudden fraternity, "am Potter Scunsthorpe. Investor, speculator, developer, and now rightful owner of this land."

Malone turned to him. Between the mountain man's unblinking stare and his personal aroma, Scunsthorpe was tempted to retreat. But he held his ground.

"By what right d'you claim this family's land?" the giant asked him.

Though it was nothing more than a piece of paper, Scunsthorpe held the deed out before him as if it were made of steel. "By right of this, as attested to under the laws of the great state of Wisconsin and the United States of America!"

"With your permission?" Without waiting for it, the mountain man took it from a startled Scunsthorpe's hand as deftly as if plucking a petal from a daisy.

"If you damage that," the speculator warned the giant, "I can have you arrested! Not that it would be of any consequence anyway. There are perfect copies on file with the county clerk."

The mountain man chuckled once. "Last time anyone tried t' arrest me were the Maharaja of Jaipur. Claimed I'd stolen one o' his fancy aigrettes right off his turban. Tried t' feed me to his pet tigers, he did."

Nearly oblivious now to the adults around him, Eli Hargrave stared wide-eyed at the visitor. "Tigers! What happened?"

His beard preceding his smile, Malone peered down at the boy. "Why, we ended up sharin' a meal instead."

"You and the maharaja?" Eli murmured wonderingly.

"Nope. Me an' the tigers." Holding the document up to the light, Malone studied it carefully. Looking on in silence, Owen Hargrave was plainly puzzled, his wife suddenly afflicted with an unreasoning hope, while Scunsthorpe quietly marveled that the excessively hirsute creature who had appeared among them could actually read.

When the giant finally lowered the deed and turned to the farmer, his tone was solemn. "I'm afeared this 'ere fella has you legally dead to rights, Mr. Hargrave."

"Ah, you see?" Scunsthorpe relaxed. The wanderer's intrusion was after all to prove nothing more than a momentary, and in its own way entertaining, interruption. "I have told you nothing less than the truth, Hargrave."

"Well, mebbe not entirely all of it, as I sees it." Malone held out the document.

Scunsthorpe frowned. It was an expression he used often and did not have to practice. "I fail to follow your meaning, sir."

A finger that might have come off one of the nearby oaks lightly tapped the deed. "As I read it here, says you can't take possession fer

at least five years an' not at all after ten if the property in question
has been properly cleared and prepared fer farmin'."

A country bumpkin, Scunsthorpe thought to himself. Verily a
great huge one, but a bumpkin nonetheless. "Quite so, sir, quite so.
I must commend the accuracy of your swift perusal. Preparation for
farming means clearing, by which one must take to mean felling the
obstructing timber. Which of its own accord is most certainly of
considerable value. In the case of such clearing, transfer of ownership is indeed denied for a minimum of five years and forbidden,
upon full payment of terms by the designated mortgage holder, after
ten." Struggling not to chortle aloud, he turned to his left and once
again gestured at the dense, unbroken forest.

"If Mr. Hargrave can, as noted, fell all of the timber under
discussion, I will most certainly be compelled to withdraw my
present claim to the property. All he must do in satisfaction of the
terms of the deed is accomplish this by the time specified thereon."
He made a show of squinting at the document. "I perceive that to
be ten o'clock on the first of October." He smiled humorlessly.
"That date falls, I believe, on Tuesday morrow."

Malone nodded at the paper. "Then we're all bein' in agreement,
sir."

Scunsthorpe was by turns now baffled as well as irritated. "Once
again, I fail to follow your reasoning, sir."

Malone indicated the wall of untouched woodland. "If the
timber on Mr. Hargrave here's land is felled by ten o'clock tomorrow, you'll take your leave o' him and his family and leave them and
this land in peace."

The colored gentleman broke out in an unrestrained guffaw
while his giant baby of an associate looked bemused and, not
entirely comprehending the proceedings, commenced to employ a
forefinger to mine a portion of his soft, undersized nose in search of
unknown ore. Scunsthorpe stared, grunted, and then grinned.

"Verily, Mr. Malone, sir, you are a man who hews to the letter of
the law, even if it be for nothing more than one's amusement." In
lieu of a better stage, he was reduced to sighing dramatically. "So be
it, then. I had hoped to conclude this awkward business today. But

on your insistence, and as a matter of common courtesy, I will delay, not returning tomorrow until the appointed hour." His expression narrowed, sharp as the cleft in a tomahawked skull. "I shall bring along for company and purposes of expeditiousness the sheriff of Newhope, in case any further fine-tuning of legalities shall be desired."

"Lookin' forward to it," Malone replied impassively.

Having previously seen to the hitching of their own horses at the Hargrave barn, Scunsthorpe marched off in that direction, trailed by his silent but intimidating associates. As Malone watched them go, a dubious Owen Hargrave ignored the reek that emanated from the giant and sidled up to him.

"While I appreciate your intervention, Mr. Malone, I fear it to be as futile as it was timely. That viper will return tomorrow, as his promises are as assured as his demeanor is detestable. You have bought us time for a last supper, if nothing else."

"Don't say that, Hargrave." Having started toward his mount, Malone found himself accompanied by the farmer and his wife while their three children attended his long, massive legs. "There still be time to perhaps fulfill the terms o' your deed."

"Now you jest with us, Mr. Malone," declared Louisa Hargrave. "Or do I take it you propose to level a quarter section of woodland in a night? Anyone who would put forth such a notion might well be called mad."

"He might indeed, m'am, while likewise takin' no offense at the designation." Reaching his animal, Malone began to hunt through one of the oversized backpacks while simultaneously advising Eli's oldest sister. "I'd keep my distance from Worthless's mouth, young missy."

Blond, precious, and wide-eyed, the girl replied solemnly even as she peered up at the wide-lipped tooth-filled aperture hovering above her. "Why, mister? Will he bite me?"

"I think not. But Worthless, he has a disgraceful tendency t' drool, and sometimes it burns."

As if to counter this assertion, the huge black head bent low. A thick tongue emerged to lick the face of the little girl, who hastily backed away, wiping frantically at her cheek while shrieking delight-edly. The stallion then turned one jaundiced eye on its master, snorted, and resumed cropping the weeds near its forelegs.

"Hungry, he is. That's most usual his condition." The mountain man looked thoughtful, as if contemplating something of more profound potential than a bag of oats. "Kin I impose on you fer some feed, Mr. Hargrave?"

"Yes. Yes, of course, Mr. Malone." Turning, the farmer barked at his son. "Eli! Get the wagon. Load it with hay and bring it back here."

"Yes, Pa!" As the boy turned to go, Malone called to him.

"And barley, boy. If you kin find any barley, Worthless dotes on the stuff. I usually don't feed it t' him becausewell, he'd keep eatin' it until he were 'bout ready t' explode. But bring it if you kin find some."

"I will do so, sir!" And with that the lad was sprinting over the rise in the direction of his home.

From the saddlebag the mountain man removed a hinged length of shaped and polished wood. As the farmer looked on with interest Malone snapped it straight, the metal hinge that connected the two lengths locking securely in place. From the trim and design it was easy enough to divine its purpose: it was an axe handle. Rummaging deeper in the same saddlebag, the visitor drew forth the corre-sponding blade. It was double-bitted and slid tightly onto the busi-ness end of the handle.

Hargrave studied the reconstituted tool. "Never seen anything quite like that, Mr. Malone. That wood—looking at it, I'd say it had to be black walnut."

"A reasonable guess, but an invalid one, sir." Malone made certain the twinned blade was secured to the handle. "This be *m'pinga*, a type of wood from near the coast of East Africa. Some folks calls it ironwood, but there's all manner of wood called that. This kind is too heavy t' float, and too tough to break."

The farmer considered the massive implement. "And that head, that must be at least a four-pounder. Or is it five? And as strange a steel as I've ever seen."

"Twenty." Malone held the implement out at arm's length to check the straightness of the handle. Held it out with one hand. "Made the blade meself, from the body of a fallin' star."

Hargrave laughed. "Begging your pardon, sir, but there's no such thing as a twenty-pound axe-head. Double-bitted or otherwise. Isn't no man could swing one."

"Probably you be right, sir. I'm just funnin' you." So saying, Malone lifted the axe without apparent effort and rested it on his right shoulder. Removing his wolf's-head cap, he placed it in the same saddlebag from which he had extracted the components of the axe and started off toward the nearby woods. Looking back over his shoulder, he called out.

"Y'kin lend a hand if you wish, Mr. Hargrave, but in any event I aim t' render what service I kin before the designated time o' surrender tomorrow."

Halting before the first tree, a noble red pine, the mountain man unlimbered the axe, brought it back, and swung. Entering the tree parallel to the ground, the massive steel cutting edge sliced halfway through the thick trunk.

"Mercy!" Putting her free hand to her chest as if she had contracted a sudden case of the vapors, Louisa Hargrave gasped aloud. For his part, her husband uttered a word that was as uncharacteristic of him as it was of considerably greater potency than those he normally employed in the presence of wife and family. Whereupon he whirled and raced off in the direction of their simple yet comforting homestead.

"Owen!" his wife called out. "Where are you going, husband?"

He yelled back at her. "To get my axe! And to hurry the boy along!" He looked beyond her, stumbling as he ran, and raised his voice. "We're going to need the team to shift timber!"

- - -

All the rest of that morning and on into the cloudy, slightly muggy afternoon, Amos Malone and Owen Hargrave cut and chopped, chopped and cut. According to the terms of the mortgage as deciphered by the mountain man, it was not necessary for the farmer to clear the timber off his land in order to satisfy the terms of the deed: it was only required that he cut it down to prove that he intended to develop it. Pine after pine, oak after oak, came crashing to the earth as the two men toiled. Malone paused only once, to place a heavy blanket across the back of his vigorously feeding steed and secure it tightly in place. Hargrave admired the mountain man's concern for his animal, though he did wonder at the need for a blanket in such mild weather. The farmer felled one tree to every ten of the big man's, until finally his aching arms gave out and the fiery blisters he had raised on his palms prevented him from wielding the axe any longer.

He nearly broke down when young Eli bravely attempted to take up the slack. Though he struggled manfully, the boy could barely raise his father's axe, let alone swing it.

Taking a break to down a full quart of the cold well water periodically fetched by Mrs. Hargrave, Malone concluded the imposing draft by wiping the back of a massive hand across his mouth. Then, unbuttoning his buckskin jacket, he slithered out of it and handed it to the boy, who all but collapsed under the load. Shirt followed jacket and lastly, after assuring the boy's mother the deeply stained attire contained nothing likely to imperil her son's life or future mental development, Malone divested himself of a cotton under-shirt from which any hint of the original whiteness had long since fled screaming.

"Here, son: if 'tis work you want, set yourself to seein' that those there garments get tidied up a bit, as they ain't been washed in quite a spell."

Standing nearby, holding the water bucket and striving with all her might to look anywhere save directly at the massive spread of hairy chest, shoulders, and muscular arms now revealed before her, Louisa Hargrave had the presence of mind to remark, "Have they truly *ever* been washed, Mr. Malone?"

The mountain man turned reflective. "Memory plays tricks on a man." His expression brightened. "I do recollect on one occasion fallin' in the course of a serious bad storm into the Upper Mississippi one time last year. Pulled meself out reasonable clean some-where in the vicinity of St. Louis." He smiled down at her and at the mound of clothing in whose approximate locality her eldest son was presently submerged. "I reckon that this time, a touch o' soap wouldn't be out o' line."

"Come, Eli." She turned back toward the homestead. "I'll do what I can for your garments, Mr. Malone, but upon initial appraisal I fear I must confess that we may have better luck with prayer."

As soon as Hargrave was able to resume work alongside his towering visitor, his axe handle promptly cracked. This forced a quick trip into town. He was unable to keep the amazing story to himself, so word quickly spread from the general store to the general populace. Eventually it settled upon the large, sporadically mobile ears of Potter Scunsthorpe, who determined that despite the unlikelihood of there being any truth to the farmer's tall tale, it would require but little effort to check it out.

Upon arriving at the land that was to be his upon the morrow, he was startled to see the progress that the two men had made. Instead of starting at one end of the property and attempting to clear-cut their way across it, they were taking down the largest trees first. While a wholly sensible stratagem, Scunsthorpe felt that it would in the end avail them nothing. There were simply too many trees for two men to fell by the following day even if one of them was as strong as a team of oxen. One would have thought that the mountain man would have utilized his heavy horse to help pull down trees that were partially cut through, but that most eccentric steed remained off to one side working its way through an immense pile of hay, barley, and feed grain. Scunsthorpe could do no more than shake his head at the sight. While he could not fathom the giant's ultimate intent, he had no intention of leaving anything to chance.

Scunsthorpe was not alone that evening in choosing to observe the unprecedented demonstration of lumberjacking talent. On buckboards and wagons, other townsfolk had come out to watch and marvel at the exhibition, for entertainment of any kind was scarce and much appreciated in that part of the country.

Approaching a fine buggy he knew well, the lanky speculator smiled and tipped his hat to its single occupant.

"Afternoon, Miss Pettiview."

"Mr. Scunsthorpe." A parasol of turquoise hue moved aside to reveal a visage of winsome grace dominated by cornflower-blue eyes, lips painted carmine, a diminutive and slightly upturned nose, and much speculation. "I am not surprised to find you here. Everyone knows of your interest in and intent to take the Hargrave property for your own."

He pursed his lips. "Does that news displease you?"

"It is nothing to me. My business lies elsewhere."

Scunsthorpe's gaze dropped. "Everyone is aware of where your business lies, Miss Pettiview. It is in knowledge of that estimable topography that I would engage your talents on a matter of some concern."

Teeth white as the chalk their owner employed in her occasional engagement as a schoolteacher flashed in the light of the setting sun. "How then may I be of service to you, Mr. Scunsthorpe?"

The speculator pointed toward the slowly shrinking line of forest off to the west. "Farmer Hargrave has found himself some assistance in his senseless attempt to satisfy the terms of the mortgage that I hold."

Raising a blue-gloved hand to shield her eyes, Pettiview gazed in the indicated direction. A slight intake of breath followed hard upon her detection of the two distant figures who were laboring among the woods. Scunsthorpe noted the inhalation and swallowed his disgust.

"If by 'assistance,'" she murmured, "you are referring to a most striking Herculean figure who is presently taking down a white pine as if it were a stalk of asparagus, then I follow your meaning quite clearly."

Once again Scunsthorpe tipped his hat to her. "It is of course impossible that any two men should reduce one hundred and sixty acres of forest in a single day and night of effort, but in my profession I have learned to take no chances. To that end it would be useful if the hulking great stranger who calls himself Amos Malone were for a while to have his attention diverted from the practice of forestry to ... other pursuits."

Reaching into an inner pocket of his fine suit, he removed a couple of heavy coins that glinted gold in the fading light. These promptly vanished into Miss Pettiview's elegantly beaded purse as deftly as if manipulated by a riverboat card shark. Extending a hand, she allowed Scunsthorpe to help her down from the buggy seat, smiling reassuringly at him as his other hand availed itself of the opportunity to clutch fleetingly at the backside of her powder-blue dress.

Parasol in hand, she made her way past murmuring townsfolk and down into the partially cut-over section of forest until she could resume her observations much nearer the two men than either Hargrave or his wife would have liked. But the farmer said nothing, and continued to hack away at the base of a red maple.

"You are quite the specimen, Mr. Amos Malone." Her forwardness would have surprised none who knew her.

Bare-chested and perspiring like a Brazilian rainforest, Malone paused in mid-swing to set the head of his massive axe on the ground. Wiping sweat from his forehead, he responded with a nod.

"And if m'lady will pardon an old reprobate such as myself, you be as trim a vessel as these watery eyes have set upon since a distant week spent in San Francisco."

"Oohhh ... 'm'lady,' he says! 'Tis quite the gentleman you are, Amos Malone. And you have been to San Francisco, too? I would love someday to make the acquaintance of that fabled metropolis."

"San Francisco, yes." Malone swung the axe. Wood chips flew, from which celluloid assault Pettiview had to defend herself with her parasol. "And ... elsewhere."

"I know one place you haven't been," she said coquettishly. The tip of one painted fingernail teased the slight space between her front teeth.

"An' where might that be, m'lady?"

"'Melissa' will do for you, if you will do for me."

He paused once again. "I don't follow you, m'laMelissa."

"Such strenuous exertions on the part of such excessive musculature must engender a healthy appetite. I would be pleased to satisfy such, if you would but extend me the courtesy."

"I *am* tendin' a mite to the famished," he murmured. "What would a good meal cost me?" He looked past her. "I would ask it of the wife Hargrave, but she already has five mouths t' feed."

"Whereas I have naught to occupy me save to stand ready to prepare your supper." Pettiview pivoted, the parasol twirling over her shoulder as she looked back, eyelids fluttering. "Come with me then, Mr. Malone, and I will see to it that you find rest, food, and succor for as much of this evening as should be necessary to satisfy your needs."

"A most temptin' offer, and one I fear it would be impolite t' refuse." So saying, he leaned the colossal axe against a nearby solitary ash. "I should recover the rest of my clothes, if they be dry enough."

"No need to bother, sir." She led him out of the woods and toward the waiting buggy, whose horse eyed the approach of Malone's mass nervously. "I am quite comfortable with dining informally, as you shall see." Whereupon she turned briefly to him and breathed deeply, thereby expanding the top of her dress to such an extent that anyone within range of some half dozen forthright buttons might not unreasonably be expected to have to dodge them, as by inhaling any further she might effortlessly turn them into weapons imbued with lethal velocity.

When Hargrave saw his possible savior leaving in the company of the notorious Pettiview, he all but surrendered to despair. Only the mountain man's encouraging shout of "I'll be back in time, Hargrave!" offered the most forlorn hope. But that was now forlorn indeed. Not that they'd had much of a chance of felling the entire quarter section of forest before morning anyway, but it had been something to work for, something to work *toward*. Now, the despondent Hargrave felt he had nothing.

Slumping down on a stump, he would not allow himself to weep. Only then did it occur to him that he, too, was starved for nourishment. With a heavy sigh he left behind his newly bought axe and staggered exhaustedly toward his unassuming homestead. He would make himself enjoy whatever Mrs. Hargrave had managed to muster for supper.

If for no other reason than it was likely the last one he would ever get to enjoy in the house he had raised up with his own hands.

———

Sunrise brought renewed hope in the form of the giant mountain man. As good as his word, Malone had returned. Having admired his now spotlessly clean undershirt, shirt, and jacket, upon all three of which Mrs. Hargrave had indeed worked miracles, Malone forbore from filthying them again so soon, carefully removing them and setting them aside before he resumed work in the woods. Hargrave joined him, even though it was plain to see that while they had done an impressive job of thinning the quarter section of forest, within the designated boundary line hundreds of smaller trees still remained rooted and standing. The farmer doubted the ploy would be sufficient to satisfy the avaricious Scunsthorpe. The deed said that all the hundred sixty acres had to be cleared. Despite their yeoman efforts, this he and Malone had plainly failed to do.

So it was that at precisely nine forty-five, the wicked Scunsthorpe made his presence known. He was accompanied this time not only by his two hulking underlings of dubious ancestry but also by Hander Cogsworth, sheriff of the town of Newhope. All was patently lost, an exhausted Hargrave realized. Malone might fast-talk even Scunsthorpe, but with the law at his side, the insatiable speculator would not hesitate to take immediate possession.

Malone joined the exhausted farmer in confronting the officious arrivals, glancing at the nearby hillside as he did so. "Where at the moment might be your family, Hargrave?"

The farmer was inconsolable. "Back at the housefor the last time. Saying their good-byes. Making their peace with the sorrowful inevitable." He gazed mournfully toward the crest of the low rise. "Louisa will be directing the children to gather up their things, and has no doubt commenced the packing of her own humble body of possessions." He looked up at the mountain man.

"Of myself, I have but little beyond wife and children that any longer holds meaning for me. My sole concern now is to see them safely on the train to Milwaukee, and thence to Chicago, where she at least may throw herself on the sympathy of family members. As for myself"—he swallowed hard—"I too shall go to the city, there to look for whatever work I may be so fortunate as to obtain, in order that I may somehow continue to contribute to the upkeep of my family."

"Are you not bein' a mite premature, Hargrave?" Malone looked skyward. "I make it t' be not quite ten o'clock. Y'all are still rightful owner of this land."

"For another fifteen minutes." Hargrave let out a snort of dejection. "Years of work, of dreaming, of what might one day be: all gone now because of a lack of time and a bad winter." A sudden thought made him blink. "What of the schoolteacher Pettiview? Did she not beguile you sufficiently?"

"Beguilin' be a knack that works both ways, friend Hargrave." Raising his gaze, Malone peered in the direction of distant Newhope. "Her cookin' weren't much to my likin', but I fear she may have treated herself to overmuch dessert. Last I saw her she were takin' herself off to the town doctor. To treat a condition recently acquired, I believe she said." He looked down. "Anyway, I am here. Now let us greet this itch that persists in troublin' you. A mite further to the eastward, I calculate."

"To the east? But why?" Hargrave eyed him uncomprehendingly.

Malone turned a fixed gaze in the opposite direction. The farmer followed the mountain man's stare, but saw only forest and brush, cloud and sky. That, and the mountain man's idiosyncratic steed. Unbelievably, it was still feeding. Insofar as Hargrave could recall, it had not stopped eating all night, having ingested a veritable mountain of silage. The animal was, if truth be told, looking more than a little bloated. Hargrave did not begrudge it or its owner the fodder; only marveled at an equine appetite the likes of which could scarce be imagined had he not observed its progression for himself.

With sheriff and minions in tow, a triumphant Scunsthorpe presented himself, deed in hand, before mountain man and farmer.

Eyeing the moderately thinned forest, the speculator pronounced himself well satisfied.

"The time is at hand, gentlemen." A snake could not smirk, but Scunsthorpe came close as he looked up at the silent Malone. "The precise time, as you wished it, sir. I can even say, with all honesty, that I am thankful for having met you and for your noteworthy if malodorous presence." With a wave of one hand he took in the thinned woods. "As you have by your remarkable yet pointless labors saved me a good deal of money by felling such a quantity of valuable timber for me."

"And I can even say," Malone replied, "with all honesty, that it were no pleasure whatsoever to havin' made your acquaintance, though yours is a type I know well, Scunsthorpe."

The investor shrugged. "Insult me as you wish. I have no time to take offense, for I must perforce take full possession of my new lands."

Malone nodded, checked the sun, and said, "Five minutes remain, Scunsthorpe. I would advise strongly they be used to move over this way." Indicating the crest of the nearby hill, he started off in the other direction, toward his placid steed. Uncomprehending and uncaring, a devastated and benumbed Owen Hargrave followed the mountain man's directions, striding slowly toward the hill and the homestead that were no longer his. So, too, did the sheriff, a heavily mustachioed man who was pleased beyond measure that his intercession would apparently not be required with so formidable a force as the towering stranger.

Uncertain at first, Scunsthorpe's minions started to follow the disconsolate farmer. Their master, however, betook himself in the other direction, his long legs allowing him to catch up to Malone.

"And get this disgusting excuse of an animal off my property immediately!" Scunsthorpe said loudly as he stomped toward Malone's placidly munching mount.

Having already reached the stallion, Malone unfastened the stays that secured the heavy horse blanket and flipped it up over his saddle and saddlebags. This small chore accomplished, he whirled and unexpectedly took off in Hargrave's wake. At a run.

"This way, Scunsthorpe! Follow me while time remains!"

"*Pfagh!* You try to toy with me, Malone, but Potter Scunsthorpe is not a man to be played with! If you won't move your swollen fat cow pile of an animal, I'll move it for you!" Passing the mountain man, he continued toward Worthless, one arm raised preparatory to delivering a sound slap to the horse's rump.

"Try if you must, Scunsthorpe!" Malone yelled back as he quickened his pace. "But fer your own sake, move round to 'is bow now!"

Scunsthorpe scoffed as he continued his approach. "What's he going to do, Malone? Kick me? Do you think me so immersed in the law of the land that I am ignorant of the nature of horses?"

"Then y'all will note, and right soon," shouted Malone as he hastily ducked down behind the top of the rise, "the consequences of his interminable consumption, proceeding without interruption from yesterday morning until this moment, which are presently about to deliver themselves not as a bout of colic, but in the form of ...!"

Worthless's tail rose, perhaps semaphoring a warning. That, more so than any of the mountain man's admonitions, drew Scunsthorpe's attention. He hesitated, his eyes widening, and turned abruptly away from the gravely bloated animal.

He was too late.

That noble if unclassifiable creature did not so much break wind as shatter it, destroy it, and biblically obliterate the entire atmosphere directly astern.

A fart of tectonic dimensions lifted the stunned Scunsthorpe off the ground. It blew him backward through the forest in company with the hundreds of treespine and ash, maple and oakthat the unquantifiable expression of equine flatulence summarily flattened. It blew him over the horizon and clear out of sight.

Great was the chanting among the local Indians at this brief if invisible manifestation of the sacred Thunderbird. Frantic were the cries of bewildered townsfolk as far away as Eau Claire, whose eau remained claire even if the air they breathed did not. Stunned pike dove deeper into Lake Winnebago, crowding the catfish for space near the bottom. It is said that ten thousand dead frogs washed ashore that day on the beaches of Green Bay.

Though they were both protected and upwind, the sheriff, Scunsthorpe's underlings, and Owen Hargrave were not entirely spared. The colored gentleman commenced crying and could not stop, while his putty-faced counterpart began retching and did not cease so doing for a good thirty minutes, long after the contents of his stomach had been voided. Blessedly for him, the sheriff had simply passed out, while Hargrave had the foresight to quickly cover his face with a bandanna. As for Malone, being used as he was to the occasional explosive hindgut disquisitions of his mount, he simply rose and brushed at something sensed but unseen in front of his face. It dissipated with thankful rapidity.

Having summarily and volcanically relieved himself of a truly astonishing buildup of gas subsequent to his owner's granting him permission to do so through the simple mechanism of raising the uniquely restrictive blanket, and apparently none the worse for the episode, Worthless astoundingly resumed his feeding on what little remained of Farmer Hargrave's reserves.

"What ...?" It was all Hargrave, being the only one of the group presently capable of coherent speech due to the fact that his lungs had remained relatively untrammeled, could muster.

"Normally, Worthless eats ... normally," Malone explained as he topped the rise to scrutinize the completely flattened quarter sectionand moreof forest. "But if I let him, the stupid sack of silly soak will just continue t' eat, an' eat, an' eat. Until his internal mechanisms, which are as abnormal in their way as the rest o' him, kin no longer appropriately process their contents. They therefore release at one go all the ignoble effluvia they have unaccountably accumulated, in a volume and at a velocity that would stun any zoologist and cause the most sober veterinarian to forswear his chosen profession on the spot. 'Tis a regrettable social imperfection that Worthless and I usually have no difficulty avoidin', as I have a care to regulate his feeding carefully. In this instance, however, I considered that lettin' his appetite run free might in its own perverse fashion prove useful, and relatively harmless bein' as we are in a relatively unpopulated region.

"And now, if y'all please, I think it both safe and pleasant for you, Mr. Hargrave, t' see to your fine family and wife, and for me t' have the distinct pleasure o' donning, for the first time in some while, clothing thet has been properly cleaned and disinfected."

A dazed Hargrave surveyed his one hundred and sixty acres: felled and, if not stacked, at least neatly aligned all in one direction. Why, he mused wonderingly, the force of the equine eruption had even cleanly topped the fallen trees. He had lumber aplenty for his own use, good timber to sell, and cleared forest land sufficient to satisfy the demands of the unrelentingly greedy Scuns....

He looked around.

Where was the unpleasant stick of a speculator, anyway?

He was found several days later, wandering the western shore of Lake Winnebago, a glazed look upon his eye. Save for a broken right arm, a sprained left knee, and a lack of intact clothing, he was apparently unharmed. Wrinkling their collective noses and keeping their distance, his rescuers proceeded to burn his surviving attire while offering the benumbed survivor food and drink. For the latter he was most volubly grateful, but for the former somewhat uncertain.

It appeared most strange to his rescuers, and while a cause could not immediately be determined, it was clear to one and all in attendance that the man's olfactory senses had been irrevocably damaged, for he could not smell so much as one of his own farts.

Certain things in life are unavoidable. The weather. Falling in love. Summer sniffles. Jokes that begin with "A priest, a rabbi, and an imam walk into a bar ... ," "A pilot, a truck driver, and a boat captain walk into a bar ... ," "An ecdysiast, an enthusiast, and an entrepreneur walk into a bar...."

Well, you're out of luck: I don't know any of those.

But I do know that one day, bereft of inspiration, I was thinking about those jokes I don't know, and Amos Malone came to mind, and I mused, "A mountain man and a ... walk into a bar."

I just didn't have anything to put in place of that central "..."

But our seven cats did.

A MOUNTAIN MAN AND A CAT WALK

W hat're you starin' so hard at, old-timer?" Malone asked as
he swung his buckskin-clad left leg up and over the vertigi-
nous back of his mount. Dust motes erupted from where his boot
whumped into the unpaved main street of the central Kansas town.
The impact left an imprint, much as an elephant might do in the
soft mud of Lake Victoria's foreshore.

His leathery, weathered visage much softened by the early light
of evening, the curious senior squinted at the enormous horse from
which its equally gargantuan rider had just dismounted.

"Tryin' to decide which of you is bigger, your animal or you."
Turning his head to his left, he spat into the street. The tobaccoid
spittle immediately sank and vanished into a dry wagon rut several
inches deep. "That's a might interestin'-looking critter you're
riding." He raised a slender but muscular arm and pointed. "What's
that leather patch across his forehead for?"

Malone tugged at the wide, silver-studded belt that struggled to
encircle his waist. "He gets sunburned easy."

"Ain't you goin' to tie 'im up?"

Swaying toward the entrance of the hotel saloon like a China
clipper battling a Force 8 gale, Malone glanced back briefly to
where he had left thick reins hanging loose.

"Worthless ain't goin' nowhere. He'll stay put."

The old man continued masticating the unnameable. "Well, what if somebody takes a hankerin' to make off with 'im?" He grinned with the remainder of his teeth, between which there was ample space for whistling and perhaps the occasional misguided flying insect. "Me, for example."

Malone lowered his gaze, the wolf's head that covered his scalp sliding slightly forward. "Why then, I reckon you'd stay put, too." He nodded once in the direction of his seemingly somnolent horse. "Anyways, I wouldn't try it. We been on the trail awhile and Worthless, he's gettin' on to bein' a mite hungry."

The old man started to chuckle. "That so? What's he gonna do? Mistake me for a bucket o' oats?"

The towering mountain man just smiled back, his own orthodonture flashing surprisingly white among the surrounding jungle of gray-flecked black beard. Then he turned, stepped up onto the protesting wood plank sidewalk, ducked his head, and pushed through the double doors leading into the saloon.

The old man looked after him for a moment, then turned back to the untethered horse that was part Percheron, part Arabian, and parts of something other. Appraising the reins falling vertical and unsecured, he took a step toward them. Swinging its head around, the unclassifiable quadruped closed one eye, squinted out of the other, and gave a snort. That did not give the tough oldster pause. What did was the puff of smoke that emerged from both equine nostrils to feather away into the early evening air.

Abruptly smacked upside the head with second thoughts, the old man turned around right quick and began to walk away. Swiftly, with an occasional nervous glance back over his shoulder. Seeing that the horse was still watching him and perhaps detecting a flicker of red in that single squinting eye, the oldster proceeded to accelerate his pace accordingly.

Malone just did avoid nudging the cat with his right foot as he entered the saloon's main room. A fleeting glance in the animal's direction as it darted in off the street and dashed past him showed an ordinary tabby of average size. Its coat was in surprisingly good shape for a street cat, in coloration falling somewhere between gold and tan, with a distinctive black swath running across its upper back from shoulder to shoulder. Hugging the baseboard while striving to be as inconspicuous as possible, it raced away from Malone to disappear among the tables.

These were occupied by the usual assortment of cardplayers, double-dealers, braggarts, liars, cowpokes, military veterans, military deserters, failed gold miners, unremarkable townsfolk, and a sprinkling of seriously underdressed women who had lately been deficient in regular church attendance. The volume of their conversation dropped by about half when Malone lumbered into the room. He disliked the effect his size and appearance had on regular folks, but there was nothing much he could do about it.

Making his way to the far end of the bar, he quietly settled down on the last, empty bar stool. This prompted a rush by the half dozen or so patrons seated nearby to vacate their stools, the occupants thereof having experienced a sudden mutual desire to betake themselves somewhere else. When the rest of the crowd saw that the enormous newcomer wasn't about to pull off anyone's leg and start gnawing on it, the usual energetic conversation was resumed by the room's relieved populace.

"Whiskey," Malone told the barkeep politely. When that uneasy but admirably professional attendant produced a bottle that looked as if it might have been filled at a horse trough, a frown crossed Malone's face. "Better." Pulling a less unsanitary container from a shelf on the backbar, the rotund bartender placed it in front of Malone and removed its predecessor. *"Better,"* the mountain man reiterated.

This time the barkeep dug under the bar until he found and brought forth a stoppered glass bottle immaculate of shape and label. Malone examined it with a practiced eye, then nodded approvingly. "That'll do. Leave it and a glass." The barkeep was relieved to comply.

An hour or so passed in silent contemplation. Apart and away from the now-isolated Malone, money was lost, temporary assignations were forged, two men were thrown out for fighting, two women were cheered on for fighting. Vociferous accusations of cheating at cards were resolved without the use of gunplay, which in contrast to the way it was portrayed in dime novels was noisy, dangerous, and counterproductive for all concerned. A steady stream of regulars and visitors came and went.

One of the latter drew more than the usual casual looks, mostly because the fellow had his dog with him. A handsome black chow, it trotted along behind its owner as they made for the bar. The animal certainly was in better shape than its human, who was tall but of a girth suggestive of a pampered life in the city, and not one spent toiling at manual labor. He had two chins or three depending on whether he was looking up or down, an absurdly long thin mustache more suited to the face of a riverboat gambler, and piercing blue eyes that were small and sharp. His nose was plump and red, as if a ripe plum had been plucked from its tree and glued to his face. When he removed his handsome but oversized wide-brimmed hat, it was to reveal a pate ornamented with a flourish of carefully coiffured blond curls. As near as anyone could tell, they were actually growing out of his head and were not the result of some desultory scalping of an anonymous ten-year-old girl.

Defying caution and present convention, he took a seat once removed from where Malone, a mountainous figure wreathed in buckskins, wolf headdress, and Zen, sat steadily working his way through the bottle in front of him. The chow did not sit. Instead, it took up an alert stance directly beside its owner's stool. The newcomer ordered, took a sip from his glass, had the barkeep pour him another. Looking over, Malone nodded in the direction of the chow.

"Judgin' by his attitude, your dog don't seem t' like me much."

Jowls aquiver, the man turned blue eyes to him. "It isn't you." With evident deliberation, he lowered his gaze. "It's your cat. Elehzub doesn't like cats."

A surprised Malone looked down at his feet. Sprawled half on, half off the upper portion of his right boot was the tabby over whom he had nearly stumbled while entering the saloon. It lay on the battered leather with its eyes shut, one paw under its jaw, purring contentedly. Occasionally it would move its head, rubbing against Malone's ankle. Given the profound panoply of odors that clung to that outsized footwear, the feline's response was not surprising.

The newcomer's attitude, which until now had ranged from placid to outright indifferent, turned suddenly unpleasant. The blue eyes narrowed. "I don't like cats, either. In fact, I hate cats."

Deploying a massive shrug, Malone returned to his contemplation of the backbar. A sizable painting hanging there displayed its creator's modest competency in oils. It showed a somewhat thickset woman lying on a bed in a typically clichéd yet no less pleasant state of complete deshabille.

"Not my cat."

Having got hold of the issue, the newcomer seemed unwilling to let go of it. "Then what's it doing lolling in simpering disgust all over your foot?"

Malone did not turn from the aesthetic that was currently holding his attention. "Why don't you ask the cat?"

It was plain that the visitor was not used to being so casually dismissed. One hand pushed away the half-filled glass resting on the bar before him.

"You are toying with me, sir. Know that I am Gustavus Eyvind Hudiksvall, and I am not one to be toyed with." He waved in the general direction of the crowd. "Unlike these simpletons, I am not intimidated by your great unhygienic bulk. Would you like to know why?" When Malone chose not to respond, Hudiksvall continued.

"You see this fine animal standing proudly beside me, that has no hesitation in expressing its dislike for *your cat*? I am not only its master. I am a master of all the dogs of the Americas. It is my profession. It is my avocation. I know American dogs. I understand American dogs. I perceive them and their inner selves in ways that you and others cannot imagine. I comprehend their needs, their desires, their innermost being! Yea, even their thoughts, for those who believe that dogs do not think know nothing of the animal."

Lovely, Malone thought as he continued to gaze at the painting. He sighed. Just lovely. Someone he had not known, but would have wished to. "Cats think also. They just don't jump around stupidly and brag about it."

The color of Hudiksvall's cheeks began to approach that of the rugoid bulbosity attached to the center of his face. "You persist in playing me for a fool, sir. Well, I will not be played." He peered down at the chow that was growling softly. A most disagreeable smile creased his wide, wide face. "Neither will Elehzub. I think ... I think I will let him eat your cat."

"Not my cat." Malone did not shift his attention from the painting.

"Then you won't mind."

Leaning over and grunting with the effort, Hudiksvall whispered something in the chow's direction. Tongue hanging and eyes eager, it perked its black ears up intently. Whatever the fat man was whispering clearly made an impression on the animal. It tensed as it listened and its soft growling took on a new, more lethal aspect.

The sound was enough to wake the tabby. Eyes snapping open, they shifted to focus on the eager dog. Rising from where it had been slumbering while contentedly inhaling the inexpressibly powerful effluvia from Malone's boot, it moved behind the mountain man's leg. Its ears flattened against its head and its back arched as it hissed warningly.

Malone took a swallow from his glass. "Looks like your animal might have a fight on its hands."

If Hudiksvall was concerned, he didn't show it. "I thought something like this might happen." His eyes zeroed in on the alarmed cat, twin blue gunsights targeting prey unable to escape. "Did I not tell you I was a master of dogs?"

Leaning over once more, still straining from the effort, he whispered something else to the chow. Something more than mere communication this time. Something powerful and private and ancient that would be known only to an individual possessed of some special and unique knowledge. Malone caught the gist of it and reacted. By which is to say a couple of black whiskers twitched among their multitudinous companions.

"Et pugnare crescere." Hudiksvall revealed impressive elocution in commanding his animal. *"Pugnare, et interficere!"*

A dark, dank, flea-free cloud began to coalesce around the chow. Small bursts of miniature lightning flashed within the murk, each one accompanied not by thunder but by a short, sharp bark. The vapor continued to darken until the chow could no longer be seen. Two men seated nearby arguing over the ownership of a mining claim noted this unexpected manifestation of necromancy and stared, but did not flee.

The miasma began to dissipate. In its place Hudiksvall's dog still stood as before, only it had been transformed. In place of the black chow there now squatted a massive, wide-shouldered bulldog. When it growled, the sound was deeper and far more menacing than anything that had been expressed by its previously chowly form. A collar of taupe leather studded with two-inch-long spikes encircled its thick neck. In response to its master's command, the revamped dog's eyes and attention were now focused exclusively on the cat that had taken shelter behind Malone's right leg.

Hudiksvall's grin arose directly from the nastiness of his soul. "This won't take but a moment, sir. When this strapping expression of Elehzub gets done, there'll be nothing left of your cat save a few picked-over bones."

"Not my cat," Malone reiterated. Thick dark brows drew together over eyes as black as the lowermost reaches of a failed Montana copper mine. "On the other hand, I *like* cats. I also don't much cotton to an unfair contest."

It was a remarkable thing to see a man as big as Malone, who stood just shy of seven feet and whose weight approached three hundred pounds, bend nearly in half. But that was the kind of astonishing flexibility he proceeded to display. He bent over, bent some more, and whispered something to the hissing cat. As a surprised Hudiksvall looked on, a swirl of gold and white opacity coiled up around the cat. Light twinkled within, flashing and blinking, accompanied by a sound like the boiler of a small Mississippi riverboat letting off steam. Or it might have been an extremely attenuated feline hiss.

As Malone straightened and returned to his drinking, the white-gold mist faded away. Where the tabby had stood before now stoodanother cat. Much larger than its former self, it was heavily spotted and thickly muscled, with a high butt, short tail, and unmistakable dark tufts rising from the tips of its ears. It snarled more impressively than any street cat while simultaneously displaying very impressive teeth.

Having initially taken a step forward, the bulldog, now finding itself confronted by a decidedly more imposing opponent, whimpered once and retreated.

Hudiksvall's anger was palpable, but he was not about to withdraw with a nonexistent tail between his legs.

"So! A man of learning and cleverness you are, also. One would not gainsay it from your uncouth appearance. It seems then it is to be tit for tat, cat for cat. I have no fear of that, for I grasp the soul of such conjuring. Just as you must know that only a cat native to America can counter a transformative American dog and vice the versa. It is written so, in aged tomes I suspect you may also have read." He eyed the lynx that now stepped out from behind the mountain man's leg. "While your adroit alteration is a fine example of the wild continental feline kind, it remains no less only a cat for all that. You think I am done? Then observe, learn, and prepare to sweep up the scraps!"

Once more bending low, this time over the bulldog, Hudiksvall murmured anew, now with more energy than before.

"Surgens autem, vinco inferno, et occidas!"

For a second time a dark cloud ballooned to life around Hudiksvall's companion. It swallowed up the bulldog, obscuring its canine reality. The cloud itself grew larger, much larger than before, until when it finally evaporated there stood in its wake a dog of truly imposing proportions. It was huge, with a blunt, powerful face and a tail that curled up over its rump. It looked down, down at the lynx, which held its ground, albeit with an effort.

"American mastiff." Hudiksvall's triumphant smile was wider this time. "Bred to protect herds of sheep and cattle." Piggish eyes blinking, he gazed expectantly down from his seat at the lynx standing firm beside Malone's leg. "Bigger bones will be left this time, but bones nonetheless."

"Dogs be dogs and cats be cats." With a shrug, Malone bent over once again to whisper something to the lynx. Tufted ears flicked immediately in his direction.

A miniature cumulus colored gold and ivory enveloped the lynx even as the mastiff started forward, drool dripping from its powerful jaws. Then it halted and began backing up, until it was standing, though still growling, behind its master, whose buttocks overflowed both sides of the bar stool.

Having come to the decision that it was about time that they pushed their argument off to another day, the two miners who had been looking on abandoned their table in favor of a joint quick-march in the direction of the saloon entrance. Simultaneously, several ladies of the evening determined that it was time to embrace the lateness of the hour, if not potential customers, whereupon they proceeded to hightail it up the nearby stairs in a concerted rush for the second-floor back rooms. Torn between fear and fascination by the increasingly ominous transformations taking place at the bar, the rest of the saloon's motley population mostly remained, transfixed.

Standing beside Malone, its smooth tan back rising to a level not far below the height of the bar, the puma fastened bright yellow eyes on the mastiff and hissed loudly enough to be heard out in the street. Exhibiting unified homage to the true frontier spirit, no one outside proved dumb enough to enter and investigate the sound.

By now the newcomer was beside himself, near apoplectic with frustration. "I am Gustavus Eyvind Hudiksvall, master of American canines and all knowledge thereto related, and no stinking moun-tain of a man and his cat will best me this night or any other! It is the nature of existence that dog should lord it over cat, that the latter should run before the former, and I swear it will be so this night as it is on every other night!"

Holding his glass between thumb and forefinger of his left hand, Malone took a half swallow of the good whiskey while with his right

hand he reached down and stroked the back of the neck of the fully
alert cougar. It growled in response.

"Not my cat."

Sliding off the stool, an avalanche of fat, Hudiksvall squatted in
front of the mastiff in order to look directly into its eyes. Reaching
out with thick fingers, he grasped both ears of the dog. This time he
did not even try to murmur. Instead, his voice rose until it rattled
around the saloon.

"FORMARE MAXIME AUTEM!" The fat man's bellow rattled
the second-floor rafters and shook dust on those seated below.
"FRATRES, DE DENTE, ET INIMICOS TUOS INTERFICERE!"

At this, the one couple in the saloon that was actually married
rose from their table and departed in haste, leaving behind the
uneaten remnants of their supper. A well-dressed rancher of some
means swore mightily in a foreign language. Everyone else could
only sit and stare, half-paralyzed. The situation had turned serious.
Spittoons were missed.

As with its predecessors, the cloud that rose around the mastiff
was dark with bark and lit with snarls, but this time the vaporous
manifestation fractured, splitting into two, three, and many more
distinct upwellings. Straightening, a sweaty but confident
Hudiksvall surveyed his canine handiwork. In time each cloud
began to dissipate, swept away by the fat man's sinister and
definitive necromancy.

"Or should I say, and this I suspect you know," he told Malone,
"simply *'Cave canum.'*"

Growling to themselves, the pack assembled beside Hudiksvall.
Tongues hanging out, panting, they flashed sharp teeth set in jaws
strong enough to bring down a bear or a bison. More than a dozen
of the huge timber wolves began to spread out, forming a semicircle
in front of Malone and the cougar in preparation for an attack.

Whereas until now the mystical, inexplicable manifestation of
dogs and cats of increasingly larger species had served largely to
enthrall the majority of the saloon's patrons, the appearance of the
wolf pack succeeded in emptying the establishment of its remaining
customers. Libations were left unimbibed, poker chips were scat-

tered, chairs were overturned, screams and curses were essayed with a mixture of vehemence and panic, and at least two heretofore atheistic shopkeepers competed in a footrace to see who could arrive first at the Baptist church that was located at the far end of the town's central thoroughfare.

"Maybe," a heavily perspiring but expectant Hudiksvall ventured maliciously, "your cat will not be sufficient to satisfy the appetite of my pets, and they will express a desire to taste man as well. They are certain to find attractive the jambalaya of effluvia that clings to you." He licked thick lips expectantly. "Well, sir, I await your response. Your final response. Is it again to be 'Not my cat'? Or perhaps, if you grovel with sufficient eloquence, I may command the pack to spare you. Though not, to be sure, this current, final, and failed iteration of your unfortunate feline."

By way of response Malone carefully set down his glass. The bottle before him was now empty, the liquid warmth it had dispensed a pleasant glow deep within his belly. Turning, he regarded with sad eyes the bloated boaster before him.

"A true necromancer knows how to fight fair." Raising a huge, callused hand, he gestured at the pack that was systematically positioning itself prior to rushing in for the kill. "Twelve against one ain't hardly fair. But if that is how it is to be ..."

Bending toward the cougar, he commenced once more to speak softly.

Hudiksvall was neither impressed nor worried. "What is to be now, sir? I know you cannot do the same spell of multiplicity as I, for I sense it, and I have the perception of the animals for whom I care. What single local feline will you draw upon now, to counter the kings of canines, who cooperate in a fight better than any other of their kind? I await your last and best counter, prior to your animal's and possibly your own dismemberment!"

A strange sound began to seep into the saloon. It came from outside the building as Malone continued to whisper—never shouting, never raising his voice. It took a moment for those who had fled outside to identify it. It was in no wise alien; they had all heard it before. It was the collective symphony of cats yowling every cat in town and onward to its outskirts screeching and hollering at the tops of their lungs.

The golden cloud that enveloped the cougar was darker than any that had preceded it. As Malone looked on with interest and Hudiksvall's gaze narrowed uncertainly, the vaporous mist grew and expanded, becoming larger, vaster, immenser (if you will), until eventually it passed into the realm of the ridiculous. At last it began to clear, revealing ... a cat.

It was a tabby, of sorts, albeit one that weighed about half a ton and might've been thirteen feet from its wet black nose to the tip of its tail. Colored somewhere between gold and tan, it showed a distinctive black ruff across its upper shoulders. A black ruff that was thick and wide and flaring. More of a mane, really. Lowering its head and dipping its brow forward, the beast contracted its mouth into a most terrible expression: death writ in wrinkles. Then it opened its jaws, revealing teeth that were large enough to chomp a man in half with one bite.

Having anticipated, called forth, and recognized the breed, Malone nodded to himself with satisfaction.

Rooted to the spot, one hand held out defensively before him, a terrified Hudiksvall stumbled backward. The pack of timber wolves were already gone, having vanished under and through the saloon's swinging doors. One, caught at the back of the pack as the other eleven struggled to squeeze through the portal simultaneously, opted for leaping through a flanking window in order to escape the room and the gargantuan feline that had materialized before them. That the window in question happened to be closed at the time did not in any way forestall the wolf's decision. Their judicious flight was accompanied by a notable absence of growls and much frantic whining.

Overweight and underpowered, Hudiksvall had no such opportunity. It was to his credit that despite his fear, it was his curiosity that came to the fore.

"That ... that monstrous beast is not an American cat! It is not possible for you to call forth a feline expression from the African continent to confront American canines. It refutes the magikal canon and cannot be so!"

"Wal now," Malone drawled as he used his right hand to ruffle the ruff of the massive creature standing beside him, "you are right correct about thet, Mr. Hudiksvall." Despite Malone's efforts to calm him, the gigantic cat continued to incline murderously toward the other man, barely restraining itself. "This here is an American lion. *Felis atrox*, if you will. First dug up by a fella name of Bill Huntington near Natchez in 1836 but not described in much detail until ol' Doc Joseph Leidy wrote somethin' up on 'em in 1852. Lot bigger than their African cousins, they are." He leaned forward. "Danged impressive teeth, ain't they?"

Advancing on paws each one of which was more than broad enough to completely cover a man's head and face, the lion took a step toward Hudiksvall and let out a single ... *ROAR*.

The folks who heard it over in the next county thought it was a storm a-brewing. The church bell in town shivered out a couple of desultory clangs that did nothing to reassure the pair of shopkeeper converts who huddled inside. Children woke up crying, in which exercise of their tear ducts they were equaled by a significant number of mothers. Strong men quaked in their boots and the town sheriff hurried to lock the jail door from the inside.

Gustavus Eyvind Hudiksvall turned positively white (well, whiter than he had been previously, anyhow) and suddenly found his feet. Despite the effort required, they conveyed him with admirable rapidity to the saloon's entrance, which portal he exited with such velocity that one of the swinging doors was knocked askew on its hinges.

Having nothing else to confront or on which to focus its attention, the splendidly immense example of *Felis atrox* turned back toward Amos Malone. A relic of an age only recently bygone, the great jaws parted. With interest, Malone peered down the throat thus revealed.

The tongue that emerged licked the mountain man's face and copious beard so that both were soon dripping with leonine saliva, until Malone finally had to put a stop to the display of primeval affection. Reaching out, he dug his right hand into the vast black mane and began scratching. Like all its kind, the lion could not purr, but it lowered its head contentedly.

"It were that black ruff o' yours," he murmured to the big cat. "I saw the connection right off, but 'tweren't no reason at the time t' pursue it." He nodded toward the damaged doorway. "Until it were forced. On the both of us." Leaning forward, he whispered into the lion's right ear.

This time the cloud shrank instead of expanding. Which was a fortunate adjustment, because it was unlikely the town itself would have survived a cat-thing of any greater dimension. When the last of the gilded cloud vanished, it left behind on the tobacco-stained floor a tabby of normal size, gold and tan in color, with an odd black streak in its hair that stretched from shoulder to shoulder. It shook itself, licked one paw to briefly groom the fur on its forehead, and then began to arch its back and rub against Malone's right boot. Reaching down, the mountain man picked it up and placed it gently on the now-deserted sweep of mahogany bar. Then he leaned forward and over to peer down behind the barrier.

"Barkeep."

Trembling visibly, the bartender rose from where he had been hiding. He looked at Malone, at the cat sitting contentedly near the giant's right hand, then back at Malone.

"Wh-wh-wh-what'll it be ... sir?"

"Whiskey. Same label." Malone indicated the serene feline seated nearby. "And a saucer of milk for my friend. Straight up."

The barkeep managed to nod. "This ... this is a saloon, sir. Milk, I'm not so sure ..."

"This here's also a hotel, friend. Got t' be some milk or cream on ice in the kitchen." He leaned forward slightly, lowering his voice. "Go find it. And you'd best come back."

No one else entered the saloon that night. No one else came near the saloon that night. Its interior was occupied solely by its shaky proprietor, a mountain man of measureless smells and unsuspected abilities, and the gold and tan cat seated comfortably on the bar off to his right. Not his cat. Together the three passed the remainder of the evening undisturbed and mostly in silence, until the time finally came for Malone to exit. At this the bartender allowed himself to faint gratefully and with some grace. He did not hit the floor too hard.

The cat followed Malone outside. After the mountain man finished admonishing his horse for eating half the hitching post, he turned to look back at the plank sidewalk. The cat was sitting there, its tail switching slowly back and forth, staring at him in the unblinking, fearless manner of cats everywhere. For certain a most ordinary cat.

"G'night, puss. Got t' be on my way. Watch your step. Don't eat any mice I wouldn't eat."

The cat turned to depart, looking back only once to meow.

That is generally remembered as the Manhattan, Kansas, earth-quake of 1867.

Has anyone ever asked you, "If you could be reincarnated, what creature would you come back as?" Oddly enough, I always knew the answer. Or least, I have ever since my family visited the Sierra Nevada's national parks when I was seven years old. From that time on I knew what I would wish to come back as. It's a choice that hasn't changed in the intervening sixty-four years.

Of course, even among such imposing life-forms there are bound to be those inclined less to conviviality than irritability. I would hope that, should such a reincarnation occur, I could be more accommodating than the example set forth in this story. Especially if I were to be granted the opportunity to meet Amos Malone. And equally so, his human counterpart in this final tale.

Without question the grove of cinnamon-red, giant trees was one of the most beautiful, inspiring, soul-rejuvenating, spirit-calming, downright sacred places Amos Malone had ever visited. At least, it was until he heard the cry for help.

STUCK

Riding astride Worthless, who was less than happy with the limited flavors of the local undergrowth and ventured his opinion by occasionally spitting out something the horse deemed not worthy of dissolution by his digestive juices, Malone had made his way up into the fabulous mountain country that had been described to him down in the valley. If anything, the farmers with whom he had spoken had understated the majesty of the untouched sequoia forest. The gargantuan ginger-toned columns that towered around him on either side reminded him less of other trees and more of the massive stone columns of the great temple at Luxor.

The cool lingering droplets of a just-concluded Sierra storm still perspired from branches high overhead and mushed beneath Worthless's huge feet. Swathed in his buckskin and furs, Malone was quite comfortable. Familiar with the vagaries of mountain weather, he suspected that by midmorning he would need to doff his outer raiment lest he begin to sweat himself. This dermatological exposure would inevitably set free a personal bouquet which he, from experience, was reluctant to inflict even on a passel of passing marmots, far less upon another human being. Fortunately, there appeared to be none of the latter about, and so his questionable personal hygiene would remain a matter for he himself.

There was, however, the possible intrusion on his solitude of someone unknown calling out for help.

Despite the notoriety the giant trees had begun to acquire, lack of ready accessibility to their mountain vastness had kept the grove through which he was currently wandering free of all but the most determined adventurer. That was a situation that would likely change with time, he knew, but for the moment the peace and tranquility of his surroundings remained inviolate. Except for the intermittent cry for assistance.

Pulling back lightly on the reins, he brought Worthless to a halt, leaned forward, and listened intently. There was no panic in the shouts he was hearing, no intimation of fear. Whoever was calling for aid was not being attacked by a catamount nor clinging perilously to the knife edge of a cliff. It was a measured, periodic yelp, forceful and determined but absent of panic.

Yet a cry for help was a cry for help, Malone knew. Straightening in the saddle and tugging again on the reins, Malone inclined Worthless in its direction. Responding with a characteristic squint eye, the muscular mélange of Percheron, quarterhorse, Shire, Arabian, Indian pony, and something not of the current reality as most folks know it, turned and headed in the indicated direction, picking up the pace as he did so. All the while, Malone listened, adjusting his mount's path according to the perceived location of each periodic outcry.

It wasn't long before they entered a small glade within a cathedral-like grove of the gigantic trees. It was there that the calls for help seemed to resound the loudest. A quick survey of the surroundings revealed no supplicant. It was dead silent, if one discounted Worthless's intermittent passing of horse gas. It was not soon after their arrival, however, that the voice Malone had been hearing once again called out strong and clear.

"Up here!"

Leaning slightly back in his saddle, Malone looked up. And up, and up, having to squint almost as hard as Worthless. It took a moment for him to spot the man standing where a branch emerged from the mighty trunk some two hundred and fifty feet above the

ground. While Malone's vision was sharp, the distance and intervening verdure made it difficult to distinguish details. What he
could see of the caller revealed a man of about Malone's own age,
but smaller and slenderer. Even at that distance it could be seen that
he boasted a beard of impressive proportions. One that in length, at
least, surpassed Malone's own equally lush facial undergrowth.

"Let me guess," Malone shouted upward. "You have conquered
this 'ere imposin' ascent only t' find you are unable to make your
way down again, either by your original route or any other."

Peering down, the man high up the tree called back emphatically. "Not at all, sir. I am more familiar than most with all manner
of trees in these mountains, and would have no difficulty making my
way down the imposing bole of this one, save for one entirely unexpected peculiarity."

Malone pursed his lips. "Perhaps I kin be of assistance. I am by
way o' experience somewhat acquainted with unexpected peculiari-
ties, Mr. ...?"

"John," came down the voice from above. "Call me John.
Everyone does. John of the mountains, sometimes."

"Then I will partake o' the general verdict, John, and call you
thet. If you will instruct me as to the particular peculiarity that
prevents you descendin' from your elevated perch, I will endeavor t'
lend a hand. Most particular, I have to ask ... *why* can't you come
down?"

"This most obstinate and infuriating tree won't let me."

"I see." It was then that Malone's vision noted the pair of
smaller branches that were wrapped respectively around the man's
chest and thighs, pinning him to a trunk that was still impressive in
girth even at altitude. He pondered a moment. Worthless glanced
back at him, snorted, and bent to masticate pinecones. The consequent crunching, which produced a sound like boots punching
through a crust of new-frozen snow, echoed through the forest.
"Why not?"

"Och, how should I know?" came the somewhat exasperated
voice from on high. The Scottish burr was unmistakable.

"Well now." Malone scratched at the back of his neck where

something small and multilegged was presently attempting to set up residence without paying rent. "Have you tried askin' the tree?"

A moment's silence preceded the slowly considered reply. "There are some who say that I am mad, sir, for doing things like climbing trees to experience the full fury of a thunderstorm in the mountains. That was the specific situation that brought me to my present inexplicable condition and finds me trapped here. But know that I am not mad when I say that as soon as I tried to descend, branches of this giant caught me tight round the body and have held me captive here for some hours now." The speaker paused, then added, "I fear that in addition to increasing thirst and hunger, I am in some desperate need of a change of undergarments."

Malone nodded to himself. "There be some also t' say that *I* am mad, John of the mountains, so it appears we are brothers in insanity. I reiterate: have you tried asking the tree?"

"Many are the birds whose calls I can imitate, and the cry of the bobcat and the warnings of the deer as well," came the response, "but while I have addressed terms of admiration and endearment to a wide assortment of growths, I have never yet managed to evoke a reply. Nor, I venture, has any human being."

"A good deal of it, John," Malone called back, "has t' do with the accent. Pine is soft and spoken wholly with the lips, birch speech more of a whispering, while cypress talk must first be begun with a growl and a murmur." Whereupon the mountain man formed his lips, tongue, palate, and epiglottis into such a wholesale confusion of body parts that any physician able to observe the result would have fainted dead away at the sheer impossibility of the biology. When everything physiological was in place, Malone formally addressed the sequoia.

"'Ere now, you great overgrown slab o' termite grub: what's behind this discourteous business o' holdin' prisoner that poor thirsty, hungry, soiled feller you've got caught in your upstairs?"

There issued from the depths of the ancient growth a rumbling so deep, so subsonic, that it would have made the private cursing of the African elephant seem positively falsetto. John up the tree did not hear it ... but he felt it. The blue jays hunting beetles in the needle piles did not hear it. Neither did the fish, nor the fox, nor the ants underfoot hear it. Only Malone possessed the learning and the sensitivity to understand the voice that came forth, seemingly formed of the very earth itself.

"HIS PRESENCE ... OFFENDS ME."

Malone pushed the wolf's-head cap back off his forehead and wiped away sweat. "Wal now, I didn't know a tree could take offense."

"YOU ARE, LIKE THE REST OF YOUR KIND, IGNORANT OF THE WORLD AROUND YOU."

"Hold on there, big twig. I may be many things, but ignorant ain't one o' them. If I'm so ignorant, how come I'm talkin' t' you right now?"

There was a pause, then, "I CONCEDE THAT YOU MAY BE MARGINALLY LESS UNKNOWING THAN THE REST OF YOUR KIND."

Malone decided to be satisfied with that. Arguing with an obstinate sequoia would get him nowhere, nor would it provide the captive John with his much-desired change of underwear.

"If you don't mind my askin', what precisely about your visitor's presence offends you so much that you refuse t' let him down?"

"HE CAME UP WITHOUT ASKING. THAT IS HOW I HAVE SEEN HUMANS TREAT MY KIND. THEY DO WHATEVER THEY DESIRE, WITHOUT ASKING."

Ever since their arrival in the glade, a pair of brother wolves had been stalking the new arrivals. They were very close now, crouched just behind a thick clump of bushes. Tongues lolling, they charged, aiming for Worthless's copious hindquarters. Snarling, they leaped with mouths agape and fangs dripping. Malone spared them a brief glance before returning his attention to the sequoia.

Without looking back, Worthless kicked out with his hind right leg. It caught the first wolf under his jaw. The impact caused the unfortunate predator to describe four complete backward somersaults before finally landing in a dense copse of gooseberry from which subsequently only a confused whimpering could be heard. Lunging for a leg, the second wolf found itself pinned beneath an

oversized hoof. With Worthless's weight atop it, it scrabbled frantically at the ground with its paws, fighting for breath, as the horse
calmly resumed his methodical devastation of nearby grass, prim-
rose, and bracken fern.

"This John, he strikes me as a good sort o' feller," Malone
continued. "One who holds nothin' but the greatest respect fer all
Nature, and especially fer trees. I'm sure he'd be happy to apologize
fer any imposition."

"TOO LATE!" the sequoia roared. Upper branches shook while
lower branches that were themselves greater in diameter than the
surrounding pines and firs trembled ever so slightly. "I HAVE
MADE MY DECISION! LET HIS REMAINS BE A LESSON TO
ANY WHO SHOULD COME AND TRY TO DO LIKEWISE. I
WILL HOLD HIM CLOSE UNTIL WIND AND RAIN AND
TIME HAVE REDUCED HIM TO WORM FOOD!"

"Now, now," murmured Malone soothingly, "turnin' admirin' visitors into worm food ain't very hospitable. There'll likely be more a-
comin' t' gape at you and yours, and no matter how many you try to
worm-food-ize, 'tis likely you'll fail to do 'em all." He gestured with
a huge, gnarled hand. "Fer one thing, you're somewhat handicapped
by a noticeable lack o' digits. You just got lucky when John here
decided t' favor you with a visit."

"I WILL FIND A WAY!" The entire enormous bulk of the
sequoia quivered slightly. "I WILL HOLD THEM ALL, ONE BY
ONE, UNTIL THEY LEARN THE WISDOM OF KEEPING
THEIR DISTANCE!" Silence was followed by a comment that
sounded somewhat uncertain. "YOUR ANIMAL IS DEFILING
MY ROOTS."

Leaning over, Malone glanced down at the ground beneath
Worthless, then straightened. "That by its simple liquid self ought t'
prove to you that if a visitor don't make contact with you directly,
there ain't much you can do. Oh, I suppose you could drop a branch
or two on 'em, but self-mutilation has its limits. Why not try bein' a
mite friendlier instead?" Rising slightly in the saddle, he took in the
rest of the magnificent grove with a single sweeping gesture. "Your
relations hereabouts don't seem near half as aggrieved as yourself."

"THEY CHOOSE TO REMAIN STUPID, IGNORANT, AND SILENT, INDIFFERENT TO INTRUSION."

Malone shook his head sadly as he sat back down. "You'd suppose thet after a couple o' thousand years o' sittin' in one place and jest thinkin', you'd have developed a better sense o' community." Slipping his left leg up and over the pommel, he dropped clear of the saddle and down to the ground.

"WHAT ARE YOU DOING?" The great tree was unafraid, but wary.

"Why, since you won't let poor John go, I reckon I'm goin' to have t' come up and git him," Malone replied as he twiddled his fingers at one of the saddlebags that was slung over Worthless's back. The buckle obediently came open.

"YOU WILL NEVER REACH HIM. YOU WILL NOT SURVIVE!"

Ignoring the threat, Malone slipped the steel tree spurs onto his boots. Though fire-resistant, almost bug-proof, and sometimes more than two feet thick, the auburn-colored bark of the giant sequoia was comparatively soft and fibrous. The spurs would find excellent purchase. Pulling a coil of rope from the same saddlebag, Malone slung it over his right shoulder.

Walking up to the base of the tree, he had to lean back to locate the most promising way upward. Without preamble, he began to climb. His thick, powerful fingers dug almost as deeply into the tree's outer layer as did the sharp metal of the spurs. The sequoia of course felt no discomfort. But it was wholly aware of Malone's presence as he ascended.

The mountain man was far above the ground before he reached the first enormous branch. This extended outward as if a full-size Douglas fir had been jammed sideways into the trunk. Repositioning his grip, Malone started to swing himself up and onto the curved, waiting platform.

It jerked violently, intending to throw him off and send him on a death spiral toward the ground.

As he clung with fingers and spurs to the sheer face of the tree, a worried voice called down from above.

"Hoy, sir! Are you all right?"

Malone glanced down at the ground. It was very far away and its surface appeared unwelcoming. For one of the few times he could recall, Worthless looked ... small. Mouth tightening, he resumed his climb.

Searching upward, he finally spied what he had been hoping for: a stub of a smaller, broken branch that projected stolidly from the side of the tree not far from where its unwilling guest was being restrained. Balancing himself against another branch that remained blessedly immobile, Malone unlimbered the lariat he had brought with him. Leaning back, he formed one end into a loop and flung it swiftly upward. It caught around the stub first try. Snugging it tight gave Malone a speedier way upward. This he proceeded to use to his advantage.

He had ascended half the remaining distance to the captive when the stub abruptly retracted into the side of the tree. The rope that had been looped around it promptly fell free.

Bereft of its support, Malone found himself falling. Looking down, he saw one massive branch rising to meet him and prepared himself for the impact.

Emitting a woody, groaning sound, it twisted out of his way, revealing only bare ground below.

Gritting his teeth, Malone yanked the looped end of the rope toward him. In a single twisting motion he passed the other end through the loop and tossed it over the branch that had contorted out of his way. The loop he still held in his hand. The shock traveled hard through his shoulders as the rope caught tight around the lassoed branch.

Clinging to the rope's free end with both hands, he let his momentum carry him around in a sweeping arc beneath the branch. At the apex of the swing, he let go, timing his release with unnatural precision. The centrifugal force of the swing carried him up, up, until he once again began to descend toward the ground.

Instead, he landed cleanly on the sturdy branch that protruded outward from beneath the feet of the tree's startled captive. As

Malone proceeded to shake free and reel in the unnaturally robust lariat, the still-immobilized prisoner gawked at him in amazement.

"I venture to say, sir, that was the most extraordinary bit of aerial prestidigitation I have ever had the pleasure of beholding! Where in God's name did you master such a technique?"

Malone shrugged as he coiled the rope, which displayed no sign of the stress it had been asked to absorb. "Here and there, friend. A bit o' physics, a touch o' the circus, a smidgen o' magic."

"'Magic'?" The prisoner eyed his rescuer uncertainly.

Malone smiled, revealing teeth that were surprisingly white in stark contrast to the rest of his sun-burned visage. "Mebbe better t' say a not-so-little birdie taught me. If we ever should have occasion t' spend a bit o' time together, I might try to explain." He turned his attention to the ground, now far below. "But first order o' business is to git down from where we are, most preferably in one piece. This here tree had a try or two at preventin' me from comin' up. I reckon it'll make something of an effort t' keep us from gettin' down."

"I shall be forever in your debt, Mr. ....?"

"Malone. Amos Malone. You kin call me Amos. Or Mad. Where monikers are concerned, I ain't particular. Kinda like Worthless."

As the mountain man unsheathed an enormous bowie knife and began to saw at the branches curled around the captive's body, John looked down toward the ground.

"Your horse? Strange name for a horse." He squinted as the branch around his chest came away, cut through. "If it is a horse. At this distance I can't be certain."

"Like names, distance don't matter where Worthless is concerned. You'll find his appearance jest as puzzlin' close up. Most folks do, though the majority choose not t' git too close." Under Malone's ministrations, the lower branch soon fell away. "There." He put out a massive hand to steady the former captive, whose muscles were cramped and knotted from hours of being held motionless against the trunk. "Easy. Watch your step. You climbed up. Reckon you kin climb down?"

Rocking his head from side to side to loosen his neck and shoulders, shaking his arms, John smiled. "There isn't a tree in the Sierra

I can't climb or descend. At least, when they're not actively engaged in countering my efforts."

Malone nodded approvingly. "Then let's be about it, afore this fathe. o' clothespins cogitates up some further mischief t' keep us from shinnyin' back down t' mother earth."

Despite Malone's unease the tree did nothing to hinder their downward progress. This they accomplished at admirable speed, with Malone marveling at John's talent for finding every possible hand- and foothold in the bark and branches. They were almost to the ground when something with the force of a spring-loaded bear trap slammed shut against Malone's right hand.

Nearby, he heard John yell. A glance sideways showed the other man still some ten feet above the ground, only inches from the easy footpath that would have been provided by the nearest bulging root mass. Just his face, hands, and feet were visible. The rest of him was trapped *within* the side of the tree. Two opposing flaps of the deeply fluted bark had slammed shut around his body, pinning him in place.

Even as he deciphered what he was seeing, Malone found himself caught between a pair of similar parallel, vertical ridges. Though he reacted with speed astonishing for such a big man, his hips and back were still caught by the enfolding strips of bark. Soft it might be, but sequoia bark was also tough. Malone's hands were free, but his knife was caught up within the fibrous restraints. He could kick at the tree, which he did, and he could slam his huge fists against the bark, which he did. He might as well have been kicking and punching the side of a mountain. Which in a sense he was, only in this instance the mountain was made of wood.

Imprisoned within opposing folds of thick bark, the two men were well and truly trapped.

He tried whispering certain words of power he knew. But they were intended only for the hearing of the great kauri of Aotearoa. He tried spit and curses suitable for persuading the inscrutable ginkgo. He tried forgotten languages and refulgent pleas. He recited relevant phrases from the *Kalevala* and Theophrastus's *Enquiry*. Nothing worked.

The tree spoke: slow, subsonic, and triumphant. "BOTH WORM FOOD NOW."

"Let us go." Malone was dead serious. "Let us go or it will end badly for you."

The sequoia could not laugh, but managed to express its amusement, nonetheless. "MEATFOOD FOR WORMS, BLOOD AND BONE FOR ME. BUT I WILL LET YOU GO. IN A THOUSAND YEARS. PERHAPS."

A more normal voice, one that propagated through the air, reached the trapped mountain man. "I am sorry to have gotten you into this, Amos Malone." Straining forward and looking to his right, Malone could just see the other man's face peering out from within the bark coffin that imprisoned him. "I have always gotten along well with trees, until now. Until this one."

"It's an ornery cuss fer sure," Malone replied calmly. "Mighty tetchy personality fer a hunk o' wood. I reckon it needs to be taught some politeness. You said you could call deer and bobcat. Any other critters?"

"Birds," came the reply from across the tree. "Many birds."

Malone shook his head sadly. "I reckon a few chickadees won't be of much assistance in our current situation. More forceful intervention is demanded. Somethin' considerable more powerful."

Turning away from the other man and pursing his lips, he whistled sharply.

"CALL WHAT YOU WISH," the exultant tree challenged him. "A DOZEN MOUNTAIN LIONS COULD NOT CLAW YOU FREE. A HUNDRED BEARS COULD NOT RELEASE YOU. A THOUSAND WAPITI WOULD NOT MOVE ME AN INCH!"

From the mountain man's mouth came forth such a stream of sounds that the other prisoner could only listen, marvel, and try to identify them. In addition to whistles of varying pitch and tone, there were a series of clicks, a kind of toothy chatter, a multitude of chirps, and a positive profusion of peeps and patterings. To John it all sounded at once familiar and alien, as if he had heard the very same sounds only arranged in a different order, in different harmonies.

It was then that something drew the attention of his sight instead of his hearing. A line was coming toward them—a line just under the ground. The upraised soil formed a positive streak, as if whatever was causing it just beneath the surface was moving with unnatural urgency. A second line soon appeared, then another, and another, all converging at the base of the tree ... where they proceeded, in silence, to disappear.

Looking up from his browsing, a querulous Worthless inclined his head toward his imprisoned master. With a knowing snort, he resumed demolishing the nearby ground cover. As he did so, he kicked irritably at the ground with a back foot. Thus inadvertently relieved of the massive steed's unrelenting weight, the wolf that had remained pinned under the horse's rear left hoof let out a long, tremulous wheeze and gasped several times for air. Righting itself, it staggered shakily toward the clump of brush that contained its badly bruised and still-whimpering brother.

John continued to struggle against his immovable wooden bonds while wondering what the whistling, chirping, chit-chitting mountain man was up to. And what could be the significance of those converging lines in the earth?

"What's going on?"

Ceasing what John could only describe as an infernal chittering, Malone looked over at him.

"In the mountains, the catamount is more ferocious, the bear stronger, the wapiti more numerous. But those are the dangerous critters you see." He cast his gaze downward. "Not everything thet eats, not everything with sharp teeth, likes t' show itself. Try listenin'."

John hesitated, then decided to do as the mountain man instructed. He heard nothing beyond the ordinary midday song of the Sierra: scolding jays, the songs of smaller birds, the intermittent sigh of the wind in the branches. He said as much to Malone.

"Try harder," the mountain man advised him. "Focus. Listen deep."

Closing his eyes, the other man complied, straining to hear whatever it was to which Malone was alluding. More of the same, it was. Except ... just there, just then. Something else. Something below him. A sound in multiples, deep beneath, and this time recognizable.

The sound of chewing.

While he considered himself a man of many words, and good ones at that, John peered across the breadth of the tree at Malone and found that at that moment he had none. Leastwise, none that were suitable, or could be expressed in polite company.

Finding its way into Malone's mouth, a wandering caterpillar quickly saw itself expectorated halfway into the next county.

"You say y'know about all the trees hereabouts, John of the mountains. Then you know that despite their great size, these giants soarin' around us have one weakness and one only. Their roots are shallow." He peered downward, listening intently even as he spoke. "'Tis all about the teeth, John-friend. Not as sharp as catamount teeth, not as powerful as a bear's, but plenty sharp enough to do their daily work. One pair can't cut much. A dozen pair would do better work still. A few hundred or so, now, all gnawin' away together ... After a bit o' hard work, why, I reckon thet kind o' activity would be sufficient t' get the attention o' any growth. Even one as humungous and disagreeable as our captor here."

As sure as the color of Millie's bloomers matched the flush of her cheeks, the great tree spoke up once again.

"WHAT IS HAPPENING? MAKE IT ... STOP."

"Let us go." Malone's tone was quiet but demanding.

"I WILL NOT.... YOU MUST MAKE IT STOP!" A shudder traveled through the entire length and breadth of the enormous bole. "MAKE IT STOP NOW!"

"Let us go ... now." Malone was resolute. Nearby, Worthless let out a complementary whinny.

There came a rippling around him. Thick folds of bark drew back, back, until he could move freely once again. Swinging his arms and stretching, he climbed down the side of the aboveground mass of the nearest root. A glance showed that John, unprompted, was doing likewise.

Standing once more emancipated and on solid ground, Malone

turned his attention not to the root he had just descended but to the earth at its base. As John looked on, the mountain man pursed his lips and emitted a series of chirps and whistles not unlike those that had emanated from him prior to their liberation. At his command, a single body popped out of the earth to stare at him, then another, and another, until at least a dozen of the subterranean denizens had responded to his calling.

John looked on in silent amazement as his towering companion knelt. The multitude of tiny saviors, a fraction of those who had done the necessary work, swarmed over and around him: ground squirrels, gophers, moles, and voles, their diminutive tongues licking and tasting of the mountain man. Two badgers emerged from the ground, wandered over, and nuzzled Malone's boots. Then, one and all, they scampered and scattered back into their holes in the earth and disappeared.

In his life of observant wandering, John had seen many wonders, but nothing to compare with what had just revealed itself before him.

"Magic. There can be no other rational explanation."

"Rationality's somethin' I find is frequently overused by way o' explanation." Malone indicated the temple of silent redwood giants beneath which they stood. "Now, these trees, this here placethat be a true definition o' magic." Rising from his crouch, he put a hand on the other man's shoulder, his leathery open palm completely covering it. "Will you be all right now, John-friend?" He shook a chiding finger at his new acquaintance. "No more climbin' trees in thunderstorms?"

Behind his impressive beard, the other man grinned. "Not without first asking permission of the tree in question, anyways. I thank you for my freedom, Mr. Malone. I think I shall write about you in my journal."

The mountain man let out a grunt. "Waste o' time, methinks. Nobody'd believe such a story. Doesn't make no sense." His face broke out in a huge grin.

"Until their existence was witnessed and reported upon," John murmured reverently, "no one believed that such trees as these endured, either."

Malone nodded once in solemn agreement. "Kin I give you a ride somewhere, John o' the mountains?"

Having turned, the other man was already striding off toward the north. "Thank you, but no. My kit is nearby and hung well out of the reach of wandering bears. Also, I confess that the thought of being in any closer proximity to your steed unsettles my stomach even more than does spending time atop a tree in a Sierra thunderstorm. Good traveling to you, Mr. Malone, sir." Halfway to the nearby ridge, he looked over at the singular sequoia that had imprisoned him, and for a while also, at Malone. "I can, however, assure you that in these mountains there is at least one tree that I will not be ascending again any time soon."

Swinging himself up and into the saddle on Worthless's back, Malone gripped the reins loosely in his right hand. At a gentle flick of the leather strands, the enigmatic steed started forward, a clutch of purple lupine hanging incongruously from his mouth. Raising a hand, Malone waved at the rapidly disappearing form of the other man and called out to him.

"I wouldn't be too hard on the woody old grouch," he shouted. "Even if his bark was worse than his height."

ABOUT THE AUTHOR

Alan Dean Foster is the author of 125 books, hundreds of pieces of short fiction, essays, columns reviews, the occasional op-ed for the NY Times, and the story for the first Star Trek movie. Having visited more than 100 countries, he is still bemused by the human condition. He lives with his wife JoAnn and numerous dogs, cats, coyotes, hawks, and a resident family of bobcats in Prescott, Arizona.

PERVIOUS PUBLICATION INFORMATION

IF YOU LIKED ...
Mad Amos Malone, you might also enjoy:

Oshenerth
by Alan Dean Foster

The Taste of Other Dimensions
by Alan Dean Foster

The Gamearth Trilogy
by Kevin J. Anderson

OTHER WORDFIRE PRESS TITLES BY ALAN DEAN FOSTER

Oshenerth

The Taste of Other Dimensions

The Flavor of Other Worlds

Our list of other WordFire Press authors and titles is always
growing. To find out more and to see our selection of titles, visit
us at:
wordfirepress.com